THE BEST
HORROR OF THE YEAR

VOLUME FOUR

Also Edited by Ellen Datlow

A Whisper of Blood
A Wolf at the Door (with Terri Windling)
Alien Sex
Black Heart, Ivory Bones (with Terri Windling)
Black Swan, White Raven (with Terri Windling)
Black Thorn, White Rose (with Terri Windling)
Blood is Not Enough: 17 Stories of Vampirism
Blood and Other Cravings
Darkness: Two Decades of Modern Horror
Digital Domains: A Decade of Science Fiction and Fantasy
Haunted Legends (with Nick Mamatas)
Inferno: New Tales of Terror and the Supernatural
Lethal Kisses
Little Deaths
Lovecraft Unbound
Naked City: Tales of Urban Fantasy
Nebula Awards Showcase 2009
Off Limits: Tales of Alien Sex
Omni Best Science Fiction: Volumes One through *Three*
Omni Books of Science Fiction: Volumes One through *Seven*
OmniVisions One and *Two*
Poe: 19 New Tales Inspired by Edgar Allan Poe
Ruby Slippers, Golden Tears (with Terri Windling)
Salon Fantastique: Fifteen Original Tales of Fantasy (with Terri Windling)
Silver Birch, Blood Moon (with Terri Windling)
Sirens and Other Daemon Lovers (with Terri Windling)
Snow White, Blood Red (with Terri Windling)
Supernatural Noir
Swan Sister (with Terri Windling)
Tails of Wonder and Imagination: Cat Stories
Teeth: Vampire Tales (with Terri Windling)
The Beastly Bride: And Other Tales of the Animal People (with Terri Windling)
The Best Horror of the Year: Volume One
The Best Horror of the Year: Volume Two
The Best Horror of the Year: Volume Three
The Beastly Bride: Tales of the Animal People
The Coyote Road: Trickster Tales (with Terri Windling)
The Dark: New Ghost Stories
The Del Rey Book of Science Fiction and Fantasy
The Faery Reel: Tales from the Twilight Realm
The Green Man: Tales of the Mythic Forest (with Terri Windling)
Troll's Eye View: A Book of Villainous Tales (with Terri Windling)
Twists of the Tale
Vanishing Acts
The Year's Best Fantasy and Horror (with Terri Windling, Gavin J. Grant, and Kelly Link)

THE BEST
HORROR OF THE YEAR

VOLUME FOUR

EDITED BY ELLEN DATLOW

NIGHT SHADE BOOKS
SAN FRANCISCO

The Best Horror of the Year: Volume Four
© 2012 by Ellen Datlow

This edition of *The Best Horror of the Year: Volume Four*
© 2012 by Night Shade Books

Cover art by Allen Williams
Interior layout and design by Amy Popovich
Photo of Ellen Datlow by Gregory Frost

Introduction, author bios, and arrangement © 2012 by Ellen Datlow.

Pages 385–387 represent an extension of this copyright page.

First Edition

ISBN: 978-1-59780-399-1

Night Shade Books

www.nightshadebooks.com

ACKNOWLEDGMENTS

I'd like to thank Melody Chamlee for being my first reader. I'd like to thank Stefan Dziemianowicz for his generosity and his time and Charles Tan for bringing material from the Philippines to my attention. Also thanks to Andrew Alford, Nick Mamatas, and Michael Kandel for their suggestions.

I'd like to acknowledge the following magazines and catalogs for invaluable information and descriptions of material I was unable to obtain: *Locus, Publishers Weekly, British Fantasy Society Journal, S.F. Commentary*, and *Prism* (the quarterly journal of fantasy given with membership to the British Fantasy Society). I'd also like to thank all the editors who made sure I saw their magazines during the year, the webzine editors who provided printouts, and the book publishers who provided review copies in a timely manner. Also, the writers who sent me printouts of their stories when I was unable to acquire the magazine or book in which they appeared.

Thanks to Merrilee Heifetz and Sarah Nagel at Writers House.

And a very special thank you to Jeremy Lassen, Jason Williams, and Ross Lockhart.

TABLE OF CONTENTS

on his other wasted, flabby, scarred leg.

"Actually, two of them," Newsome said. "One was that it was very good to be alive, although I understood—even before the pain that's been my constant companion for the last two years started to eat through the shock—that I had been badly hurt. The second was that the word *imperative* is used very loosely by most people, including my former self. There are only two imperative things. One is life itself, the other is freedom from pain. Do you agree, Reverend Rideout?" And before Rideout could agree (for surely he would do nothing else), Newsome said in his waspy, hectoring, old man's voice: "Not so goddam *tight*, Kat! How many times do I have to tell you?"

"Sorry," she murmured, and loosened the strap. *Why do I even try?*

Melissa, the housekeeper, looking trim in a white blouse and high-waisted white slacks, came in with a coffee tray. Jensen accepted a cup, along with two packets of artificial sweetener. The new one, the bottom-of-the-barrel so-called reverend, only shook his head. Maybe he had some kind of holy coffee in his lunchbox Thermos. Kat didn't get an offer. When she took coffee, she took it in the kitchen with the rest of the help. Or in the summerhouse… only this wasn't summer. It was November, and wind-driven rain lashed the windows.

"Shall I turn you on, Mr. Newsome, or would you prefer that I leave now?"

She didn't want to leave. She'd heard the whole story many times before—the imperative meeting, the crash, how Andrew Newsome had been ejected from the burning plane, about the broken bones, chipped spine, and dislocated neck, most of all about the twenty-four months of unrelieved suffering, which he would soon get to—and it bored her. But Rideout didn't. Other charlatans would undoubtedly follow, now that all reputable relief resources had been exhausted, but Rideout was the first, and Kat was interested to see how the farmer-looking fellow would go about separating Andy Newsome from a large chunk of his cash. Or how he would try. Newsome hadn't amassed his obscene piles of cash by being stupid, but of course he wasn't the same man he had been, no matter how real his pain might be. On that subject, Kat had her own opinions, but this was the best job she'd ever had. At least in terms of money. And if Newsome wanted to continue suffering, wasn't that his choice?

"Go ahead, honey, turn me on." He waggled his eyebrows at her. Once the lechery might have been real (Kat thought Melissa might have information on that subject), but now it was just a pair of shaggy eyebrows working on muscle memory.

Kat plugged the cords into the control unit and flicked the switch. Properly attached, the TENS units would have sent a weak electrical current into Newsome's muscles, a therapy that seemed to have some ameliorative effects… although no one could say exactly why, or if they were entirely of the placebo variety. Be that as it might, they would do nothing for Newsome tonight. Hooked up as loosely as they were, they had been reduced to the equivalent of joy-buzzers. Expensive ones.

"Shall I—?"

"Stay!" he said. "Therapy!"

The lord wounded in battle commands, she thought, *and I obey.*

She bent over to pull her chest of goodies out from under the bed. It was filled with tools many of her past clients referred to as implements of torture. Jensen and Rideout paid no attention to her. They continued to look at Newsome, who might (or might not) have been granted revelations that had changed his priorities and outlook on life, but who still enjoyed holding court.

He told them about awakening in a cage of metal and mesh. There were steel gantries called fixators on both legs and one arm to immobilise joints that had been repaired with "about a hundred" steel pins (actually seventeen; Kat had seen the X-rays). The fixators were anchored in the outraged and splintered femurs, tibiae, fibulae, humerus, radius, ulna. His back was encased in a kind of chain-mail girdle that went from his hips to the nape of his neck. He talked about sleepless nights that seemed to go on not for hours but for years. He talked about the crushing headaches. He told them about how even wiggling his toes caused pain all the way up to his jaw, and the shrieking agony that bit into his legs when the doctors insisted that he move them, fixators and all, so he wouldn't entirely lose their function. He told them about the bedsores and how he bit back howls of hurt and outrage when the nurses attempted to roll him on his side so the sores could be flushed out.

"There have been another dozen operations in the last two years," he said with a kind of dark pride. Actually, Kat knew, there had been five, two of those to remove the fixators when the bones were sufficiently healed. Unless you included the minor procedure to re-set his broken fingers, that was. Then you could say there were six, but she didn't consider surgical stuff necessitating no more than local anaesthetic to be "operations." If that were the case, she'd had a dozen herself, most of them while listening to Muzak in a dentist's chair.

Now we get to the false promises, she thought as she placed a gel pad in the crook of Newsome's right knee and laced her hands together on the hanging hot-water bottles of muscle beneath his right thigh. *That comes next.*

"The doctors promised me the pain would abate," Newsome said. "That in six weeks I'd only need the narcotics before and after my physical therapy sessions with the Queen of Pain here. That I'd be walking again by the summer of 2010. *Last* summer." He paused for effect. "Reverend Rideout, those were false promises. I have almost no flexion in my knees at all, and the pain in my hips and back is beyond description. The doctors—*ah! Oh!* Stop, Kat, *stop*!"

She had raised his right leg to a ten-degree angle, perhaps a little more. Not even enough to hold the cushioning pad in place.

"Let it go down! Let it *down*, goddammit!"

Kat relaxed her hold on his knee, and the leg returned to the hospital bed. Ten degrees. Possibly twelve. Whoop-de-do. Sometimes she got it all the way to fifteen—and the left leg, which was a little better, to twenty degrees of flex—before he started hollering like a kid who sees a hypodermic needle in a school nurse's hand. The doctors guilty of false promises had not been guilty of false advertising; they had told him the pain was coming. Kat had been there as a silent onlooker during several of those consultations. They had told him he would swim in pain before those crucial tendons, shortened by the accident and frozen in place by the fixators, stretched out and once again became limber. He would have plenty of pain before he was able to get the bend in his knees back to ninety degrees. Before he would be able to sit in a chair or behind the wheel of a car, that was. The same was true of his back and his neck. The road to recovery led through the Land of Pain, that was all.

These were true promises Andrew Newsome had chosen not to hear. It was his belief—never stated baldly, in words of one syllable, but undoubtedly one of the stars he steered by—that the sixth-richest man in the world should not have to visit the Land of Pain under any circumstances, only the Costa del Sol of Full Recovery. Blaming the doctors followed as day follows night. And of course he blamed fate. Things like this were not supposed to happen to guys like him.

Melissa came back with cookies on a tray. Newsome waved a hand—twisted and scarred in the accident—at her irritably. "No one's in the mood for baked goods, 'Lissa."

Here was another thing Kat MacDonald had discovered about the mega-rich, those dollar-babies who had amassed assets beyond ordinary comprehension: they felt very confident about speaking for everyone in the room.

Melissa gave her little Mona Lisa smile, then turned (almost pirouetted) and left the room. *Glided* from the room. She had to be at least forty-five, but looked younger. She wasn't sexy; nothing so vulgar. Rather there was an ice-queen glamour about her that made Kat think of Ingrid Bergman. Icy or not, Kat supposed men would wonder how that chestnut hair would look freed from its clips, and lying all mussed up on a pillow. How her coral lipstick would look smeared on her teeth and up one cheek. Kat, who considered herself dumpy, told herself at least once a day that she wasn't jealous of that smooth, cool face. Or that heart-shaped bottom.

Kat returned to the other side of the bed and prepared to lift Newsome's left leg until he yelled at her again to stop, goddammit, did she want to kill him? *If you were another patient, I'd tell you the facts of life,* she thought. *I'd tell you to stop looking for shortcuts, because there are none. Not even for the sixth-richest man in the world. You have me—I'd help you if you'd let me—but as long as you keep looking for a way to pay yourself out of the shit, you're on your own.*

She placed the pad under his knee. Grasped the hanging bags that should have been turning back into muscle by now. Began to bend the leg. Waited for him to scream at her to stop. And she would. Because five thousand dollars a week added up to a cool quarter-mil a year. Did he know that part of what he was buying was her silence? How could he not?

Now tell them about the doctors. Geneva, London, Madrid, Mexico City, et cetera, et cetera.

"I've been to doctors all over the world," he told them. Speaking primarily to Rideout now. Rideout still hadn't said a word, just sat there with the red wattles, his overshaved neck hanging over his buttoned-to-the-neck country preacher shirt. He was wearing big yellow workboots. The heel of one almost touched his black lunchbox. "Teleconferencing would be the easier way to go, given my condition, but of course that doesn't cut it in cases like mine. So I've gone in person, in spite of the pain it causes me. We've been everywhere, haven't we, Kat?"

"Indeed we have," she said, very slowly continuing to bend the leg. On which he would have been walking by now, if he weren't such a child about the pain. Such a spoiled baby. On crutches, yes, but walking. And in another year, he would have been able to throw the crutches away. Only in another year he would still be here in this two hundred thousand dollar state-of-the-art hospital bed. And she would still be with him. Still taking his hush-money. How much would be enough? Two million? She told herself that now, but she'd told herself half a million would be enough not so long ago, and had since moved the goalposts. Money was wretched that way.

"We've seen specialists in Mexico, Geneva, London, Rome, Paris… where else, Kat?"

"Vienna," she said. "And San Francisco, of course."

Newsome snorted. "Doctor there told me I was manufacturing my own pain. 'To keep from doing the hard work of rehabilitation,' he said. But he was a Paki. And a queer. A queer Paki, how's that for a combo?" He gave a brief bark of laughter, then peered at Rideout. "I'm not offending you, am I, Reverend?"

Rideout rotated his head side-to-side in a negative gesture. Twice. Very slowly.

"Good, good. Stop, Kat, that's enough."

"A little more," she coaxed.

"Stop, I said. That's all I can take."

She let the leg subside and began to manipulate his left arm. That he allowed. He often told people both of his arms had also been broken, but this wasn't true. The left one had only been sprained. He also told people he was lucky not to be in a wheelchair, but the all-the-bells-and-whistles hospital bed suggested strongly that this was luck he had no intention of capitalising on in the near future. The all-the-bells-and-whistles hospital bed *was* his wheelchair. It rolled. He had ridden all over the world in it.

Neuropathic pain, Kat thought. *It's a great mystery. Perhaps insoluble. The drugs no longer work.*

"The consensus is that I'm suffering from neuropathic pain."

And cowardice.

"It's a great mystery."

Also a good excuse.

"Perhaps insoluble."

Especially when you don't try.

"The drugs no longer work and the doctors can't help me. That's why I've brought you here, Reverend Rideout. Your references in the matter of... er... healing... are very strong."

Rideout stood up. Kat hadn't realised how tall he was. His shadow scared up behind him on the wall even higher. Almost to the ceiling. His eyes, sunken deep in their sockets, regarded Newsome solemnly. He had charisma, of that there could be no doubt. It didn't surprise her, the char-latans of the world couldn't get along without it, but she hadn't realised how much or how strong it was until he got to his feet and towered over them. Jensen was actually craning his neck to see him. There was move-ment in the corner of Kat's eye. She looked and saw Melissa standing in the doorway. So now they were all here except for Tonya, the cook.

Outside, the wind rose to a shriek. The glass in the windows rattled.

"I don't heal," Rideout said. He was from Arkansas, Kat believed—that was where Newsome's latest Gulfstream IV had picked him up, at least—but his voice was accentless. And flat.

"No?" Newsome looked disappointed. Petulant. Maybe, Kat thought, a little scared. "I sent a team of investigators, and they assure me that in many cases—"

"I *expel*."

Up went the shaggy eyebrows. "I beg your pardon."

Rideout came to the bed and stood there with his long-fingered hands laced loosely together at the level of his flat crotch. His deep-set eyes looked sombrely down at the man in the bed. "I exterminate the pest from the wounded body it's feeding on, just as a bug exterminator would exterminate pests—termites, for instance—feeding on a house."

Now, Kat thought, *I have heard absolutely everything*. But Newsome was fascinated. *Like a kid watching a three-card monte expert on a streetcorner,* she thought.

"You've been possessed, sir."

"Yes," Newsome said. "That's what it feels like. Especially at night. The nights are… very long."

"Every man or woman who suffers pain is possessed, of course, but in some unfortunate people—you are one—the problem goes deeper. The possession isn't a transient thing but a permanent condition. One that worsens. Doctors don't believe, because they are men of science. But *you* believe, don't you? Because you're the one who's suffering."

"Yous bet," Newsome breathed. Kat, sitting beside him on her stool, had to restrain herself from rolling her eyes.

"In these unfortunates, pain opens the way for a demon god. It's small, but dangerous. It feeds on a special kind of hurt produced only by certain special people."

Genius, Kat thought, *he's going to love that.*

"Once the god finds its way in, pain becomes agony. It feeds just as termites feed on wood. And it will eat until you are all used up. Then it will cast you aside, sir, and move on."

Kat surprised herself by saying, "What god would that be? Certainly not the one you preach about. That one is the God of love. Or so I grew up believing."

Jensen was frowning at her and shaking his head. He clearly expected an explosion from the boss… but a little smile had touched the corners of Newsome's lips. "What do you say to that, Rev?"

"I say that there are many gods. The fact that our Lord, the Lord God of Hosts, rules them all—and on the Day of Judgment will *destroy* them all—does not change that. These little gods have been worshipped by people both ancient and modern. They have their powers, and our God sometimes allows those powers to be exercised."

As a test, Kat thought.

"As a test of our strength and faith." Then he turned to Newsome and said something that surprised her. Jensen, too; his mouth actually dropped open. "You are a man of much strength and little faith."

Newsome, although not used to hearing criticism, nevertheless smiled. "I don't have much in the way of Christian faith, that's true, but I have faith in myself. I also have faith in money. How much do you want?"

Rideout returned the smile, exposing teeth that were little more than tiny eroded gravestones. If he had ever seen a dentist, it had been many moons ago. Also, he was a tobacco-chewer. Kat's father, who had died of mouth cancer, had had the same discoloured teeth.

"How much would you pay to be free of your pain, sir?"

"Ten million dollars," Newsome replied promptly. Kat heard Melissa gasp. "But I didn't get to where I am by being a sucker. If you do whatever it is you do—expelling, exterminating, exorcising, call it what you want—you get the money. In cash, if you don't mind spending the night. Fail, and you get nothing. Except your first and only roundtrip on a private jet. For that there will be no charge. After all, *I* reached out to *you*."

"No." Rideout said it mildly, standing there beside the bed, close enough to Kat so she could smell the mothballs that had been recently keeping his dress pants (maybe his only pair, unless he had another to preach in) whole. She could also smell some strong soap.

"No?" Newsome looked frankly startled. "You tell me no?" Then he began to smile again. This time it was the secretive and rather unpleasant smile he wore when he made his phone calls and did his deals. "I get it. Now comes the curveball. I'm disappointed, Reverend Rideout. I really hoped you were on the level." He turned to Kat, causing her to draw back a bit. "You, of course, think I've lost my mind. But I haven't shared the investigators' reports with you. Have I?"

"No," she said.

"There's no curveball," Rideout said. "I haven't performed an expulsion in five years. Did your investigators tell you that?"

Newsome didn't reply. He was looking up at the thin, towering man with a certain unease.

Jensen said, "Is it because you've lost your powers? If that's the case, why did you come?"

"It's God's power, sir, not mine, and I haven't lost it. But an expulsion takes great energy and great strength. Five years ago I suffered a major heart attack shortly after performing one on a young girl who had been in a terrible car accident. We were successful, she and I, but the cardiologist I consulted in Jonesboro told me that if I ever exerted myself in such a way again, I might suffer another attack. This one fatal."

Newsome raised a gnarled hand—not without effort—to the side of his mouth and spoke to Kat and Melissa in a comic stage-whisper. "I think he wants twenty million."

"What I want, sir, is seven hundred and fifty thousand."

Newsome just stared at him. It was Melissa who asked, "Why?"

"I am pastor of a church in Titusville. The Church of Holy Faith, it's called. Only there's no church anymore. We had a dry summer in my part of the world. There was a wildfire, probably started by campers. And probably drunk. That's usually the case. My church is now just a concrete footprint and a few charred beams. I and my parishioners have been worshipping in an abandoned gas station-convenience store on the Jonesboro Pike. It is not satisfactory during the winter months, and there are no homes large enough to accommodate us. We are many but poor."

Kat listened with interest. As con-man stories went, this was a good one. It had the right sympathy-hooks.

Jensen, who still had the body of a college athlete (he also served as Newsome's bodyguard) and the mind of a Harvard MBA, asked the obvious question. "Insurance?"

Rideout once more shook his head in that deliberate way: left, right, left, right, back to center. He still stood towering over Newsome's state-of-the-art bed like some country-ass guardian angel. "We trust in God."

"In this case, you might have been better off with Allstate," Melissa said.

Newsome was smiling. Kat could tell from the stiff way he held his body that he was in serious discomfort—his pills were now half an hour overdue—but he was ignoring it because he was interested. That he *could* ignore it was something she'd known for quite awhile now. He could battle the pain if he chose to. He had resources. She had thought she was merely irritated with this, but now, probably prompted by the appearance of the charlatan from Arkansas, she discovered she was actually infuriated. It was so *wasteful*.

"I have consulted with a local builder—not a member of my flock, but a man of good repute who has done repairs for me in the past and quotes a fair price—and he tells me that it will cost approximately six hundred and fifty thousand dollars to rebuild. I have taken the liberty of adding one hundred thousand dollars, just to be on the safe side."

Uh-huh, Kat thought.

"We don't have such monetary resources, of course. But then, not even a week after speaking with Mr. Kiernan, your letter came, along with the video-disc. Which I watched with great interest, by the way."

I'll bet you did, Kat thought. *Especially the part where the doctor from San Francisco says the pain associated with his injuries can be greatly alleviated by physical therapy.* Stringent *physical therapy.*

It was true that nearly a dozen other doctors on the DVD had claimed themselves at a loss, but Kat believed Dr. Dilawar was the only one with the guts to talk straight. She had been surprised that Newsome had allowed the disc to go out with that interview on it, but since his accident, the sixth-richest man in the world had slipped a few cogs.

"Will you pay me enough to rebuild my church, sir?"

Newsome studied him. Now there were small beads of sweat just below his receding hairline. Kat would give him his pills soon, whether he asked for them or not. The pain was real enough, it wasn't as though he were faking or anything, it was just…

"Would you agree not to ask for more? Gentleman's agreement. We don't need to sign anything."

"Yes." Rideout said it with no hesitation.

"Although if you're able to remove the pain—*expel* the pain—I might well make a contribution of some size. Some *considerable* size. What I believe you people call a love offering."

"That would be your business, sir. Shall we begin?"

"No time like the present. Do you want everyone to leave?"

Rideout shook his head again: left to right, right to left, back to center. "I will need assistance."

Magicians always do, Kat thought. *It's part of the show.*

Outside, the wind shrieked, rested, then shrieked again. The lights flickered. Behind the house, the generator (also state-of-the-art) burped to life, then stilled.

Rideout sat on the edge of the bed. "Mr. Jensen there, I think. He looks strong and quick."

"He's both," Newsome said. "Played football in college. Running back. Hasn't lost a step since."

"Well… a few," Jensen said modestly.

Rideout leaned toward Newsome. His dark, deeply socketed eyes studied the billionaire's scarred face solemnly. "Answer a question for me, sir. What color is your pain?"

"Green," Newsome replied. He was looking back at the preacher with fascination. "My pain is green."

Rideout nodded: up, down, up, down, back to center. Eye-contact never lost. Kat was sure he would have nodded with exactly the same look of grave confirmation if Newsome had said his pain was blue, or as purple as the fabled Purple People-Eater. She thought, with a combination of dismay and real amusement: *I could lose my temper here. I really could. It would be the most expensive tantrum of my life, but still—I could.*

"And where is it?"

"Everywhere." It was almost a moan. Melissa took a step forward, giving Jensen a look of concern. Kat saw him shake his head a little and motion her back to the doorway.

"Yes, it likes to give that impression," Rideout said, "but it's not so. Close your eyes, sir, and concentrate. Look for the pain. Look past the false shouts it gives—ignore the cheap ventriloquism—and locate it. You can do this. You *must* do it, if we're to have any success."

Newsome closed his eyes. For a space of ninety seconds there was no sound but the wind and the rain spattering against the windows like handfuls of fine gravel. Kat's watch was the old-fashioned wind-up kind, a nursing school graduation present from her father many years ago, and when the wind lulled, the room was quiet enough for her to hear its self-important ticking. And something else: at the far end of the big house, elderly Tonya Andrews singing softly as she neatened up the kitchen at the end of another day: *Froggy went a-courtin' and he did ride, mmm-hm.*

At last Newsome said, "It's in my chest. High in my chest. Or at the bottom of my throat, just below the windpipe."

"Can you see it? Concentrate!"

Vertical lines appeared on Newsome's forehead. Scars from the skin that had been flayed open during the accident wavered through these grooves of concentration. "I see it. It's pulsing in time to my heartbeat." His lips pulled down in an expression of distaste. "It's nasty."

Rideout leaned closer. "Is it a ball? It is, isn't it? A green ball."

"Yes. Yes! A little green ball that *breathes!*"

Like the rigged-up tennis ball you undoubtedly have either up your sleeve or in that big black lunchbox of yours, Rev, she thought.

And, as if she were controlling him with her mind (instead of just deducing where this sloppy little playlet would go next), Rideout said: "Mr. Jensen, sir. There's a lunchbox under the chair I was sitting in. Get it and open it and stand next to me. You need to do no more than that for the moment. Just—"

Kat MacDonald snapped. It was a snap she actually heard in her head. It sounded like Roger Miller snapping his fingers during the intro to 'King of the Road'.

She stepped up beside Rideout and shouldered him aside. It was easy. He was taller, but she had been turning and lifting patients for nearly half her life, and she was stronger. "Open your eyes, Andy. Open them right now. Look at me."

Startled, Newsome did as she said. Melissa and Jensen (now with the lunchbox in his hands) looked alarmed. One of the facts of their working lives—and Kat's own, at least until now—was that you didn't command the boss. The boss commanded you. You most certainly did not startle him.

But she'd had quite enough, thank you. In another twenty minutes she might be crawling after her headlights along stormy roads to the only motel in the vicinity, a place that looked like the avatar of all roach-traps, but it didn't matter. She simply couldn't do this any longer.

"This is bullshit, Andy," she said. "Are you hearing me? Bullshit."

"I think you better stop right there," Newsome said, beginning to smile—he had several smiles, and this wasn't one of the good ones. "If you want to keep your job, that is. There are plenty of other nurses in Vermont who specialise in pain therapy."

She might have stopped there, but Rideout said, "Let her speak, sir." It was the gentleness in his tone that drove her over the edge.

She leaned forward, into his space, and the words spilled out in a torrent.

"For the last sixteen months—ever since your respiratory system improved enough to allow meaningful physiotherapy—I've watched you lie in this goddamned expensive bed and insult your own body. It makes me sick. Do you know how lucky you are to be alive, when everyone else on that airplane was killed? What a miracle it is that your spine wasn't severed, or your skull crushed into your brain, or your body burned—no, *baked*, baked like an apple—from head to toe? You would have lived four days, maybe even two weeks, in hellish agony. Instead you were thrown clear. You're not a vegetable. You're not a quadriplegic, although you choose to act like one. You won't do the work. You look for some easier way. You want to pay your way out of your situation. If you died and went to Hell, the first thing you'd do is look for a tollgate."

Jensen and Melissa were staring at her in horror. Newsome's mouth hung open. If he had ever been talked to in such a fashion, it had been long ago. Only Rideout looked at ease. *He* was the one smiling now. The way a father would smile at his wayward four year old. It drove her crazy.

"You could have been walking by now. God knows I've tried to make you understand that, and God knows I've told you—over and over—the kind of work it would take to get you up out of that bed and back on your feet. Dr. Dilawar in San Francisco had the guts to tell you—he was the only one—and you rewarded him by calling him a faggot."

"He *was* a faggot," Newsome said pettishly. His scarred hands had balled themselves into fists.

"You're in pain, yes. Of course you are. It's manageable, though. I've seen it managed, not once but many times. But not by a lazy rich man who tries to substitute his sense of entitlement for the plain old hard work and tears it takes to get better. You refuse. I've seen that, too, and I know what always happens next. The quacks and confidence men come, the way leeches come when a man with a cut leg wades into a stagnant pond. Sometimes the quacks have magic creams. Sometimes they have magic pills. The healers come with trumped-up claims about God's power, the way this one has. Usually the marks get partial relief. Why wouldn't they, when half the pain is in their heads, manufactured by lazy minds that only understand it will hurt to get better?"

She raised her voice to a wavering, childlike treble and bent close to him. "Daddy, it *hurrr-rrrts!* But the relief never lasts long, because the muscles have no tone, the tendons are still slack, the bones haven't thickened enough to accommodate weight-bearing. And when you get this guy on the phone to tell him the pain's back—if you can—do you know what he'll say? That you didn't have *faith* enough. If you used your brains on this the way you did on your manufacturing plants and various invest-ments, you'd know there's no little living tennis ball sitting at the base of your throat. You're too fucking old to believe in Santa Claus, Andy."

Tonya had come into the doorway and now stood beside Melissa, staring with wide eyes and a dishwiper hanging limp in one hand.

"You're fired," Newsome said, almost genially.

"Yes," Kat said. "Of course I am. Although I must say that this is the best I've felt in almost a year."

"Don't fire her," Rideout said. "If you do, I'll have to take my leave."

Newsome's eyes rolled to the Reverend. His brow was knitted in perplexity. His hands now began to knead his hips and thighs, as they always did when his pain medication was overdue.

"She needs an education, praise God's Holy Name." Rideout leaned toward Newsome, his own hands clasped behind his back. He reminded Kat of a picture she'd seen once of Washington Irving's schoolteacher, Ichabod Crane. "She's had her say. Shall I have mine?"

Newsome was sweating more heavily, but he was smiling again. "Have at her, Rideout. I believe I want to hear this."

Kat faced him. Those dark, socketed eyes were unsettling, but she met them. "So do I."

Hands still clasped behind his back, pink skull shining mutedly through his thin hair, long face solemn, Rideout examined her. Then he said: "You've never suffered yourself, have you, miss?"

Kat felt an urge to flinch at that, or look away, or both. She suppressed it. "I fell out of a tree when I was eleven and broke my arm."

Rideout rounded his thin lips and whistled: one tuneless, almost toneless note. "Broke an *arm* while you were *eleven*. Yes, that must have been excruciating."

She flushed. She felt it and hated it but couldn't stop the heat. "Belittle me all you want. I based what I said on years of experience dealing with pain patients. It is a *medical* opinion."

Now he'll tell me he's been expelling demons, or little green gods, or whatever they are, since I was in rompers.

But he didn't.

"I'm sure," he soothed. "And I'm sure you're good at what you do. I'm sure you've seen your share of fakers and posers. You know their kind. And I know yours, miss, because I've seen it many times before. They're usually not as pretty as you—" Finally a trace of accent, *pretty* coming out as *purty*. "—but their condescending attitude toward pain they have never felt themselves, pain they can't even conceive of, is always the same. They work in sickrooms, they work with patients who are in varying degrees of distress, from mild pain to deepest, searing agony. And after awhile, it all starts to look either overdone or outright fake to them, isn't that so?"

"That's not true at all," Kat said. What was happening to her voice? All at once it was small.

"No? When you bend their legs and they scream at fifteen degrees—or even at ten—don't you think, first in the back of your mind, then more and more toward the front, that they are lollygagging? Refusing to do the hard work? Perhaps even fishing for sympathy? When you enter the room and their faces go pale, don't you think, 'Oh, now I have to deal with *this* lazy thing again?' Haven't you—who once fell from a tree and broke your *arm*, for the Lord's sake—become more and more disgusted when they beg to be put back into bed and be given more morphine or whatever?"

"That's so unfair," Kat said… but now her voice was little more than a whisper.

"Once upon a time, when you were new at this, you knew agony when you saw it," Rideout said. "Once upon a time you would have believed in what you are going to see in just a few minutes, because you knew in your heart that malignant outsider god was there. I want you to stay so I can refresh your memory… and the sense of compassion that's gotten lost somewhere along the way."

"Some of my patients *are* whiners," Kat said, and looked defiantly at Rideout. "I suppose that sounds cruel, but sometimes the truth *is* cruel. Some *are* malingerers. If you don't know that, you're blind. Or stupid. I don't think you're either."

He bowed as if she had paid him a compliment—which, in a way, she supposed she had. "Of course I know. But now, in your secret heart, you believe *all* of them are malingerers. You've become inured, like a soldier who's spent too long in battle. Mr. Newsome here has been infested, I tell you, *invaded*. There's a demon inside him so strong it has become a god, and I want you to see it when it comes out. It will improve matters for you considerably, I think. Certainly it will change your outlook on pain." To Newsome: "Can she stay, sir?"

Newsome considered. "If you want her to."

"And if I choose to leave?" Kat challenged him.

Rideout smiled. "No one will hold you here, Miss Nurse. Like all of God's creatures, you have free will. I would not ask others to constrain it, or constrain it myself. But I don't believe you're a coward, merely calloused. Case-hardened."

"You're a fraud," Kat said. She was furious, on the verge of tears.

"No," Rideout said, once more speaking gently. "When we leave this room—with you or without you—Mr. Newsome will be relieved of the agony that's been feeding on him. There will still be pain, but once the agony is gone, he'll be able to deal with the pain. Perhaps even with your help, miss, once you've had the necessary lesson in humility. Do you still intend to leave?"

"I'll stay," she said, then said: "Give me the lunchbox."

"But—" Jensen began.

"Give it over," Rideout said. "Let her inspect it, by all means. But no more talk. If I am meant to do this, it's time to begin."

Jensen gave her the long black lunchbox. Kat opened it. Where a workman's wife might have packed her husband's sandwiches and a little Tupperware container of fruit, she saw an empty glass bottle with a wide mouth. Inside the domed lid, held by a wire clamp meant to secure a Thermos, was a green aerosol can. There was nothing else. Kat turned to Rideout. He nodded. She took the aerosol out and looked at the label, nonplussed. "Pepper spray?"

"Pepper spray," Rideout agreed. "I don't know if it's legal in Vermont—probably not would be my guess—but where I come from, most hardware stores stock it." He turned to Tonya. "You are—?"

"Tonya Marsden. I cook for Mr. Newsome."

"Very nice to make your acquaintance, ma'am. I need one more thing before we begin. Do you have a baseball bat? Or any sort of club?"

Tonya shook her head. The wind gusted again; once more the lights flickered and the generator burped in its shed behind the house.

"What about a broom?"

"Oh, yes, sir."

"Fetch it, please."

Tonya left. There was silence except for the wind. Kat tried to think of something to say and couldn't. Droplets of clear perspiration were trickling down Newsome's narrow cheeks, which had also been scarred in the accident. He had rolled and rolled, while the wreckage of the Gulfstream burned in the rain behind him. *I never said he wasn't in pain*, she told herself. *Just that he could manage it, if he'd only muster half the will he showed during the years he spent building his empire.*

But what if she was wrong?

That still doesn't mean there's some sort of living tennis ball inside him, sucking his pain the way a vampire sucks blood.

There were no vampires, and no gods of agony… but when the wind blew hard enough to make the big house shiver in its bones, such ideas almost seemed plausible.

Tonya came back with a broom that looked like it had never swept so much as a single pile of floor-dirt into a dustpan. The bristles were bright blue nylon. The handle was painted wood, about four feet long. She held it up doubtfully. "This what you want?"

"I think it will do," Rideout said, although to Kat he didn't sound entirely sure. It occurred to her that Newsome might not be the only one in this room who had slipped a few cogs lately. "I think you'd better give it to our sceptical nurse. No offence to you, Mrs. Marsden, but younger folks have quicker reflexes."

Looking not offended in the slightest—looking relieved, in fact—Tonya held out the broom. Melissa took it and handed it to Kat.

"What am I supposed to do with it?" Kat asked. "Ride it?"

Rideout smiled, briefly showing the stained and eroded pegs of his teeth. "You'll know when the time comes, if you've ever had a bat or raccoon in the room with you. Just remember: first the bristles. Then the stick."

"To finish it off, I suppose. Then you put it in the specimen bottle."

"As you say."

"So you can put it on a shelf somewhere with the rest of your dead gods, I suppose."

He smiled without humor. "Hand the spray-can to Mr. Jensen, please."

Kat did so. Melissa asked, "What do I do?"

"Watch. And pray, if you know how. On my behalf, as well as Mr. Newsome's. For my heart to be strong."

Kat, who saw a fake heart attack coming, said nothing. She simply moved away from the bed, holding the handle of the broom in both hands. Rideout sat down beside Newsome with a grimace. His knees popped like pistol-shots. "You, Mr. Jensen."

"Yes?"

"You'll have time—it will be stunned—but be quick, just the same. As quick as you were on the football field, all right?"

"You want me to Mace it?"

Rideout once more flashed his brief smile, but now there was sweat on his brow as well as his client's. "It's not Mace—that *is* illegal where I come from—but that's the idea, yes. Now I'd like silence, please."

"Wait a minute." Kat propped the broom against the bed and ran her hands first up Rideout's left arm, then his right. She felt only plain cotton cloth and the man's scrawny flesh beneath.

"Nothing up my sleeve, Miss Kat, I promise you."

"Hurry *up*," Newsome said. "This is bad. It always is, but the goddam stormy weather makes it worse."

"Hush," Rideout said. "All of you, hush."

They hushed. Rideout closed his eyes. His lips moved silently. Twenty seconds ticked past on Kat's watch, then thirty. Her hands were damp with perspiration. She wiped them one at a time on her sweater, then took hold of the broom again. *We look like people gathered at a deathbed*, she thought.

Outside, the wind howled along the gutters.

Rideout said, "For Jesus' sake I pray," then opened his eyes and leaned close to Newsome.

"God, there is an evil outsider in this man. An outsider feeding on his flesh and bones. Help me cast it out, as Your Son cast out the demons from the possessed man of the Gadarenes. Help me speak to the little green god of agony inside Andrew Newsome in your own voice of command."

He leaned closer. He curled the long fingers of one arthritis-swollen hand around the base of Newsome's throat, as if he intended to strangle him. He leaned closer still, and inserted the first two fingers of his other hand into the billionaire's mouth. He curled them, and pulled down the jaw.

"Come out," he said. He had spoken of command, but his voice was soft. Silky. Almost cajoling. It made the skin on Kat's back and arms prickle. "Come out in the name of Jesus. Come out in the names of all the saints and martyrs. Come out in the name of God, who gave you leave to enter and now commands you to leave. Come out into the light. Leave off your meal and come out."

There was nothing. He began again.

"Come out in the name of Jesus. Come out in the names of the saints and martyrs." His hand flexed slightly, and Newsome's breath began to rasp. "No, don't go deeper. You can't hide, thing of darkness. Come out into the light. Jesus commands you. The saints and martyrs command you. God commands you to leave your meal and come out."

A cold hand gripped Kat's upper arm and she almost screamed. It was Melissa. Her eyes were huge. Her mouth hung open. In Kat's ear, the housekeeper's whisper was as harsh as bristles. "*Look.*"

A bulge like a goiter had appeared in Newsome's throat just above Rideout's loosely grasping hand. It began to move slowly mouthward. Kat had never seen anything like it in her life.

"That's right," Rideout almost crooned. His face was streaming with sweat; the collar of his shirt had gone limp and dark. "Come out. Come out into the light. You've done your feeding, thing of darkness."

The wind rose to a scream. Rain that was now half-sleet blasted the windows like shrapnel. The lights flickered and the house creaked.

"The God that let you in commands you to leave. Jesus commands you to leave. All the saints and martyrs—"

He let go of Newsome's mouth, pulling his hand back the way a man does when he's touched something hot. But Newsome's mouth stayed open. More: it began to widen, first into a gape and then into a soundless howl. His eyes rolled back in his head and his feet began to jitter. His urine let go and the sheet over his crotch went as dark as Rideout's collar.

"Stop," Kat said, starting forward. "He's having a seizure. You have to st—"

Jensen yanked her back. She turned to him and saw his normally ruddy face had gone as pale as a linen napkin.

Newsome's jaw had dropped all the way to his breastbone. The lower half of his face disappeared into a mighty yawn. Kat heard temporomandibular tendons creak as knee-tendons did during strenuous physical therapy: a sound like dirty hinges. The lights in the room stuttered off, on, off, then on again.

"Come out!" Rideout shouted. "Come out!"

In the darkness behind Newsome's teeth, a bladderlike thing rose like water in a plugged drain. It was pulsing. There was a rending, splintering crash and the window across the room shattered. Coffee cups fell to the floor and broke. Suddenly there was a branch in the room with them. The lights went out. The generator started up again. No burp this time but a steady roar. When the lights came back, Rideout was lying on the bed with Newsome, his arms flung out and his face planted on the wet patch in the sheet. Something was oozing from Newsome's gaping mouth, his teeth dragging grooves in its shapeless body, which was stippled with stubby green spikelets.

Not a tennis ball, Kat thought. *More like one of those Kooshes the kids play with.*

Tonya saw it and fled back down the hall with her head hunched forward, her hands locked at the nape of her neck, and her forearms over her ears.

The green thing tumbled onto Newsome's chest.

"*Spray it!*" Kat screamed at Jensen. "*Spray it before it can get away!*" Yes. Then they would put it in the specimen bottle and screw the lid down tight. *Very* tight.

Jensen's eyes were huge and glassy. He looked like a sleepwalker. Wind blew through the room. It swirled his hair. A picture fell from the wall. Jensen pistoned out the hand holding the can of pepper spray and triggered the plastic nub. There was a hiss, then he leaped to his feet, screaming. He tried to turn, probably to flee after Tonya, but stumbled and fell to his knees. Although Kat felt too dumbfounded to move—to even stir a hand—part of her brain must still have been working, because she knew what had happened. He had gotten the can turned around. Instead of pepper-spraying the thing that was now oozing through the unconscious Reverend Rideout's hair, Jensen had sprayed himself.

"*Don't let it get me!*" Jensen shrieked. He began to crawl blindly away from the bed. "*I can't see, don't let it get me!*"

The wind gusted. Dead leaves lifted from the tree-branch that had come through the window and swirled around the room. The green thing dropped from the nape of Rideout's creased and sunburned neck onto the floor. Feeling like a woman underwater, Kat swiped at it with the bristle end of the broom. She missed. The thing disappeared under the bed, not rolling but slithering.

Jensen crawled headfirst into the wall beside the doorway. "*Where am I? I can't see!*"

Newsome was sitting up, looking bewildered. "What's going on? What happened?" He pushed Rideout's head off him. The reverend slid bonelessly from the bed to the floor.

Melissa bent over him.

"*Don't do that!*" Kat shouted, but it was too late.

She didn't know if the thing was truly a god or just some weird kind of leech, but it was fast. It came out from under the bed, rolled along Rideout's shoulder, onto Melissa's hand, and up her arm. Melissa tried to shake it off and couldn't. *Some kind of sticky stuff on those stubby little spikes*, the part of Kat's brain that would still work told the part—the much larger part—that still wouldn't. *Like the glue on a fly's feet.*

Melissa had seen where the thing came from and even in her panic was wise enough to cover her own mouth with both hands. The thing skittered up her neck, over her cheek, and squatted on her left eye. The wind screamed and Melissa screamed with it. It was the cry of a woman drowning in the kind of pain the charts in the hospitals can never describe. The charts go from one to ten; Melissa's agony was well over one hundred—that of someone being boiled alive. She staggered backwards, clawing at the thing on her eye. It was pulsing faster now, and Kat could hear a low, liquid sound as the thing resumed feeding. It was a *slushy* sound.

It doesn't care who it eats, she thought, just as if this made sense. Kat realised she was walking toward the screaming, flailing woman, and observed this phenomenon with interest.

"Hold still! *Melissa, HOLD STILL!*"

Melissa paid no attention. She continued to back up. She struck the thick branch now visiting the room and went sprawling. Kat went to one knee beside her and brought the broomhandle smartly down on Melissa's face. Down on the thing that was feeding on Melissa's eye.

There was a splatting sound, and suddenly the thing was sliding limply down the housekeeper's cheek, leaving a wet trail of slime behind. It moved across the leaf-littered floor, intending to hide under the branch the way it had hidden under the bed. Kat sprang to her feet and stepped on it. She felt it splatter beneath her sturdy New Balance walking shoe. Green stuff shot out in both directions, as if she had stepped on a small balloon filled with snot.

Kat went down again, this time on both knees, and took Melissa in her arms. At first Melissa struggled, and Kat felt a fist graze her ear. Then Melissa subsided, breathing harshly. "Is it gone? Kat, is it gone?"

"I feel better," Newsome said wonderingly from behind them, in some other world.

"Yes, it's gone," Kat said. She peered into Melissa's face. The eye the thing had landed on was bloodshot, but otherwise it looked all right. "Can you see?"

"Yes. It's blurry, but clearing. Kat... the pain... it was all through me. It was like the end of the world."

"Somebody needs to flush my eyes!" Jensen yelled. He sounded indignant.

"Flush your own eyes," Newsome said cheerily. "You've got two good legs, don't you? I think I might, too, once Kat throws them back into gear. Somebody check on Rideout. I think the poor sonofabitch might be dead."

Melissa was staring up at Kat, one eye blue, the other red and leaking tears. "The pain... Kat, you have no idea of the pain."

"Yes," Kat said. "Actually, I do. Now." She left Melissa sitting by the branch and went to Rideout. She checked for a pulse and found nothing, not even the wild waver of a heart that is still trying its best. Rideout's pain, it seemed, was over.

The generator went out.

"Fuck," Newsome said, still sounding cheery. "I paid seventy thousand dollars for that Jap piece of shit."

"*I need someone to flush my eyes!*" Jensen bellowed "*Kat!*"

Kat opened her mouth to reply, then didn't. In the new darkness, something had crawled onto the back of her hand.

◄○►

STAY

LEAH BOBET

She felt the storm come in, in her kneecaps, then her thighs. By eight o'clock, it blew from the north into Sunrise, January-hard and fine like sand, and Cora's hip was aching.

She asked Johnny Red for a smoke break and limped out back to the storeroom, kneading the hip with her right hand while her left cupped the cigarette. The storeroom was cold and cluttered, a tiny junkyard of boxes and broken chairs, but normally it was quiet; the rattle of pots in Johnny Red's kitchen didn't quite reach through the door. Tonight, though, the back door banged like an angry drunk; the snow hissed and ground at metal, brick, bone. Cora lit a second thin-rolled smoke off the first and listened to the rattle of the heartbroke wind.

When she came back through the storeroom door, half her tables had up and left.

"Better service across the street?" she asked. The plates were half-full, still steaming. There was nothing across the street. There was nowhere else to eat in the whole town: just the service stations, the Tutchos' grocery, and the snow.

"Transport truck's gone off the road," Johnny said behind the counter, and crimped a new coffee filter into the brew basket. A few hairs pulled loose from his straight black ponytail and drifted into his face;

he brushed them back with a callused brown hand. "The boys went to haul it to Fiddler's."

Georgie Fiddler ran one of the two service stations in town. Mike Blondin, who ran the other, was still at his table, hands wrapped thin around a chipped blue pottery mug. He held it up and Cora grabbed the stained coffeepot.

"I want the fresh stuff," he complained; she didn't answer, just filled the mug with sour, black coffee. He waved her off before it hit the brim and flipped open the dented metal sugar tin.

"You didn't go out with them," she said. Not a question.

Mike Blondin's fingers moved like a stonecarver's, measured sugar with chisel precision: one pinch, two. He had big hands. "Wouldn't want to just abandon you," he grinned. There'd been a time, not too many years past, when Mikey Blondin's grin had got him whatsoever he desired anywhere from Sunrise to the Alberta border.

"Thoughtful," she said, dry, just as Johnny Red hit the percolator button and called out, "What'm I, chopped liver?" Gertie Myers, back at the corner table, rolled her eyes. Cora ignored it all and covered the cooling plates.

An hour passed before the menfolk trickled back in, red-faced and damp with winter-sweat. "Hey," Johnny Red said, and ladled out eight bowls of steaming chicken soup. "What's the news?"

"Went hard into the ditch," Fred Tutcho replied, and sucked back soup straight from the bowl. The steam set the ice in his eyelashes to melting. "Georgie got the tow and we managed to fish it out, but the front axle's pretty busted."

"The driver?" Cora asked.

"Got him up at Jane's." Jane Hooker ran the Treeline Motel, which was ten rooms and a Dene crafts shop, old-style porcupine quill-and-hair work, out by Blondin's. In the deep wintertime most of her rooms were closed; the only visitors to Sunrise in January were family and the odd long-haul trucker. "She'n Georgie are checking him out."

"I'll bring them something, then," Cora said, and ducked into the kitchen. She filled three thermoses and screwed the lids on tight, shrugged on her long, thick, battered coat. She wound three scarves and a hat about her head before stepping out into the storm.

It wasn't enough. The storm cut. It had blown in from the north, where there weren't no buildings or shrubs—whitebark pines or larches—to beat down the wind. Even breathing through thick wool, Cora's nostrils froze together at the first sucked-in breath, and her jeans were stiff by the time she reached the Treeline Motel. There was only one light on. Cora hunkered deeper into her scarves and scooted, knees-bent against the slippery gravel, down the battered row of doors with fingers clamped around her canvas bag.

Room six had been converted into a warm and stuffy sickroom. Jane Hooker leaned over the bed, obscuring her patient from the knees on up, and Georgie Fiddler tinkered with the steam radiator, coaxing out a whining, clanking heat. The warm air made Cora sneeze, and two heads turned sharp around the double bed. She waggled the canvas bag and groped with her free hand for a tissue.

Her fingers were still stiff when she unscrewed the thermos caps and set them on the nightstand. Jane shifted over to make room, and she finally got a look at the driver.

He had soft, sweaty, messy hair. It fell dark across a white man's flattened cheekbones and was tamped down in a line where his cap would sit. The cap was on the dresser: white and faded red, damp from the roadside snow. The brim was bent almost double, into a fist.

Jane had the man's jackets off—one for winter and a checked old lumber jacket—and her broad hand felt the shape of his ribs. "Good enough," she said to Georgie with a nod, and he let out a little sigh; probably happy he didn't have to call to Hay River for the doctor.

Cora poured them half-chilled chicken soup and passed the mugs into reddened hands. "From Johnny," she said. Jane took hers with a nod, distracted; Georgie caught his up and resumed his regular pacing. She cupped her hands around a third mug, stealing what heat it had left, and leaned back against the wall to watch.

"Enough left for our boy here?" Jane asked, and Cora nodded. She'd ladled Johnny's soup pot dry. "Good," Jane replied, and stood with a long, loose breath. The lines around her eyes were windburned and deep. "I get the feeling he'll wake up hungry. Got a pretty good crack on the head."

"Lucky he didn't break those ribs too," Georgie said.

"Speaking of." Jane paused. "You find his seatbelt on?"

"He was clear across the cab." Georgie looked up at her, at Jane, and his brow creased into three fine canyons over his greying eyebrows. "I'll look over the truck tomorrow."

Jane nodded. "You're a good man, George Fiddler."

She didn't need to say it. But Georgie pinkened anyways over the rim of his mug, and those terrible fissures came out of his face.

"Hey," he said sudden, and both Jane and Cora looked up. "I think he's waking up."

Cora leaned in soon enough to see his eyes flicker. They were folded, turned a touch at the corners. Métis then, not white, but whatever blood he had, it wasn't Dene or Inuit. The nose was too narrow, the face too thin. Too thin for his own cheekbones, she realized. The man looked gaunt. Hungry.

"Hello?" she asked softly, then: "Wotziye?"

The creased eyelids opened.

The eyes behind them were bright and black, bone-sharp. They darted right and left like a trapped hunting bird's, taking in ceiling, walls, triple-paned window with the air of something captive. Cora jerked back and they tracked her movement. The gaze stung like wind-whipped ice on the edge of her cheek.

Cora had once, before she moved to Sunrise, seen a polar bear hunt. It crouched by a seal's breathing hole silent, waiting, waiting for a seal to draw breath, and then reached in and crushed its skull.

Those black winter eyes rested upon her, and she didn't breathe.

"Hey there," Jane said beside her, terribly far away. "How you feeling?"

That terrible watching, January-cold and fine like sand, *moved*.

Nothing happened. Jane Hooker, solid and dependable, didn't lean back or recoil. "Thought we'd lost you there," she said, all good cheer and good sense.

Cora exhaled, and for a brief second, her breath steamed in the air.

She felt a hand on her elbow and jumped; Georgie Fiddler, standing an arm's-length back. "You all right there?"

No. "Yeah," she said. Her jaw was numb, and it ached. Those wicked eyes looked at Jane Hooker and they were just brown: too-bright and confused, flicking back and forth between faces and the pitted white ceiling. The pupils were overlarge, crowding the skin-brown iris, dark and deep but normal.

It wasn't the pupil, Cora thought distinctly, and rubbed her palm against her cheek. The man's mouth shaped a question, and it was not at all the same.

Georgie quirked an eyebrow. "Go on, Cor. Johnny probably needs you back."

"Thanks," she said. There was gooseflesh on her hands. She stuffed them in her coat pockets and went.

She was ten steps into the crunching, wailing snow, her second scarf only half-wrapped around her ears, when she heard the bird cry.

There was a raven perched on the Treeline Motel's roof, still as an animal killed five miles from home and frozen rictus. The storm beat against it, passed around it, let it through. It cocked its head—a beak-shadow, a change in the darkness—and laughed at her once more, biting.

Oh hell, she thought.

And then it blurred against the snowfall, its wings black against white against bottomless black, and she ran.

⟨o⟩

"I saw a raven on the Treeline's roof last night," Cora said, no preamble, when she came into the diner the next morning.

Johnny Red was in the kitchen, fumbling for something that clattered and bumped and made him swear. "It's minus thirty," he said when he surfaced.

"Yeah," Cora said.

She felt his eyes on her as she hung up her coat and tied on her soft, worn-down apron. It was just the two of them here this time of day, but he still kept his voice low. "Think it's something?"

She pulled the knot tight, tugged at each of the loops to make sure they wouldn't give. The sun was brilliant outside, halfway through the sky and already falling: subarctic noontime. It turned the snow to pure light and slanted anti-shadow across the pale blue tabletops. "I don't know medicine, Johnny."

"Sometimes you don't have to," he replied, ducking back onto his haunches behind the counter and clattering some more. She had all the table settings in place and he'd started the soup before she said, "Yeah. I think it's something."

His mouth pulled down, grimmer. He didn't reply.

Georgie Fiddler came in right at the lunchtime open, pink with cold and puffy-eyed. He nodded to Cora and bellied up to the old-fashioned lunch counter. "Thanks for the soup last night," he said, and set the bag of empty thermoses on the counter.

Johnny waved it off, ladle in hand. "How's damages?"

"Bent front axle," he said, and tugged off his gloves. "Be a day or two before I can run up to Hay River for the new axle brackets. They haven't cleared the highways yet."

Cora looked out the restaurant's triple-paned windows at the glittering snow: knee-high if it was an inch. Terrible driving weather. "How's our trucker?"

"Awake," he said; the glance he cast her was only a little concerned. "Jane said he's just staring." He didn't need to say more; there was only one kind of stare in a town like this. Cora'd first seen it young, in an uncle home after a turn in Grande Cache who'd stayed only a week before drifting off one night to freeze. After that it showed up on mothers, friends, the boys who sniffed gasoline in tool sheds on long winter nights; it blurred.

"You reach his people yet?" Johnny Red asked.

"Jane don't think he's got any people. The only number in his wallet was the trucking company."

"That's a shame," Johnny Red said evenly, in a way someone else might have thought idle.

Cora lifted an eyebrow. He put his long chef's knife against the curve of a withered onion and said nothing.

Georgie Fiddler did. "Everything all right there, John?"

Johnny's knife paused. "Cora saw a raven on the motel roof last night."

"Johnny—" she said, sharp enough to surprise herself. His jaw twitched a little below the curve of his ear; the look he cast her said *sorry*, and *no*. She let out a breath and noticed her hand at her own jaw, rubbing it like a feeding baby's back. She put it in her apron pocket. She needed a smoke.

"It's thirty below," Georgie said.

Johnny Red nodded and snipped the shoot end off his onion.

Georgie Fiddler frowned. "So what's that mean?" He was one of the few fully white men in Sunrise, come up from north Saskatchewan twelve and a half years back. Nobody begrudged him for it—he paid better wages and kept better hours than Mike Blondin, after all—but it meant sometimes he needed a thing explained that should never need explaining.

"The problem with Raven," Johnny Red said delicately, "is that you're never sure *what* you're going to get."

"Oh," Georgie Fiddler said, in a way that meant he hadn't grasped the half of it. Cora couldn't blame him. *She'd* barely grasped the half of it.

"Anyways," Johnny said, brushing onion from his cutting board, "It'll go better when he's gone."

The silence puddled a little, chilly, on the tiled black and white floor.

"Well," Georgie said, stiff, "it'll be a good while for that. The other driver on the route went missing last week, just up and vanished from the depot, and they can't send another until next week. *If* they clear the highway tomorrow. So try to keep it under your hat, man."

Johnny's expression didn't change. "So that truck's gonna sit in your garage for a week?" he said as if he'd not heard Georgie at all.

Cora shot Georgie a *look*. He took the hint. "Looks like," he said, and ran a hand through his thin hair. "Northbest'll be pretty pissed. It's a perishable load, and boy is it gonna perish."

"What's so perishable?" she asked.

Georgie Fiddler smiled dryly. "Fruit. Veg. Stuff I've never even seen before. Don't know how good it'll be after another night in this weather."

Johnny put his knife down. "So you've got the phone number for this Northbest man."

Georgie set a torn slip of paper down on the Formica counter. "That's what I came to bring you," he said, still a little cool. "And to ask if you could run lunch for two down to Jane's."

"For him," Johnny said.

"And Daisy."

"I'll go," Cora said.

"Cor—" Johnny started.

"Not even Raven lives on thin air just yet." Her voice stayed level. The colour rose behind his windburned brown cheeks, but he tipped her a nod.

"I can do sandwiches," he said, and disappeared into his kitchen.

"You sure you're all right?" Georgie Fiddler asked, and she wasn't sure if he meant Johnny Red or last night or Raven on the Treeline's roof, laughing bitter dark.

Cora untied her apron and let out a long breath. "If I don't come back," she said, "break all the eggs."

Inside the kitchen, Johnny Red snorted.

⟨○⟩

Daisy Blondin was in with the trucker when Cora tapped on the door. "Lunch," Cora said, stomping snow off her boots.

The trucker was propped up in Jane Hooker's clean white bed, tee-shirt thin and rumpled, bruise-dark shadows underneath his eyes. Light brown stubble was coming in on his cheek; someone would have to find a razor. Too far away to see his eyes, but Georgie was right: staring.

"Lunch!" Daisy said, and put aside a creased copy of *Canadian Technician*. Her feet were on the bed; two brown toes peeked out of a hole in her red-and-white striped socks. "No chance you could take over? Jane's sleeping and my brother's gonna kill me."

Cora unbuttoned her coat, but didn't take it off. Tough words in the presence of Johnny Red or not, she wasn't staying a minute farther than she had to. "I can't. It's lunch rush."

Daisy sighed. "All right. Let me go to the can." She wandered around the foot of the bed to the bathroom, and there was silence for a moment after the bathroom door slammed. Cora heard the click of the toilet lid hitting the tank, and another sound: the steady thud of an axe against a whitebark pine. Her forehead wrinkled. It was cold for cutting trees this afternoon, and as far as she knew, the gas for the furnaces wasn't anywhere near that precarious yet.

The heater pinged and muttered. It was cold in here, too. Her hip ached. The man on the bed pushed himself up to sitting, and she forced herself to stay still. "Lunch?" she asked, and it fell into the silence like a stone.

He was a big man; she hadn't noticed that last night. Tall and rangy enough that his feet stuck out over the edge of the double bed, his forearms pale but ropy and strong. It made the hollows under his cheekbones stand out even sharper. His shoulders hunched around his chin as if he wished himself disappeared. His nod was a ghost.

"So what do I call you?" she asked, trying to keep her voice normal.

"Aidan," he said. He sounded hoarse, quiet; like someone half out of the habit of talking.

"I'm Cora." She forced herself to hand him the waxed-paper package. He stared at it for a second, cupped in his two hands, before picking it open with a dirty fingernail.

"You were here last night," he said suddenly, and Cora realized he was watching her from behind that fall of mussed-up hair. She rubbed her jaw, little circles like Johnny Red cleaning his counter.

"I was," she said careful.

He rolled bread into a tiny ball between thumb and forefinger. He wasn't eating.

The sound of wood chopping was closer now, in the room, and heater or not, her breath steamed. She stepped backwards once, twice.

"You feeling better, then?" she asked to cover it, and he looked up at her full for the first time. He talked like a shut-in, but he stared like a resting lynx.

"Yeah," he said, soft and creaking, and the chill sound of trees falling, wood splintering in rhythm—*heartbeat rhythm*—almost drowned it out.

Her ears were ringing. Her tongue didn't want to move, and his eyes were so big, nighttime-big, dark as raven's-feather and sharp as a polar bear's, waiting. Waiting. "Well, we'll take good care of you," she blurted.

He stopped. Everything stopped.

The dizzying cold shattered.

"I… pardon?" he choked out. His face was dirty pale, hands shaking. The sandwich was squashed flat between his fingers.

What did I say?

Cora sucked in a breath. Her hip was burning with cold, wedged hard against the motel's plaster wall. She was shivering. She couldn't get warm. "They ain't coming to get you for a week. I just didn't want you to worry, that we wouldn't take good care of you—"

She was babbling. She was panicking.

She hadn't thought he could look any sicker.

"A week?" he asked, and there were funerals in his brown, big, human eyes.

The toilet flushed, and Daisy banged out of the washroom, Jane's bathroom towel trailing from her hand. "Thanks, Cor. Tell Mikey I'm here if you see him?"

"Yeah," she said unsteady, and Daisy Blondin, only six years younger than her but about twenty more invincible, flicked up an eyebrow and looked each to each.

"Everything all right?" she asked.

"Yeah," Cora said, automatic, regretting it a split-second after. "I gotta run." She had three smokes left in the pack. She'd counted them last night.

The skies were clear on the walk from the Treeline Motel to the Sunrise Restaurant. She scanned the skies and rooflines as she walked, and smoked them all.

◄◦►

There were things in the back of the produce truck that Cora had never seen: mangoes, persimmons, fine nubbly oranges, not to mention the vegetables she couldn't name. She and Johnny loaded a good third of the Northbest crates onto service station wagons after the lunch crowd trickled away, and then helped Magda Tutcho wrestle the rest into the General Store. It wouldn't last long—a week and a half at most, Magda said—but there was always Gertie's canning apparatus, and besides, it'd be a hell of a week.

Cora hand-lettered a sign for the Sunrise Restaurant's door—*Tropical Party 7pm Tonite: $15 Full Meal*—and tacked it firmly down by all four corners. Sunrise was a small town. Word would get around.

They sorted the oddest fruits on the countertop, next to the spine-cracked chef school cookbook left behind, mouldering, by the last owner of the Sunrise Restaurant. "What's this one?" she asked, balancing a red, round weight in one hand.

"Pomegranate," Johnny Red said. He'd worked as a cook down in Calgary for three years before he took over the Sunrise Restaurant. By the second year up north he'd mostly stopped complaining about how everything came in tins, but when he took the pomegranate from her hand, the look on his face was like the first day of spring. "All the rage out in BC. White ladies in workout pants beat down your door for them."

He waggled his eyebrows, and she laughed. It came out bad; forced. There was something cold stuck inside her. The sound of a chopped-down tree, creaking, falling.

"Cor?" he asked, and his eyebrows drew down. She shook her head.

"It's the trucker, isn't it?"

"Johnny—" she started.

"You didn't have to go out there."

"Pomegranate," she said, firm, and crossed her arms.

He split it with his chef's knife, and a dribble of red juice wandered across the counter. The seeds were packed in tight, nestled together for warmth or love or safekeeping. They didn't part easy: Johnny had to dig in with two fingers and pry a cluster out. They were translucent when alone, and bruised easily. She held them to the light before popping them in her mouth.

"Sour," she said when she could speak again. Her mouth felt washed-out, astringent. They burned warm all the way down.

"That," Johnny Red said, "is the fruit that trapped a white girl down in Hell at the beginning of the world."

She ran her tongue over her lips. "Now you tell me."

He smiled, lopsided. "White people medicine only works on white people, dontcha know."

"I'm half that," she replied, mild.

Johnny Red sized her up for a moment, a stare that echoed like Aidan the trucker man's but much, much warmer. "Well," he said. "That means half of you is going to be bound three whole months to me and this town. So better decide if it's the top half or the bottom."

This time she really did laugh. "Oh, you'd like *that*."

He waggled his eyebrows again—Groucho Marx had never had a Dene man's sharp eyebrows, but it worked out—and leaned over the counter at her. She leaned back a little, shook her head smiling. "Nuh-uh."

He sighed, overtheatrical, and dusted his palms on his jeans. They left smears and smudges of red. "What's a guy have to do?"

"Give me a raise," Cora replied, but her lungs had stopped aching. *Thank you, Johnny Red.* She rolled a green-red oval at him across the counter. "Next?"

◄◦►

People started showing up come half past seven: fashionably late for a party in Sunrise. Johnny Red took their cash at the counter and Cora steered them to their tables, each stacked with the three-course menu they'd done in two shades of blocky handwriting. It was fresh veg and mangoes, orange juice not from a can; wedges of pineapple cut and perched on scratched plastic glasses. There wasn't no pomegranate on it; either Johnny Red hadn't found a use for it in time or he just didn't plan on sending the whole town to white-man Hell.

Nate Okpik brought his fiddle, and Daisy Blondin her drum, and by eight the whole place was hopping, Johnny slinging plates as fast as he could. Cora dodged the odd dancer, coffeepot and empty soup bowls balanced, rock-certain she wasn't getting no smoke break tonight.

People streamed in and out, took seats, moved chairs, left them for other tables; nobody sat alone. Nobody was *quiet*. She noticed, then, the little puddle of silence at the corner table; the little draft of cold air.

Aidan the bird-eyed trucker was hunched alone over a menu.

He was pale, even for a sick man—a sick half-white man with a crack on the head the size of a trailer. He looked up, hunting-hawk quick, and saw her. Two spots of red bloomed in his face: frozen, helpless embarrassment. She reached out to steady herself and caught the handle of the coffeepot, waitress's self-defence. There was no pretending she hadn't seen him. No turning away.

She approached the table, holding the pot out like a shield. "Coffee?"

"Sure," he mumbled, tilting his head away.

She poured. The stream of coffee arced into the cup: it only trembled a little, only spilled a drop. "Sugar's on the table," she said, unnecessary. "You take milk?"

He shook his head. He still wouldn't look at her. It made the back of her neck prickle in a way that Mike Blondin's too-big smiles never had. "No milk," he said, and fingered the edge of the menu. "This is from my truck?"

Nate Okpik, next table over, turned and grinned broadly over the booth's back. "That's right. You're drinking free tonight."

Aidan's shoulders folded in like a deflated accordion. "Let him be," Cora snapped. *Leave him alone. He's dangerous.*

"Fine, fine," Nate said, big and rumbling and good-natured, and turned back to his wife and boys.

Aidan had retreated even farther into himself, fingers plaited together as if groping for something to hold on to and finding only each other. "Sorry 'bout that," she said, and he flashed a wan, anxious smile. He looked like hell. Who was supposed to be watching him—Magda? Gertie? The man shouldn't have been out of bed.

It'll be better when he's gone, Johnny Red's voice echoed, and she shook her head. *Come off it. Do your job.*

She swallowed, tried to force up a smile. "Get you the special?"

He nodded, lifting his gaze from her knees to her belly, the apron tied snug about it. A whisper of chill wind wandered across her hip.

"Cor?" Johnny Red's voice rose sharp and tense across the floor. She looked up and he was right behind the lunch counter, ladle clenched in his hand like a weapon. "Need you over here, please."

Cora shivered with relief and steered back across the restaurant. The muscles of Johnny's face eased like she'd just walked back off a highway median. Behind him, over at table thirteen, Georgie Fiddler watched them and frowned.

Grandma Okpik had said Johnny had a bit of the medicine once, back when he'd rolled into town on the Tuesday Greyhound with nothing but a few changes of clothes and a set of knives that'd make your hair stand up until you found out they were for the kitchen. It wasn't the kind of thing she'd got around to asking about, and this was, unfortunately, not the time for a hearty and extended chat about what it was Johnny Red saw.

"What d'you want to do?" she asked.

Johnny looked over her shoulder; watching him. "I don't know yet," he said, and went to whisper in Mike Blondin's ear.

Aidan No-Last-Name picked at his food; the violent green vegetable soup Johnny Red had fixed for starter was barely below the rim when she came back to refill the coffee. His spoon leaned unused on his napkin. "He your boyfriend?" Aidan asked through a fall of brown hair.

"No," Cora said, though Johnny Red had managed to kiss her in the storeroom once or twice, and she'd not turned away. "He just likes having people to boss around. Everything all right here?"

His hands stilled. He looked up at her. Opened his mouth and shut it again. *He knows,* she realized, sharply. Everything was not at all right. *He's scared.*

"Something I can do?" she asked carefully.

His hands were still on the table. He was staring, and she realized, not at her; past her, out the big windows of the Sunrise Restaurant, into the snow. She turned, and on the featureless white there was a splotch of black; low to the ground, ruffled, feathered.

The raven hopped one step, two, in the soft-packed January snow. It twisted its head near backwards, like birds do, and cawed a wicked laugh at the both of them.

Something dropped from its sharp little beak and landed in the snow: long, and thin, and red.

Aidan scrambled up against the back of the booth and *howled,* all the voice of wolves and snuffling bears and winter, eyes big and black and wide, and the cold spiralled out of him. The cold rushed in.

The raven fluttered into the night laughing, its wings snapping like falling trees. The coffeepot slid out of Cora's hand and rang on the black and white tile. Coffee splashed her trousers, her shoes. She flinched back from the window, the raven, the boiling hot liquid on the floor. The fiddle had stopped, and the drum. Every head in Sunrise turned to stare out into the dark.

He took one step towards her. Two.

And ran.

Aidan jostled past her, between tables and chairs, out the oak front doors. "Hey!" she called, slipping in coffee, limping after him. The cold air hit like a knife to the throat. "Wait!" she managed, before she doubled over coughing.

He didn't wait. Coatless, hatless, Aidan ran across the path and to the highway, head down and legs working like all the wickedness in the world was right behind him. His breath misted, a little plume to follow, and then her hip tightened sharp and he was disappearing, farther away. Going, smaller and smaller. Gone.

"Shit!" she said, and the footsteps behind her caught up: Johnny Red and Georgie Fiddler, one after the other, Johnny still with his fat blue oven mitts on.

"Cora," he said, and threw an arm full around her to keep her from falling, or maybe just running any further. "What the hell?"

"He got away. The raven," she said, and burst out again coughing. "It was out here. It dropped something—"

"I felt it," he said. *Felt, not saw.*

"He's scared," she said. "It scared him."

"We need coats," Georgie called, and they picked their way back over the broken snow. Their feet had churned up the bird-tracks.

"It wasn't too far." Her teeth were chattering. She curled out of Johnny's bracing arm and picked her way back to the parking lot: back under the edges of the sodium lights. Nothing. Nothing—

And then the wind rose and ruffled the snow, stirred it up and out and away, and Cora looked down at the smooth brown finger, slowly turning blue in the January snow.

◄o►

The search party came back cold and empty-handed, and Johnny Red had nothing left over for soup.

"We found Gertie," Jane Hooker said, staring at the specials board and the remains of Tropical Party Night. Her right mitten dangled from a string on her coat sleeve. "She's…"

Mike Blondin swallowed. "We're gonna need to call her nephew."

Bile nudged into Cora's throat. She forced it back. "Oh," Daisy said, and it sounded like all the air had left her lungs forever. Johnny held his coffee filter between thumb and finger for one long moment, turned it around, and crumpled it in his fist.

"I went by Jane's. We got an APB 'bout an hour ago," Georgie Fiddler said, his face sallow and sick. Smudged fax paper fluttered from his left hand, limp as a dead child. "From the Mounties over in High Level."

Cora took the paper. She read it briefly, like a dry goods manifest or a power bill. "Suspicion of murder and—" her voice failed. Johnny Red took the page from her. "Desecration of a corpse?" he finished, both eyebrows up high.

Jane's cheeks were red: bright and hot and burning. The tears in her eyes were probably scalding. "Her fingers were missing," she said, out from somewhere far away. "And her stomach—"

"Hey," Georgie said, and held up one hand. Big Mike Blondin looked like he planned to be sick.

"Wendigo," Johnny Red said quiet, and it cut every voice in the restaurant dead.

Cora felt for her pack, dipped into it with chilly fingers: empty. "Bum a smoke?" she asked Mike Blondin quietly, and he didn't even try to make her give him a smile for it. She rolled it between her fingers like a raven's trophy, held onto it like there was nothing else to hold.

"What do you mean?" Georgie Fiddler said. He was sweating. "Wendigo's a monster. They're made up."

She shook her head. She couldn't explain wendigo to Georgie Fiddler, not now. Jane stepped in smoothly, taking his arm. "Wendigo aren't made up," she said softly. "My grandpa knew one."

"What happened?" Georgie asked.

Jane hesitated. "They found him at the river and shot him down."

"We can't—that's murder. He's a person."

"Not anymore," Fred Tutcho said softly.

Poor Georgie Fiddler looked around the circle for backup; found none. "Maybe he won't come back," he said weakly.

Johnny Red shook his head. "He'll come back." There was no food or shelter for two hundred miles in any direction, and he had no jacket, and he was unarmed. Cora didn't know a whole lot about wendigo, but there were ways in which they were just like people: they wanted above everything to live through the night.

"So what do we do?" Georgie asked.

"We get the shotguns," Jane said, and shoved the restaurant door open, letting in the night.

"He's still a person," Georgie muttered, and the cigarette between Cora's fingers bent and tore.

◄◦►

There were seven shotguns in the town of Sunrise. Six of them worked. The six shotguns and their owners gathered close in the Sunrise Restaurant with the other eighty-three townsfolk crammed in around them. They locked the doors and turned the outside lights on full. Whatever came, if it threw a shadow, they'd see it coming.

Jane and Georgie and Nate and Daisy and Fred Tutcho and Johnny Red stood behind the counter, lining up ammunition. It was most of it deershot: there weren't no licences to carry for much else in this small a town. "They're hard to kill," Johnny Red said softly; loud enough for Cora to hear where she was pouring hot cocoa into salvaged and washed-up mugs. "You got to shoot and shoot again. Don't stop, even if he's got his hands up. Don't stop 'til he stops moving."

Cora popped one more marshmallow into the cocoa mug and drifted back to the counter, to the always-filling coffeepot. "Have a minute, Johnny?"

He looked down at her with a frown she hadn't seen before; tense, old. Tired. "What's up?"

She glanced around at her people, her family: the Okpiks and Tutchos and Blondins and Hookers and Fiddlers and Johnny Red Antoine from down south in the plains. "Georgie's right," she said. "He's still a person."

"You didn't see what he did to Gertie," Nate said, and she held up a hand, but gently.

"I looked into his eyes," she said, swallowing back the thought of fingers snapped at the bottommost joint, of intestines looped and gnawed, teeth marks like wolves'. "The real ones. And… that's still a person. He's scared." She hesitated, gathered her breath. "This isn't old times, where you could just hunt someone down by the river. The Mounties'll come. They'll have an inquest. And you know what that means."

It'd change Sunrise. Knowing everyone by name, knowing their children. Leaving your door unlocked at night. The way a man like Mikey Blondin was bad, but roll-your-eyes bad, and how people didn't get run out of town or live on welfare or huff rubber cement or sneak liquor before noontime.

It'd change everything.

"He knows something's wrong," she finished, weakly. "He's terrified."

"We could deal with an inquest later," Fred Tutcho said, but his heart wasn't all in. "He's out there, and the kids—"

"You don't want to do this," Cora said, soft. "I will not let no wendigo or man or Raven make me someone I'm ashamed to be."

A moment passed. Fred Tutcho let out a breath. He shook his head.

Johnny Red squinted at her. "So what then?" A real question, not a challenge.

"We heal him up," she said, faltering now. She didn't know what then. She'd never expected them to say yes. "We find a way to drive it out, or keep him tucked away until the Mounties get here. He was raised a white man. It's like as he doesn't know what's happened to him."

Georgie made a little noise of protest. "C'mon, Cor."

She patted his hand, absently. "There's knowing and there's knowing, George."

Johnny Red's shoulders were tight-wound. "Cor," he said. "You don't do medicine."

She didn't, and *Sometimes you don't have to* wouldn't cut no ice with Johnny. Grandma Okpik had been the first and last in Sunrise and she hadn't taught it; this wasn't an old community, where people could say *This is where my father's house sat,* or *Here's a spot cleared by ancestors.* Nobody here passed down traditions. Sunrise had been built, deliberate and slow like a snow dune: people washed up from the highway between north Alberta and the city, smelling the bad coffee, the music, something. The right ones stayed.

"We'll put the word out. Ask for help," she said. "We've gotta try."

Johnny Red looked at her for a long moment, then nodded once, slow.

"All right," Mike Blondin said. "We'll try not to shoot."

"Thank you," Cora said, and went back to washing dishes.

Johnny Red came into the kitchen a few minutes later. He bellied up to the sink beside her and dipped his arms in to the sleeve line. "You thinking something?"

"Yeah," she said. "A bit."

He didn't say anything. He didn't have to.

"You trust me?" she said anyways.

He rinsed a plate. Set it in the rack. "Yeah."

She nodded. "Okay." Behind them was the hum of worried voices; the clink of cutlery both in the sink and outside. Her elbow brushed his as they passed plates and bowls from the battered aluminum sink to the draining board. Water splashed and rustled, and outside, the wind.

Behind it all a sound, faint and creaking, like the chopping of a white-bark pine.

Cora slid her hands out of the water, dusted them gently on the front of her apron. "Going for a smoke," she said to Johnny Red, and walked slow and straight down the little hall past the kitchen that led to the storeroom door.

"She didn't have any left. Wait—" she heard behind her, but she didn't turn around.

When she passed the kitchen counter, she picked up a drying wedge of pomegranate and tucked it into her pocket.

◄◦►

She felt it right away in her kneecaps, her thighs: cramp and twist. The burn of cold so hard it wrapped your body like heat.

Storm coming.

She closed the storeroom door behind her cautiously, sharp for any unfamiliar sound. The wind scuttled 'round the corners, wearing the heart out of the buildings inch by creeping inch. She stumbled into her milk crates, swore, and righted the top one before it fell. Plastic scraped plastic, terrifically loud. She let it go with shaking hands.

"Aidan," she said soft. Shifted her weight to her good leg, trying not to feel the burn. "C'mon, I know you're back here."

Something rustled behind the old stacked-up chairs. Silence.

"I can hear your heart," she whispered.

The blow blacked out her vision for two long, falling seconds, and then he was on top of her.

Aidan was sobbing. He wept like an animal, his hips pinning hers, his hands groping for her flailing wrists to hold them down. She tried to push with her leg, but her leg wouldn't work; the hurt turned to paralysis, muscles shutting down, giving up, playing dead. The back of her head felt bitter, bitter cold, and then it was nothing but pain; he must have hit her with something. He slammed her left wrist to the floor, and she gasped. It had only been his bare hands after all.

Too strong.

Oh, hell.

She screamed, and it was tiny; his chest was on hers too, pushing the air out, sinking the chill of every January night she'd ever known down through her ribcage, her bones. She couldn't scream. She couldn't get enough air.

"Why did you say that?" he said, and it took a second before she could make out the words through his shuddering, terrified tears. "Why'd you say it?"

"Say what?" she gasped, and his teeth glinted in the thin light. Man's teeth, not a predator's: dull and blunt and slow. It wouldn't be quick or clean, this. It would hurt like five thousand years of Hell.

"Why'd you say you'd take care of me!" he burst, and his hands were moving wildfire, moving without will; they spread her own hand out, palm up, on the floor. The specks cleared from her vision, and his eyes were black, all pupil, black as a raven's wing. "Nobody can take care of *this*—"

His voice failed. The hands grew steadier, firmer, and she hadn't realized that they were shaking until they weren't; that the look on his face had been the same that Jane Hooker'd worn when she talked about Gertie cut down. Broken in two, like a little child.

And now it was fading into something monstrous. Something not a person anymore.

"Aidan, stay—" she managed, and the smell of wind, the winter-mask that used to be a person's face faltered.

"What?" he whispered, pupils shrinking abrupt and small.

Oh please. A plan. A bit of a plan.

Cora rolled herself hard right and jammed a knee up against his thigh. Those brown man's eyes went wide—wide and betrayed—and his grip broke: just a man's again, weak and changeable, not a monster's anymore. Cora fumbled in her pocket, grabbed, slid out her weapon before the hand came down and smashed her skull against the concrete once, twice, three times.

She held on like it was the only thing left in the world.

There was a raven in the roof, shuffling its feathers, watching the wendigo in Aidan's flesh pry open that hand, lean down close, bare his teeth. Its eyes were bright and staring. It was curiously silent.

The monster growled through Aidan's throat. It flung itself down and bit.

Pain spiked through her fingers: second, middle, ring. They unclenched, unwilling, and then willing, and then she jammed a full wedge of pomegranate into his open mouth.

The seeds crunched between his teeth like bones, like something living. He choked.

She twitched out from under him, wheezing; she couldn't roll anymore, couldn't move right. Her leg was a dead weight, and her head wouldn't lift. There was winter in her lungs, and she couldn't cough it out.

"Once upon a time when the world was young," she forced out, rattle-quick and low, because white-people medicine needed invocations, needed words, "a white girl ate six pomegranate seeds and was trapped down six months in Hell."

His eyes went big. He knew this story, knew it to the bone. He spat, reflexive, and she let slip a grin through the tears. Too late.

"Now you're bound to us," she said. Her vision was blurring. She couldn't see half of him, couldn't see the dark that was from the dark that wasn't. "See all those seeds? Each one's a month. That's how long you're bound to me and this town."

His mouth was stained red. Some of it was thin and some thick, drying. Some of it was hers: her hand stung, burned on three flat points on the ridge of each long finger. It'd all stain.

"Stay with me," she said, and cradled her bleeding hand; tried to say it like Grandma Okpik, like medicine, like somebody who loved you. "Stay people."

He opened his mouth, and the moan that came out was terrible, ter-rible, but not animal. Only the sound of a human being, pushed horrible miles too far.

"Good boy," she whispered, and leaned back against the hard, freezing floor. There were footsteps somewhere outside, footsteps in the hallway she could hear now that the sound of trees falling, wood breaking, living things dying was gone. The raven's eyes regarded her, black on black on black, and then one blink to the next, they were gone.

They broke down the door.

Shadows flicked across her vision: friends and neighbours, friends with guns. "Down!" Jane Hooker was shouting. "Stay *down!*"

"I'm done now," Aidan sobbed, rocking, hands clasped over his ears, mouth torn and bleeding fruit and flesh and saliva. "I'm all done. I want to go *home*—"

"Don't shoot," Cora whispered.

And then Johnny was beside her, gathering her up and calling for Jane, for Georgie, for the doctor from Hay River. She blinked slow and long and his face was above hers, lined with stark terror. "He won't be no trouble," she managed, and Johnny Red looked like he was about to be sick.

"*That* was your plan?" he said.

"He needs a bowl of soup," she told him, cradled lopsided in his arms, and the world went black as wings departing.

◄◦►

She came to in room five of the Treeline Motel, the last set of buildings standing before the end of roots and leaves and life and hope. Sunlight speckled across the ceiling, ice-light, winter-light, and the trees outside swayed quiet, and she was still alive.

She let out a sigh, long and shuddering.

Johnny Red was at her bedside in an instant. "You okay?" he said. His voice was snow-brush soft. He looked like he hadn't slept for at least a day or three.

She licked her lips. Dry. "Who's got the restaurant?" she croaked, and he went for a glass of water. He wet her lips, her bruised throat.

"Nobody," he said, and there was a rawness in it now. "Talk to me."

She stretched, cautiously; nothing broken. Jane Hooker's careful hands would have made sure of it. Her eyes wouldn't quite focus, but that was all right. There were three tidy, thick bandages wrapped about the fingers of her right hand. "I've had worse," she said.

Johnny Red flinched. "Don't tell me that."

His hand slipped down to her good one. Held on. She didn't shake it off.

"He's outside." Johnny's mouth twisted with something: fear, anger, distaste. The edges of a terrible hatred. "Has been all day, and all yesterday too. Crying like a dog."

"How much does he remember?" she asked after a second.

Johnny Red opened his mouth, shut it with a snap. "All of it."

"Did Jane call the Mounties?"

Johnny's expression went even flatter. "Not yet."

Cora leaned back against the soft pillows; heard a half-wendigo voice sobbing, burning, asking *Why did you say that to me? Why'd you say you'd take care—*

"It's gone now," she said. Then hesitated, turned her head to him half an inch. "It is, right?"

Johnny Red's lips pressed together. "Hard to tell. This could just be—" he paused with distaste "—a stronger claim. How long do we have?"

There were a lot of seeds in that pomegranate, nestled together like lovers, like houses perched on the edge of the highway to Hay River. It was past too late to find out how many he'd spit, how many he'd swallowed down. "I don't know," she said. "I guess we'll find out."

He didn't answer. He didn't answer for long enough that she turned her head another agonizing space, and saw him sitting in a chair beside her, elbows on his knees, head buried in his hands.

"The raven left," he said muffled. "Maybe that means something."

It means, she thought, *we're on our own now.*

"How much medicine d'you have?" she asked.

He looked up. There were tears in his eyes: sheer frustration, pain. Relief. "Not enough," he said. "Not half enough to make this safe."

"We'll be fine," she said, faintly.

Johnny Red stood up, all six feet of him, and leaned over her slowly, bracing himself with a hand on the yielding mattress. The kiss he left on her mouth wasn't hard—she was bandaged up too much for hard right now—but it didn't brook no questions.

"You," he said, "are bound to me three months, and next time you *talk* to me about the plan."

She didn't talk back to that.

Johnny Red went to the door, swung the hinges wide. She felt the cold air blow in, cold but not terrible bitter, and heard voices exchanged low, terse, cautious. One set of footsteps faded, and another stepped inside. Shut the door. Moved, soft and tremulous, along the faded carpet runner to the bedside.

The light was so much better now. It had to be past three. Spring coming, eventually.

"Hey," Aidan said, standing two feet away, hands clasped in front of him like they were the only thing in the world to hold; eyes big and brown and human and terrified and whole.

"Hey," she said. "You stayed."

◄◦►

THE MORAINE

SIMON BESTWICK

The mist hit us suddenly. One moment we had the peak in sight; the next, the white had swallowed up the crags and was rolling down towards us.

"Shit," I said. "Head back down."

For once, Diane didn't argue.

Trouble was, it was a very steep climb. Maybe that was why we'd read nothing about this mountain in the guidebooks. Some locals in the hotel bar the night before had told us about it. They'd warned us about the steepness, but Diane liked the idea of a challenge. All well and good, but now it meant we had to descend very slowly; one slip and you'd go down the mountainside, arse over apex.

That was when I saw the faint desire-line that led off, almost at right angles to the main path, running sideways and gently downwards.

"There, look," I said, pointing. "What do you reckon?"

Diane hesitated, glancing down the main path then up at the fast-falling mist. "Let's try it."

So we did.

"Look out," I said. Diane was lagging a good four or five yards behind me. "Faster."

"I'm going as fast as I bloody can, Steve."

I didn't rise to the bait, just turned and jogged on. The gentler slope meant we could run, but even so, we weren't fast enough. Everything went suddenly white.

"Shit," Diane said. I reached out for her hand—she was just a shadow in the wall of white vapour—and she took it and came closer. The mist was cold, wet and clinging, like damp cobwebs.

"What now?" Diane said. She kept her voice level, but I could tell it wasn't easy for her. And I couldn't blame her.

Don't be fooled by Lakeland's picture-postcard scenery; its high mountains and blue tarns, the boats on Lake Windermere, the gift shops and stone-built villages. You come here from the city to find the air's fresher and cleaner, and when you look up at night you see hundreds, thousands more stars in the sky because there's no light pollution. But by the same token, fall on a slope like this and there'll be no-one around, and your mobile won't get a signal. And if a mist like this one comes down and swallows you up and you don't know which way to go—it doesn't take that long, on a cold October day, for hypothermia to set in. These fells and dales claimed lives like ours each year.

I took a deep breath. "I think…"

"You OK?" she asked.

"I'm fine." I was a little nettled she'd thought otherwise; she was the one who'd sounded in need of reassurance, but I wasn't going to start bickering now. It occurred to me—at the back of my head, and I'd have denied it outright if anyone had suggested it to me—that this might be a blessing in disguise; if I could stay calm and lead us to safety, I could be a hero in her eyes. "We need to get to some lower ground."

"Yes, I *know*," she said, as if I'd pointed out the stupidly obvious. Well, perhaps I had. I was just trying to clarify the situation. Alright, I wanted to impress her, to look good. But I wanted to do the right thing as well. Honestly.

So I pointed down the trail—the few feet of it we could see where it disappeared into the mist. "Best off keeping on. Keep our heads and go slowly."

"Yes, I worked that bit out as well." I recognised her tone of voice; it was the one she used to take cocky students down a peg. There'd been a time when I used to slip into her lectures, even though I knew nothing, then or now, about Geology; I just liked hearing her talk about her favoured subject. I couldn't remember ever seeing her in any of *my* lectures—not that she was interested in Music. Maybe it had never been what I'd thought it was. Maybe it had never been for either of us.

Not an idea I liked, but one I'd kept coming back to far too often lately. As had Diane. Hence this trip, which was looking less and less like a good idea all the time. We'd spent our honeymoon here; I suppose we'd hoped to recapture something or other, but there's no magic in places. Only people, and precious little of that; less and less the older you get.

And none of that was likely to get us safely out of here. "OK then," I said. "Come on."

◦

Diane caught the back of my coat and pulled. I wheeled to face her and swayed, off-balance. Loose scree clattered down into the mist; the path had grown rockier underfoot. She caught my arm and steadied me. I yanked it free, thoroughly pissed off. "What?"

"Steve, we're still walking."

"I noticed. Well, actually, we're not just now, since you just grabbed me."

She folded her arms. "We've been walking nearly twenty minutes." I could see she was trying to stop her teeth chattering. "And I don't think we're much closer to ground level. I think we might be a bit off course."

I realised my teeth had started chattering too. It was hard to be sure, but I thought she might have a point; the path didn't look like it was sloping down any longer. If it'd levelled off, we were still halfway up the damned mountain. "Shit."

I felt panic threatening, like a small hungry animal gnawing away inside my stomach, threatening to tear its way up through my body if it let it. I wouldn't. Couldn't. Mustn't. If we panicked we were stuffed.

At least we hadn't come completely unprepared. We had Kendal Mint Cake and a thermos of hot tea in our backpacks, which helped, but they could only buy a little more time. We either got off this mountain soon, or we never would.

We tried our mobiles, but it was an exercise; there was no reception out here. They might as well have been bits of wood. I resisted the temptation to throw mine away.

"Should've stayed on the main path," Diane said. "If we'd taken it slow we'd have been OK."

I didn't answer. She glanced at me and rolled her eyes.

"What?"

"Steve, I wasn't having a go at you."

"Fine."

"Not everything has to be about that."

"I said, fine."

But she wouldn't leave it. "All I said was that we should've stuck to the main path. I wasn't saying this was all your fault."

"*Okay.*"

"I wasn't. If I'd seen that path I would've probably done the same thing. It looked like it'd get us down faster."

"Right."

"I'm just saying, looking back, we should've gone the other way."

"Okay. Alright. You've made your point." I stood up. A sheep bleated faintly. "Can we just leave it now?"

"*Okay.*" I saw her do the eye roll again, but pretended not to. "So now what? If we backtrack…"

"Think we can make it?"

"If we can get back to the main path, we should be able to find our way back from there."

If we were very lucky, perhaps; our hotel was a good two miles from the foot of this particular peak, and chances were the mist would be at ground level too. Even off the mountain we'd be a long way from home and dry, but it seemed the best choice on offer. If only we'd taken it sooner; we might not have heard the dog bark.

But we did.

We both went still. Diane brushed her dark hair back from her eyes and looked past me into the mist. I looked too, but couldn't see much. All I could see was the rocky path for a few feet ahead before it vanished into the whiteout.

The sheep bleated again. A few seconds later, the dog barked.

I looked at Diane. She looked back at me. A sheep on its own meant nothing—most likely lost and astray, like us. But a dog—a dog most likely had an owner.

"Hello?" I called into the mist. "Hello?"

"Anybody down there?" Diane called.

"Hello?" A voice called back.

"Thank god for that," Diane whispered.

We started along the rattling path, into the mist. "Hello?" called the voice. "Hello?"

"Keep shouting," I called back, and it occurred to me that we were the ones who sounded like rescuers. Maybe we'd found another fell-walker, caught out in the mists like us. I hoped not. What with the dog barking as well, I was pinning my hopes on a shepherd out here rounding up a lost sheep, preferably a generously-disposed one with a warm, nearby cottage complete with a fire and a kettle providing hot cups of tea.

Scree squeaked and rattled underfoot as we went. I realised the surface of the path had turned almost entirely into loose rock. Not only that, but it was angling sharply down after all. Diane caught my arm. "Careful."

"Yeah, okay, I know." I tugged my arm free and tried to ignore the long sigh she let out behind me.

The mist cleared somewhat as we reached the bottom. We could see between twenty-five and thirty yards ahead, which was a vast improvement, although the whiteout still completely hid everything beyond that point. The path led down into a sort of shallow ravine between our peak and its neighbour. The bases of the two steep hillsides sloped gently downwards to a floor about ten yards wide. It was hard to be certain as both the floor and those lower slopes were covered in a thick layer of loose stone fragments.

The path we'd followed petered out, or more into accurately disappeared into that treacherous surface. Two big, flat-topped boulders jutted out of the scree, one about twenty yards down the ravine floor, the other about fifteen yards on from that, at the mouth of a gully that gaped in the side of our peak.

The mist drifted. I couldn't see any sign of man or beast. "Hello?" I called.

After a moment, there was a click and rattle somewhere in the ravine. Rock, pebbles, sliding over one another, knocking together.

"Bollocks," I said.

"Easy," Diane said. "Looks like we've found some low ground anyway."

"That doesn't mean much. We've lost our bearings."

"There's somebody around here. We heard them. Hello?" She shouted the last—right down my earhole, it felt like.

"Ow."

"Sorry."

"Forget it."

There was another click and rattle of stone. And the voice called out "Hello?" again.

"There," said Diane. "See?"

"Yeah. Okay."

There was a bleat, up and to our left. I looked and sure enough there was the sheep we'd heard, except it was more of a lamb, picking its unsteady way over the rocks on the lower slopes of the neighbouring peak.

"Aw," said Diane. "Poor little thing." She's one of those who goes all gooey over small furry animals. Not that it stops her eating them; I was nearly tempted to mention the rack of lamb in red wine jus she'd enjoyed so much the night before. Nearly.

The lamb saw us, blinked huge dark eyes, bleated plaintively again.

In answer, there were more clicks and rattles, and an answering bleat from further down the ravine. The lamb shifted a bit on its hooves, moving sideways, and bleated again.

After a moment, I heard the rocks click again, but softly this time. It lasted longer too, this time. Almost as if something was moving slowly, as stealthily as the noisy terrain allowed. The lamb was still, looking silently up the ravine. I looked too, trying to see past where the scree faded into the mist.

The rocks clicked softly, then were silent. And then a dog barked, twice.

The lamb tensed but was still.

Click click click, went the rocks, and the dog barked again.

The lamb bleated. A long silence.

Diane's fingers had closed round my arm. I felt her draw breath to speak, but I turned and shushed her, fingers to her lips. She frowned; I touched my finger back to my own lips and turned to look at the lamb again.

I didn't know why I'd done all that, but somehow knew I'd had to. A moment later we were both glad of it.

The click of shifting rocks got louder and faster, almost a rustle, like grass parting as something slid through it. The lamb bleated and took a few tottering steps back along the slope. Pebbles clattered down. The rock sounds stopped. I peered into the mist, but I couldn't see anything. Then the dog barked again. It sounded very close now. More than close enough to see, but the ravine floor was empty. I looked back at the lamb. It was still. It cocked its head.

A click of rocks, and something bleated.

The lamb bleated back.

Rocks clattered again, deafeningly loud, and Diane made a strangled gasp that might have been my name, her hand clutching my arm painfully, and pointed with her free hand.

The ravine floor was moving. Something was humped beneath the rocks, pushing them up as it went so they clicked and rattled in its wake. It was like watching something move underwater. It raced forward, arrowing towards the lamb.

The lamb let out a single terrified bleat and tried to turn away, but it never stood a chance. The humped shape under the scree hurtled towards it, loose stone rattling like dice in a shaken cup, and then rocks sprayed upwards like so much kicked sand where the lamb stood. Its bleat became a horrible squealing noise—I'd no idea sheep could make sounds like that. The shower of rubble fell back to earth. The lamb kept squealing. I could only see its head and front legs; the rest was buried under the rock. The front legs kicked frantically and the head jerked about, to and fro, the lips splaying back horribly from the teeth as it squealed out its pain. And then a sudden, shocking spray of blood spewed out from under the collapsing shroud of rocks like a scarlet fan. Diane clapped a hand to her mouth with a short, shocked cry. I think I might have croaked 'Jesus', or something along those lines, myself.

The lamb's squeals hit a new, jarring crescendo that hurt the ears, like nails on a blackboard, then choked and cut off. Scree clattered and hissed down the slope and came to rest. The lamb lay still. Its fur was speckled red with blood; its eyes already looked fixed and unblinking, glazing over. The rocks above and around it glistened.

With any luck it was beyond pain. I hoped so, because in the next moment the lamb's forequarters were yanked violently, jerked further under the rubble, and in the same instant the scree seemed to surge over it. The heaped loose rock jerked and shifted a few times, rippled slightly and was still. Even the stones splashed with blood were gone, rolled under the surface and out of sight. A few glistening patches remained, furthest out from where the lamb had been, but otherwise there was no sign that it'd even existed.

"Fuck." I definitely said it this time. "Oh fucking hell."

There was a moment of silence; I could hear Diane drawing breath again to speak. And then there was that now-familiar click and rattle as something moved under the scree. And from where the lamb had been a voice, a low, hollow voice called "Hello?"

◄⊙►

Diane put her hand over my mouth. "Stay quiet," she whispered.

"I know that," I whispered back, muffled by her hand.

"It hunts by sound," she whispered. "Must do. Vibration through the rocks."

There was a slight, low hump where the lamb had been killed; you had to look hard to see it, and know what it was you were trying to spot. A soft clicking sound came from it. Rock on rock.

"It's under the rocks," she whispered.

"I can *see* that."

"So if we can get back up onto solid ground, we should be okay."

"Should."

She gave me an irritated look. "Got any better ideas?"

"Okay. So we head back?"

"Hello?" called the voice again.

"Yes," whispered Diane. "And very, very slowly, and carefully and quietly."

I nodded.

The rocks clicked and shifted, softly. Diane raised one foot, moved it upslope, set it slowly, gently down again. Then the other foot. She turned and looked at me, then reached out and took my hand. Or I took hers, as you prefer.

I followed her up the slope. We climbed in as near silence as we could manage, up towards the ravine's entrance, towards the solidity of the footpath. Rocks slid and clicked underfoot. As if in answer, the bloodied rocks where the lamb had died clicked too, knocking gently against one another as something shifted under them.

"Hello?" I heard again as we climbed. And then again: "Hello?"

"Keep going," Diane whispered.

The rocks clicked again. With a loud rattle, a stone bounced down to the ravine floor. "John?" This time it was a woman's voice. Scottish, by the accent. "John?"

"Fucking hell," I muttered. Louder than I meant to and louder than I should have, because the voice sounded again. "John? John?"

Diane gripped my hand so tight I almost cried out. For a moment I wondered if that was the idea– make me cry out, then let go and run, leave the unwanted partner as food for the thing beneath the rocks while she made her getaway, kill two birds with one stone. But it wasn't, of course.

"Shona?" This time the voice was a man's, likewise Scottish-accented. "Shona, where are ye?"

Neither of us answered. A cold wind blew. I clenched my teeth as they tried to start chattering again. I heard the wind whistle and moan. Shrubs flapped and fluttered in the sudden gale and the surrounding terrain became a little clearer, though not much. Then the wind dropped again, and a soft, cold whiteness began to drown the dimly-glimpsed outlines of trees and higher ground again.

Stones clicked. A sheep's bleat sounded. Then a cow lowed.

Diane tugged my hand. "Come on," she said, "let's go."

The dog barked two, three times as we went, sharp and sudden, startling me a little and making me sway briefly for balance. I looked at Diane, smiled a little, let out a long breath.

We were about nine feet from the top when a deafening roar split the silence apart. I don't know what the hell it was, what kind of animal sound—but even Diane cried out, and I stumbled, and sending a mini-landslide slithering back down the slope.

The broken slate heaved and rattled, and then surged as something flew across, under, *through* the ravine floor towards us.

"Run!" I heard Diane yell, and I tried, we both did, but the shape was arrowing past us. We saw that at the last moment; it was hurtling past us to the edge of the scree, the point where it gave way to the path.

Diane was already starting back down, pushing me behind her, when the ground erupted in a shower of stone shrapnel. I thought I glimpsed something, only for the briefest of moments, moving in the hail of broken stone, but when it fell back into place there was no sign of anything—except, if you looked, a low humped shape.

Diane shot past me, still gripping my hand, pelting along the ravine. Behind us I heard the stones rattle as the thing gave chase. Diane veered towards the nearest of the boulders—it was roughly the size of a small car, and looked like pretty solid ground.

"Come on!" Diane leapt—pretty damned agile for a woman in her late thirties who didn't lead a particularly active life—onto the boulder, reached back for me. "Quick!"

The shape was hurtling towards us, slowing as it neared us. Its bow-wave of loose stones thickened, widened; it was gathering speed. I could see what was coming; I grabbed Diane and pushed her down flat on the boulder. She didn't fight, so I'm guessing she'd reached the same conclusions as me.

There was a muffled thud and the boulder shook. For a moment I thought we'd both be pitched onto the scree around it, but the boulder held, too deeply rooted to be torn loose. Rocks rained and pattered down on us; I tucked my head in.

I realised I was clinging on to Diane, and that she was doing to the same to me. I opened my eyes and looked at her. She looked back. Neither of us said anything.

Behind us, there were clicks and rattles. I turned slowly, sliding off Diane. We both sat up and watched.

There was a sort of crater in the layer of loose rocks beside the boulder, where the thing had hit. The scree at the bottom was heaving, shifting, rippling. The crater walls trembled and slid. After a moment, the whole lot collapsed on itself. The uneven surface rippled and heaved some more, finally stopped when it looked as it had before—undisturbed, except of course for the low humped shape beneath it.

Click went the stones as it shifted in its tracks, taking stock. Click click as it moved and began inching its way round the boulder. "John? Shona? Hello?" All emerged from the shifting rocks, each of those different voices. Then the bleat. Then the roar. I swear I felt the wind of it buffet me.

"Christ," I said.

The rocks clicked, softly, as the humped shape began moving, circling slowly round the boulder. "Christ," my own voice answered me. Then another voice called, a child's. "Mummy?" Click click click. "Shona?" Click. "Oh, for God's sake, Marjorie," came a rich, fruity voice which sounded decidedly pre-Second World War. If not the First. "For God's sake."

Click. Then silence. The wind keened down the defile. Fronds of mist drifted coldly along. Click. A high, thin female voice, clear and sweet, began singing 'The Ash Grove.' Very slowly, almost like a dirge. "*Down yonder green valley where streamlets meander…*"

Diane clutched my wrist tightly.

Click, and the song stopped, as if a switch had been thrown. Click click. And then there was a slow rustling and clicking as the shape began to move away from the boulder, moving further and further back. Diane gripped me tighter. The mist was thickening and the shape went slowly, so that it was soon no longer possible to be sure exactly where it was. Then the last click died away and there was only the silence and the wind and the mist.

-◦-

Time passed.

"It's not gone far," Diane whispered. "Just far enough that we've got some freedom of movement. It wants us to make a move, try to run for it. It knows it can't get us here."

"But we can't stay here either," I pointed out in the same whisper. My teeth were already starting to chatter again, and I could see hers were too. "We'll bloody freeze to death."

"I know. Who knows, maybe it does too. Either way, we'll have to make a break for it, and sooner rather than later. If we leave it much longer we won't stand a chance."

"What the hell do you think it is?" I asked.

She scowled at me. "You expect me to know? I'm a geologist, not a biologist."

"Don't suppose you've got the number for a good one on your mobile?"

She stopped and stared at me. "We're a pair of fucking idiots," she said, and dug around in the pocket of her jeans. Out came her mobile. "Never even thought of it."

"There's no signal."

"There wasn't before. It's worth a try."

Hope flared briefly, but not for long; it was the same story as before.

"Okay," I said. "So we can't phone a friend. Let's think about this then. What do we know about it?"

"It lives under the rocks," Diane said. "Moves under them."

"Likes to stay under them, too," I said. "It was right up against us before. *That* far from us. It could've attacked us easily just by coming up out from under, but it didn't. It'd rather play it safe and do the whole waiting game thing."

"So maybe it's weak, if we can get it out of the rocks. Vulnerable." Diane took off her glasses, rubbed her large eyes. "Maybe it's blind. It seems to hunt by sound, vibration."

"A mimic. That's something else. It's a mimic, like a parrot."

"Only faster," she said. "It mimicked you straight away, after hearing you once."

"Got a good memory for voices, too," I whispered back. "Some of those voices…"

"Yes, I think so too. And that roar it made. How long's it been since there was anything roaming wild in this country, could make a noise like that?"

"Maybe a bear," I offered, "or one of the big sabre-toothed cats."

Diane looked down at the scree. "Glacial till," she said.

"What?"

"Sorry. The stones here. It's what's called glacial till—earth that's been compressed into rock by the pressure of the glaciers coming through here." She looked up and down the ravine.

"So?"

The look she gave me was equal parts hurt and anger. "So… nothing much, I suppose."

Wind blew.

"I'm sorry."

She shrugged. "S'okay."

"No. Really."

She gave me a smile, at least, that time. Then frowned, looked up at the way we'd come in—had it only been in the last hour? "Look at that.

You can see it now."

"See what?"

She pointed. "This is a moraine."

"A what?"

"Moraine. It's the debris—till and crushed rock—a glacier leaves behind when it melts. All this would've been crushed up against the mountainsides for god knows how long…"

I remembered Diane telling me about the last Ice Age, how there'd have been two miles of ice above the cities we'd grown up in. How far down would all this have been? And would—*could*—anything have lived in it?

I was willing to bet any of our colleagues in the Biology Department would have snorted at the idea. But even so… life is very tenacious, isn't it? It can cling on in places you'd never expect it to.

Maybe some creatures had survived down here in the Ice Age, crawling and slithering between the gaps in the crushed rock. And in every food chain, something's at the top—something that hunted blindly by vibration and lured by imitation. Something that had survived the glaciers' melting, even prospered from it, growing bigger and fatter on bigger, fatter prey.

The lost lamb had saved us by catching its attention. Without that, we'd have had no warning and would've followed that voice—no doubt belonging to some other, long-dead victim—into the heart of the killing ground.

Click click click, went the rocks in the distance, as the creature shifted and then grew still.

And Diane leant close to me, and breathed in my ear: "We're going to have to make a move."

—◦—

To our left was the way we'd come, the scree-thick path sloping up before blending with the moraine. Twenty yards. It might as well have been ten miles.

The base of the peak was at our backs. It wasn't sheer, not quite, but it may as well have been. The only handholds were the occasional rock or root; even if the fall didn't kill you, you'd be too stunned or injured to stand a chance. The base of the opposite peak—even if we *could* have got past the creature—was no better.

To our right, the main body of the ravine led on, thick with rubble, before vanishing into the mist. Running along that would be nothing short of suicide, but there was still the gully we'd seen before. From what I could see the floor of it was thickly littered with rubble, but it definitely angled upwards, hopefully towards higher ground of solid earth and grass, where the thing from the moraine couldn't follow. Better still, there was that second boulder at the gully mouth, as big and solidly rooted-looking as this one, if not bigger. If we could make it that far—and we might, with a little luck—we had a chance to get out through the gully.

I looked at the boulder and back to Diane. She was still studying it. "What do you reckon?" I breathed.

Click click click, came softly, faintly, gently in answer.

Diane glanced sideways. "The bastard thing's fast," she whispered back. "It'll be a close thing."

"We could distract it," I suggested. "Make a noise to draw it off."

"Like what?"

I nodded at the rocks at the base of the boulder. "Pick a spot and lob a few of them at it. Hopefully it'll think it's another square meal."

She looked dubious. "S'pose it's better than nothing."

"If you've got any better ideas."

She looked hurt rather than annoyed. "Hey…"

"I'm sorry." I was, too. I touched her arm. "We've just got to make that boulder."

"And what then?"

"We'll think of something. We always do."

She forced a smile.

Reaching down to pick up the bits of rubble and rock wasn't pleasant, mainly because the thing had gone completely silent and there was no knowing how close it might be now. Every time my hands touched the rocks I was convinced they'd explode in my face before something grabbed and yanked me under them.

But the most that happened was that once, nearby, the rocks clicked softly and we both went still, waiting, for several minutes before reaching down again after a suitable pause. At last we were ready with half a dozen good-sized rocks apiece.

"Where do we throw them?" Diane whispered. I pointed to the footpath; we'd be heading, after all, in the opposite direction. She nodded.

"Ready?"

Another nod.

I threw the first rock. We threw them all, fast, within a few seconds, and they cracked and rattled on the slate. The slate nearby rattled and hissed as something moved.

"Go," Diane said; we jumped off the boulder and ran for the gully mouth.

Diane'd often commented on my being out of condition, so I was quite pleased that I managed to outpace her. I overtook easily, and was soon a good way ahead. The boulder was two more strides away, three at most, and then—

The two sounds came together; a dismayed cry from Diane, and then that hiss and click and rattle of displaced scree, rising to a rushing roar as a bow wave of broken rocks rose up behind Diane and bore down on her.

I screamed at her to run, covering the rest of the distance to the boulder and leaping onto it, turning, holding my hands out to her, as if that was going to help. But what else could I have done? Running back to her wouldn't have speeded her up, and—

Oh. Yes. I could've tried to draw it off. Risked my own life, even sacrificed it, to save hers. Yes, I could've done that. Thanks for reminding me.

It got to her as I turned. There was an explosion of rubble, a great spray of it, and she screamed. I threw up my hands to protect my face. A piece of rock glanced off my forehead and I stumbled, swayed, losing balance, but thank God I hadn't ditched my backpack—the weight dragged me back and I fell across the boulder.

Rubble rained and pattered about us as I stared at Diane. She'd fallen face-down on the ground, arms outstretched. Her pale hands, splayed out on the earth, were about three feet from the boulder.

I reached out a hand to her, leaning forward as far as I dared. I opened my mouth to speak her name, and then she lifted her head and looked up. Her glasses were askew on her pale face, and one lens was cracked. In another moment I might have jumped off the boulder and gone to her, but then she screamed and blood sprayed from the ground where her feet were covered by a sheet of rubble. Her back arched; a fingernail split as she clawed at the ground. Red bubbled up through the stones, like a spring.

Diane was weeping with pain; she tried to twist round to see what was being done to her, but jerked, shuddered and cried out before she could complete it. She twisted back to face me, lips trembling, still crying.

I leant forward, hands outstretched, but couldn't reach. Then I remembered the backpack and struggled out of it, loosening the straps to give the maximum possible slack, gripping one and holding the backpack as far out as I could, so that the other dangled closer to her. "Grab it," I whispered. "I'll pull you in."

She shook her head hard. "No," she managed at last. "Don't you get it?"

"What?" We weren't whispering anymore. Didn't seem much point. Besides, her voice was ragged with pain.

"It wants you to try. Don't you see? Otherwise it would've dragged me straight under by now."

I stared at her.

"Steve… it's using me as bait." Her face tightened. She bit her lips and fresh tears leaked down her pale cheeks. Her green eyes squeezed shut. When they opened again, they were red and bloodshot. "Oh God. What's it done to my legs? My feet?"

"I don't know," I lied.

"Well, that's it, don't you see?" She was breathing deeply now, trying to get the agony under control. "I've had it. Won't get far, even if it did let me go to chase after you. Can't get at you up there. So stay put."

"But… but…" Dimly I realised I was crying too. This was my wife. My *wife*, for Christ's sake.

Diane forced a smile. "Just stay put. Or try… make a getaway."

"I'm not leaving you."

"Yes, you are. It'll go after you. Might be able… drag myself there." She nodded at the boulder. "You could go get help. Help me. Might stand a chance."

I looked at the blood still bubbling up from the stones. She must have seen the expression on my face. "Like that, is it?"

I looked away. "I can try." My view of the gully was still constricted by my position. I could see the floor of it sloping up, but not how far it ultimately went. If nothing else, I could draw it away from her, give her a chance to get to the boulder.

And what then? If I couldn't find a way out of the gully? If there wasn't even a boulder to climb to safety on, I'd be dead and the best Diane could hope for was to bleed to death.

But I owed her a chance of survival, at least.

I put the backpack down, looked into her eyes. "Soon as it moves off, start crawling. Shout me when you're here. I'll keep making a racket, try and keep it occupied."

"Be careful."

"You too." I smiled at her and refused to look at her feet. We met at University, did I tell you? Did I mention that? A drunken discussion about politics in the Student Union bar. More of an argument really. We'd been on different sides but ended up falling for each other. That pretty much summed up our marriage, I supposed. "Love you," I managed to say at last.

She gave a tight, buckled smile. "You too," she said back.

That was never something either of us had said easily. Should've known it'd take something like this. "Okay, then," I muttered. "Bye."

I took a deep breath, then jumped off the boulder and started to run.

◄◦►

I didn't look back, even when Diane let out a cry, because I could hear the rattle and rush of slate behind me as I pelted into the gully and knew the thing had let her go—let her go so that it could come after me.

The ground's upwards slope petered out quite quickly and the walls all around were a good ten feet high, sheer and devoid of handholds, except for at the very back of it. There was an old stream channel—only the thinnest trickle of water made it out now, but I'm guessing it'd been stronger once, because a mix of earth and pebbles, lightly grown over, formed a slope leading up to the ground above. A couple of gnarled trees sprouted nearby, and I could see their roots breaking free of the earth—thick and twisted, easy to climb with. All I had to do was reach them.

But then I noticed something else; something that made me laugh wildly. Only a few yards from where I was now, the surface of the ground changed from a plain of rubble to bare rock. Here and there earth had accumulated and sprouted grass, but what mattered was that there was no rubble for the creature to move under.

I chanced one look behind me, no more than that. It was hurtling towards me, the huge bow-wave of rock. I ran faster, managed the last few steps, and then dived and rolled across blessed solid ground.

Rubble sprayed at me from the edge of the rubble and again I caught the briefest glimpse of something moving in there. I couldn't put any kind of name to it if I tried, and I don't think I want to.

The rubble heaved and settled. The stones clicked. I got up and started backing away. Just in case. Click, click, click. Had anything ever got away from it before? I couldn't imagine anything human doing so, or men would've come back here with weapons, to find and kill it. Or perhaps that survivor hadn't been believed. Click. Click, click. Click, click, click.

Click. A sheep bleated.

Click. A dog barked.

Click. A wolf howled.

Click. A cow lowed.

Click. A bear roared.

Click. "John?"

Click. "Shona? Shona, where are ye?"

Click. "Mummy?"

Click. "Oh, for God's sake, Marjorie. For God's sake."

Click. *"Down yonder green valley where streamlets meander..."*

Click. "Christ." My voice. "Christ."

Click. "Steve? Get help. Help me." Click. "Steve. Help me."

I turned and began to run, started climbing. I looked back when I heard stones rattling. I looked back and saw something, a wide shape, moving under the stones and heading away, back towards the mouth of the gully.

"Diane?" I shouted. "Diane?"

There was no answer.

⫷⚬⫸

I've been walking now, according to my wristwatch, for a good half-hour. My teeth are chattering and I'm tired and all I can see around me is the mist.

Still no signal on the mobile. They can trace your position from a mobile call these days. That'd be helpful. I've tried to walk in a straight line, so that if I find help I can just point back the way I came, but I doubt I've kept to one.

I tell myself that she must have passed out—passed out from the effort and pain of dragging herself onto that boulder. I tell myself that the cold must have slowed her circulation down to the point where she might still be alive.

I do not think of how much blood I saw bubbling out from under the stones.

I do not think of hypothermia. Not for her. I'm still going, so she still must have a chance there too, surely?

I keep walking. I'll keep walking for as long as I can believe Diane might still be alive. After that, I won't be able to go on, because it won't matter anymore.

I'm crawling, now.

We came out here to see if we still worked, the two of us, under all the clutter and the mess. And it looks like we still did.

There's that cold comfort, at least.

◄○►

BLACKWOOD'S BABY

LAIRD BARRON

Late afternoon sun baked the clay and plaster buildings of the town. Its dirt streets lay empty, packed as hard as iron. The boarding house sweltered. Luke Honey sat in a chair in the shadows across from the window. Nothing stirred except flies buzzing on the window ledge. The window was a gap bracketed by warped shutters and it opened into a portal view of the blazing white stone wall of the cantina across the alley. Since the fistfight, he wasn't welcome in the cantina although he'd seen the other three men he'd fought there each afternoon, drunk and laughing. The scabs on his knuckles were nearly healed. Every two days, one of the stock boys brought him a bottle.

Today, Luke Honey was drinking good strong Irish whiskey. His hands were clammy and his shirt stuck to his back and armpits. A cockroach scuttled into the long shadow of the bottle and waited. An overhead fan hung motionless. Clerk Galtero leaned on the counter and read a newspaper gone brittle as ancient papyrus, its fiber sucked dry by the heat; a glass of cloudy water pinned the corner. Clerk Galtero's bald skull shone in the gloom and his mustache drooped, sweat dripping from the tips and onto the paper. The clerk was from Barcelona and Luke Honey heard the fellow had served in the French Foreign Legion on the Macedonian Front during the Great War, and that he'd been clipped in the arm and that was why it curled tight and useless against his ribs.

A boy entered the house. He was black and covered with the yellow dust that settled upon everything in this place. He wore a uniform of some kind, and a cap with a narrow brim, and no shoes. Luke Honey guessed his age at eleven or twelve, although his face was worn, the flesh creased around his mouth, and his eyes suggested sullen apathy born of wisdom. Here, on the edge of a wasteland, even the children appeared weathered and aged. Perhaps that was how Luke Honey himself appeared now that he'd lived on the plains and in the jungles for seven years. Perhaps the land had chiseled and filed him down too. He didn't know because he seldom glanced at the mirror anymore. On the other hand, there were some, such as a Boer and another renowned hunter from Canada Luke Honey had accompanied on many safaris, who seemed stronger, more vibrant with each passing season, as if the dust and the heat, the cloying jungle rot and the blood they spilled fed them, bred into them a savage vitality.

The boy handed him a telegram in a stiff white envelope with fingerprints all over it. Luke Honey gave him a fifty cent piece and the boy left. Luke Honey tossed the envelope on the table. He struck a match with his thumbnail and lighted a cigarette. The light coming through the window began to thicken. Orange shadows tinged black slid across the wall of the cantina. He poured a glass of whiskey and drank it in a gulp. He poured another and set it aside. The cockroach fled under the edge of the table.

Two women descended the stairs. White women, perhaps English, certainly foreign travelers. They wore heavy, Victorian dresses, equally staid bonnets, and sheer veils. The younger of the pair inclined her head toward Luke Honey as she passed. Her lips were thinned in disapproval. She and her companion opened the door and walked though its rectangle of shimmering brilliance into the furnace. The door swung shut.

Clerk Galtero folded the newspaper and placed it under the counter. He tipped his glass toward Luke Honey in a sardonic toast. "The ladies complained about you. You make noise in your room at night, the younger one says. You cry out, like a man in delirium. The walls are thin and she cannot sleep, so she complains to me."

"Oh. Is the other one deaf, then?" Luke Honey smoked his cigarette with the corner of his mouth. He sliced open the envelope with a pocket knife and unfolded the telegram and read its contents. The letter was an invitation from one Mr. Liam Welloc Esquire to partake in an annual private hunt in Washington State. The hunt occurred on remote ancestral property, its guests designated by some arcane combination of pedigree and longstanding association with the host, or by virtue of notoriety in hunting circles. The telegram chilled the sweat trickling down his face. Luke Honey was not a particularly superstitious man; nonetheless, this missive called with an eerie intimacy and struck a chord deep within him, awakened an instinctive dread that fate beckoned across the years, the bloody plains and darkened seas, to claim him.

He stuck the telegram into his shirt pocket, then drank his whiskey. He poured another shot and lighted another cigarette and stared at the window. The light darkened to purple and the wall faded, was almost invisible. "I have nightmares. Give the ladies my apologies." He'd lived in the boarding house for three weeks and this was the second time he and Clerk Galtero had exchanged more than a word in passing. Galtero's brother Enrique managed the place in the evening. Luke Honey hadn't spoken to him much either. After years in the wilderness, he usually talked to himself.

Clerk Galtero spilled the dregs of water on the floor and walked over with his queer, hitching step, and poured the glass full of Luke Honey's whiskey. He sat in one of the rickety chairs. His good arm lay atop the table. His hands and arm were thickly muscled. The Legion tattoos had begun to elongate as his flesh loosened. "I know you," he said. "I've heard talk. I've seen your guns. Most of the foreign hunters wear trophies. Your friends, the other Americans, wear teeth and claws from their kills."

"We aren't friends."

"Your associates. I wonder though, why you have come and why you stay."

"I'm done with the bush. That's all."

"This place is not so good for a man such as yourself. There is only trouble for you here."

Luke Honey smiled wryly. "Oh, you think I've gone native."

"Not at all. I doubt you get along with anyone."

"I'll be leaving soon." Luke Honey touched the paper in his pocket. "For the States. I suppose your customers will finally have some peace."

They finished their drinks and sat in silence. When it became dark, Clerk

Galtero rose and went about lighting the lamps. Luke Honey climbed the stairs to his stifling room. He lay sweating on the bed and dreamed of his brother Michael, as he had for six nights running. The next morning he arranged for transportation to the coast. Three days later he was aboard a cargo plane bound for Morocco. Following Morocco there would be ships and trains until he eventually stood again on American soil after half a lifetime. Meanwhile, he looked out the tiny window. The plains slowly disappeared into the red haze of the rim of the Earth.

◄◦►

Luke Honey and his party arrived at the lodge not long before dark. They'd come in two cars and the staff earned its keep transferring the mountain of bags and steamer trunks indoors before the storm broadsided the valley. Lightning sizzled from the vast snout of fast approaching purple-black clouds. Thunder growled. A rising breeze plucked leaves from the treetops. Luke Honey leaned against a marble colonnade and smoked a cigarette, personal luggage stacked neatly at his side. He disliked trusting his rifles and knives to bellhops and porters.

The Black Ram Lodge towered above a lightly wooded hillside overlooking Olde Towne. The lodge and its town lay in the folds of Ransom Hollow, separated from the lights of Seattle by miles of dirt road and forested hills. "Backward country," one of the men had called it during the long drive. Luke Honey rode with the Brits Bullard and Wesley. They'd shared a flask of brandy while the car left the lowlands and climbed toward the mountains, passing small, quaint townships and ramshackle farms tenanted by sober yeoman folk. Wesley and Bullard snickered like a pair of itinerant knights at the potato pickers in filthy motley, bowed to their labor in dark, muddy fields. Luke Honey didn't share the mirth. He'd seen enough bloody peasant revolts to know better. He knew also that fine cars and carriages, horses and guns, the gloss of their own pale skin, cursed the nobility with a false sense of well-being, of safety. He'd removed a bullet from his pocket. The bullet was made for a .454 rifle and it was large. He'd turned it over in his fingers and stared out the window without speaking again.

After supper, Dr. Landscomb and Mr. Liam Welloc, co-proprietors of the lodge, entertained the small group of far-flung travelers who'd come for the annual hunt. Servants lighted a fire in the hearth and the eight gentlemen settled into grand oversized chairs. The parlor was a dramatic landscape of marble statuary and massive bookshelves, stuffed and mounted heads of ferocious exotic beasts, liquor cabinets and a pair of billiard tables. Rain and wind hammered the windows. Lights flickered dangerously, promising a rustic evening of candlelight and kerosene lamps.

The assembly was supremely merry when the tale-telling began.

"We were in Mexico," Lord Bullard said. Lord Bullard hailed from Essex; a decorated former officer in the Queen's Royal Lancers who'd fought briefly in the Boer War, but had done most of his time pacifying the "wogs" in the Punjab. Apparently his family was enormously wealthy in lands and titles, and these days he traveled to the exclusion of all else. He puffed on his cigar while a servant held the flame of a long-handled match steady. "Summer of 1919. The war had just ended. Some Industrialist friends of mine were visiting from Europe. Moaning and sulking about the shutdowns of their munitions factories and the like. Beastly boring."

"Quite, I'm sure," Dr. Landscomb said. The doctor was tall and thin. He possessed the ascetic bearing of Eastern European royalty. He had earned his degree in medicine at Harvard and owned at least a quarter of everything there was to own within two counties.

"Ah, a trying time for the makers of bombs and guns," Mr. Liam Welloc said. He too was tall, but thick and broad with the neck and hands of the ancient Greek statues of Herakles. His hair and beard were bronze and lush for a man his age. His family owned half again what the Landscombs did and reportedly maintained ancestral estates in England and France. "One would think there are enough territorial skirmishes underway to keep the coins flowing. The Balkans, for example. Or Africa."

"Exactly. It's a lack of imagination," Mr. Williams said. A bluff, weather-beaten rancher baron attired in Stetson boots, corduroys and impressive buckle, a starched shirt with ivory buttons, and an immaculate Stetson hat. He drank Jack Daniel's, kept the bottle on a dais at his side. He'd come from Texas with Mr. McEvoy and Mr. Briggs. McEvoy and Briggs were far more buttoned down in Brooks Brothers suits and bowlers; a banker and mine owner, respectively. Williams drained his whiskey and poured another, waving off the ever-hovering servant. "That's what's killing you boys. Trapped in the Renaissance. Can't run an empire without a little imagination."

"Besides, Germany is sharpening its knives," Mr. Briggs said. "Your friends will be cranking up the assembly lines inside of five years. Trust me. They've the taste for blood, those Krauts. You can't beat that outta them. My mistress is Bavarian, so I know."

Lord Bullard thumped his cigar in the elegant pot near his foot. He cleared his throat. "Harrumph. Mexico City, 1919. Bloody hot. Miasma, thick and gray from smokestacks and chimneys of all those hovels they heap like ruddy anthills."

"The smog reminded me of home," Wesley said. Wesley dressed in a heavy linen coat and his boots were polished to a high gloss. His hair was slick and parted at the middle and it shone in the firelight. When Luke Honey looked at him, he thought *Mr. Weasel.*

"A Mexican prince invited us to a hunt on his estate. He was conducting business in the city, so we laid over at his villa. Had a jolly time."

Mr. Wesley said, "Tubs of booze and a veritable harem of randy strumpets. What was not to like? I was sorry when we departed for the countryside."

"Who was it, Wes, you, me, and the chap from York… Cantwell? Cotter?"

"Cantwell."

"Yes, right then. The three of us were exhausted and chafed beyond bearing from frantic revels at the good Prince's demesne, so we ventured into the streets to seek new pleasures."

"Which, ironically, constituted the pursuit of more liquor and fresh strumpets."

"On the way from one particularly unsavory cantina to another, we were accosted by a ragtag individual who leaped at us from some occulted nook in an alley. This person was of singularly dreadful countenance; wan and emaciated, afflicted by wasting disease and privation. He smelled like the innards of a rotting sheep carcass, and his appearance was most unwelcome. However, he wheedled and beseeched my attention, in passable English, I must add, and clung to my sleeve with such fervor it soon became apparent the only way to rid myself of his attention was to hear him out."

"We were confounded upon learning this wretch was an expatriate American," Mr. Wesley said.

"Thunderstruck!"

"Ye Gods," Dr. Landscomb said. "This tale bears the trappings of a penny dreadful. More, more, gentlemen!"

"The man's name was Harris. He'd once done columns for some paper and visited Mexico to conduct research for a story he never got around to writing. The entire tale of his fall from grace is long and sordid. It's enough to say he entered the company of disreputable characters and took to wickedness and vice. The chap was plainly overjoyed to encounter fellow speakers of English, but we soon learned there was much more to this encounter than mere chance. He knew our names, where we intended to hunt, and other details I've put aside."

"It was uncanny," Mr. Wesley said.

"The man was obviously a grifter," Luke Honey said from his spot near the hearth where he'd been lazing with his eyes mostly shut and thinking with mounting sullenness that the pair of Brits were entirely too smug, especially Lord Bullard with his gold rimmed monocle and cavalry saber. "A spy. Did he invite you to a séance? To predict your fortune with a handful of runes?"

"In fact, he did inveigle us to join him in a smoky den of cutthroats and thieves where this ancient crone read the entrails of chickens like the pagans read Tarot cards. It was she who sent him into the streets to track us." Lord Bullard fixed Luke Honey with a bloodshot stare. "Mock as you will, it was a rare experience."

Luke Honey chuckled and closed his eyes again. "I wouldn't dream of mocking you. The Romans swore by the custom of gutting pigeons. Who am I to argue?"

"Whom indeed? The crone scrabbled in the guts, muttering to herself while Harrison crouched at her side and Harrison translated. He claimed the hag dreamed of our arrival in the city for some time and that these visions were driving her to aggravation. She described a 'black cloud' obscuring the future. There was trouble awaiting us, and soon. Something about a cave. We all laughed, of course, just as you did, Mr. Honey." Lord Bullard smiled a wry, wan smile that accentuated the creases of his face, his hangdog mouth. "Eventually, we extricated ourselves and made for the nearest taproom and forgot the whole incident. The Prince returned from his business and escorted us in style to a lavish country estate deep in the central region of the country. Twelve of us gathered to feast at his table, and in the morning he released boars into the woods."

"Twelve, you say?" Mr. Williams said, brows disappearing under his big hat. "Well, sir, I hope one of you boys got a picture to commemorate the occasion."

"I need another belt to fortify myself in the face of this heckling," Lord Bullard said, snapping his fingers as the servant rushed over to fill his glass. The Englishman drained his glass and wagged his head for another. "To the point then: we shot two boars and wounded another—the largest of them. A prize pig, that one, with tusks like bayonets and the smoothest, blackest hide. Cantwell winged the brute, but the boar escaped and we were forced to spend the better part of two days tracking it through a benighted jungle. The blood trail disappeared into a mountain honeycombed with caves. Naturally, honor dictates pursuing wounded quarry and dispatching it. Alas, a brief discussion with the Prince and his guides convinced us of the folly of descending into the caverns. The system extended for many miles and was largely uncharted. No one of any sense attempted to navigate them. We determined to return home, satisfied with the smaller boars."

"Eh, the great white hunters balked at the precipice of the unknown?" Luke Honey said. "Thank God Cabot and Drake couldn't see you fellows quailing in the face of fear."

Lord Bullard spluttered and Mr. Wesley rose quickly, hand on the large ornamented pistol he wore holstered under his coat. He said, "I demand satisfaction!" His smile was sharp and vicious and Luke Honey had little doubt the man yearned for moments such as these.

Dr. Landscomb smoothly interposed himself, arms spread in a placating manner. "Gentlemen, gentlemen! This isn't the Wild West. There'll be no dueling on these premises. Mr. Wesley, you're among friends. Please, relax and have another drink. Mr. Honey, as for you, perhaps a bit of moderation is in order."

"You may be correct," Luke Honey said, casually sliding his revolver back into its shoulder holster. He looked at Mr. Williams who nodded approvingly and handed him the rapidly diminishing bottle of Jack Daniel's. Luke Honey took a long pull while staring at Mr. Wesley.

Mr. Wesley sat, folding himself into the chair with lethal grace, but continued to smile through small, crooked teeth. "Go on, Arthur. You were getting to the good part."

Lord Bullard wiped his red face with a handkerchief. His voice scarcely above a mutter, he said, "An American named Henderson had other ideas and he convinced two Austrians to accompany him into the caves while the rest of us made camp for the night. The poor fools slipped away and were gone for at least an hour before the rest of us realized what they'd done. We never saw any of them again. There was a rescue mission. The Mexican Army deployed a squadron of expertly trained and equipped mountaineers to investigate, but hard rains came and the tunnels were treacherous, full of rockslides and floodwater. It would've been suicide to persist, and so our comrades were abandoned to their fates. This became a local legend and I've reports of peasants who claim to hear men screaming from the caves on certain, lonely nights directly before a storm."

The men sat in uncomfortable silence while the windows rattled and wind moaned in the flue. Mr. Liam Welloc eventually stood and went to a bookcase. He retrieved a slim, leather bound volume and stood before the hearth, book balanced in one hand, a crystal goblet of liquor in the other. "As you may or may not know, Ian's grandfather and mine were among the founders of this town. Most of the early families arrived here from places like New York and Boston, and a few from California when they discovered the golden state not quite to their taste. The Black Ram itself has gone through several incarnations since it was built as a trading post by a merchant named Caldwell Ellis in 1860 on the eve of that nasty business between the Blue and the Gray. My grandfather purchased this property in 1890 and renovated it as the summer home for him and his new bride, Felicia. Much of this probably isn't of much interest to you, so I'll not blather on about the trials and tribulations of my forebears, nor how this grand house became a lodge. For now, let me welcome you into our most sacred tradition and we wish each of you good fortune on the morrow."

Dr. Landscomb said, "I concur. As you know, there are plenty of boar and deer on this preserve, but assuredly you've come for the great stag known as Blackwood's Baby—"

"Wot, wot?" Mr. Wesley said in mock surprise. "We're not here for the namesake of this fine establishment? What of the Black Ram?"

Mr. Liam Welloc smiled, and to Luke Honey's mind there was something cold and sinister in the man's expression. Mr. Liam Welloc said, "There was never a black ram. It's a euphemism for…Well, that's a story for another evening."

Dr. Landscomb cleared his throat politely. "As I said—the stag is a mighty specimen—surely the equal of any beast you've hunted. He is the king of the wood and descended from a venerable line. I will note, that while occasionally cornered, none of these beasts has ever been taken. In any event, the man who kills the stag shall claim my great grandfather's Sharps model-1851 as a prize. The rifle was custom built for Constantine Landscomb III by Christian Sharps himself, and is nearly priceless. The victorious fellow shall also perforce earn a place among the hallowed ranks of elite gamesmen the world over."

"And ten thousand dollars, sterling silver," Mr. Wesley said, rubbing his hands together.

"Amen, partner!" Mr. McEvoy said. "Who needs another round?"

It was quite late when the men said their goodnights and retired.

◄◦►

The rain slackened to drizzle. Luke Honey lay with his eyes open, listening to it rasp against the window. He'd dreamed of Africa, then of his dead brother Michael toiling in the field of their home in Ingram, just over the pass through the Cascades. His little brother turned to him and waved. His left eye was a hole. Luke Honey had awakened with sick fear in his heart.

While the sky was still dark he dressed and walked downstairs and outside to the barn. The barn lay across the muddy drive from the lodge. Inside, stable hands drifted through the silty gloom preparing dogs and horses for the day ahead. He breathed in the musk of brutish sweat and green manure, gun oil and oiled leather, the evil stink of dogs swaggering in anticipation of murder. He lighted a cigarette and smoked it leaning against a rail while the air brightened from black to gray.

"There you are, mate." Mr. Wesley stepped into the barn and walked toward Luke Honey. He wore workmanlike breeches, a simple shirt, and a bowler. He briskly rolled his sleeves.

Luke Honey didn't see a gun, although Mr. Wesley had a large knife slung low on his hip. He smiled and tapped the brim of his hat and then tried to put out the Brit's eye with a flick of his flaming cigarette. Mr. Wesley flinched, forearms raised, palms inverted, old London prizefighter style, and Luke Honey made a fist and struck him in the ribs below the heart, and followed that with a clubbing blow to the side of his neck. Mr. Wesley was stouter than he appeared. He shrugged and trapped Luke Honey's lead arm in the crook of his elbow and butted him in the jaw. Luke Honey wrenched his arm loose and swiped his fingers at Mr. Wesley's mouth, hoping to fishhook him, and tried to catch his balance on the rail with his off hand. Rotten wood gave way and he dropped to his hands and knees. Light began to slide back and forth in the sky as if he'd plunged his head into a water trough. Mr. Wesley slammed his shin across Luke Honey's chest, flipping him onto his back like a turtle. He sprawled in the wet straw, mouth agape, struggling for air, his mind filled with snow.

"Well. That's it, then." Mr. Wesley stood over him for a moment, face shiny, slick hair in disarray. He bent and scooped up his bowler, scuffed it against his pants leg and smiled at Luke Honey. He clapped the bowler onto his head and limped off.

"Should I call a doctor, kid?" Mr. Williams struck a match on the heel of his boot, momentarily burning away shadows around his perch on a hay bale. A couple of the stable hands had stopped to gawk and they jolted from their reverie and rushed to quiet the agitated mastiffs who whined and growled and strutted in their pens.

"No, he's okay," Luke Honey said when he could. "Me, I'm going to rest here a bit."

Mr. Williams chuckled. He smoked his cigarette and walked over to Luke Honey and looked down at him with a bemused squint. "Boy, what you got against them limeys anyway?"

The left side of Luke Honey's face was already swollen. Drawing breath caused flames to lick in his chest. "My grandfather chopped cotton. My father picked potatoes."

"Not you, though."

"Nope," Luke Honey said. "Not me."

‹o›

The lord of the stables was named Scobie, a gaunt and gnarled Welshman whose cunning and guile with dogs and horses, and traps and snares, had elevated him to the status of a peasant prince. He dressed in stained and weathered leather garments from some dim Medieval era and his thin hair bloomed in a white cloud. Dirt ingrained his hands and nails, and when he smiled his remaining teeth were sharp and crooked. His father had been a master falconer, but the modern hunt didn't call for birds any more.

The dogs and the dog handlers went first and the rest of the party entered the woods an hour later. Luke Honey accompanied the Texans and Mr. Liam Welloc. They rode light, tough horses. Mr. McEvoy commented on the relative slightness of the horses and Mr. Welloc explained that the animals were bred for endurance and agility.

The forest spread around them like a cavern. Well-beaten trails criss-crossed through impenetrable underbrush and unto milky dimness. Water dripped from branches. After a couple of hours they stopped and had tea and biscuits prepared by earnest young men in lodge livery.

"Try some chaw," Mr. Briggs said. He cut a plug of hard tobacco and handed it to Luke Honey. Luke Honey disliked tobacco. He put it in his mouth and chewed. The Brits stood nearby in a cluster talking to Dr. Landscomb and Mr. Liam Welloc. Mr. Briggs said, "You in the war? You look too young."

"I was fifteen when we joined the dance. Just missed all that fun."

"Bully for you, as the limeys would say. You can shoot, I bet. Everybody here either has money or can shoot. Or both. No offense, but I don't have you pegged for a man of means. Nah, you remind me of some of the boys in my crew. Hard-bitten. A hell-raiser."

"I've done well enough, in fact."

"He's the *real* great white hunter," Mr. Williams said. "One of those fellers who shoots lions and elephants on the Dark Continent. Fortunes to be won in the ivory trade. That right, Mr. Honey?"

"Yeah. I was over there for a while."

"Huh, I suppose you have that look about you," Mr. Briggs said. "You led safaris?"

"I worked for the Dutch."

"Leave it be," Mr. Williams said. "The man's not a natural braggart."

"Where did you learn to hunt?" Mr. McEvoy said.

"My cousins. They all lived in the hills in Utah. One of them was a sniper during the war." Luke Honey spat tobacco into the leaves. "When my mother died I went to live with my uncle and his family and those folks have lots of kin in South Africa. After college I got a case of wanderlust. One thing led to another."

"Damned peculiar upbringing. College even."

"What kid doesn't dream of stalking the savanna?" Mr. Briggs said. "You must have a hundred and one tales."

"Surely, after that kind of experience, this trip must be rather tame," Mr. McEvoy said.

"Hear, hear," Mr. Briggs said. "Give up the ivory trade for a not-so-likely chance to bag some old stag in dull as dirt U.S.A.?"

"Ten thousand sterling silver buys a lot of wine and song, amigos," Mr. Williams said. "Besides, who says the kid's quit anything?"

"Well, sir, I *am* shut of the business."

"Why is that?" Mr. Briggs said.

Luke Honey wiped his mouth. "One fine day I was standing on a plain with the hottest sun you can imagine beating down. Me and some other men had set up a crossfire and plugged maybe thirty elephants from this enormous herd. The skinners got to work with their machetes and axes. Meanwhile, I got roaring drunk with the rest of the men. A newspaper flew in a photographer on a biplane. The photographer posed us next to a pile of tusks. The tusks were stacked like cordwood and there was blood and flies everywhere. I threw up during one of the pictures. The heat and the whiskey, I thought. They put me in a tent for a couple of days while a fever fastened to me. I ranted and raved and they had to lash me down. You see, I thought the devil was hiding under my cot, that he was waiting to claim my soul. I dreamt my dear dead mother came and stood at the entrance of the tent. She had soft, magnificent wings folded against her back. White light surrounded her. The light was brilliant. Her face was dark and her eyes were fiery. She spat on the ground and the tent flaps flew shut and I was left alone in darkness. The company got me to a village where there was a real doctor who gave me quinine and I didn't quite die."

"Are you saying you quit the safaris because your mother might disapprove from her cloud in heaven?" Mr. Briggs said.

"Nope. I'm more worried she might be disapproving from an ice floe in Hell."

⟼◦⟻

In the afternoon, Lord Bullard shot a medium buck that was cornered by Scobie's mastiff pack. Luke Honey and Mr. Williams reined in at a remove from the action. The killing went swiftly. The buck had been severely mauled prior to their arrival. Mr. Wesley dismounted and cut the animal's throat with his overlarge knife while the dogs sniffed around and pissed on the bushes.

"Not quite as glorious as ye olden days, eh?" Mr. Williams said. He took a manly gulp of whiskey from his flask and passed it to Luke Honey.

Luke Honey drank, relishing the dark fire coursing over his bloody teeth. "German nobles still use spears to hunt boars."

"I wager more than one of those ol' boys gets his manhood torn off on occasion."

"It happens." Luke Honey slapped his right thigh. "When I was younger and stupider I was gored. Hit the bone. Luckily the boar was heart shot— stone dead when it stuck me so I didn't get ripped in two."

"Damn," Mr. Williams said.

Mr. Briggs and Mr. McEvoy stared at Luke Honey with something akin to religious awe. "Spears?" Mr. Briggs said. "Did you bring one?"

"Nope. A couple of rifles, my .45, and some knives. I travel light."

"I'm shocked the limeys put up with the lack of foot servants," Mr. Briggs said.

"I doubt any of us are capable of understanding you, Mr. Honey," Mr. Williams said. "I'm beginning to think you may be one of those rare mysteries of the world."

⟼◦⟻

An hour before dusk, Scobie and a grimy boy in suspenders and no shirt approached the hunters while they paused to smoke cigarettes, drink brandy, and water the horses.

Scobie said, "Arlen here came across sign of a large stag yonder a bit. Fair knocked the bark from trees with its antlers, right boy?" The boy nodded and scowled as Scobie tousled his hair. "The boy has a keen eye.

How long were the tracks?" The boy gestured and Lord Bullard whistled in astonishment.

Mr. Williams snorted and fanned a circle with his hat to disperse a cloud of mosquitoes. "We're talking about a deer, not a damned buffalo."

Scobie shrugged. "Blackwood's Baby is twice the size of any buck you've set eyes on, I'll reckon."

"Pshaw!" Mr. Williams cut himself a plug and stuffed it into his mouth. He nudged his roan sideways, disengaging from the conversation.

"I say, let's have at this stag," Mr. Wesley said, to which Lord Bullard nodded.

"Damned tooting. I'd like a crack at the critter," Mr. Briggs said.

"The dogs are tired and it's late," Scobie said. "I've marked the trail, so we can find it easy tomorrow."

"Bloody hell!" Lord Bullard said. "We've light yet. I've paid my wage to nab this beastie, so I say lead on!"

"Easy, now," Mr. Welloc said. "Night's on us soon and these woods get very, very dark. Crashing about is foolhardy, and if Master Scobie says the dogs need rest, then best to heed his word."

Lord Bullard rolled his eyes. "What do you suggest, then?"

Scobie said, "Camp is set around the corner. We've got hunting shacks scattered along these trails. I'll kennel the hounds at one and meet you for another go at daybreak."

"A sensible plan," Mr. McEvoy said. As the shadows deepened and men and horses became smoky ghosts in the dying light, he'd begun to cast apprehensive glances over his shoulder.

Luke Honey had to admit there was a certain eeriness to the surroundings, a sense of inimical awareness that emanated from the depths of the forest. He noted how the horses flared their nostrils and shifted skittishly. There were boars and bears in this preserve, although he doubted any lurked within a mile after all the gunfire and barking. He'd experienced a similar sense of menace in Africa near the hidden den of a terrible lion, a dreaded man eater. He rubbed his horse's neck and kept a close watch on the bushes.

Mr. Landscomb clasped Scobie's elbow. "Once you've seen to the animals, do leave them to the lads. I'd enjoy your presence after supper."

Scobie looked unhappy. He nodded curtly and left with the boy.

Camp was a fire pit centered between two boulders the size of carriages. A dilapidated lean-to provided a dry area to spread sleeping bags and hang clothes. Stable boys materialized to unsaddle the horses and tether them behind the shed. Lodge workers had ignited a bonfire and laid out a hot meal sent from the chef. This meal included the roasted heart and liver from the buck Lord Bullard brought down earlier.

"Not sure I'd tuck into those vittles," Mr. Williams said, waving his fork at Lord Bullard and Mr. Wesley. "Should let that meat cool a day or two, else you'll get the screamin' trots."

Mr. McEvoy stopped shoveling beans into his mouth to laugh. "That's right. Scarf enough of that liver and you'll think you caught dysentery."

Lord Bullard spooned a jellified chunk of liver into his mouth. "Bollocks. Thirty years afield in the muck and the mud with boot leather and ditchwater for breakfast. My intestines are made of iron. Aye, Wes?"

"You've got the right of it," Mr. Wesley said, although sans his typical enthusiasm. He'd set aside his plate but half finished and now nursed a bottle of Laphroaig.

Luke Honey shucked his soaked jacket and breeches and warmed his toes by the fire with a plate of steak, potatoes and black coffee. He cut the meat into tiny pieces because chewing was difficult. It pleased him to see Mr. Wesley favoring his own ribs whenever he laughed. The Englishman, doughty as he was, seemed rather sickly after a day's exertion. Luke Honey faintly hoped he had one foot in the grave.

A dank mist crept through the trees and the men instinctively clutched blankets around themselves and huddled closer to the blaze, and Luke Honey saw that everyone kept a rifle or pistol near to hand. A wolf howled not too far off and all eyes turned toward the darkness that pressed against the edges of firelight. The horses nickered softly.

Dr. Landscomb said, "Hark, my cue. The wood we now occupy is called Wolfvale and it stretches some fifty miles north to south. If we traveled another twelve miles due east, we'd be in the foothills of the mountains. Wolfvale is, some say, a cursed forest. Of course, that reputation does much to draw visitors." Dr. Landscomb lighted a cigarette. "What do you think, Master Scobie?"

"The settlers considered this an evil place," Scobie said, emerging from the bushes much to the consternation of Mr. Briggs who yelped and half drew his revolver. "No one logs this forest. No one hunts here except for the lords and foolish, desperate townies. People know not to come here because of the dangerous animals that roam. These days, it's the wild beasts, but in the early days, it was mostly Bill."

"Was Bill some rustic lunatic?" Mr. Briggs said.

"We Texans know the type," Mr. Williams said with a grin.

"Oh, no, sirs. Black Bill, Splayfoot Bill, he's the devil. He's Satan and those who carved the town from the hills, and before them the trappers and fishermen, they believed he ruled these dark woods."

"The Indians believed it too," Mr. Welloc said. "I've talked with several of the elders, as did my grandfather with the tribal wise men of his era. The legend of Bill, whom they referred to as the Horned Man, is most ancient. I confess, some of my ancestors were a rather scandalous lot, given to dabbling in the occult and all matters mystical. The town library's archives are stuffed with treatises composed by the more adventurous founders, and myriad accounts by landholders and commoners alike regarding the weird phenomena prevalent in Ransom Hollow."

Scobie said, "Aye. Many a village child vanished, an' grown men an' women, too. When I was wee, my father brought us in by dusk an' barred the door tight until morning. Everyone did. Some still do."

Luke Honey said, "A peculiar arrangement for such a healthy community."

"Aye, Olde Towne seems robust," Lord Bullard said.

Dr. Landscomb said. "Those Who Work are tied to the land. A volcano won't drive them away when there's fish and fur, crops and timber to be had."

"Yeah, and you can toss sacrificial wretches into the volcano, too," Mr. McEvoy said.

"This hunt of ours goes back for many years, long before the lodge itself was established. Without exception, someone is gravely injured, killed, or lost on these expeditions."

"Lost? What does "lost" mean, precisely?" Mr. Wesley said.

"There are swamps and cliffs, and so forth," Dr. Landscomb said. "On occasion, men have wandered into the wilds and run afoul of such dangers. But to the point. Ephraim Blackwood settled in Olde Towne at the time of its founding. A widower with two grown sons, he was a furrier by trade. The Blackwoods ran an extensive trap line throughout Ransom

Hollow and within ten years of their arrival, they'd become the premier fur trading company in the entire valley. People whispered. Christianity has never gained an overwhelming mandate here, but the Blackwoods' irreligiousness went a step beyond the pale in the eyes of the locals. Inevitably, loose talk led to muttered accusations of witchcraft. Some alleged the family consorted with Splayfoot Bill, that they'd made a pact. Material wealth for their immortal souls."

"What else?" Mr. Williams said to uneasy chuckles.

"Yes, what else indeed?" Dr. Landscomb's smile faded. "It is said that Splayfoot Bill, the Old Man of the Wood, required most unholy indulgences in return for his favors."

"Do tell," Lord Bullard said with an expression of sickly fascination.

"The devil takes many forms and it is said he is a being devoted to pain and pleasure. A Catholic priest gave an impromptu sermon in the town square accusing elder Blackwood of lying with the Old Man of the Wood, who assumed the form of a doe, one night by the pallor of a sickle moon, and the issue was a monstrous stag. Some hayseed wit soon dubbed this mythical beast "Blackwood's Git." Other, less savory colloquialisms sprang forth, but most eventually faded into obscurity. Nowadays, those who speak of this legend call the stag "Blackwood's Baby." Inevitably, the brute we shall pursue in the morn is reputed to be the selfsame animal."

"Sounds like that Blackwood fella was a long way from Oklahoma," Mr. Williams said.

"Devil spawn!" Luke Honey said, and laughed sarcastically.

"Bloody preposterous," Lord Bullard said without conviction.

"Hogwash," Mr. Briggs said. "You're scarin' the women and children, hoss."

"My apologies, good sir," Dr. Landscomb said. He didn't look sorry to Luke Honey.

"Oh, dear." Lord Bullard lurched to his feet and made for the woods, hands to his belly.

The Texans guffawed and hooted, although the mood sobered when the wolf howled again and was answered by two more of its pack.

Mr. Williams scowled, cocked his big revolver and fired into the air. The report was queerly muffled and its echo died immediately.

"That'll learn 'em," Mr. Briggs said, exaggerating his drawl.

"Time for shut eye, boys," Mr. Williams said. Shortly the men began to yawn and turned in, grumbling and joshing as they spread their blankets on the floor of the lean-to.

Luke Honey made a pillow of the horse blanket. He jacked the bolt action and chambered a round in his *Mauser Gewher 98*, a rifle he'd won from an Austrian diplomat in Nairobi. The gun was powerful enough to stop most things that went on four legs and it gave him comfort. He slept.

The mist swirled heavy as soup and the fire had dwindled to coals when he woke. Branches crackled and a black shape, the girth of a bison or a full grown rhino, moved between shadows. It stopped and twisted an incomprehensibly configured head to survey the camp. The beast huffed and continued into the brush. Luke Honey remained motionless, breath caught in his throat. The huff had sounded like a chuckle. And for an instant, the lush, shrill wheedle of panpipes drifted through the wood. Far out amid the folds of the savanna, a lion coughed. A hyena barked its lunatic bark, and much closer.

Luke Honey started and his eyes popped open and he couldn't tell the world from the dream.

⊰⊙⊱

Lord Bullard spent much of the predawn hours hunkered in the bushes, but by daybreak he'd pulled himself together, albeit white-faced and shaken. Mr. Wesley's condition, on the other hand, appeared to have worsened. He didn't speak during breakfast and sat like a lump, chin on his chest.

"Poor bastard looks like hell warmed over," Mr. Williams said. He dressed in long johns and gun belt. He sipped coffee from a tin cup. A cigarette fumed in his left hand. "You might've done him in."

Luke Honey rolled a cigarette and lighted it. He nodded. "I saw a fight in a hostel in Cape Town between a Scottish dragoon and a big Spaniard. The dragoon carried a rifle and gave the Spaniard a butt stroke to the midsection. The Spaniard laughed, drew his gun and shot the Scot right through his head. The Spaniard died four days later. Bust a rib and it punctures the insides. Starts a bleed."

"He probably should call it a day."

"Landscomb's a sawbones. He isn't blind. Guess I'll leave it to him."

"Been hankerin' to ask you, friend—how did you end up on the list? This is a mighty exclusive event. My pappy knew the Lubbock Wellocs before I was born. Took me sixteen years to get an invite here. And a bribe or two."

"Lubbock Wellocs?"

"Yep. Wellocs are everywhere. More of them than you shake a stick at—Nevada, Indiana, Massachusetts. Buncha foreign states too. Their granddads threw a wide loop, as my pappy used to say."

"My parents lived east of here. Over the mountains. Dad had some cousins in Ransom Hollow. They visited occasionally. I was a kid and I only heard bits and pieces... the men all got liquored up and told tall tales. I heard about the stag, decided I'd drill it when I got older."

"Here you are, sure enough. Why? I know you don't give a whit about the rifle. Or the money."

"How do you figure?"

"The look in your eyes, boy. You're afraid. A man like you is afraid, I take stock."

"I've known some fearless men. Hunted lions with them. A few of those gents forgot that Mother Nature is more of a killer than we humans will ever be and wound up getting chomped. She wants our blood, our bones, our goddamned guts. Fear is healthy."

"Sure as hell is. Except, there's something in you besides fear. Ain't that right? I swear you got the weird look some guys get who play with fire. I knew this vaquero who loved to ride his pony along the canyon edge. By close, I mean rocks crumbling under its hooves and falling into nothingness. I ask myself, what's here in these woods for you? Maybe I don't want any part of it."

"I reckon we all heard the same story about Mr. Blackwood. Same one my Daddy and his cousins chewed over the fire."

"Sweet Jesus, boy. You don't believe that cart load of manure Welloc and his crony been shovelin'? Okay then. I've got a whopper for you. These paths form a miles wide pattern if you see 'em from a plane. World's biggest pentagram carved out of the countryside. Hear that one?"

Luke Honey smiled dryly and crushed the butt of his cigarette underfoot.

Mr. Williams poured out the dregs of his coffee. He hooked his thumbs in his belt. "My uncle Greg came here for the hunt in '16. They sent him home in a fancy box. The Black Ram Lodge is first class all the way."

"Stag get him?"

The rancher threw back his head and laughed. He grabbed Luke Honey's arm. There were tears in his eyes. "Oh, you are a card, kid. You really do buy into that mumbo-jumbo horse pucky. Greg spotted a huge buck moving through the woods and tried to plug it from the saddle. His horse threw him and he split his head on a rock. Damned fool."

"In other words, the stag got him."

Mr. Williams squeezed Luke Honey's shoulder. Then he slackened his grip and laughed again. "Yeah, maybe you're on to something. My pappy liked to say this family is cursed. We sure had our share of untimely deaths."

The party split again, Dr. Landscomb and the British following Scobie and the dogs; Mr. Welloc, Luke Honey and the Texans proceeding along a parallel trail. Nobody was interested in the lesser game; all were intent upon tracking down Blackwood's Baby.

They entered the deepest, darkest part of the forest. The trees were huge and ribboned with moss and creepers and fungi. Scant light penetrated the canopy, yet brambles hemmed the path. The fog persisted.

Luke Honey had been an avid reader since childhood. Robert Louis Stevenson, M.R. James, and Ambrose Bierce had gotten him through many a miserable night in the tarpaper shack his father built. He thought of the fairy tale books at his aunt's house. Musty books with wooden covers and woodblock illustrations that raised the hair on his head. The evil stepmother made to dance in red hot iron shoes at Snow White's garden wedding while the dwarves hunched like fiends. Hansel and Gretel lost in a vast, endless wood, the eyes of a thousand demons glittering in the shadows. The forest in the book was not so different from the one he found himself riding through.

At noon, they stopped to take a cold lunch from their own saddlebags as this was beyond the range of the lodge staff. Arlen trotted from the forest, dodgy and feral as a fox, to report Scobie picked up the trail and was hoping to soon drive the stag itself from hiding. Dr. Landscomb and the British were in hot pursuit.

"Damn," Mr. Williams said.

"Aw, now that limey's going to do the honors," Mr. Briggs said. "I wanted that rifle."

"Everybody wants that rifle," Mr. McEvoy said.

Mr. Williams clapped his hands together. "Let's mount up, *muchachos*. Maybe we'll get lucky and our friends will miss their opening."

"The quarry is elusive," Mr. Liam Welloc said. "Anything is possible."

The men kicked their ponies to a brisk trot and gave chase.

◄◦►

An hour later, all hell broke loose.

The path crossed a plank bridge and continued upstream along the cut bank of a fast moving stream. Dogs barked and howled and the shouts of men echoed from the trees. A heavy rifle boomed twice. No sooner had Luke Honey and his companions entered a large clearing with a lagoon fed by a waterfall, did he spy Lord Bullard and Mr. Wesley afoot, rifles aimed at the trees. Dr. Landscomb stood to one side, hands tight on the bridle of his pony. Dead and dying dogs were strewn everywhere. A pair of surviving mastiffs yapped and snarled, muzzles slathered in foam, as Scobie wrenched mightily at their leashes.

The Brits' rifles thundered in unison. Luke Honey caught a glimpse of what at first he took to be a stag. Yet something was amiss about the shape as it bolted through the trees and disappeared. It was far too massive and it moved in a strange, top-heavy manner. Lord Bullard's horse whinnied and galloped blindly through the midst of the gawking Americans. It missed Luke Honey and Mr. Williams, collided with Mr. McEvoy and knocked his horse to the ground. The banker cursed and vaulted from the saddle, landing awkwardly. His horse staggered upright while Mr. Wesley's mount charged away into the mist in the opposite direction. Mr. Briggs yelled and pulled at the reins of his mount as it crow-hopped all over the clearing.

"What the hell was that?" Williams said, expertly controlling his horse as it half-reared, eyes rolling to the whites. "Welloc?"

Mr. Liam Welloc had wisely halted at the entrance and was supremely unaffected by the debacle. "I warned you, gentlemen. Blackwood's Baby is no tender doe."

Mr. McEvoy had twisted an ankle. He sat on a rock while Dr. Landscomb tended him. Scobie calmed his mastiffs and handed their leashes to Mr. Liam Welloc. He took a pistol from his coat and walked among the dogs who lay scattered and broken along the bank of the lagoon and in the bushes. He fired the pistol three times.

No one spoke. They rubbed their horses' necks and stared at the blood smeared across the rocks and at the savaged corpses of the dogs. Scobie began dragging them into a pile. A couple of flasks of whiskey were passed around and everyone drank in morbid silence.

Finally, Mr. Williams said, "Bullard, what happened here?" He repeated the question until the Englishman shuddered and looked up, blank-faced, from the carnage.

"It speared them on its horns. In all my years… it scooped two dogs and pranced about while they screamed and writhed on its antlers."

"Anybody get a clear shot?"

"I did," Mr. Wesley said. He leaned on his rifle like an old man. "Thought I nicked the bugger. Surely I did." He coughed and his shoulders convulsed. Dr. Landscomb left Mr. McEvoy and came over to examine him.

Mr. Liam Welloc took stock. "Two horses gone. Five dogs killed. Mr. McEvoy's ankle is swelling nicely, I see. Doctor, what of Mr. Wesley?"

Dr. Landscomb listened to Mr. Wesley's chest with a stethoscope. "This man requires further medical attention. We must get him to a hospital at once."

Scobie shouted. He ran back to the group, his eyes red, his mouth twisted in fear. "Arlen's gone. Arlen's gone."

"Easy, friend." Mr. Williams handed the older man the whiskey and waited for him to take a slug. "You mean that boy of yours?"

Scobie nodded. "He climbed a tree when the beast charged our midst. Now he's gone."

"He probably ran away," Mr. Briggs said. "Can't say as I blame him."

"No." Scobie brandished a soiled leather shoe. "This was lying near the tracks of the stag. They've gone deeper into the wood."

"Why the bloody hell would the little fool do that?" Lord Bullard said, slowly returning to himself.

"He's a brave lad," Scobie said and wrung the shoe in his grimy hands.

"Obviously we have to find the kid," Luke Honey said, although he was unhappy about the prospect. If anything, the fog had grown thicker.

"We have four hours of light. Maybe less."

"It's never taken the dogs," Scobie said so quietly Luke Honey was certain no one else heard.

◄◦►

There was a brief discussion regarding logistics where it was decided that Dr. Landscomb would escort Mr. Wesley and Mr. McEvoy to the prior evening's campsite—it would be impossible to proceed much farther before dark. The search party would rendezvous with them and continue on to the lodge in the morning. Luke Honey volunteered his horse to carry Mr. Wesley, not from a sense of honor, but because he was likely the best tracker of the bunch and probably also the fleetest of foot.

They spread into a loose line, Mr. Liam Welloc and Mr. Briggs ranging along the flanks on horseback, while Luke Honey, Scobie, and Mr. Williams formed a picket. Mr. Williams led his horse. By turns, each of them shouted Arlen's name.

Initially, pursuit went forth with much enthusiasm as Lord Bullard had evidently wounded the stag. It's blood splattered fern leafs and puddle in the spaces between its hoof prints and led them away from the beaten trails into brush so thick, Luke Honey unsheathed his Barlow knife and hacked at the undergrowth. Mosquitoes attacked in swarms. The light dimmed and the trail went cold. A breeze sighed, and the ubiquitous fog swirled around them and tracking soon became a fruitless exercise. Mr. Liam Welloc announced an end to the search on account of encroaching darkness.

Mr. Williams and Luke Honey stopped to rest upon the exposed roots of a dying oak tree and take a slug from Mr. Williams' hip flask. The rancher smoked a cigarette. His face was red and he fanned away the mosquitoes with his hat. "Greg said this is how it was."

"Your uncle? The one who died?"

"Yeah, on the second go-around. The first time he came home and talked about a disaster. Horse threw a feller from a rich family in Kansas and broke his neck."

"I reckon everybody knows what they're getting into coming to this place."

"I'm not sure of that at all. You think you know what evil is until you look it in the eye. That's when you really cotton to the consequences. Ain't no fancy shooting iron worth any of this."

"Too early for that kind of talk."

"The hell it is. I ain't faint-hearted, but this is a bad fix. The boy is sure enough in mortal danger. Judging what happened to them dogs, *we* might be in trouble."

Luke Honey had no argument with that observation, preoccupied as he was with how the fog hung like a curtain around them, how the night abruptly surged upon them, how every hair of his body stood on end. He realized his companion wasn't at his side. He called Mr. Williams' name and the branches creaked overhead.

An unearthly stillness settled around him as he pressed his hand against the rough and slimy bark of a tree. He listened as the gazelle at the waterhole listened for the predators that deviled them. He saw a muted glow ahead; the manner of light that seeped from certain fogbanks on the deep ocean and in the depths of caverns. He went forward, groping through coils of mist, rifle held aloft in his free hand. His racing heart threatened to unman him.

Luke Honey stepped into a small grove of twisted and shaggy trees. The weak, phosphorescence rose from the earth and cast evil shadows upon the foliage and the wall of thorns that hemmed the grove on three sides. A statue canted leeward at the center of the grove—a tall, crumbling marble stack, ghastly white and stained black by moss and mold, a terrible horned man, or god. This was an idol to a dark and vile Other and it radiated a palpable aura of wickedness.

The fog crept into Luke Honey's mouth, trickled into his nostrils, and his gorge rebelled. Something struck him across the shoulders. He lost balance and all the strength in his legs drained and he collapsed and lay supine, squashed into the wet earth and leaves by an imponderable force. This force was the only thing keeping him from sliding off the skin of the Earth into the void. He clawed the dirt. Worms threaded his fingers. "Get behind me, devil," he said.

The statue blurred and expanded, shifting elastically. The statue was so very large and its cruel shadow pinned him like an insect, and the voices of its creators, primeval troglodytes who'd dwelt in mud huts and made love in the filth and offered their blood to long dead gods, whispered obscenities, and images unfolded in his mind. He threshed and struggled to rise. A child screamed. The cry chopped off. A discordant vibration rippled over the ground and passed through Luke Honey's bones—a hideous clash of cymbals and shrieking reeds reverberated in his brain. His nose bled.

Fresh blood is best, the statue said, although it was Luke Honey's mouth that opened and made the words. *Baby blood, boy child blood. Rich red sweet rare boy blood. What, little man, what could you offer the lord of the dark? What you feeble fly?* His jaw contorted, manipulated by invisible fingers. His tongue writhed at the bidding of the Other. A choir of corrupt angels sang from the darkness all around—a song sweet and repellent, and old as Melville's sea and its inhabitants. Sulfurous red light illuminated the fog and impossible shapes danced and capered as if beamed from the lens of a magic lantern.

Luke Honey turned his head sideways in the dirt and saw his brother hoeing in the field. He saw himself as a boy of fourteen struggling with loading a single shot .22 and the muzzle flash exactly as Michael leaned in to look at the barrel. Luke Honey's father sent him to live in Utah and his mother died shortly thereafter, a broken woman. The black disk of the moon occulted the sun. His massive .416 Rigby boomed and a bull elephant pitched forward and crumpled, its tusks digging furrows in the dirt. Mother stood in the entrance of the tent, wings charred, her brilliant nimbus dimmed to reddish flame. Arlen regarded him from the maze of thorns, his face slack with horror. "Take me instead," Luke Honey said through clenched teeth, "and be damned."

You're already mine, Lucas. The Other cackled in lunatic merriment.

The music, the fire, the singing, all crashed and stopped.

Mr. Williams leaned over him and Luke Honey almost skewered the man. Mr. Williams leaped back, staring at the Barlow knife in Luke Honey's fist. "Sorry, boy. You were having a fit. Laughing like a crazy man."

Luke Honey clambered to his feet and put away the knife. His scooped up his rifle and brushed leaves from his clothes. The glow had subsided and the two men were alone except for the idol which hulked, a terrible lump the darkness.

"Sweet baby Jesus," Mr. Williams said. "My uncle told me about these damned things, too. Said rich townies—that weren't followers of Christ, to put it politely—had 'em shipped in and set up here and there across the estate. Gods from the Old World. There are stories about rituals in the hills. Animal sacrifices and unnatural relations. Stories like our hosts told us about the Blackwoods. To this day, folks with money and an interest in ungodly practices come to visit these shrines."

"Let's get away from this thing," Luke Honey said.

"Amen to that." Mr. Williams led the way and they might've wandered all night, but someone fired a gun to signal periodically, and the two men stumbled into the firelight of camp as Mr. Liam Welloc and Mr. McEvoy were serving a simple dinner of pork and beans. By unspoken agreement, neither Luke Honey or Mr. Williams mentioned the vile statue. Luke Honey retreated to the edge of the camp, eyeing Mr. Liam Welloc and Dr. Landscomb. As lords of the estate there could be no doubt they knew something of the artifacts and their foul nature. Were the men merely curators, or did they partake of corrupt ceremonies by the dark of the moon? He shuddered and kept his weapons close.

Dr. Landscomb and Lord Bullard had wrapped Mr. Wesley in a cocoon of blankets. Mr. Wesley's face was drawn, his eyes heavy-lidded. Lord Bullard held a brandy flask to his companion's lips and dabbed them with a handkerchief after each coughing jag.

"Lord Almighty," Mr. Williams said as he joined Luke Honey, a plate of beans in hand. "I reckon he's off to the happy hunting grounds any minute now."

Luke Honey ate his dinner and tried to ignore Mr. Wesley's groans and coughs, and poor Scobie mumbling and rocking on his heels, a posture that betrayed his rude lineage of savages who went forth in ochre paints and limed hair and wailed at the capriciousness of pagan gods.

There were no stories around the fire that evening, and later, it rained.

⟶⟨o⟩⟶

Mr. Wesley was dead in the morning. He lay stiff and blue upon the lean-to floor. Dr. Landscomb covered him with another blanket and said a few words. Lord Bullard wept inconsolably and cast hateful glances at Luke Honey.

"Lord Almighty," was all Mr. Williams could repeat. The big man stood near the corpse, hat in hand.

"The forest is particularly greedy this season," Mr. Liam Welloc said. "It has taken a good Christian fellow and an innocent child, alas."

"Hold your tongue, Mr. Welloc!" Scobie's face was no less contorted in grief and fury than Lord Bullard's. He pointed at Mr. Liam Welloc. "My grandson lives, an' I swear to uproot every stone an' every tree in this godforsaken forest to find him."

Mr. Liam Welloc gave Scobie a pitying smile. "I'm sorry, my friend. You know as well as I that the odds of his surviving the night are slim. The damp and cold alone...."

"We must continue the search."

"Perhaps tomorrow. At the moment, we are duty bound to see our guests to safety and make arrangements for the disposition of poor Mr. Wesley's earthly remains."

"You mean to leave Arlen at the tender mercy of... Nay, I'll have none of it."

"I am sorry. Our duty is clear."

"Curse you, Mr. Welloc!"

"Master Scobie, I implore you not to pursue a reckless course—"

"Bah!" Scobie made a foul gesture and stomped into the predawn gloom.

Mr. McEvoy said, "The old man is right—we can't just quit on the kid."

"Damned straight," Mr. Briggs said. "What kind of skunks would we be to abandon a boy while there's still a chance?"

Dr. Landscomb said, "Well spoken, sirs. However, you can hardly be expected to grasp the, ah, gravity of the situation. I assure you, Arlen is lost. Master Scobie is on a Quixotic mission. He won't find the lad anywhere in Wolfvale. In any event, Mr. McEvoy simply must be treated at a hospital lest his ankle grow worse. I dislike the color of the swelling."

"Surely, it does no harm to try," Mr. Briggs said.

"We tempt fate by spending another minute here," Mr. Liam Welloc said. "And to stay after sunset.... This is impossible, I'm afraid." The incongruity of the doctor's genteel comport juxtaposed with his apparent dread of the supernatural chilled Luke Honey in a way he wouldn't have deemed possible after his experiences abroad.

"Tempt fate?" Mr. Briggs said. "Not stay after sunset? What the hell is that supposed to mean, Welloc? Boys, can you make heads or tails of this foolishness?"

"He means we'd better get ourselves shut of this place," Mr. Williams said.

"Bloody right," Lord Bullard said. "This is a matter for the authorities."

Mr. Briggs appeared dumbfounded. "Well don't this beat all. Luke, what do you say?"

Luke Honey lighted a cigarette. "I think we should get back to the lodge. A dirty shame, but that's how I see it."

"I don't believe this."

"Me neither," Mr. McEvoy said. His leg was elevated and his cheeks shone with sweat. His ankle was swaddled in bandages. "Wish I could walk, damn it."

"You saw what that stag did to the dogs," Lord Bullard said. "There's something unnatural at work and I've had quite enough, thank you." He wiped his eyes and looked at Luke Honey. "You'll answer for Wes. Don't think you won't."

"Easy there, partner," Mr. Williams said.

Luke Honey nodded. "Well, Mr. Bullard, I think you may be correct. I'll answer for your friend. That reckoning is a bit farther down the list, but it's on there."

"This is no time to bicker," said Mr. Liam Welloc. "Apparently we are in agreement—"

"Not all of us," Mr. Briggs said, glowering.

"—Since we are in agreement, let's commence packing. We'll sort everything out when we return to the house."

"What about Scobie?" Mr. Briggs said.

"Master Scobie can fend for himself," Mr. Liam Welloc said, his bland, conciliatory demeanor firmly in place. "As I said, upon our return we will alert the proper authorities. Sheriff Peckham has some experience in these matters."

Luke Honey didn't believe the sheriff, or anybody else, would be combing these woods for one raggedy kid anytime soon. The yearly sacrifice had been accomplished. This was the way of the world; this was its beating heart and panting maw. He'd seen such offerings made by tribes in the jungles, just as his own Gaelic kin had once poured wine in the sea and cut the throats of fatted lambs. If one looked back far enough, all men issued from the same wellspring and every last one of them feared the dark as Mr. Liam Welloc and Dr. Landscomb and their constituency in Ransom Hollow surely did. Despite the loathsome nature of their pact, there was nothing shocking about this arrangement. To propitiate the gods, to please one's lord and master was ever the way. That expert killers such as the English and the Texans and, of course, himself, served as provender in this particular iteration of the eternal drama filled Luke Honey's heart with bitter amusement. This wry humor mixed with his increasing dread and rendered him giddy, almost drunken.

Mr. Wesley's body was laid across the saddle of Luke Honey's horse and the company began the long trudge homeward. The dreary fog persisted, although the rain had given out for the moment.

"I hope you don't think I'm a coward," Mr. Williams said. He rode beside Luke Honey who was walking at the rear of the group.

Luke Honey didn't speak. He pulled his collar tight.

"My mama raised me as a God fearin' boy. There's real evil, Mr. Honey. Not that existential crap, either. Last night, I felt somethin' I ain't felt before. Scared me spitless." When Luke Honey didn't answer, Mr. Williams leaned over and said in a low voice, "People got killed in that grove, not just animals. Couldn't you feel it coming off that idol like a draft in a slaughter yard? I ain't afraid of much, but Bullard's right. This ain't natural and that kid is a goner."

"Who are you trying to convince?" Luke Honey said, although the question was more than a little self referential. "The hunt is over. Go back to Texas and dream away the winter. There's always next year."

"No, not for me. My uncle made that mistake. Next year, I'll go to British Colombia. Or Alaska. Damned if I know, but I know it won't be Ransom Hollow." Mr. Williams clicked his tongue and spurred his mount ahead to rejoin the group.

Later, the company halted for a brief time to rest the animals and allow the men to stretch their legs. The liquor was gone and tempers short. When they remounted, Luke Honey remained seated on a mossy boulder, smoking his last cigarette. His companions rode on, heads down and dispirited, and failed to notice his absence. They disappeared around a sharp bend.

Luke Honey finished his cigarette. The sun slowly ate through the clouds and its pale light shone in the gaps of the foliage. He turned his back and walked deeper into the woods, into the darkness.

-◦-

The shrieks of the mastiffs came and went all day, and so too the phantom bellows of men, the muffled blasts of their weapons. Luke Honey resisted the urge to cover his ears, to break and flee. Occasionally, Scobie hollered from an indeterminate distance. Luke Honey thought the old man's cries sounded more substantial, more of the mortal realm, and he attempted to orient himself in their direction. He walked on, clutching his rifle.

Night came and he was lost in the endless forest.

A light glimmered to his left, sifting down through the black gallery to illuminate a figure who stood as if upon a stage. Mr. Wesley regarded him, hat clasped to his navel in both hands, hair slick and shining. His face was white. A black stain spread across the breast of his white shirt. He removed a pair of objects from inside his hat and with an insolent flourish tossed them into the bushes short of Luke Honey. Dr. Landscomb stepped into view and took Mr. Wesley by the elbow and drew him into the shadows. The ray of light blinked out of existence.

The objects were pale and glistening and as Luke Honey approached them, his heart beat faster. He leaned close to inspect them and recoiled, his courage finally buckling in the presence of such monstrous events.

Luke Honey blindly shoved his way through low hanging branches and spiky undergrowth. His clothes were torn, the flesh of his hands and face scratched and bleeding. A rifle fired several yards away. He staggered and shielded his eyes from the muzzle flash and a large animal blundered past him, squealing and roaring. Then it was gone and Scobie came tearing in pursuit and almost tripped over him. The old man swung a battered lantern. He gawked at Luke Honey in the flat yellow glare.

Scobie's expression was wild and caked in dirt. His face was nicked and bloody. He panted like a dog. He held his rifle in his left hand, its bore centered on Luke Honey's middle. In a gasping voice, he said, "I see you, Bill."

"It's me, Luke Honey."

"What's your business here?"

"I came to help you find the boy." He dared not speak of what he'd so recently discovered, an abomination that once revealed was certain to drive the huntsman into raving madness. At this range Scobie's ancient single shot rifle would cut Luke Honey in twain.

"Arlen's gone. He's gone." Scobie lowered the weapon, his arm quivering in exhaustion.

"You don't believe that." Luke Honey said with a steadiness born of staring down savage predators, of waiting to pull the trigger that would drop them at his feet, of facing certain death with a coldness of mind inherent to the borderline mad. The terror remained, ready to sweep him away.

"I'm worn to the bone. There's nothing left in me." Scobie seemed to wither, to shrink into himself in despair.

"The stag is wounded," Luke Honey said. "I think you hit it again, judging from the racket."

"It don't matter. You can't kill a thing like that." Scobie's eyes glittered with tears. "This is the devil's preserve, Mr. Honey. Every acre. You should've gone with the masters, got yourself away. We stayed too long and we're done for. He only pretends to run. He'll end the game and come for us soon."

"I had a bad feeling about Landscomb and Welloc."

"Forget those idiots. They're as much at the mercy of Hell as anyone else in Ransom Hollow."

"Got anything to drink?" Luke Honey said.

Scobie hung the lantern from a branch and handed Luke Honey a canteen made of cured animal skin. The canteen was full of sweet, bitter whiskey. The men took a couple of swigs and rested there by the flickering illumination of the sooty old lamp. Luke Honey built a fire. They ate jerky and warmed themselves as the dank night closed in ever more tightly.

Much later, Scobie said, "It used to be worse. My grandsire claimed some of the more devout folk would drag girls from their homes and cut out their innards on them stone tablets you'll find under a tree here or there." His wizened face crinkled into a horridly mournful smile. "An' my mother, she whispered that when she was a babe, Black Bill was known to creep through the yards of honest folk while they slept. She heard his nails tap-tapping on their cottage door one night."

Luke Honey closed his eyes. He thought again of Arlen's pitiful, small hands severed at the wrists and discarded in the brush, a pair of soft, dripping flowers. He heard his companion rise stealthily and creep away from camp. He slept and awakened to the old man kneeling at his side. Scobie's face was hidden in shadow. Luke Honey smelled the oily steel of a knife near his own neck. The man reeked of murderous intent. He wondered where Scobie had been, what he had done.

Scobie spoke softly, "I don't know what to do. I'm a man of God."

"Yet here we are. Look who you serve."

"No, Mr. Honey. The hunt goes on an' I don't matter none. You're presence ain't my doing. You bought your ticket. I come because somebody's got to stand up. Somebody's got to put a bullet in the demon."

"The price you've paid seems steep as hell, codger."

Scobie nodded. He remained quiet for a while. At last he said, "Come, boy. You must come with me now. He's waiting for us. He whispered to me from the dark, made a pact with me he'd take one of us in return for Arlen. I promised him you, God help me. It's a vile oath and I'm ashamed."

"Oh, Scobie." Luke Honey's belly twisted and churned. "You know how these things turn out. You poor, damned fool."

"Please. Don't make me beg you, Mr. Honey. Don't make me. Do what's right for that innocent boy. I know the Lord's in your heart."

Luke Honey reached for Scobie's arm, and patted it. "You're right about one thing. God help you."

They went. There was a clearing, its bed layered with muck and spoiled leaves. Unholy symbols were gouged into the trees; brands so old they'd fossilized. It was a killing ground of antiquity and Scobie had prepared it well. He'd improvised several torches to light the shallow basin with a ghastly, reddish glare.

Scobie took several steps and uttered an inarticulate cry, a glottal exclamation held over from his ancestors. He half turned to beckon and his face was transformed by shock when Luke Honey smashed the butt of his rifle into his hip, and sent him stumbling into the middle of the clearing.

Luke Honey's eyes blurred with grief, and Michael's shade materialized there, his trusting smile disintegrating into bewilderment, then inertness. The cruelness of the memory drained Luke Honey of his fear. He said with dispassion, "My hell is to testify. Don't you understand? He doesn't want me. He took me years ago."

Brush snapped. The stag shambled forth from the outer darkness. It loomed above Scobie, its fur rank and steaming. Black blood oozed from gashes along its flanks. Beneath a great jagged crown of antlers its eyes were black, its teeth yellow and broken. Scobie fell to his knees, palms raised in supplication. The stag nuzzled his matted hair and its long tongue lapped at the muddy tears and the streaks of drying blood upon the man's upturned face. Its muzzle unhinged. The teeth closed and there was a sound like a ripe cabbage cracking apart.

Luke Honey slumped against the bole of the oak, the rifle a dead, useless weight across his knees, and watched.

◄○►

LOOKER

DAVID NICKLE

I met her on the beach.

It was one of Len's parties—one of the last he threw, before he had to stop. You were there too. But we didn't speak. I remember watching you talking with Jonathan on the deck, an absurdly large tumbler for such a small splash of Merlot wedged at your elbow as you nodded, eyes fixed on his so as not to meet mine. If you noticed me, I hope you also noticed I didn't linger.

Instead, I took my own wineglass, filled it up properly, climbed down that treacherous wooden staircase, and kicked off my shoes. It was early enough that the sand was still warm from the sun—late enough that the sun was just dabs of pink on the dark ocean and I could tell myself I had the beach to myself.

She was, I'm sure, telling herself the same thing. She had brought a pipe and a lighter with her in her jeans, and was perched on a picnic table, surreptitiously puffing away. The pipe disappeared as I neared her. It came back soon enough, when she saw my wineglass, maybe recognized me from the party.

I didn't recognize her. She was a small woman, but wide across the shoulders and the tiniest bit chubby. Hair was dark, pulled back into a ponytail. Pretty, but not pretty enough; she would fade at a party like Len's.

"Yeah, I agree," she said to me and I paused on my slow gambol to the surf.

"It's too bright," she said, and as I took a long pull from my wine, watching her curiously, she added, "look at him."

"Look at me," I said, and she laughed.

"You on the phone?" I asked, and she dropped her head in extravagant *mea culpa*.

"No," she said. "Just…"

"Don't fret. What's the point of insanity if you can't enjoy a little conversation?"

Oh, I am smooth. She laughed again, and motioned me over, and waved the pipe and asked if I'd like to share.

Sure I said, and she scooted aside to make room on the table. Her name was Lucy. Lucille, actually, was how she introduced herself but she said Lucy was fine. I introduced myself. "Tom's a nice name," she said.

The night grew. Lungs filled with smoke and mouths with wine; questions asked, questions answered. *How do you know Len? What do you do? What brings you to the beach when so much is going on inside?* It went both ways.

Lucy knew Len scarcely at all. They'd met through a friend who worked at Len's firm. Through the usual convolutions of dinners and pubs and excursions, she'd insinuated herself onto the cc list of the *ur*-mail by which Len advertised his parties. She worked cash at a bookstore chain in town and didn't really have a lot of ambition past that right now. Which tended to make her feel seriously out of her weight class at Len's parties or so she said; the beach, therefore, was an attractive option.

She finished my wine for me, and we walked. I'd been on my way to the water's edge and Lucy thought that was a fine idea. The sun was all gone by now and stars were peeking out. One of the things I liked about Len's place—it was just far enough away from town you could make out stars at night. Not like the deep woods, or the mountains. But constellations weren't just theoretical there.

"Hey Tom," she said as the surf touched our toes, "want to go for a swim? I know we don't have suits, but…"

Why not? As you might remember, I've a weakness for the midnight dunk. We both did, as I recall.

I stepped back a few yards to where the sand was dry, set down my glass and stripped off my shirt, my trousers. Lucy unbuttoned her blouse, the top button of her jeans. I cast off my briefs. "Well?" I said, standing *in flagrante delicto* in front of her.

"Get in," she said, "I'll be right behind you."

It didn't occur to me that this might be a trick until I was well out at sea. Wouldn't it be the simplest thing, I thought, as I dove under a breaking wave, to wait until I was out far enough, gather my trousers, find the wallet and the mobile phone, toss the clothes into the surf and run to a waiting car? I'm developing my suspicious mind, really, my dearest—but it still has a time delay on it, even after everything...

I came up, broke my stroke, and turned to look back at the beach.

She waved at me. I was pleased—and relieved—to see that she was naked too. My valuables were safe as they could be. And Lucy had quite a nice figure, as it turned out: fine full breasts—wide, muscular hips—a small bulge at the tummy, true... but taken with the whole, far from offensive.

I waved back, took a deep breath and dove again, this time deep enough to touch bottom. My fingers brushed sea-rounded rock and stirred up sand, and I turned and kicked and broke out to the moonless night, and only then it occurred to me—how clearly I'd seen her on the beach, two dozen yards off, maybe further.

There lay the problem. There wasn't enough light. I shouldn't have seen anything.

I treaded water, thinking back at how I'd seen her... glistening, flickering, with tiny points of red, of green... winking in and out... like stars themselves? Spread across not sky, but flesh?

I began to wonder: Had I seen her at all?

There was no sign of her now. The beach was a line of black, crowned with the lights from Len's place, and above that... the stars.

How much had I smoked? I wondered. What had I smoked, for that matter? I hadn't had a lot of wine—I'd quaffed a glass at Len's before venturing outside, and I'd shared the second glass with Lucy. Not even two glasses...

But it *was* Len's wine.

I'd made up my mind to start back in when she emerged from the waves—literally in front of my face.

"You look lost," Lucy said, and splashed me, and dove again. Two feet came up, and scissored, and vanished. Some part of her brushed against my hip.

I took it as my cue and ducked.

The ocean was nearly a perfect black. I dove and turned and dove again, reaching wide in my strokes, fingers spreading in a curious, and yes, hungry grasp. I turned, and came near enough the surface that I felt my foot break it, splashing down again, and spun—

—and I saw her.

Or better, I saw the constellation of Lucy—a dusting of brilliant red points of light, defining her thighs—and then turning, and more along her midriff; a burst of blue stipple, shaping her breasts, the backs of her arms. I kicked toward her as she turned in the water, my own arms held straight ahead, to lay hold of that fine, if I may say, celestial body.

But she anticipated me, and kicked deeper, and I'd reached my lungs' limits so I broke surface, gasping at the night air. She was beside me an instant later, spitting and laughing. No funny lights this time; just Lucy, soaking wet and treading water beside me.

"We don't have towels," she said. "I just thought of that. We're going to freeze."

"We won't freeze," I said.

"It's colder than you think."

"Oh, I know it's cold. We just won't freeze."

She splashed me and laughed again and wondered what I meant by that, but we both knew what I meant by that, and after we'd not-quite tired ourselves out in the surf, we made back for the shore.

I wonder how things went for you, right then? I know that you always fancied Jonathan; I know what happened later. I hope you don't think I'm being bitter or ironic when I say I hope you had a good time with him. If he misbehaved—well, I trust you did too.

Shall I tell you how *we* misbehaved?

Well—

In some ways, it was as you might expect; nothing you haven't seen, nothing you haven't felt, my dear.

In others...

‹o›

Through the whole of it, Lucy muttered.

"He is," she would say as I pressed against her breasts and nibbled on her earlobe; and "Quiet!" as I ran my tongue along the rim of her aureole... "I said no," as I thrust into her, and I paused, and then she continued: "Why are you stopping, Tommy?"

This went on through the whole of it. As I buried my face between her legs, and she commented, "Isn't he, though?", I thought again of Lucy on the shore, under the water. "Too bright," she moaned, and I remembered my visions of the sky, on her skin.

And as I thought of these things, my hands went exploring: along her thighs, across her breasts—along her belly...

She gasped and giggled as I ran my thumb across her navel... and she said, "Tommy?" as my forefinger touched her navel again... and "What are you doing?" as the palm of my hand, making its way along the ridge of her hip-bone... found her navel once more.

I lifted my head and moved my hand slowly aside. For an instant, there was a flash of dim red light—reflecting off my palm like a candle-flame. But only an instant. I moved my hand aside and ran the edge of my thumb over the flesh there. It was smooth. "Tom?" she said sharply, and started on about unfinished business. "Shh," I said, and lowered my face—to the ridge of her hip-bone, or rather the smooth flesh inward of it. And slowly, paying minute attention, I licked her salted skin.

I would not have found it with my crude, calloused fingertips; my tongue was better attuned the task. I came upon it first as a small bump in the smooth flesh: like a pimple, a cyst. As I circled it, I sensed movement, as though a hard thing were rolling inside. Running across the tiny peak of it, I sensed a line—like a slit in the flesh, pushed tightly closed. Encouraged, I surrounded it with my lips and began to suck, as I kept probing it with my tongue. "I'm sorry," she said, and then, "Oh!" as my tongue pushed through. It touched a cool, wet thing—rolling on my tongue like an unripened berry.

And then... I was airborne... it was though I were flying up, and falling deep. And I landed hard on my side and it all resolved, the world once more. Icy water lapped against me. And Lucy was swearing at me.

I looked at her, unbelieving. She looked back.

She, and a multitude.

For now I could see that what I'd first thought were star-points, were nothing of the sort. Her flesh was pocked with eyes. They were small, and reflective, like a cat's.

Nocturnal eyes.

In her shoulders—the swell of her breasts—along the line of her throat... They blinked—some individually, some in pairs, and on her belly, six points of cobalt blue, formed into a nearly perfect hexagon. Tiny slits of pupils widened to take in the sight of me. The whole of her flesh seemed to writhe with their squinting.

It didn't seem to cause her discomfort. Far from it; Lucy's own eyes—the ones in her head—narrowed to slits, and her mouth perked in a little smile. "He is that," she said, "yes, you're right." And it struck me then: those strange things she was saying weren't intended for me or anyone else.

She was talking to the eyes.

"He can't have known," she continued, her hand creeping down to her groin, "and if he did, well now he knows better."

I drew my legs to my chest and my own hands moved instinctively to my privates, as the implications of all these eyes, of her words, came together.

These weren't her eyes; they were from another creature, or many creatures. And they were all looking upon me: naked, sea-shrivelled, crouching in the dirt.

Turning away from her, I got to my feet, ran up the beach and gathered my shirt and trousers, and clutching them to my chest, fairly bolted for the stairs. I pulled on my shirt and trousers, hunted around for my shoes, and made my way up the stairs. At the top, I looked back for the glow of Lucy. But the beach was dark.

The eyes were shut.

◄◦►

You and Jonathan were gone by the time I came back to the house.

I wasn't surprised; Len had switched to his Sarah Vaughan / Etta James play-list, and I remember how fond you are of those two. And it was late. The party had waxed and waned during my excursion with Lucy on the beach and those who remained were the die-hards: Ben and Dru, sprawled on the sectional, finishing off a bottle of Shiraz; Dennis, holding court in the kitchen with Emile and Prabh and the dates they'd not thought to introduce—at least not to me; maybe a half-dozen others that neither of us wouldn't recognize if we met them on the street. Len's party had proceeded without me.

I wasn't surprised, and I wasn't unhappy about it. Skinny dipping on the ocean and fucking on the beach are two activities that hardly leave one presentable to polite company. Best then to wait until the polite company had moved along, leaving only the depraved ones.

I made for the bathroom—the second floor bath, which yes, I know, was a *faux-pas* at Len's parties, particularly late into the evening. But there was a small crowd around the two-piece off the kitchen, and I needed to tidy up sooner, so I slipped upstairs and made for the master bath. Which, happily, was vacant. The lights flickered on as I stepped inside and I slid the pocket door shut, and confronted myself in the long mirror opposite the showers.

I didn't think I took that long; just splashed water in my face, ran a wet comb through my hair, shook the sand out of my shirt and tucked it in properly before giving myself another inspection. By my own reckoning, it couldn't have been more than five minutes. But the hammering on the door said otherwise.

It was Kimi, Len's Kimi.

In a week, she'd be on a plane back to New York, done with all of us, gone from Len's circle for good. That party, she was on the verge of it. I slid open the door and apologized. "You shouldn't be up here," she said, "not this time of night," and I agreed.

"Ask forgiveness not permission? That it, Tommy?" she said and brushed past me. She had been spending time in Len's rooms, and it had gone about as badly as it did toward the end. You could tell. Do you remember that time Len had us all on that boat he'd hired for the summer? And she came hammering on our cabin door—with that fish-hook stuck in just below the collar-bone? And when you opened it, she was so quiet, asking if you knew where they kept the first-aid kit on the boat because "Len isn't sure." You knew something awful had happened, I knew something awful had happened. We talked about it after we got the hook out and the wound cleaned and bandaged and Kimi, smiling brightly, had excused herself and skipped back to the cabin she and Len were sharing. What did you say? "One day, that armour of hers is going to crack. When it does, she'll either leave or she'll die."

It was a good line; I laughed as hard as you did.

Well there in the upstairs bath, the armour was cracking. And Kimi wasn't dead. But she wasn't leaving either. She leaned against the vanity, arms crossed over her chest. She was wearing a short black skirt. Her shoulders, arms, and legs were bare. There were no visible bruises. No fish-hooks either. She studied me, maybe looking for the same things.

"You go for a swim?" she said finally. "You look like you went for a swim in the ocean."

"Guilty."

Her eyes flickered away a moment as she waved a hand. "Nobody's guilty of taking a fucking swim. And it's a good look for you." Then she looked again, reassessing. "But you didn't just go for a swim."

"You were right. I took a fucking swim," I said, and started to laugh, and she got it and laughed too.

"How's your night going?" I asked. She made a little sneer with her lips—as if she was trying to fish a piece of food out of her teeth. Put her bare feet together on the slate tile floor, made a show of inspecting the nails.

"Len's very tired," she said.

I raised my eyebrows. "Oh dear. That doesn't sound good."

"It's not as bad as that."

"If you say so."

She looked at me. "Are you hitting on me, Tommy?"

I said I wasn't.

"Then why the fuck are you still here?"

There was an answer to that question, but not one I could really articulate—not the way she was looking at me then. I wanted to talk to her about Lucy, about the eyes… I thought—hoped—that she would be able to help me parse the experience somehow. Or failing that, help me put it away, someplace quiet.

But her armour was cracked. She had nothing to offer me. And although I wouldn't know for sure until a week later—she wasn't leaving that night, she stayed the whole time—she was almost certainly planning her escape.

So I left her to it. "I'm very tired too," I said, and stepped into the hall. That one didn't get a laugh. The bathroom door slid shut behind me, hitting the door-jamb hard enough to quiver in its track.

"You're still thinking about *her*," said Kimi through the wood. "Well give it up, Tommy. It's obvious to everybody. She's done with you."

◄○►

Oh, don't worry. I know you're done with me. I'm done with you too.

◄○►

I joined the conversation in the kitchen, or rather hovered at its edge. Dennis had stepped away, and now Emile was talking about Dubai, which was hardly a new topic for him. But the girls he and Prabh had brought were new. They hung on every word. I leaned against the stove, poured myself the dregs of a Chardonnay into a little plastic cup and swallowed the whole thing. Prabh found me a Malbec from Portugal and poured a refill.

"Yeah, you look like shit," he said. "Bad night?"

"Not exactly bad," I said. "Strange. Not exactly bad."

Prabh nodded and turned back to his girl. She was very pretty, I had to hand it to him: tall, with streaked blond hair and a dancer's body. Twenty-seven years old, no older. I'd turn back to her too.

So I kept drinking, and Prabh kept filling my cup, and after awhile, I'd moved from the periphery of the conversation to the juicy middle. And there, I asked as innocently as I could manage: "Any of you know Lucy?"

Shrugs all around. I showed a level hand to indicate her height. Another to show how long her hair was. "We don't know her, Tom," said Emile, and Prabh poured me another glass. "Maybe you want to sit down?" asked one of the girls.

It was an excellent suggestion. I made my way to the sectional in the living room with only a little help here and there, as necessary.

Really, I don't think I made *that* much of a spectacle of myself. But I had had too much to drink and I'd had it all too quickly. I was speaking extemporaneously you might say. So I concluded it be best not to speak at all.

I fitted myself into the corner of the sectional. Dru and Ben a few feet to my left, made a point of staying engrossed in one another—and as soon as it was polite to do so, got up and found spots at the dining room table. And I was left to myself.

By this time it was well past midnight. You know how that is. It's a time when you start asking questions about things that in the light of day you wouldn't consider twice. It's a time... well, we both know how it goes, in the dark hour.

I was left to myself.

◄o►

I began to feel badly about leaving Lucy on the beach. I wondered if I might have handled things differently. I worried that I might have impregnated her, or caught a venereal disease. Briefly, I worried that some of those eyes might have migrated from her skin to mine—if I'd caught a case of leaping, burrowing and uniquely ocular crabs. If I closed my own eyes, would I see a thousand dim refractions of the room from the point of view of my belly?

The notion made me laugh—a little too loudly, I think. Dennis, reeking of weed and vodka cooler, just about turned on his heel at the sight of me and fled back to the deck. But it got me back wondering at the nature of Lucy's peculiar disease, if that's what it was. If not she, then who was looking out through those eyes? And so, in circles, went my thoughts.

The front door opened and closed once, twice, five times. Water ran in the kitchen sink. Lights dimmed in rooms not far from this one.

"Hey Tom. How you keeping?"

I looked up and blinked.

"Hey Len," I said. "Haven't seen you all night."

He nodded. "I've been a rotten host."

Len was wearing his kimono, that red one with the lotus-design. He'd lost a lot of weight—you couldn't mistake it, the kimono hung so loose on him. His hair was coming back in, but it was still thin, downy. He sat down beside me.

"You met Lucille," he said.

"How did you know?" I asked, but I didn't need to; as I spoke, I saw Kimi over the breakfast bar in the kitchen, putting glasses into the dishwasher. She'd told him about our conversation in the washroom. He'd put it together.

"Yeah," said Len, "you were on the beach. Two of you. Had yourself a time, didn't you Tom?"

"We had ourselves a time."

Len put a bony hand on my thigh, gave it a squeeze of surprising strength, and nodded.

"Now you're drunk in my living room, when everybody else has had sense to get out. Too drunk to drive yourself, am I right?"

That was true.

"And you don't have cab fare, do you?"

I didn't have cab fare.

"You're a fucking leech, Tom. You *smell* like a fucking leech."

"It's the ocean," I said.

Kimi turned her back to us, lowered her head and raised her shoulder blades, like wings, as she ran water in the kitchen sink.

"Yeah, we know that's not so," said Len. "You smell of Lucy." He licked his lips, and not looking up, Kimi called out, "that's not nice, Len," and Len chuckled and jacked a thumb in her direction and shrugged.

"Did she leave?" I asked. "Lucy I mean."

"Miss her too now?" Did I miss her like *you*, he meant, obviously.

"I just didn't see her leave."

"What'd I just say? *Everybody else* had the sense to get out."

A plate clattered loudly in the sink. Len shouted at Kimi to *be fuckin' careful with that.* Then he coughed and turned an eye to me. His expression changed.

"You saw," he said quietly. "Didn't you?"

"I saw."

He looked like he wanted to say more. But he stopped himself, the way he does: tucking his chin down, pursing his lips… like he's doing some math, which is maybe close to the mark of what he is doing until he finally speaks.

"Did she tell you how we met?"

"Friend of a friend," I said, then remembered: "Not just a friend; one of your partners. And then you just kept inviting her out."

"Always that simple, isn't it?"

"It's never that simple," I said, "you're going to tell me."

"It is that simple," he said. "Lucille Carroll is a high-school friend of Linda James. Linda isn't a partner now and I won't likely live to see the day that she is. But she did work for me. With me. And she used to come out sometimes. And she brought Lucille one day. And not long after, Linda stopped coming around. Lucille still shows up." He sighed. "Simple."

Kimi flipped a switch under the counter and the dishwasher hummed to life. "I'm turning in," she announced, and when Len didn't say anything, she climbed the stairs.

"It's not that simple," I said when Kimi was gone. Now, I thought, was the time when Len would spell it out for me: tell me what had happened, really.

"And she doesn't like to talk about it," was what he said instead. "It's private, Tom."

What came next? Well, I might have handled it better. But you know how I hate it when my friends hide things from me. We both remember the weekend at the lake, with your sister and her boys. Did I ever properly apologize for that? It's difficult to, when all I've spoken is God's truth.

But I could have handled it better.

"It's not private," I said, "it's the opposite. She's the least private person I've met. The eyes…"

"Her skin condition you mean."

"You do know about them." I may have jabbed him in the chest. That may have been unwise. "Maybe you like them? Watching everything you do? Maybe they flatter your vanity…"

Len shook his head. He stopped me.

"You know what, Tom? I'm sick of you. I've been sick of you for a long time. But I'm also sick, and I'll tell you—that clarifies things for a man. So here's what I see:

"You come here to my house—you moon around like some fucking puppy dog—you drink my wine… the friends of mine you don't fuck, you bother with your repetitive, self-involved shit. Jesus, Tom. You're a leech."

"I'm sorry," I said, because really—what else do you say to something like that? To someone like Len, for Christ's sake?

"Yeah," he said. "Heard that one before. Lucy's a special girl, Tom. She's helping me in ways you couldn't imagine. And it has nothing to do with my fucking vanity. Not a fucking thing. Lucy's my… assurance. And she's always welcome here."

"I'm sorry."

"I got that. Now are you okay to drive yet, Tom?"

I wasn't. But I said sure.

"Then you get out of my house. Get back to your place. Stay there. I don't think you should come back here again."

◄◦►

Yes. That's why you hadn't seen me at Len's after that. He cast me out—into the wilderness—left me to my own devices.

I wasn't avoiding you.

Far from it.

◄◦►

Lucy wasn't that hard to find.

She had a Facebook page, and I had enough information to narrow her down from the list of those other Lucy Carrolls who said they were from here. So I sent her a note apologizing for being such an asshole, and she sent me a friend request and I agreed—and she asked me to pick a place, and that's where we met. It's the Tokyo Grill in the Pier District. I don't think we ever went there, you and I. But at 12:15 on a Tuesday in June, it's very bright.

Lucy wore a rose print dress, not quite as pale as her skin. She had freckles and her hair was more reddish than brunette. Perhaps it was the effect of wearing a dress and not a pair of jeans, but she seemed more svelte on the patio than she did that night on the beach. *Her* eyes were hazel.

Do you remember how I courted you? Did you ever doubt that I was anything but spontaneous? That when I laughed so hard at that joke of yours, it was because I thought it was the funniest thing I'd ever heard?

You didn't? You should have. I'm not good at everything in life, oh that I'll admit. But I am good at this part. I am smooth.

And that's how I was at the Tokyo Grill that Tuesday.

Lucy wasn't sure about me and she made that explicit pretty early. I'd seemed nice at first, but running off like that… well, it had been hurtful. It made her feel as though there was something wrong with her, and as she made explicit somewhat later on, there wasn't anything wrong with her.

"It's not you—it's the rest of the world," I said, and when she took offense, I explained I wasn't making fun.

"The world's an evil place. Lots wrong with it. Look at… think about Len, as an example."

"What do you mean?"

"Well. How he treats people. How he uses them. Like Kimi."

"He's an important man," she said quickly. "I imagine it takes a toll. All those clients he's got to look after." She sighed. "Clients can be very demanding."

"Clients." I made a little smile. "That's a good word. Len has clients like other people have friends."

Yes, I suppose I was being dramatic. But Lucy didn't think so; she laughed, very hard, and agreed.

"So what about you?" she asked. "Are you client or friend?"

"Something else."

I explained how Lucy wasn't the only one I'd offended with my bad behaviour that night—and again, I layered contrition on top of itself, and doing so took another step to winning her over.

Working through it, I could almost forget that Lucy was a woman containing a multitude—that as she sat here opposite me in the Pier District, the lids up and down her body squinted shut like tiny incision scars against the bright daylight.

Like clients.

I had to forget. Because I couldn't mention them; Len was right—she didn't want to talk about it. She may not have even been capable.

And keeping silent on the subject, and knowing of that alien scrutiny, resting behind translucent lids…

I couldn't have done what I had to do.

Lucy's next shift at the bookstore was Wednesday afternoon, so she had the rest of the day to herself, and as we finished our sashimi, she made a point of saying the afternoon shift meant she could stay out as late as she liked.

So we took a walk. We found my car. We drove back to my apartment. And behind drawn blinds, we stripped off our clothes and lay down together on fresh white sheets.

Oh dear. I can tell you're upset—not by anything I've done, but what you think I'm about to do: relay some detailed account of how it was for

Lucy and I, rutting on the very same sheets where you and I lolled, those long Sunday mornings, when… well, before you came to your senses is how you might put it…

I'll try and be circumspect.

◄○►

Lucy talked through it all, same as she had on the beach: those half-formed statements: "He's the same," and "The third floor," and "I do not agree." Of course, she was talking to them—fielding questions: *Is he the handsome fellow from the beach? On what floor is this fellow's apartment? Don't you think he's a bit much—being too…*

too…

To which she answered: *I do not agree.*

I'd drawn the curtains in my rooms, to make it dim enough for the curious eyes to open without being blinded—and sure enough, this is what they did. As I ran my tongue along her shoulder-blade, I found myself looking into a tiny blue orb, no bigger than a rat's. It blinked curiously at me as I moved past, to the nape of her neck, and there, in the wispy curls at the base of her skull, I uncovered two yellow eyes, set close together, in the forest of her hair. Were they disapproving? I imagine they must have been, affixed on Lucy's skull, less than an inch from her brain. I winked and moved on.

"Tell them," I whispered into her ear, looking into a squinting, infinitely old eye fixed in her temple, "that I understand."

"He understands," she murmured.

"Tell them I'm not afraid."

"He's not afraid."

"Tell them," I said, before I moved from her ear to her mouth, and rolled her onto her back, and slid atop her, "that I'm ready."

◄○►

And the rest of it?

Well, I did tell you I'd be circumspect. Suffice it to say… just as poor old Len would, not long after…

I *entered* her.

◄○►

You looked good at my funeral. You and Jonathan both. The dress you wore—was it new? Did you buy it especially for the occasion? It would be nice to think that you had.

In any event, I must say that Jonathan was very supportive of you. He held your hand so very tightly through the eulogies. Had you needed it, I'm sure he would have provided a handkerchief; if it had rained at the graveside, he'd have held the umbrella. He seems that sort of upright fellow. A real keeper.

You look great now, too. You have a lovely smile, you always have, and the shorter haircut—it suits you. It really frames your face. I can't hear what you're saying, here in Emile's house in town, over the dregs of what I recall as being an acceptable cab-franc from Chile.

Still, you're laughing, and that's good. You've left Kimi and poor dying Len behind. You're cementing new friendships... with Prabh and Emile and, perhaps, Lucy?

Perhaps.

It's impossible to say of course—I haven't been at this long enough to learn how to read lips, particularly with that damned brooch in the way. I never could guess your mind on this sort of thing. But you seem... open to it, to this new friend who works the cash in your favourite bookstore. You are. Aren't you?

Ah well. I must learn patience here in my new place. After all, Lucy will tell me everything—in due time, in a quiet moment, when the lights are low:

She says she misses you. She says she can't believe she let you go. Now that you're gone.

She says that she and I will be great friends.

And then, if all goes well... if you and Lucy really do hit it off...

I can't promise, other than to say I'll do my best. I'll try not to let my gaze linger.

◄○►

THE SHOW

PRIYA SHARMA

The camera crew struggled with the twisting, narrow stairs. Their kit was portable, steadicams being all the rage. They were lucky that the nature of their work did not require more light. Shadows added atmosphere. Dark corners added depth. It was cold down in the cellar. It turned their breath to mist, which gathered in the stark white pools shed by the bare bulbs overhead.

Martha smiled. It was sublime. Television gold.

Tonight there'd been a crowd. Word had got out. She'd have to find out who blabbed. There had been only a few fans at the start but now they needed security to keep them back.

She'd joined the presenter, Pippa and her producer-husband Greg at the barrier. The three of them had posed for photographs and signed autographs. Pip had been strict about that. Be nice to the public. The audience would make or break the show, not studio executives.

Martha laughed out loud when a woman produced a photo of Pip and Greg in their previous incarnation as chat show hosts.

"Nice haircuts," she said as they both signed it. Their fashionable styles dated this period of fame but Martha was careful when she joked about their pasts. It was Pippa's new idea that had reinvented their careers.

Pippa was popular but it was really Martha the crowd wanted. She recognised the faithful amid the curious locals. The ones who wanted to touch her hand, as if it were a blessing. To ask her help to reach the dead, to say what they'd left unsaid.

A man reached out as Martha tried to leave, snatching at her coat sleeve.

"Good luck," he said. "May God keep you through the night."

－◦－

Martha leant against the cellar wall to watch Pippa in discussion with the team. She could tell Pippa was well pleased. The first part of the show comprised of interviews. The bar staff had been verbose in their remembering. The tall tales of the spooked. The cellar had fallen fallow. Too many broken beer bottles. Boxes overturned, alcopops leaking on the floor. Too many barmaids emerging with bruises flowering on their arms. Too many accusations. Too many resignations.

Yes, it was horrible down here. Its history appalled. The chill seeped from the floor, through her boot soles and crept into her feet. She fastened up her coat. Red cashmere. She'd decided to live a vivid life. She wouldn't exist in shades of grey. She'd no longer bow or obey. She'd promised herself good money. In the bank. Not tatty fivers from someone's housekeeping, like the ones her mother would take with embarrassment and stuff into the chipped teapot on the dresser. Iris never asked for more. Only barely enough. *You can't abuse the gift.* Cheap meat on Sundays as a treat. For Martha and her sister Suki, white knee socks gone grey, but still too good to throw away.

The second part of the show was a vigil. The team were busy setting up thermometers and motion sensors to add the illusion of science but it was Martha that added the something special to the mix.

"Don't forget," Pippa would say, face tight into the lens, "Martha, our psychic, doesn't know our destination. She'll be brought here and do a reading, blind."

Martha stamped her feet to expel the cold. Pippa was busy with her preparations. Vocal exercises. Shaking her limbs. If Martha channelled spirits, then Pippa channelled the audience. With the cameras on, Pippa (like Martha) became a true believer. Her range spanned from nervous to hysterical. Her tears of fear turned her heavy eye makeup to muddy pools. Her performance heightened suggestibility and atmosphere.

"Have you destroyed them?" Greg sidled up to Martha. He was talking about the copy of his research notes that he always gave her.

"Don't treat me like I'm an amateur. You know I learn them and then burn them."

These were hot readings, as they were called within the trade, when a medium was already primed. Martha would reveal the memorised histories of suicidal serving girls, murdered travellers and Victorian serial killers.

Martha's key was subtlety. She was frugal with the facts. Too direct and the show would be a pantomime. Too detailed and she'd be reciting by rote. And what couldn't be confirmed couldn't be denied, which was useful when the truth wasn't juicy enough to appeal. All Martha needed was a name, a date, a hard fact around which to embroider her yarns. Greg, who also played on-screen researcher, would fake surprise with widened eyes, saying such as, "Yes, Martha, there was a third son here by the name of Walter, but we can't corroborate there was a maid by the name Elaine whom he killed on Midsummer's Day."

"New coat?" Greg's fingers stroked her collar.

"Keep your paws off."

"Watch it. Pippa will think we're paying you too much."

Greg was clumsy where Pippa's angling had been more oblique. Martha had chosen to ignore her jibes and hints, having stuck to the deal made when they were all green and keen. She'd not allow Greg to change the terms.

"You're not and I'm worth every penny."

Worth a better time slot and channel. Worth another series.

"How many personal clients do you have now? How much for your last tour?"

A lot. The world was ripe. She'd weighed it in her palm.

"None of your business."

Martha was brisk. Even with her clients she was sharp. She'd not pander to their fantasies that mediums were soft and ethereal.

"Take care. We built you up and we can pull you down."

Her laughter echoed around the empty cellar. Pip turned and stared at them.

"You won't. You can't."

To reveal Martha as a fraud was to expose them all. The true believers would be incensed. Most viewers though were sceptics, they would already suspect, but the fun lay in the possibility of doubt. The chance that Martha might be real. So, not perjury, not a lie to shatter worlds, but was it one to shatter careers?

"We can find someone new. You'd be easy to replace."

"Don't threaten me. I'll send you all to hell."

"Keep it down," Pippa stalked over. "Do you want everyone to hear? We'll talk about this later. Do you understand, Martha? There are things to be addressed. Now get ready, it's time to start the show."

◦

Martha had learnt from watching Iris and Suki. Both had reigned at Lamp Street, lumpish in their muddy coloured cardigans, giving readings to anyone who called. Muttering thanks to spirit guides. Turning tatty Tarot cards.

Martha had no claim to special gifts. She learnt to read the hands and face, the gestures that betrayed need and greed. The skill of deciphering a tic, interpreting a pause. Martha studied hard and learnt how to put on a show.

"Yes, David. Thanks."

Made-up-David helped Martha to the other side. A fictional spirit guide to help usher in an imaginary spectral presence or fake demonic possession. David was a friar. Shaman. Priest. Rabbi. Denomination was irrelevant. People seemed to find religious men more comforting in the afterlife than in the flesh. David was based on an engraving that Iris kept by her bed. A monk with his hands folded in prayer.

"What do you make of it?" Pippa asked, now in character.

"It's a big place." Martha sniffed. "It smells bad. Like something's rotted down here."

The low ceiling pressed down on them, while the walls stretched out into shadow. Martha rubbed her temples, where pain had started to gather. She walked to the opposite wall, as if in search of something. It was her trick. The camera was forced to follow and the others had to orbit her to stay in shot.

"Brother David, help me." Martha gained momentum. She covered her ears with flat hands. "Make them stop. They're deafening me."

"What is it?"

"Clanging. Fit to wake the dead. The sound of banging metal." She winced as if uncomfortable. Tonight had to be special. She had a point to prove. "It's claustrophobic. Too many souls in too small a space. A strong sense of punishment."

Pippa made a display of her excitement, trying to reclaim screen time for her and Greg. "Greg, can you tell us more?"

"It's a fascinating place. A gruesome history. It was a prison in the eighteenth century."

His eyes shone in the viewfinder.

"What about the clanging?" Pippa asked. More professional than Greg, she'd not prove a point at the show's expense.

"An inmate, Samuel Greenwood, was questioned by the prison board. One of them, shocked, recorded the interview in his diary. The main gates were locked but down here the doors were all open. New arrivals were greeted by the banging of the cell doors." He mimed a man clutching bars and rattling them. "An unholy din by all accounts."

Martha took off her gloves and trailed her fingers along the crumbling mortar of the wall, talking continually to David as she went. Her eyes closed in concentration. The camera loved the gesture.

"Of course. I see it now." She stopped and the spotlight overshot her. "There's so much misery here. Pain. Searing. Physical."

The cameraman tripped up on an empty crate. The world was up-ended as an explosion of panicked feathers went off in his face. Too stunned to scream, Pippa did it for him. The bird, in its eagerness to escape incarceration in the upturned crate, sprang up and hit the ceiling. It landed with a dull thud upon the floor. It jerked and flapped, a reflex of the fleshly dead, until finally it came to rest. Martha knelt and picked it up. It was a scrawny thing, its feet deformed, head lolling on its broken neck.

Pippa had stopped screaming, looking over Martha's shoulder.

"I wonder how it got down here. And how long ago."

Martha laid the carcass back on the crate. She shook her head in disbelief. Sickened by this small, crushed life, her headache was suddenly much worse. She'd never experienced a full-blown migraine but recognised the signs. Lights danced at the periphery of her vision. Strange patterns hovered in the air. It interfered with coherent thought. She tried to reassert herself.

"This is no ordinary prison, is it, Greg? All these voices cry out but no-one comes. No-one keeps the peace."

"Samuel Greenwood said the inmates ran the place. The authorities didn't get in their way."

Martha tasted bile rising in her throat. *I'll not be sick. I'll not be sick.* Not a mantra but a command. She'd last vomited in childhood. Its associations were too painful to encounter. Not like this. Not here. Martha fought it back.

"There's uncontrolled rage within these walls. Frenzy. Violation." She turned on Greg as if he were to blame. "Men, women, children, all mixed in together."

"Yes," Greg's voice was serious and low. "Murderers and thieves," he savoured the words, "cheats and fraudsters."

Martha wasn't listening. The lingering odour of decay she'd noted was getting worse. It was rotting flowers, fungi and burnt sugar. The pain in her head was punctuated by explosions. Monstrous white blooms contracted and expanded before her eyes. She clutched the wall with one hand, bent double, and threw her stomach contents upon the floor.

The sensation of muscles moving in her throat, of acid burning in her nose, evoked the shock and grief of that distant summer her father died. Passed over was the term they used at home. Martha despised this euphemism, even though it was part of her work's vocabulary. Not long after her father's sudden death, she had been burnt up by a fever. She'd vomited without relief. She had the same sensations now as then, like she'd died and was floating out of reach.

"Where's Daddy?" Hot and hallucinating, Martha was emphatic. She wanted her father, not her mother's comforts.

"Daddy's here," Iris replied. "He's in the room. He's telling you he loves you. Can't you hear?"

"No," Martha whimpered. Had there been a time when the world was full of voices? She couldn't recall.

"Oh, my sweetheart," and under her breath, Iris spoke the damaging, damning words that separated Martha from her tribe, "you used to be like us. You used to see but now you're blind."

So Martha was left in darkness, Iris and Suki in the light.

Martha dabbed her mouth, vomit dripping on her coat. Greg motioned for the filming to continue. Pippa ladled on concern.

"Are you okay?"

"I'm sorry. It's the smell."

"It's bad, isn't it? Maybe there's a dead bird or rat that's rotting." Then, because Martha's pallor couldn't be feigned, "Do you want us to stop?"

Martha clutched a crumpled tissue to her mouth to stem the swelling tide. She recognised the smell now. It was death. Bedridden Iris, nursed by her girls in the front parlour, had been rank with it. Devoured by a cancer in her breast that had ulcerated and wept pus throughout her long slide towards a terrible demise.

People still came, even at the end. To see her. Just for a minute. Just to ask advice. Women whose daughters followed Suki and Martha home from school. Hair pullers, name callers, shin kickers who loved to plague the pair of witches. These same mothers would sit and wait, watching the girls no older than their own, move around the unclean kitchen, washing their mother's soiled sheet in the sink. Not a single one offered aid.

Suki started reading to give Iris peace. So this wall-eyed girl who was clumsy at PE and hated school inherited her mother's mantle and the regulars. She stayed at home and read the cards, while Martha passed her exams and got into fights with anyone who looked at her askew.

"I'm dying, a little more each day. There's no need to be afraid." Iris had beckoned Martha over. "They're waiting for me on the other side. Suki will be just fine. She has the gift but what will become of you, Martha? What will you do?"

Yes, Martha was familiar with the smell. It was enough to make her turn and vomit once again before the floor rose up to meet her. She felt her bones crunch with the impact.

"Martha, can you hear me?"

She was shaken back to consciousness by rough, frightened hands. The pain had gone and left her empty headed, her brain replaced by cotton wool, her mouth with acid and sand.

"Thank God. What happened?" Greg motioned for the crew to stand back and give her air. She tried to sit.

"Just a faint."

In the seconds she was away the cellar had reassembled itself. She could see anew. The investigators were still there. The bare bulbs still shed their light but there was a whole world superimposed upon their own. A past that occupied the present, which shared their time and space. Figures moved around them, weak imprints on here and now. She had peeled back the skin of the world and was looking underneath. When one of these shadow prisoners walked through Martha, she shuddered. It felt like cobwebs were being brushed against her skin.

"There's a lot of residual energy here." The stock phrase had been given shape. Martha wanted to cry. Something locked away was liberated. Was this how Iris saw the world? She realised it has been six years since she last spoke with Suki. How much they had to share. "This place was a health hazard. They're all filthy."

Ragged figures milled around or else they squatted in huddles. Food was piled in troughs as though for swine. There was a gentle buzz. They were too afraid to speak up.

A group of convicts emerged from the far end of the prison, the overlords of this peculiar hell. These self tattooed, beribboned demons strutted with such swagger that Martha quailed with fear. They singled out a shadow-boy for sport. They hauled him up and took their time at play. One swung his knife about and it passed through Martha's chest, making her gasp, even though it was only a projection of things past. Another one unfolded his razor and the boy's face was devastated. The crime he suffered for most was his prettiness.

"Martha, what is it?"

"A gang ran this place." She found her voice. She talked too loudly so she could hear herself above the shrieks and jeers.

"They kept the peace," Greg said.

"Not peace. I wouldn't call it that."

Martha struggled to her feet. She tipped and tilted until the horizon righted.

"Jimmy Bailey, Michael O'Connor, Kit Williams, Simeon Weaver…" Martha repeated the names as they were shouted at roll call.

"I don't have it here but there is a ledger…" Greg fumbled with his notes.

"Check if you want. They'll all be there."

Greg twitched. This was unexpected. She had raised the stakes. He hadn't thought she'd do her own research.

"Emma Parker," Martha's eyes were horrified. Emma lay on the floor. Slit from pubic bone to ribcage, her blood sprayed upon the walls. "They were animals. When she fell pregnant they opened her up with a knife. They cut out her womb and watched her bleed to death."

Greg frowned at her nasty embellishments. After all, this was a family show.

"The smell. It's death."

She walked back towards the twisted stairs. She had been shocked but now she was afraid. Something was missing from this nether, neither world. Someone was missing.

"There's something about this spot." She strained to listen to the henchman who stood beside the steps like a lackey at some royal court making proclamations. "Thomas the Knife, that's his name."

It sparked of recognition. The name in Greg's notes was Thomas Filcher. Where was he?

"Close. Thomas the Blade." Greg was glad of her return to the script. "He sat waiting for new inmates to be brought down. Tapping on his boot heel with a knife."

Martha pushed her fists against her eyes. Where was the architect of this regime? Why could she not see him?

The clearing of a throat. It was a quiet sound.

"Did you hear that?" Pip piped up. "Who's there? We mean no harm. Give us a sign."

It came again. This time between a chuckle and a growl.

"Did you hear it?"

Greg was normally subtle in the projections of his voice, but in for a penny, in for a pound.

Cold trickled down Martha's spine. What did it mean that the others could hear him too? There came a laugh, cruel and amused. Martha held up a hand to silence Pip. "Come out. Show yourself. Or else leave us well alone."

He rose to her challenge, stepping from shadow into light. Thomas the Knife stood before her, denser than the other shades. There was enough of him to trip a movement sensor. It called out in alarm.

"What is it?" Pippa hissed.

They can hear him, Martha thought, but they can't see him.

"Everyone, step back towards the stairs."

"Why?"

"Just do it." Martha could smell her own stale vomit and fear. "This isn't residual energy. It's active. He's here."

The crew started to retreat but Pip hovered by her side. She'd not be upstaged.

"Martha, tell us what you see."

"He's tall. Handsome." Thomas smirked at that. "Well dressed and fed compared to the rest. A dandy in a blood splattered shirt."

He was a gentleman butcher, linen stained by the evidence of his industry. Long hair tied back and boots up to his thighs. Even dead, he bristled with an energy Martha rarely saw in men. She watched him like he was a predator. Magnificent and unpredictable. Her eyes were fixed on him in retreat. She clasped Pippa's elbow but the presenter shook her off.

"He's King down here. He thrived. He sniffed out the proudest and the most delicate. Broke their spirit as if it were a game." Martha looked up, a line of girls crucified upon the bars, their modesty and disfigurements on display. "He's full of hate and it's women that he hates the most."

Martha knew the cleansing rituals, protective circles and holy chants. Iris had been most insistent that they learn, even if Martha wasn't blessed with special sight. Arrogant and adamant in her disbelief, she'd come down here totally unarmed.

"We have to get out now."

Too late. Too late. Thomas the Knife wanted company. His boots fell heavily on stone. Surprisingly loud, considering he was a ghost.

All the lights went out, leaving only sounds. Pip's screaming and struggling. Greg shouting for her. The metallic crunch as a camera hit the ground. One of the bulbs shattered overhead, showering them in glass. Tiny fragments lodged in Martha's face. A dozen tiny stings.

"Leave her alone." Martha tried to help, calling over muffled cries. "Please stop. Don't hurt her."

He did stop. Eventually. Then the movement sensors were set off one by one, marking Thomas' progress around the room. Martha found the wall and groped along it in the direction of the stairs. Greg shouted out, a single cry of pain.

The lights came on and the carnage was revealed. Greg was within Martha's reach, lying on the floor. She crouched beside him, dabbing at his wound. A neat line joined his ear to the corner of his mouth, blood oozing from the deep wedge of red flesh revealed.

"Where's Pip?" Greg, dizzy and disorientated, struggled to lift his head.

They followed the soft sobbing to the corner. This was not Pippa's TV histrionics but the heartbreak of the truly wounded. Thomas stood back, well satisfied with his work.

Pip was revealed in the dim circle of the lamp. She was curled against the wall, bare torso revealed. Thomas had remade her. When the blood crusted and the scabs fell off, she would be a work of art. That a single, common blade could carve such detail was remarkable. She was etched with arcane calligraphy. Profane flourishes. No plastic surgeon could eradicate his dirty graffiti. But that would be for later. For now she was slick and slippery with snot and tears and blood. Martha slipped her coat off to cover her. Greg moved to enclose her in his arms. Nothing could diminish her distress until the paramedics arrived and she slipped into the dreams of deep sedation.

◄◦►

The traffic was streaks of light. Neon discoloured the night. The police kept the crowds at bay. Greg went to where Martha stood alone. Her hair, soaked with perspiration, stuck to her head in unflattering curls.

"You did this, didn't you? When I find out how, I'll kill you."

A policeman came over, casting them a warning look.

"Miss Palmer. We're taking everyone in for questioning. It's time for you to come along with me."

"Greg, he says you got it wrong." Her last words to him. "It's Thomas the Knife. Not Thomas the Blade."

Martha settled into the slippery car seat. Her new travelling companion by her side. They stared at one another, neither speaking. Iris' lessons came to mind.

A medium must take care. The opening of consciousness is a special time in a girl's life. When a spirit guide is acquired. Don't be scared. I'll be here to keep you safe.

Suki had smirked when it was her time. The advent of Martha's menstruation seemed paltry by comparison.

You'll never want for company.

You'll never be alone.

For all those years, I believed all the things you said, Martha thought. *You're not the gifted one. You're not gifted.* It was always you and Suki, talking to voices I couldn't hear.

Talking to Dad.

If only you could see me now, Iris. If only you could see me now.

◄o►

MULBERRY BOYS

MARGO LANAGAN

So night comes on. I make my own fire, because why would I want to sit at Phillips's, next to that pinned-down mulberry?

Pan-flaps, can you make pan-flaps? Phillips plopped down a bag of fine town flour and gave me a look that said, *Bet you can't. And I'm certainly too important to make them.* So pan-flaps I make in his little pan, and some of them I put hot meat-slice on, and some cheese, and some jam, and that will fill us, for a bit. There's been no time to hunt today, just as Ma said, while she packed and packed all sorts of these treats into a sack for me—to impress Phillips, perhaps, more than to show me favour, although that too. She doesn't mind me being chosen to track and hunt with the fellow, now that I'm past the age where he can choose me for the other thing.

We are stuck out here the night, us and our catch. If I were alone I would go back; I can feel and smell my way, if no stars and moon will show me. But once we spread this mulberry wide on the ground and fixed him, and Phillips lit his fire and started his fiddling and feeding him leaves, I knew we were to camp. I did not ask; I dislike his sneering manner of replying to me. I only waited and saw.

He's boiled the water I brought up from the torrent, and filled it with clanking, shining things—little tools, it looks like, as far as I can see out of the corner of my eye. I would not gratify him with looking directly. I stare into my own fire, the forest blank black beyond it and only fire-lit smoke above, no sky though the clouds were clearing last I looked. I get out my flask and have a pull of fire-bug, to settle my discontentments. It's been a long day and a weird, and I wish I was home, instead of out here with a half-man, and the boss of us all watching my every step.

"Here, boy," he says. He calls me *boy* the way you call a dog. He doesn't even look up at me to say it.

I cross from my fire to his. I don't like to look at those creatures, mulberries, so I fix instead on Phillips, his shining hair-waves and his sharp nose, the floret of silk in his pocket that I know is a green-blue bright as a stout-pigeon's throat, but now is just a different orange in the fire's glow. His white, weak hands, long-fingered, big-knuckled—oh, they give me a shudder, just as bad as a mulberry would.

"Do you know what a loblolly boy is?"

He knows I don't. I hate him and his words. "Some kind of insulting thing, no doubt," I say.

"No, no!" He looks up surprised from examining the brace, which is pulled tight to the mulberry's puffed-up belly, just below the navel, when it should dangle on an end of silk. "It's a perfectly legitimate thing. Boy on a ship, usually. Works for the surgeon."

And what is a surgeon? I am not going to ask him. I stare down at him, wanting another pull from my flask.

"Never mind," he says crossly. "Sit." And he waves where; right by the mulberry, opposite himself.

Must I? I have already chased the creature five ways wild today; I've already treed him and climbed that tree and lowered him on a rope. I'm sick of the sight of him, his round stary face, his froggy body, his feeble conversation, trying to be friendly.

But I sit. I wonder sometimes if I'm weak-minded, that even one person makes such a difference to me, what I see, what I do. When I come to the forest alone, I can see the forest clear, and feel it, and everything in it. If I bring Tray or Connar, it becomes the ongoing game of us as big men in this world—with the real men left behind in the village, so they don't show us up. When I come with Frida Birch it is all about the inside of her mysterious mind, what she can be thinking, what has she noticed that I haven't about some person, some question she has that would never occur to me. It's as if I cannot hold to my own self, to my own forest, if another person is with me.

"Feed him some more," says Phillips, and points to the sack beside me. "As many as he can take. We might avoid a breakage yet if we can stuff enough into him."

I untie the sack, and put aside the first layer, dark leaves that have been keeping the lower, paler ones moist. I roll a leaf-pill—the neater I make it, the less I risk being bitten, or having to touch lip or tongue. I wave it under his nose, touch it to his lips, and he opens and takes it in, good mulberry.

Phillips does this and that. Between us the mulberry's stomach grumbles and tinkles with the foreign food he's kept down. Between leaf-rollings, I have another pull. "God, the smell of that!" says Phillips, and spares a hand from his preparations to wave it away from his face.

"It's good," I say. "It's the best. It's Nat Culloden's."

"How old are you anyway?" He cannot read it off me. Perhaps he deals only with other men—I know people like that, impatient of the young. Does he have children? I'd hate to be his son.

"Coming up fifteen," I say.

He mutters something. I can't hear, but I'm sure it is not flattering to me.

Now there's some bustle about him. He pulls on a pair of very thin-stretching gloves, paler even than his skin; now his hands are even more loathsome. "Right," he says. "You will hold him down when I tell you. That is your job."

"He's down." Look at the spread cross of him; he couldn't be any flatter.

"You will hold him *still*," says Phillips. "For the work. When I say."

He pulls the brace gently; the skein comes forth as it should, but— "Hold him," says Phillips, and I hook one leg over the mulberry's thigh and spread a hand on his chest. He makes a kind of warning moan. Phillips pulls on, slowly and steadily like a mother. "*Hold* him," as the moaning rises, buzzes under my hand. "Christ above, if he makes this much of a fuss *now*."

He pulls and pulls, but in a little while no more silk will come. He winds what he has on a spindle and clamps it, tests the skein once more. "No? Well. Now I will cut. Boy, I have nothing for his pain." He looks at me as if *I* forgot to bring it. "And I need him utterly still, so as not to cut the silk or his innards. Here." He hands me a smooth white stick, of some kind of bone. "Put that crosswise between his teeth, give him something to bite on."

I do so; the teeth are all clagged with leaf-scraps, black in this light. Mulberries' faces are the worst thing about them, little round old-children's faces, neither man nor woman. And everything they are thinking shows clear as water, and this one is afraid; he doesn't know what's happening, what's about to be done to him. Well, I'm no wiser. I turn back to Phillips.

"Now get a good weight on him, both ends."

Gingerly I arrange myself. He may be neither man nor woman, but still the creature is naked, and clammy as a frog in the night air.

"Come on," says Phillips. He's holding his white hands up, as if the mulberry is too hot to touch. "You're plenty big enough. Spread yourself out there, above and below. You will need to press here, too, with your hand." He points, and points again. "And this foot will have some work to do on this far leg. Whatever is loose will fight against what I'm doing, understand?"

So he says, to a boy who's wrestled tree-snakes so long that his father near fainted to see them, who has jumped a shot stag and ridden it and killed it riding. Those are different, though; those are wild, they have some dignity. What's to be gained subduing a mulberry, that is gelded and a fool already? Where's the challenge in that, and the pride upon having done it?

"Shouldn't you be down there?" I nod legs-wards.

"Whatever for, boy?"

"This is to let the food out, no?"

"It is to let the food out, *yes*." He cannot speak without making me lesser.

"Well, down there is where food comes out, yours and mine."

"Pity sake, boy, I am not undoing all *that*. I will take it out through his silk-hole, is the plan."

Now I am curled around the belly, with nowhere else to look but at Phillips's doings. All his tools and preparations are beyond him, next to the fire; from over there he magics up a paper packet. He tears it open, pulls from it a small wet cloth or paper, and paints the belly with that; the smell nips at my nostrils. Then he brings out a bright, light-as-a-feather-looking knife, the blade glinting at the end of a long handle.

"Be ready," he says.

He holds the silk aside, and sinks the blade into the flesh beside it. The mulberry-boy turns to rock underneath me; he spits out the stick, and howls to the very treetops.

◄◦►

Mulberry *boys* we call them. I don't know why, for some begin as girls, and they are neither one nor the other once they come out of Phillips's hut by the creek. They all look the same, as chickens look all the same, or goats. *Nonsense,* says Alia the goat woman, *I know my girls each one, by name and nature and her pretty face.* And I guess the mothers, who tend the mulberries, might know them apart. This one is John Barn, or once was called that; none of them truly have names once they've been taken.

Once a year I notice them, when Phillips comes to choose the new ones and to make them useful, from the boys among us who are not yet sprouted towards men, and the girls just beginning to change shape. The rest of the year, the mulberries live in their box, and the leaves go in, and the silk comes out on its spindles, and that is all there is to it.

They grow restless when he comes. Simple as they are, they recognise him. *They can smell their balls in his pocket,* says James Pombo, and we hush him, but something like that is true; they remember.

Some have struggled or wandered before, and these are tied to chairs in the box, but you have to watch the others. Though they have not much equipment for it, they have a lot of time to think, and because their life is much the same each day and month and year, they see the pattern and the holes in it through which they might wangle their way.

Why the John Barn one should take it into his head after all these years, I don't know. He was always mulberry, ever since I knew to know, always just one of the milling amiables in that warm box.

Oh, I remember him, says Pa. *Little straw-haired runabout like all them Barns. Always up a tree. Climbed the top of Great Grandpa when he couldn't have been—what, more than three years, Ma? Because his sister Gale did it, and she told him he was too little. That'll send a boy up a tree.*

Last year when I was about to sprout, it was the first year Phillips came instead of his father. When he walked in among us we were most uneasy at the size of him, for he is delicately made, hardly taller than a mulberry himself, and similar shaped to them except in lacking a paunch. Apart from the shrinkage, though, you would think him the same man as his father. He wore the same fine clothes, as neat on him as if sewn to his body directly, and the fabrics so fine you can hardly see their weave. He had the same wavy hair, but brown instead of silver, and a beard, though not a proper one, trimmed almost back to his chin.

The mothers were all behind us and some of the fathers too, putting their children forward. He barely looked at me, I remember, but moved straight on to the Thaw children; there are lots of them and they are very much of the mulberry type already, without you sewing a stitch on them. I remember being insulted. The man had not *bothered* with me; how could he know I was not what he wanted, from that quick glance? But also I was ashamed to be so obviously useless, so wrong for his purposes—because whatever those purposes were, he was from the town, and he was powerfuller in his slenderness and his city clothes than was any bulky man among us, and everyone was afraid of him. I wanted a man like that to recognise me as of consequence, and he had not.

But then Ma put her arm over my shoulder and clamped me to her, my back against her front. We both watched Phillips among the Thaws, turning them about, dividing some of them off for closer inspection. The chosen ones—Hinny and Dull Toomy, it was, that time, those twins—stood well apart, Pa Toomy next to them arms folded and face closed. They looked from one of us to another, not quite sure whether to arrange their faces proudly, or to cry.

Because it is the end of things, if you get chosen. It is the end of your line, of course—all your equipment for making children is taken off you and you are sewn up below. But it is also the end of any food but the leaves—fresh in the spring and summer, sometimes in an oiled mash through autumn if you are still awake then. And it is the end of play, because you become stupid; you forget the rules of all the games, and how to converse in any but a very simple way, observing about the weather and not much more. You just stay in your box, eating your leaves and having your stuff drawn off you, which we sell, through Phillips, in the town.

It is no kind of life, and I was glad, then, that I had not been taken up for it. And Ma was glad too, breathing relieved above me as we watched him sort and discard and at length choose Arvie Thaw. I could feel Ma's gladness in the back of my head, her heart knocking hard in her chest, even though all she had done was stand there and seem to accept whatever came.

◄◦►

While we tracked John Barn today, I was all taken up impressing Phillips. The forest and paths presented me trace after trace, message after message, to relay to the town-man, so's he could see what a good tracker I was. I felt proud of myself for knowing, and scornful of him for not—yet I was afraid, too, that I would put a foot wrong, that he would somehow catch me out, that he would see something I had missed and make me a nobody again, and worthy of his impatience.

So John Barn himself was not much more to me than he'd always been; he was even somewhat less than other animals I hunted, for he had not even the wit to cut off the path at any point, and he left tracks and clues almost as if he wanted us to catch him, things he had chewed, and spat out or brought up from his stomach, little piles of findings—stones, leaves, seed-pods—wet-bright in the light rain. He might as well have lit beacon-fires after himself.

Climbing up to him in the tree, I could see his froggy paunch pouching out either side of the branch, and his skinny white legs around it, and then of course his terrible face watching me.

"Which one are you?" he said in that high, curious way they have. They can never remember a name.

"I am George," I said, "of the Treadlaws."

"Evening's coming on, George," he said, watching as I readied the rope. This was why I had been brought, besides for my tracking. Mulberries won't flee or resist anyone smaller than themselves (unless he is Phillips, of course, all-over foreign), but send a grown man after them and they will throw themselves off a cliff or into a torrent, or climb past pursuing up a tree like this. It is something about the smell of a grown man sets them off, which is why men cannot go into the box for the silk, but only mothers.

I busied myself with the practicalities, binding Barn and lowering him to Phillips, which was no small operation, so I distracted myself from my revulsion that way. And then, when I climbed down, Phillips took up all the air in the clearing and in my mind with his presence and purposefulness, which I occupied myself sulking at. Then when I had to press the creature down, to lie with him, lie *on* him, everything in me was squirming away from the touch but Phillips's will was on me like an iron, pinning me as fast as we'd pinned the mulberry, and I was too angry and unhappy at being made as helpless as John Barn, to think how he himself might be finding it, crushed by the weight of me.

But when he stiffened and howled, it was as if I had been asleep to John Barn and he woke me, as if he had been motionless disguised in the forest's dappled shadows, but then my eye had picked out his frame, distinct and live and sensible in there, never to be unseen again. All that he had said, that we had dismissed as so much noise, came back to me: *I don't like that man, George. Yes, tie me tight, for I will struggle when you put me near him. It's getting dark. It hurts me to stretch flat like this. My stomach hurts. An apple and a radish, I have kept both down. I stole them through a window; there was meat there too; meat was what I mostly wanted. But I could not reach it. Oh, it hurts, George.* I had done as Phillips did, and not met the mulberry's eye and not answered, doing about him what I needed to do, but now all his mutterings sprang out at me as having been said by a person, a person like me and like Phillips; there were three of us here, not two and a creature, not two and a snared rabbit, or a shot and struggling deer.

And the howl was not animal noise but voice, with person and feeling behind it. It went through me the way the pain had gone through John Barn, freezing me as Phillips's blade in his belly froze him, so that I was locked down there under the realising, with all my skin a-crawl.

I stare at Phillips's hands, working within their false skins. The fire beyond him lights his work and throws the shadows across the gleaming-painted hill-round of Barn's belly. Phillips cuts him like a cloth or like a cake, with just such swiftness and intent; he does not even do as you do when hunting, and speak to the creature you have snared or caught and are killing, and explain why it must die. The wound runs, and he catches the runnings with his wad of flock and cloth, absentmindedly and out of a long-practised skill. He bends close and examines what his cutting has revealed to him, in the cleft, in the deeps, of the belly of John Barn.

"Good," he says—to himself, not to me or Barn. "Perfect."

He puts his knife in there, and what he does in there is done in me as well, I feel so strongly the tremor it makes, the fear it plays up out of Barn's frame, plucking him, rubbing him, like a fiddle-string. His breath, behind me, halts and hops with the fear.

Phillips pierces something with a pop. Barn yelps, surprised. Phillips sits straighter, and waves his hand over the wound as he waved away the smell of my grog before. I catch a waft of shit-smell and then it's gone, floated up warm away.

He goes to his instruments. "That's probably the worst of it, for the moment," he says to them. "You can sit up if you like. Stay by, though; you never know when he'll panic."

I sit up slowly, a different boy from the one who lay down. I half-expect my own insides to come pouring out of me. John Barn's belly gapes open, the wound dark and glistening, filling with blood. Beyond it, his flesh slopes away smooth as a wooden doll between his weakling thighs, which tremble and tremble.

Phillips returns to the wound, another little tool in his hand—I don't know what it is, only that it's not made for cutting. I put my hand on Barn's chest, trying to move as smoothly and bloodlessly as Phillips.

"George, what has he done to me?" John Barn makes to look down himself.

Quick as light, I put my hand to his sweated brow, and press his head to the ground. "He's getting that food out," I say. "If it stays in there, it'll fester and kill you. He's helping you."

"Feed him some more," says Phillips, and bends to his work. "Keep on that."

So I lie, propped up on one elbow, rolling mulberry pills and feeding them to Barn. He chews, dutifully; he weeps, tears running back over his ears into his thin hair. He swallows the mulberry mush down his child-neck. *Hush,* I nearly say to him, but Phillips is there, so I only think it, and attend to the feeding, rolling the leaves, putting them one by one into Barn's obedient mouth.

I can't help but be aware, though, of what the man is doing there, down at the wound. For one thing, besides the two fires it is the only visible activity, the only movement besides my own. For another, for all that the sight of those blood-tipped white hands going about their work repels me, their skill and care, and the life they seem to have of their own, are something to see. It's like watching Pa make damselfly flies in the firelight in the winter, each finger independently knowing where to be and go, and the face above all eyes and no expression, the mind taken up with this small complication.

The apple and the radish, all chewed and reduced and cooked smelly by John Barn's body's heat, are caught in the snarled silk. Phillips must draw them, with the skein, slowly lump by lump from Barn's innards, up into the firelight where they dangle and shine like some unpleasant necklace. Sprawled beside John Barn, in his breathing and his bracing himself I feel the size of every bead of that necklace large and small, before I see it drawn up into the firelight on the shining strands. Phillips frowns above, fire-fuzz at his eyebrow, a long streak of orange light down his nose, his closed lips holding all his thoughts, all his knowledge, in his head—and any feelings he might have about this task. Is he pleased? Is he revolted? Angry? There is no way to tell.

"Do you have something for their pain, then," I say, "when you make them into mulberries?"

"Oh yes," he says to the skein, "they are fully anaesthetised then." He hears my ignorance in my silence, or sees it in my stillness. "I put them to sleep."

"Like a chicken," I say, to show him that I know something.

"Not at all like that. With a chemical."

All is quiet but for fire-crackle, and John Barn's breath in his nose, and his teeth crushing the leaves.

"How do you learn that, about the chemicals, and mulberry-making? And mulberry-fixing, like this?"

"Long study," says Phillips, peering into the depths to see how the skein is emerging. "Long observation at my father's elbow. Careful practice under his tutelage. Years," he finishes and looks at me, with something like a challenge, or perhaps already triumph.

"So *could* you unmake one?" I say, just to change that look on him.

"Could I? Why *would* I?"

I make myself ignore the contempt in that. "Supposing you had a reason."

He draws out a slow length of silk, with only two small lumps in it. "Could I, now?" he says less scornfully. "I've never considered it. Let me think." He examines the silk, both sides, several times. "I could perhaps restore their digestive functioning. The females' reproductive system *might* re-establish its cycle, with a normal diet, though I cannot be sure. The males' of course…" He shrugs. He has a little furnace in that hut of his by the creek. There he must burn whatever he cuts from the mulberries, and all his blood-soaked cloths and such. Once a year he goes in there with the chosen children, and all we know of what he does is the air wavering over the chimney. The men speak with strenuous cheer to each other; the mothers go about thin-lipped; the mothers of the chosen girls and boys close themselves up in their houses with their grief.

"But what about their… Can you undo their thinking, their talking, what you have done to that?"

"Ah, it is coming smoother now, look at that," he says to himself. "What do you mean, boy, 'undo'?" he says louder and more scornfully, as if I made up the word myself out of nothing, though I only repeated it from him.

I find I do not want to call John Barn a fool, not in his hearing as he struggles with his fear and his swallowing leaf after leaf, and with lying there belly open to the sky and Phillips's attentions. "They… haven't much to say for themselves," I finally say. "Would they talk among us like ourselves, if you fed them right, and took them out of that box?"

"I don't know what they would do." He shrugs again. He goes on slowly drawing out silk, and I go on hating him.

"Probably not," he says carelessly after a while. "All those years, you know, without social stimulus or education, would probably have impaired their development too greatly. But possibly they would regain something, from moving in society again." He snorts. "Such society as you *have* here. And the diet, as you say. It might perk them up a bit."

Silence again, the skein pulling out slowly, silently, smooth and clean white. Barn chews beside me, his breathing almost normal. Perhaps the talking soothes him.

"But then," says Phillips to the skein, with a smile that I don't like at all, "if you 'undid' them all, you would have no silk, would you? And without silk you would have no tea, or sugar, or tobacco, or wheat flour, or all the goods in tins and jars that I bring you. No cloth for the women, none of their threads and beads and such."

Yes, plenty of people would be distressed at that. I am the wrong boy to threaten with such losses, for I hunt and forage; I like the old ways. I kept myself fed and healthy for a full four months, exploring up the glacier last spring—healthier than were most folk when I arrived home, with their toothaches and their coughs. But others, yes, they rely wholly on those stores that Phillips brings through the year. When he is due, and they have run short of tobacco, they go all grog and temper waiting, or hide at home until he should come. They will not hunt or snare with me and Tray and Pa and the others; take them a haunch of stewed rabbit, and if they will eat it at all they will sauce it well with complaints and wear a sulking face over every bite.

"And no food coming up, for all those extra mouths you'd have to feed," says Phillips softly and still smiling, "that once were kept on mulberry leaves alone. Think of that."

What was I imagining, all my talk of undoing? The man cannot make mulberries back into men, and if he could he would never teach someone like me, that he thought so stupid, and whose folk he despised. And even if he taught us, and worked alongside us in the unmaking, we would never get back the man John Barn was going to be when he was born John Barn, or any of the men and women that the others might have become.

"You were starving and in rags when my father found you," says Phillips, sounding pleased. "Your people. You lived like animals."

"We had some bad years, I heard." *And we* are *animals,* I nearly add, *and so are you. A bear meets you, you are just as much a meal to him as is a berry-bush or a fine fat salmon. What are you, if not animal?*

But I have already lost this argument; he has already dismissed me. He draws on, as if I never spoke, as if he were alone. Good silk is coming out now; all the leaves we've been feeding into John Barn are coming out clean, white, strong-stranded; he is restored, apart from the great hole in him. Still I feed him, still he chews on, both of us playing our parts to fill Phillips' hands with silk.

"Very well," says Phillips, "I think we are done here. Time to close him up again."

I'm relieved that he intends to. "Should I lie on him again?"

"In a little," he says. "The inner parts are nerveless, and will not give him much pain. When I sew the dermal layers, perhaps."

It is very much like watching someone wind a fly, the man-hands working such a small area and mysteriously, stitching inside the hole. The thread, which is black, and waxed, wags out in the light and then is drawn in to the task, then wags again, the man concentrating above. His fingers work exactly like a spider's legs on its web, stepping delicately as he brings the curved needle out and takes it back in. I can feel from John Barn's chest that there is not pain exactly, but there is sensation where there should not be, and the fear that comes from not understanding makes Phillips's every movement alarming to him.

I didn't quite believe that Phillips would restore John Barn and repair him. I lie across Barn again and watch the stitching-up of the outer skin. With each pull and drag of thread through flesh Barn exclaims in the dark behind me. "Oh. Oh, that is bad. Oh, that feels dreadful." He jerks and cries out at every piercing by the needle.

"He's nearly finished, John," I say. "Maybe six stitches more."

And Phillips works above, ignoring us, as unmoved as if he were sewing up a boot. A wave of his hair droops forward on his brow, and around his eyes is stained with tiredness. It feels as if he has kept us in this small cloud of firelight, helping him do his mad work, all the night. There is no danger of me sleeping; I am beyond exhaustion; Barn's twitches wake me up brighter and brighter, and so does the fact that Phillips can ignore them so thoroughly, piercing and piercing the man. And though a few hours ago I would happily have left Barn to him, now I want to be awake and endure each stitch as well, even if there is no chance of the mulberry ever knowing or caring.

Then it is done. Phillips snips the thread with a pair of bright-gold scissors, inspects his work, draws a little silk out past all the layers of stitching. "Good, that's good," he says.

I lever myself up off Barn, lift my leg from his. "He's done with you," I tell him, and his eyes roll up into his head with relief, straight into sleep.

"We will leave him tied. We may as well," says Phillips, casting his used tools into the pot on the fire. "We don't want him running off again. Or getting infection in that wound." He strips off his horrid gloves and throws them in the fire. They wince and shrivel and give off a few moments' stink.

I feel as if I'm floating a little way off the ground; Phillips looks very small over there, his shining tools faraway. "There are others, then?" I say.

"Others?" He is coaxing his fire up to boil the tools again.

"'Careful practice,' you said, by your father's side. Yet we never saw you here. So there are other folk like ours, with their mulberries, that you practised on? In other places in the mountains, or in the town itself? I have never been there to know."

"Oh," he says, and right at me, his eyes bright at mine. "Yes," he says. "Though there is a lot to be learned from… books, you know, and general anatomy and surgical practice." He surveys the body before us, up and down. "But yes," he says earnestly to me. "Many communities. Quite a widespread practice, and trade. Quite solidly established."

I want to keep him talking like this, that he cares what he says to me. For the first time today he seems not to scorn me for what I am. I'm not as clear to him as John Barn has become to me, but I am more than I was this morning when he told Pa, *I'll take your boy, if you can spare him.*

"Do you have a son, then," I say, "that you are teaching in turn?"

"Ah," he says, "not as yet. I've not been so blessed thus far as to achieve the state of matrimony." He shows me his teeth, then sees that I don't understand. Some of his old crossness comes back. "I have no wife. Therefore I have no children. That is the way it is done in the town, at least."

"When you have a son, will you bring him here, to train him?" Even half-asleep I am enjoying this, having his attention, unsettling him. He looks as if he thought *me* a mulberry, and now is surprised to find that I can talk back and forth like any person.

"I dare say, I dare say." He shakes his head. "Although I'm sure you understand, it is a great distance to come, much farther than other… communities. And a boy—their mothers are terribly attached to them, you know. My wife—my wife *to be*—might not consent to his travelling so far, from her. Until he is quite an age."

He waits on my next word, and so do I, but after a time a yawn takes me instead, and when it is over he is up and crouched by his fire. "Yes, time we got some rest. Excellent work, boy. You've been most useful." He seems quite a different man. Perhaps he is too tired to keep up his contempt of me? Certainly *I* am too tired to care very much. I climb to my feet and walk into the darkness, to relieve myself before sleep.

⟶⟨⟩⟶

I wake, not with a start, but suddenly and completely, to the fire almost dead again and the forest all around me, aslant on the ridge. Dawn light is starting to creep up behind the trees, and stars are still snagged in the high branches, but here, close to me, masses of darkness go about their growing, roots fast in the ground around my head, thick trunks seeming to jostle each other, though nothing moves in the windless silence.

I am enormous myself, and wordless like the forest, yet full of burrows and niches and shadows where beasts lie curled—some newly gone to rest, others about to move out into the day—and birds roost with their breast-feathers fluffed over their claws. I am no fool, though that slip of a man with his tiny tools and his sneering took me for one. I see the story he spun me, and his earnest expectation that I would believe it. I see his whole plan and his father's, laid out like paths through the woods, him and his town house and his tailor at one end there, us and our poor mulberries at the other, winding silk and waiting for him. A widespread trade? No, just this little pattern trodden through from below. Many communities? No, just us. Just me and my folk, and our children.

I sit up silently. I wait until the white cross of John Barn glimmers over there on the ground, until the smoke from my fire comes clear, a fine grey vine climbing the darkness without haste. I think through the different ways I can take; there are few enough of them, and all of them end in uncertainty, except for the first and simplest way that came to me as I slept—which is now, which is here, which is me. I spend a long time listening to folk in my head, but whenever I look to Barn, and think of holding him down, and his trembling, and his dutiful chewing of the leaves, they fall silent; they have nothing to say.

A red-throat tests its call against the morning silence. I get up and go to Barn, and take up the coil of leftover cord from beside him.

Phillips is on his side, curled around what is left of his fire. His hands are nicely placed for me. I slip the cord under them and pin his forearms down with my boot. As he wakes, grunts—"What are you at, boy?"—and begins to struggle, I loop and loop, and swiftly tie the cord. "How *dare* you! What do you think—"

"Up." I stand back from him, all the forest behind me, and in me. We have no regard for this man's thin voice, his tiny rage.

Staring, he pushes himself up with his bound hands, is on his knees, then staggers to his feet. He is equal the height of me, but slender, built for spider-work, while I am constructed to chop wood and haul water and bring down a running stag. I can do what I like with him.

"You are just a boy!" he says. "Have you no respect for your elders?"

"You are not my elders," I say. I take his arm, and he tries to flinch away. "This way," I say, and I make him go.

"Boy?" says John Barn from the ground. He has forgotten my name again.

"I'll be back soon, John. Don't you worry."

And that is all the need I have of words. I force Phillips down towards the torrent path; he pours *his* words out, high-pitched, outraged, neat-cut as if he made them with that little knife of his. But I am forest vastness, and the birds in my branches have begun their morning's shouting; I have no ears for him.

I push him down the narrow path; I don't bully him or take any glee when he falls and complains, or scratches his face in the underbrush, but I drag him up and keep him going. The noise of the torrent grows towards us, becomes bigger than all but the closest, loudest birds. His words flow back at me, but they are only a kind of odd music now, carrying no meaning, only fear.

He rounds a bend and quickly turns, and is in my arms, banging my chest with his bound purple hands. "You will not! You will not!" I turn him around, and move him on with all my body and legs. The torrent shows between the trees—that's what set him off, the water fighting white among the boulders.

Now he resists me with all that he has. His boots slip on the stones and he throws himself about. But there is simply not enough of him, and I am patient and determined; I pull him out of the brush again and again, and press him on. If he won't walk, I'm happy for him to crawl. If he won't crawl I'm prepared to push him along with my boot.

The path comes to a high lip over the water before cutting along and down to the flatter place where you can fill your pots, or splash your face. I bring him to the lip and push him straight off, glad to be rid of his flailing, embarrassed by his trying to fight me.

He disappears in the white. He comes up streaming, caught already by the flow, shouting at the cold. It tosses him about, gaping and kicking, for a few rocks, and then he turns to limp cloth, to rubbish, a dab of bright wet silk draggling across his chest. He slides up over a rock and drops the other side. He moves along, is carried away and down, over the little falls there, and across the pool, on his face and with blood running from his head, over again and on down.

I climb back up through the woods. It is very peaceful and straightforward to walk without him, out of the water-noise into the birdsong. The clearing when I reach it is quiet without him, pleased to be rid of his fussing and displeasure and only to stand about, head among the leaves while the two fires send up their smoke-tendrils and John Barn sleeps on.

I bend down and touch his shoulder. "Come, John," I say, "Time to make for home. Do I need to bind you?"

He wakes. "You?" His eyes reflect my head, surrounded by branches on the sky.

"George. George Treadlaw, remember?"

He looks about as I untie his feet. "That man is gone," he says. "Good. I don't like that man."

I reach across him to loosen his far hand. "Oh, George," he says "You smell bad this morning. Perhaps you'd better bind me, and walk at a little distance. That's a fearsome smell. It makes me want to run from you."

I sniff at a pinch of my shirt. "I'm no worse than I was last night."

"Yes, last night it started," he says. "But I was tied down then and no trouble to you."

I tether him to a tree-root and cook myself some pan-flaps.

"They smell nice," he says, and eats another mulberry leaf, watching the pan.

"You must eat nothing but leaves today, John," I tell him. "Anything foreign, you will die of it, for I can't go into you like Phillips and fetch it out again."

"You will have to watch me," he says. "Everything is very pretty, and smells so adventurous."

We set off home straight after. All day I lead him on a length of rope, letting him take his time. I am not impatient to get back. No one will be happy with me, that I lost Phillips. Oh, they will be angry, however much I say it was an accident, a slip of the man's boot as he squatted by the torrent washing himself. No one will want to take the spindles down to the town, and find whoever he traded them to, and buy the goods he bought. I will have to do all that, because it was I who lost the man, and I will, though the idea scares me as much as it will scare them. No one will want to hunt again, in years to come as the mulberries die off and no new ones are made; no one will want to gather roots and berries, and make nut flour, just to keep us fed, for people are all spoilt with town goods, the ease of them and the strong tastes and their softness to the tooth. But what can they do, after all, but complain? *Go down to the town yourselves,* I'll tell them. *Take a mulberry with you and some spindles; tell what was done to us. Do you think they will start it again? No, they will come up here and examine everything and talk to us as fools; they might take away all our mulberries; they might take all of us away, and make us live down the town. And they will think we did worse than lose Phillips in the torrent; they will take me off to gaol, maybe. I don't know what will happen. I don't know.*

"It is a fine day, George of the Treadlaws," John Barn says behind me. "I like to breathe, out here. I like to see the trees, and the sun, and the birds."

He is following behind obedient, pale and careful, the stitches black in his paunch, the brace hanging off the silk-end. Step, step, step, he goes with his unaccustomed feet, on root and stone and ledge of earth, and he looks about when he can, at everything.

"You're right, John." I move on again so that he won't catch up and be upset by the smell of me. "It's a fine day for walking in the forest."

◄o►

ROOTS AND ALL

BRIAN HODGE

The way in was almost nothing like we remembered, miles off the main road, and Gina and me with one half-decent sense of direction between us. *Do you need us to draw you a map,* our parents had asked, hers and mine both, once at the funeral home and again over the continental breakfast at the motel. *No, no, no,* we'd told them. *Of course we remember how to get to Grandma's.* Indignant, the way adults get when their parents treat them like nine-year-olds.

Three wrong turns and fifteen extra minutes of meandering later, we were in the driveway, old gravel over ancestral dirt. Gina and I looked at each other, a resurgence of some old telepathy between cousins.

"Right," I said. "We never speak of this again."

She'd insisted on driving my car, proving… something… and yanked the keys from the ignition. "I don't even want to speak about it now."

If everything had still been just the way it used to be, maybe we would've been guided by landmarks we hadn't even realized we'd internalized. But it wasn't the same, and I don't think I was just recalling some idealized version of this upstate county that had never actually existed.

I remembered the drive as a thing of excruciating boredom, an interminable landscape of fields and farmhouses, and the thing I'd dreaded most as a boy was finding ourselves behind a tractor rumbling down a road too narrow for us to pass. But once we were here, it got better, because my grandfather had never been without a couple of hunting dogs, and there were more copses of trees and tracts of deep woodland than the most determined pack of kids could explore in an entire summer.

Now, though…

"The way here," I said. "It wasn't always this dismal, was it?"

Gina shook her head. "Definitely not."

I was thinking of the trailers we'd passed, and the forests of junk that had grown up around them, and it seemed like there'd been a time when, if someone had a vehicle that obviously didn't run, they kept it out of sight inside a barn until it did. They didn't set it out like a trophy. I was thinking, too, of riding in my grandfather's car, meeting another going the opposite direction, his and the other driver's hands going up at the same moment in a friendly wave. Ask him who it was, and as often as not he wouldn't know. They all waved just the same. Bygone days, apparently. About all the greeting we'd gotten were sullen stares.

We stood outside the car as if we needed to reassure ourselves that we were really here. Like that maple tree next to the driveway, whose scarlet-leafed shade we parked in, like our grandfather always had—it had to have grown, but then so had I, so it no longer seemed like the beanstalk into the clouds it once was. Yet it had to be the same tree, because hanging from the lowest limbs were a couple of old dried gourds, each hollowed out, with a hole the size of a silver dollar bored into the side. There would be a bunch more hanging around behind the house. Although they couldn't have been the same gourds. It pleased me to think of Grandma Evvie doing this right up until the end. Her life measured by the generations of gourds she'd turned into birdhouses, one of many scales of time.

How long since we've been here, Gina?

Ohhh… gotta be… four or five gourds ago, at least.

Really. That long.

Yeah. Shame on us.

It was the same old clapboard farmhouse, white, always white, always peeling. I'd never seen it freshly painted, but never peeled all the way down to naked weathered wood, either, and you had to wonder if the paint didn't somehow peel straight from the can.

We let ourselves in through the side door off the kitchen—I could hardly remember ever using the front door—and it was like stepping into a time capsule, everything preserved, even the smell, a complex blend of morning coffee and delicately fried foods.

We stopped in the living room by her chair, the last place she'd ever sat. The chair was so thoroughly our grandmother's that, even as kids, we'd felt wrong sitting in it, although she'd never chased us out. It was old beyond reckoning, as upholstered chairs went, the cushions flattened by decades of gentle pressure, with armrests as wide as cutting boards. She'd done her sewing there, threaded needles always stuck along the edge.

"If you have to die, and don't we all," Gina said, "that's the way to do it."

Her chair was by the window, with a view of her nearest neighbor, who'd been the one to find her. She'd been reading, apparently. Her book lay closed on one armrest, her glasses folded and resting atop it, and she was just sitting there, her head drooping but otherwise still upright. The neighbor, Mrs. Tepovich, had thought she was asleep.

"It's like she decided it was time," I said. "You know? She waited until she'd finished her book, then decided it was time."

"It must've been a damn good book. I mean… if she decided nothing else was ever going to top it." Totally deadpan. That was Gina.

I spewed a time-delayed laugh. "You're going to Hell."

Then she got serious and knelt by the chair, running her hand along the knobbly old fabric. "What's going to happen to this? Nobody'd want it. There's nobody else in the world it even fits with. It was *hers*. But to just throw it out…?"

She was right. I couldn't stand the thought of it joining a landfill.

"Maybe Mrs. Tepovich could use it." I peered through the window, toward her house. "We should go over and say hi. See if there's anything here she'd like."

This neighborly feeling seemed as natural here as it would've been foreign back home. The old woman in that distant house… I'd not seen her in more than a decade, but it still felt like I knew her better than any of the twenty or more people within a five-minute walk of my own door.

It was easy to forget: Really, Gina and I were just one generation out of this place, and whether directly or indirectly, it had to have left things buried in us that we didn't even suspect.

◄○►

If the road were a city block, we would've started at one end, and Mrs. Tepovich would've been nearly at the other. We tramped along wherever walking was easiest, a good part of it over ground that gave no hint of having been a strawberry field once, where people came from miles around to pick by the quart.

But Mrs. Tepovich, at least, hadn't changed, or not noticeably so. She'd seemed old before and was merely older now, less a shock to our systems than we were to hers. Even though she'd seen us as teenagers she still couldn't believe how we'd grown, and maybe it was just that Gina and I looked like it had been a long time since we'd had sunburns and scabs.

"Was it a good funeral?" she wanted to know.

"Nobody complained," Gina said.

"I stopped going to funerals after Dean's."

Her husband. My best memory of him was from when the strawberries came in red and ripe, and his inhuman patience as he smoked roll-your-own cigarettes and hand-cranked a shiny cylinder of homemade ice cream in a bath of rock salt and ice. The more we pleaded, the slyer he grinned and the slower he cranked.

"I've got one more funeral left in me," Mrs. Tepovich said, "and that's the one they'll have to drag me to."

It should've been sad, this little sun-cured widow with hair like white wool rambling around her house and tending her gardens alone, having just lost her neighbor and friend—a fixture in her life that had been there half a century, one of the last remaining pillars of her past now gone.

It should've been sad, but wasn't. Her eyes were too bright, too expectant, and it made me feel better than I had since I'd gotten the news days ago. *This was what Grandma Evvie was like, right up to the end. How do you justify mourning a thing like that? It should've been celebrated.*

But no, she'd gotten the usual dirge-like send-off, and I was tempted to think she would've hated it.

"So you've come to sort out the house?" Mrs. Tepovich said.

"Only before our parents do the real job," Gina told her. "They said if there was anything of Grandma's that we wanted, now would be the time to pick it out."

"So we're here for a long weekend," I said.

"Just you two? None of the others?"

More cousins, she meant. All together, we numbered nine. Ten once, but now nine, and no, none of the others would be coming, although my cousin Lindsay hadn't been shy about asking me to send her a cell phone video of a walkthrough, so she could see if there was anything she wanted. I was already planning on telling her sorry, I couldn't get a signal up here.

"Well, you were her favorites, you know." Mrs. Tepovich got still, her eyes, mired in a mass of crinkles, going far away. "And Shae," she added softly. "Shae should've been here. She wouldn't have missed it."

Gina and I nodded. She was right on both counts. There were a lot of places my sister should've been over the past eight years, instead of... wherever. Shae should've been a lot of places, been a lot of things, instead of a riddle and a wound that had never quite healed.

"We were wondering," Gina went on, "if there was anything from over there that you would like."

"Some of that winter squash from her garden would be nice, if it's ready to pick. She always did grow the best Delicata. And you've got to eat that up quick, because it doesn't keep as long as the other kinds."

We were looking at each other on two different wavelengths.

"Well, it doesn't," she said. "The skin's too thin."

"Of course you're welcome to anything from the garden that you want," Gina said. "But that's not exactly what we meant. We thought you might like to have something from *inside* the house."

"Like her chair," I said, pretending to be helpful. "Would you want her chair?"

Had Mrs. Tepovich bitten into the tartest lemon ever grown, she still wouldn't have made a more sour face. "That old eyesore? What would I need with that?" She gave her head a stern shake. "No. Take that thing out back and burn it, is what you should do. I've got eyesores of my own, I don't need to take on anyone else's."

We stayed awhile longer, and it was hard to leave. Harder for us than for her. She was fine with our going, unlike so many people her age I'd been around, who did everything but grab your ankle to keep you a few more minutes. I guessed that's the way it was in a place where there was always something more that needed to be done.

Just this, on our way out the door:

"I don't know if you've got anything else planned for while you're here," she said, and seemed to be directing this at me, "but don't you go poking your noses anywhere much off the roads. Those meth people that've made such a dump of the place, I hear they don't mess around."

◄o►

Evening came on differently out here than it did at home, seeming to rise up from the ground and spill from the woods and overflow the ditches that ran alongside the road. I'd forgotten this. Forgotten, too, how night seemed to spread outward from the chicken coop, and creep from behind the barn, and pool in the hog wallow and gather inside the low, tin-roofed shack that had sheltered the pigs and, miraculously, was still standing after years of disuse. Night was always present here, it seemed. It just hid for a while and then slipped its leash again.

I never remembered a time when it hadn't felt better being next to somebody when night came on. We watched it from the porch, plates in our laps as we ate a supper thrown together from garden pickings and surviving leftovers from the fridge.

When she got to it, finally, Gina started in gently. "What Mrs. Tepovich said… about having anything else planned this weekend… meaning Shae, she couldn't have been talking about anything else… she wasn't onto something there, was she? That's not on your mind, is it, Dylan?"

"I can't come up here and *not* have it on my mind," I said. "But doing something, no. What's there to do that wouldn't be one kind of mistake or another?"

Not that it wasn't tempting, in concept. Find some reprobate and put the squeeze on, and if he didn't know anything, which he almost certainly wouldn't, then have him point to someone who might.

"Good," she said, then sat with it long enough to get angry. We'd never lost the anger, because it had never had a definite target. "But… if you did … you could handle yourself all right. It's what you do every day, isn't it."

"Yeah, but strength in numbers. And snipers in the towers when the cons are out in the yard."

She looked across at me and smiled, this tight, sad smile, childhood dimples replaced by curved lines. Her hair was as light as it used to get during summers, but helped by a bottle now, I suspected, and her face narrower, her cheeks thinner. When they were plump, Gina was the first girl I ever kissed, in that fumbling way of cousins ignorant of what comes next.

There was no innocence in her look now, though, like she wished it were a more lawless world, just this once, so I could put together a private army and come back up here and we'd sweep through from one side of the county to the other until we finally got to the bottom of it.

Shae was one of the ones you see headlines about, if something about their disappearance catches the news editors' eyes: MISSING GIRL LAST SEEN MONDAY NIGHT. FAMILY OF MISSING COLLEGE STUDENT MAKE TEARFUL APPEAL. Like that, until a search team gets lucky or some jogger's dog stands in a patch of weeds and won't stop barking.

Except we'd never had even that much resolution. Shae was one of the ones who never turned up. The sweetest girl you could ever hope to meet, at nineteen still visiting her grandmother, like a Red Riding Hood who trusted that all the wolves were gone, and this was all that was found: a single, bloodied scrap of a blouse hanging from the brambles about half a mile from where our mother had grown up. The rest of her, I'd always feared, was at the bottom of a mineshaft or sunk weighted into the muck of a pond or in a grave so deep in the woods there was no chance of finding her now.

I'd had three tours of duty to erode my confidence about any innate sense of decency in the human race, and if that weren't enough, signing on with the Department of Corrections had finished off the rest. For Shae, I'd always feared the worst, in too much detail, because I knew too well what people were capable of, even the good guys, even myself.

-o-

We made little progress that first evening, getting lost on a detour into some photo albums, then after an animated phone conversation with her pair of gradeschoolers, Gina went to bed early. But I stayed up with the night, listening to it awhile from Grandma Evvie's chair, until listening wasn't enough, and I had to go outside to join it.

There was no cable TV out this far, and Grandma hadn't cared enough about it for a satellite dish, so she'd made do with an ancient antenna grafted to one side of the house. The rotor had always groaned in the wind, like a weathervane denied its true purpose, the sound carrying down into the house, a ghostly grinding while you tried to fall asleep on breezy nights. Now I used it as a ladder, scaling it onto the roof and climbing the shingles to straddle the peak.

Now and again I'd see a light in the distance—the September wind parting the trees long enough to see the porch bulb of a distant neighbor, a streak of headlights on one of the farther roads—but the blackest nights I'd ever known were out here, alone with the moon and the scattershot field of stars.

So I listened, and I opened.

The memory had never left, among the clearest from those days of long summer visits—two weeks, three weeks, a month. We would sleep four and five to a room, when my cousins and sister and I were all here at once, and Grandma would settle us in and tell us bedtime stories, sometimes about animals, sometimes about Indians, sometimes about boys and girls like ourselves.

I don't remember any of them.

But there was one she returned to every now and then, and that one stuck with me. The rest were just stories, made up on the spot or reworked versions of tales she already knew, and there was nothing lingering about them. I knew that animals didn't talk; the good Indians were too foreign to me to really identify with, and I wasn't afraid the bad ones would come to get us; and as for the normal boys and girls, well, what of them when we had real adventures of our own, every day.

The stories about the Woodwalker, though... those were different.

That's just my name for it. My own grandmother's name for it, she admitted to us. *It's so big and old it's got no name. Like rain. The rain doesn't know it's rain. It just falls.*

It was always on the move, she told us, from one side of the county to the other. It never slept, but sometimes it settled down in the woods or the fields to rest. It could be vast, she told us, tall enough that clouds sometimes got tangled in its hair—when you saw clouds skimming along so quickly you could track their progress, that's when you knew—but it could be small, too, small enough to curl inside an acorn if the acorn needed reminding on how to grow.

You wouldn't see it even if you looked for it every day for a thousand years, she promised us, but there were times you could see evidence of its passing by. Like during a dry spell when the dust rose up from the fields—that was the Woodwalker breathing it in, seeing if it was dry enough yet to send for some rain—and in the woods, too, its true home, when the trees seemed to be swaying opposite the direction the wind was blowing.

You couldn't see it, no, but you could feel it, down deep, brushing the edges of your soul. Hardly ever during the day, not because it wasn't there, but because if you were the right sort of person, you were too busy while the sun was up. Too busy working, or learning, or visiting, or too busy playing and wilding and having fun. But at night, though, that was different. Nights were when a body slowed down. Nights were for noticing the rest.

What's the Woodwalker do? we'd ask. *What's it for?*

It loves most of what grows and hates waste and I guess you could say it pays us back, she'd tell us. *And makes sure we don't get forgetful and too full of ourselves.*

What happens then, if you do? Somebody always wanted to know that.

Awful things, she'd say. *Awful, awful things.* Which wasn't enough, because we'd beg to know more, but she'd say we were too young to hear about them, and promise to tell us when we were older, but she never did.

You're just talking about God, right? one of my cousins said once. *Aren't you?*

But Grandma never answered that either, at least not in any way we would've understood at the time. I still remember the look, though… not quite a no, definitely not a yes, and the wisdom to know that we'd either understand on our own someday, or never have to.

I saw the Woodwalker once, Shae piped up, quiet and awestruck. *One weekend last fall. He was looking at two dead deer.* None of us believed her, because we believed in hunters a lot more than we believed in anything called the Woodwalker. But, little as she was, Shae wouldn't back down. Hunters, she argued, didn't stand deer on their feet again and send them on their way.

I'd never forgotten that.

And so, as the night blustered on the wings of bats and barn owls, I listened and watched and took another tiny step toward believing.

"Any time," I whispered to whatever might speak up or show itself. "Any time."

◄◦►

The milk had gone bad and the bacon with it, and we needed a few other things to get us through the weekend, so that next morning I volunteered to make the run back to the store near the turnoff on the main road. I decided to take the long way, setting off in the opposite direction, because it had been years and I wanted to see more of the county, and even if I made more wrong turns than right, there were worse things than getting lost on a September Saturday morning.

Mile after mile, I drove past many worse things.

You can't remember such a place from before it got this way, can't remember the people who'd proudly called it home, without wondering what they would think of it now. Would *they* have let their homes fall to ruin with such helpless apathy? Would they have sat back and watched the fields fill with weeds? Would they have ridden two wheels, three wheels, four, until they'd ripped the low hills full of gouges and scars? Not the people I remembered.

It made me feel old, not in the body but in the heart, old in a way you always say you never want to be. It was the kind of old that in a city yells at kids to get off the lawn, but here it went past annoyance and plunged into disdain. Here, they'd done real harm. They'd trampled on memories and tradition, souring so much of what I'd decided had been good about the place, and one of them, I could never forget, had snatched my sister from the face of the Earth.

Who were the people who lived here now, I wondered. They couldn't all have come from somewhere else. Most, I imagined, had been raised here and never left, which made their neglect even more egregious.

But the worst of it was in the west of the county, where the coal once was. The underground mines had been tapped out when we were children, and while that's when I'd first heard the term strip-mining, I hadn't known what it meant, either as a process or its consequences.

It was plain enough now, though, all the near-surface coal gone too, and silent wastelands left in its wake, horizon-wide lacerations of barren land pocked with mounds of topsoil, the ground still so acidic that nothing wanted to grow there.

No matter how urgently the Woodwalker might remind the seeds what to do.

It was the wrong frame of mind to have gotten in before circling back to the store. I left my sunglasses on inside, the same way I'd wear them on cloudy days while watching the inmates in the yard, and for the same reasons, too: as armor, something to protect us both, because there was no good to come from locking eyes, from letting some people see what you think of their choices and what they'd thrown away.

The place was crowded with Saturday morning shoppers, and there was no missing the sickness here. *Those meth people that've made such a dump of the place, I hear they don't mess around,* Mrs. Tepovich had said, and for that matter, neither did the meth. I knew the look—some of the inmates still had it when they transferred from local lockups to hard time—and while it wasn't on every face in the market, it was on more than enough to make me fear it was only going to get worse here. A body half-covered with leprosy doesn't have a lot of hope for the rest of it.

The worst of them had been using for years, obviously, their faces scabbed and their bones filed sharp. With teeth like crumbling gravel, they looked like they'd been sipping tonics of sulfuric acid, and it was eating through from the inside. The rest of them, as jumpy and watchful as rats, would get there. All they needed to know about tomorrow was written in the skins of their neighbors.

It had an unexpected leveling effect.

From what I remembered of when we visited as children, the men nearly always died first here, often by a wide margin. They might go along fine for decades, as tough as buzzards in a desert, but then something caught up with them and they fell hard. They'd gone into the mines and come out with black spots on their lungs, or they'd broken their backs slowly, one sunrise-to-sunset day at a time, or had stubbornly ignored some small symptom for ten years too many. The women, though, cured like leather and carried on without them. It was something you could count on.

No longer.

The race to the grave looked like anybody's to win.

◆

When I got back to the house, I discovered we had a visitor, a surprise since there was no car in the drive. As I came in through the kitchen, Gina, over his shoulder, gave me a where-were-you-all-this-time look that she could've stolen from my ex. They were sitting at the kitchen table with empty coffee mugs, and Gina looked like the statute of limitations on her patience had expired twenty minutes earlier.

I couldn't place him, but whoever he was, he probably hadn't had the same fierce black beard, lantern jaw, and giant belly when we were kids.

"You remember Ray Sinclair," she said, then jabbed her finger at the door, and it came back in a rush: Mrs. Tepovich's great-nephew. He used to come over and play with us on those rare days that weren't already taken up with chores, and he'd been a good guide through the woods—knew where to find all the wild berries, at their peak of ripeness, and the best secluded swimming holes where the creeks widened. We shook hands, and it was like trying to grip a baseball glove.

"I was dropping some venison off at Aunt Pol's. She told me you two were over here," he said. "My condolences on Evvie. Aunt Pol thought the world of her."

I put away the milk and bacon and the rest, while Gina excused herself and slipped past, keeping an overdue appointment with some room or closet as Ray and I cleared the obligatory small talk.

"What have you got your eye on?" he asked then. "For a keepsake, I mean."

"I don't know yet," I said. "Maybe my granddad's shotgun, if it turns up."

"You do much hunting?"

"Not since he used to take me out. And after I got back from the army … let's just say I wasn't any too eager to aim at something alive and pull a trigger again." I'd done fine with my qualifications for the job, although that was just targets, nothing that screamed and bled and tried to belly-crawl away. "But I'm thinking if I had an old gun that I had some history with, maybe…" I shrugged. "I guess I could've asked for it after Granddad died, but it wouldn't have seemed right. Not that Grandma went hunting, but left alone out here, she needed it more than I did."

He nodded. "Especially after your sister."

I looked at him without being obvious about it, then realized I hadn't taken off my sunglasses yet, just like at the market. *It could've been you,* I thought. No reason to think so, but when a killing is never solved, a body never found, it can't *not* cross your mind when you look at some people, the ones with proximity and access and history. The ones you really don't know anything about anymore. If Ray had known where to find berries, he'd know where to bury a girl.

"Especially then," I said.

"Did I say something wrong?" he asked. "My apologies if I did."

He sounded sincere, but I'd been hearing sincere for years. *Naw, boss, I don't know who hid that shank in my bunk. Not me, boss, I didn't have nothing to do with that bag of pruno.* They were all sincere down to the rot at their core.

The other C.O.s had warned me early on: *There'll come a time when you look at everybody like they're guilty of something.*

I'd refused to believe this: *No, I know how to leave work at work.*

Now it was me telling the new C.O.s the same thing.

I took off the shades. "You didn't say anything wrong. A thing like that, you never really get over it. Time doesn't heal the wounds, it just thickens up the scars." I moved to the screen door and looked outside, smelled the autumn day, a golden scent of sun-warmed leaves. "It's not like it used to be around here, is it."

He shrugged. "Where is?"

I had him follow me outside, and turned my face to the sun, shutting my eyes and just listening, thinking that it at least sounded the way it had. That expansive, quiet sound of birds and wide-open spaces.

"When I was at the market, I would've needed at least two hands to count the people I'd be willing to bet will be dead in five years," I said. "How'd this get started?"

Ray eyed me hard. I knew it even with my eyes closed. I'd felt it as sure as if he'd poked me with two fingers. When I opened my eyes, he looked exactly like I knew he would.

"You're some kind of narc now, aren't you, Dylan?" he said.

"Corrections officer. I don't put anybody in prison, I just try to keep the peace once they're there."

He stuffed his hands in his pockets and rocked back and forth, his gaze on far distances. "Well... the way anything starts, I guess. A little at a time. It's a space issue, mostly. Space, privacy. We got plenty of both here. And time. Got plenty of that, too."

His great-uncle hadn't, not to my recollection. Mr. Tepovich had always had just enough time, barely, to do what needed doing. The same as my grandfather. I wondered where all that time had come from.

"How many meth labs are there around here, I wonder," I said.

"I couldn't tell you anything. All I know's what I hear, and I don't hear much."

Can't help you, boss. I don't know nothing about that.

"But if you were to get lucky and ask the right person," Ray went on, "I expect he might tell you something like it was the only thing he was ever good at. The only thing that ever worked out for him."

The trees murmured, and leaves whisked against the birdhouse gourds.

"He might even take the position that it's a blessed endeavor."

I hadn't expected this. "Blessed by who?"

His hesitation here, his uncertainty, looked like the first genuine expression since we'd started down this path. "Powers that be, I guess. Not government, not those kinds of powers. Something… higher." He tipped his head back, jammed his big jaw and bristly beard forward, scowling at the sky. "Say there's a place in the woods, deep, where nobody's likely to go by accident. Not big, but not well hid, either. Now say there's a team from the sheriff's department taking themselves a hike. Fifteen, twenty feet away and they don't see it. Now say the same thing happens with a group of fellows got on jackets that say 'DEA.' They all just walk on by like nothing's there."

He was after something, but I wasn't sure what. Maybe Ray didn't know either. They say if you stick around a prison long enough, you'll see some strange things that are almost impossible to explain, and even if I hadn't, I'd heard some stories. Maybe Ray had heard that as well, and was looking for… what, someone who understood?

"I don't know what else you'd call that," he said, "other than blessed."

"For a man who doesn't hear much, you have some surprising insights."

His gaze returned to earth and the mask went back on. "Maybe I keep my ear to the ground a little more than I let on." He began to sidle away toward his aunt's. "You take care, Dylan. Again, sorry about Evvie."

"Hey Ray? Silly question, but…" I said. "Your Aunt Polly, your own grandma, your mom, anybody… when you were a kid, did any of them ever tell you stories about something called the Woodwalker?"

He shook his head. "Nope. Seen my share of wood*peckers*, though." He got a few more steps away before he stopped again, something seeming to rise up that he hadn't thought of in twenty years. "Now that you mention it, I remember one from Aunt Pol about what she called Old Hickory Bones. It didn't make a lot of sense. 'Tall as the clouds, small as a nut,' that sort of nonsense. You know old women and their stories."

"Right."

He looked like he was piecing together memories from fragments. "The part that scared us most, she'd swear up and down it was true, from when she was a girl. That there was this crew of moonshiners got liquored up on their own supply and let the still fire get out of hand. Burned a few acres of woods, and some crops and a couple of homes with it. Her story went that they were found in a row with their arms and legs all smashed up and run through with hickory sticks… like scarecrows, kind of. And that's how Old Hickory Bones got his name. I always thought she just meant to scare us into making sure we didn't forget about our chores."

"That would do it for me," I said.

He laughed. "Those cows didn't have to wait on me for very many morning milkings, I'll tell you what." He turned serious, one big hand scrubbing at his beard. "Why do you come to ask about a thing like that?"

I gestured at the house. "You know how it is going through a place this way. Everything you turn over, there's another memory crawling out from underneath it."

ᐊᴏᐅ

Later, I kept going back to what I'd said when Gina and I had first walked in and looked at Grandma's chair: that it seemed like she'd finished her book and set it aside and peacefully resolved it was a good day to die. It's the kind of invention that gives you comfort, but maybe she really had. She kept up on us, her children and grandchildren, even though we were scattered far and wide. She knew I had a vacation coming up, knew that it overlapped with Gina's.

And we were her favorites. Even Mrs. Tepovich knew that.

So I'm tempted to think Grandma trusted that, with the right timing, Gina and I would be first to go through the house. She couldn't have wanted my mother to do it. Couldn't have wanted my father to be the first up in the attic. Some things are too cruel, no matter how much love underlies them.

Maybe she'd thought we would be more likely to understand and accept. Because we were her favorites, and even though my mother had grown up here, and my aunts and uncles too, they were so much longer out of the woods than we, her grandchildren, were.

It broke the agreeable calm of Saturday afternoon, Gina and I in different parts of the house. I was in the pantry, looking through last season's preserves and had discovered an ancient Mason jar full of coins when a warbling cry drifted down. I thought she'd come across a dead raccoon, a nest of dried-out squirrels… the kind of things that sometimes turn up in country attics.

But when Gina came and got me, her face was pale and her voice had been reduced to such a small thing I could barely hear it. *Shae,* she was saying, or trying to. *Shae.* Over and over, with effort and an unfocused look in her eyes. *Shae.*

I didn't believe her while climbing the folding attic ladder; still didn't while crossing the rough, creaking boards, hunched beneath the slope of the roof in the gloom and cobwebs and a smell like a century of dust. But after five or twenty minutes on my knees, I believed, all right, even if nothing made sense anymore.

There was light, a little, coming through a few small, triangular windows at the peaks. And there was air, slatted vents at either end allowing some circulation. And there was my sister's body, on a cot between a battered steamer trunk and a stack of cardboard boxes, covered by a sheet that had been drawn down as far as her chest.

The sheet wasn't dusty or discolored. It was clean, white, recently laundered. Eight years of washing her dead granddaughter's sheets—my head had trouble grasping that, and my heart just wanted to stop.

Gradually it dawned on me: With Shae eight years dead, we shouldn't have been able to recognize her. At best, she would've mummified in the dry heat, shriveled into a husk. At worst, all that was left would be scraps and bones, and the strawberry blonde silk of her hair. Instead, the most I could say was that she looked very, very thin, and when I touched her cheek, her skin was smooth and stiff but pliable, like freshly worked clay. I touched her cheek and almost expected her eyes to open.

She'd been nineteen then, was nineteen now. She'd spent the last eight years being nineteen. Nineteen and dead, only not decayed. She lay on a blanket and a bed of herbs. They were beneath her, alongside her. Sprigs and bundles had been stuffed inside the strips of another sheet that had been loosely wound around her like a shroud. The scent of them, a pungent and spicy smell of fields and trees, settled in my nose.

"Do you think Grandma did this?" Gina was behind me, pressing close. "Not *this* this, that's obvious, but… killed her, I mean. Not on purpose, but by accident, and she just couldn't face the rest of us."

"Right now I don't know what to think."

I shoved some junk out of the way to let more light at her. Her skin was white as a china plate, and dull, without the luster of life. Her far cheek and jaw were traced with a few pale bluish lines like scratches that had never healed. Gently, as if it were still possible to hurt her, I turned her head from side to side, feeling her neck, the back of her skull. There were no obvious wounds, although while the skin of her neck was white as well, it was a more mottled white.

"Do me a favor," I said. "Check the rest of her."

Gina's eyes popped. "Me? Why me? You're the hard-ass prison guard."

It was then I knew everything was real, because when tragedy is real, silly things cross your mind at the wrong times. *Corrections officer,* I wanted to tell her. *We don't like the G-word.*

"She's my sister. She's still a teenager," I said instead. "I shouldn't be… she wouldn't want me to."

Gina moved in and I moved aside and turned my back, listening to the rustle of cotton sheets and the crackle of dried herbs. My gaze roved and I spotted mousetraps, one set, one sprung, and if there were two, there were probably others. Grandma had done this, too. Set traps to keep the field mice away from her.

"She's, uh…" Gina's voice was shaky. "Her back, her bottom, the backs of her legs, it's all purple-black."

"That's where the blood pooled. That's normal." At least it didn't seem like she'd bled to death. "It's the only normal thing about this."

"What am I looking for, Dylan?"

"Injuries, wounds… is it obvious how she was hurt?"

"There's a pretty deep gash across her hipbone. And her legs are all scratched up. And her belly. There are these lines across it, like, I don't know… rope burns, maybe?"

Everything in me tightened. "Was she assaulted? Her privates?"

"They… look okay to me."

"All right. Cover her up decent again."

I inspected Shae's hands and fingertips. A few of her nails were ragged, with traces of dirt. Her toenails were mismatched, clean on one foot, the other with the same rims of dirt, as if she'd lost a shoe somewhere between life and death. Grandma had cleaned her up, that was plain to see, but hadn't scraped too deeply with the tip of the nail file. Maybe it just came down to how well she could see.

I returned to Shae's neck, the mottling there. Connect the dots and you could call it lines. If her skin weren't so ashen, it might look worse, ringed with livid bruises.

"If I had to guess, I'd say she was strangled," I told Gina. "And maybe not just her throat, but around the middle, too." Someone treating her like a python treats prey, wrapping and squeezing until it can't breathe.

We tucked her in again and covered her the rest of the way, to keep off the dust and let her return to her long, strange sleep.

"What do you want to do?" Gina said, and when I didn't answer: "The kindest thing we could do is bury her ourselves. Let it be our secret. Nobody else has to know. What good would it do if they did?"

For the first minute or two, that sounded good. Until it didn't. "You don't think Grandma knew that too? It's not that she couldn't have. If she was strong enough to work the soil in her garden, and to get Shae up the ladder, then she was strong enough to dig a grave. And there's not one time in the last eight years I heard her say anything that made me think her mind was off track. You?"

Gina shook her head. "No."

"Then she was keeping Shae up here for a reason."

We backed off toward the ladder, because another night, another day, wasn't going to do Shae any harm.

And that's when we found the envelope that Gina must have sent flying when she first drew back the sheet.

◄O►

How you react to what I got to say depends on who's done the finding, our Grandma Evvie had written. *I have my hopes for who it is, and if it hasn't gone that way I won't insult the rest by spelling it out, but I think you know who you are.*

First off, I know how this looks, but how things look and how things are don't always match up.

Know this much to be true: It wasn't any man or woman that took Shae's life. The easiest thing would've been to turn her over and let folks think so and see her buried and maybe see some local boy brought up on charges because the sheriff decides he's got to put it on somebody. I won't let that happen. There's plenty to pay for around here, and maybe the place would be better off even if some of them did get sent away for something they didn't do, but I can't help put a thing like that in motion without knowing whose head it would fall on.

If I was to tell you Shae was done in by what I always called the Wood-walker, some of you might believe me and most of you probably wouldn't. Believing doesn't make a thing any more or less true, it just points you toward what you have to do next.

If I was to tell you you could have Shae back again, would you believe it enough to try?

⬦

In the kitchen that evening, across the red oilcloth spread over the table, Gina and I argued. We argued for a long time. It comes naturally to brothers and sisters, but cousins can be pretty good at it too.

We argued over what was true. We argued over what couldn't possibly be real. We weren't arguing with each other so much as with ourselves, and with what fate had shoved into our faces.

Mostly, though, we argued over how far is too far, when it's for family.

⬦

Living with this has been no easy task. What happened to Shae was not a just thing. Folks here once knew that whatever we called it, there really is something alive in the woods and fields, as old as time and only halfway to civilized, even if few were ever lucky or cursed enough to see it. We always trusted that if we did right by it, it would do right by us. But poor Shae paid for other folks' wrongs.

She meant well, I know. It's no secret there's a plague here and it's run through one side of this county to the other. So when Shae found a trailer in the woods where they cook up that poison, nothing would do but that she draw a map and report it.

Till the day I die I won't ever forget the one summer when all the grandchildren were here and the night little Shae spoke up to say she'd seen the Woodwalker. I don't know why she was allowed at that age to see what most folks never do in a lifetime, but not once did I think she was making it up. I believed her.

The only thing I can fathom is this: Once she decided to report that trailer and what was going on there, the Woodwalker knew her heart, and resolved to put a stop to her intentions.

-o-

I spent half of Sunday out by myself, trying to find what Shae had found, but all I had to go by was the map she'd drawn. There was no knowing how accurate it was when it was new, and like the living things they are, woods never stop changing over time. Trees grow and fall, streams divert, brambles close off paths that were once as clear as sidewalks.

And whoever had put the trailer there had had eight years to move it. What it sounded like they'd never had, though, was a reason.

I had the map, and a bundle of sticks across my back, and like any hunter I had a shotgun—not my granddad's, since that one had yet to turn up, and it's just as well I went for the one in my trunk, carried out of habit for the job—but sometimes hunters come home empty-handed.

At least I came back with a good idea of what else I needed before going out to try again.

-o-

I don't want to say what I saw, but it was enough to know that it was no man using all those vines to drag her off toward the hog wallow, faster than I could chase after them. By the time I caught up, it had choked the life from her.

It didn't do this because it wanted to protect those men for their own sakes. I think it's because it wants the plague to continue until it finishes clearing away everybody who's got it, and there's nobody left in this county but folks who will treat the place right again.

These days you'll hear how the men who've brought this plague think they're

*beyond the reach of the law, because their hideaways can't be found. Well, I
say it's only because the Woodwalker has a harsher plan than any lawman,
and blinds the eyes of those who come from outside to look.*

But Shae always did see those woods with different eyes.

◄o►

"Remember what Grandma used to call her?" Gina asked. I was ashamed
to admit I didn't. "'Our little wood-elf,'" she said, then, maybe to make
me feel better, "That's not something a boy would've remembered. That's
one for the girls."

"Maybe so," I said, and peeled the blanket open one more time to
check my sister's face. I'd spent the last hours terrified that there had
been some magic about our grandmother's attic, and that once she was
carried back to the outside world again, the eight years of decay Shae had
eluded would find her at last.

One more time, I wouldn't have known she wasn't just dreaming.

Instead, the magic had come with her. Or maybe the Woodwalker,
spying us with the burden we'd shared through miles of woodland, knew
our hearts now, too, and opened the veil for our eyes to see. Either way,
I'd again followed where the old map led, and this time Shae had proven
to be the key.

"Do you think it goes the other way?" Gina asked.

"What do you mean?"

"If we stood up and whoever's in there looked out, would they see us
now? Or would they look straight at us and just see more trees?"

"I really don't want to put that to the test."

The trailer was small enough to hitch behind a truck, large enough for
two or three people to spend a day inside without tripping over each other
too badly. It sat nestled into the scooped-out hollow of a rise, painted
with a fading camouflage pattern of green and brown. At one time its
keepers had strung nets of nylon mesh over and around it, to weave with
branches and vines, but it looked like it had been a long time since they'd
bothered, and they were sagging here, collapsed there. It had a generator
for electricity, propane for gas. From the trailer's roof jutted a couple of
pipes that had, ever since we'd come upon it, been venting steam that had
long since discouraged anything from growing too close to it.

Eventually the steam stopped, and a few minutes later came the sound of locks from the other side of the trailer door. It swung open and out stepped two men. They took a few steps away before they stripped off the gas masks they'd been wearing and let them dangle as they seemed glad to breathe the cool autumn air.

I whispered for Gina to stay put, stay low, then stepped out from our hiding place and went striding toward the clearing in-between, and maybe it did take the pair of them longer to notice than it should've. They each wore a pistol at the hip but seemed to lack the instinct to go for them.

And the trees shuddered high overhead, even though I couldn't feel or hear a breeze.

"Hi, Ray," I called, leveling the shotgun at them from the waist.

"Dylan," he said, with a tone of weary disgust. "And here I believed you when you said you weren't no narc."

For a while I'd been wondering if he'd simply dropped by while visiting his great-aunt, and Shae had suspected him for what he was and followed him here, righteous and foolhardy thing that she could be.

I glanced at the gangly, buzz-cut fellow at his side. "Who's that you're with?"

"Him? Andy Ellerby."

"Any more still inside?"

Ray's fearsome beard seemed to flare. "You probably know as well as I do, cooking is a two-man job at most." He scuffed at the ground. "Come on, Dylan, your roots are here. You don't do this. What say we see what we can work out, huh?"

I looked at his partner. Like Ray, the edges of his face and the top of his forehead were red-rimmed where the gas mask had pressed tight, and he gave me a sullen glare. "Andy Ellerby, did I know you when we were kids?"

He turned his head to spit. "What's it matter if you did or didn't, if you can't remember my name."

"Good," I said. "That makes this much a little easier."

I snapped the riot gun to my shoulder and found that, when something mattered this much, I could again aim at something alive and pull the trigger. The range was enough for the twelve-gauge load to spread out into a pattern as wide as a pie tin. Andy took it in the chest and it flung him back against the trailer so hard he left a dent.

I'd loaded it with three more of the same, but didn't need them, so I racked the slide to eject the spent shell, then the next three. Ray looked confused as the unfired shells hit the forest floor, and his hand got twitchy as he remembered the holster on his belt, but by then I was at the fifth load and put it just beneath his breastbone, where his belly started to slope.

He looked up at me from the ground, trying to breathe with a reedy wheeze, groping where I'd shot him and not comprehending his clean, unbloodied hands.

"A beanbag round," I told him. "We use them for riot control. You can't just massacre a bunch of guys with homemade knives even if they are a pack of savages."

I knelt beside him and plucked the pistol from his belt before he remembered it, tossed it aside. Behind me, Gina had crept out of hiding with her arms wrapped around herself, peering at us with the most awful combination of hope and dread I'd ever seen.

"I know you didn't mean to, and I know you don't even know you did it, but you're still the reason my little sister never got to turn twenty." I sighed, and tipped my head a moment to look at the dimming sky, and listened to the sound of every living thing, seen and unseen. "Well… maybe next year."

I drew the hunting knife from my belt while he gasped; called for Gina to bring me the bundle of hickory sticks that my grandmother must have sharpened years ago, and the mallet with a cast-iron head, taken down from the barn wall. It would've been easier with Granddad's chainsaw, but some things shouldn't come easy, and there are times the old ways are still the best.

I patted Ray's shoulder and remembered the stocky boy who'd taken us to the fattest tadpoles we'd ever seen, the juiciest berries we'd ever tasted. "For what it's worth, I really was hoping it wouldn't be you coming out that door."

◄○►

If the family is to have Shae back again, there's some things that need doing, and I warn you, they're ugly business.

Dylan, if you're reading this, know that it was only you that I ever believed had the kind of love and fortitude in you to take care of it and not flinch from it. Whether you still had the faith in what your summers here put inside you was another matter. I figured that was a bridge we'd cross when it was time.

But then you came back from war, and whatever you'd seen and done there, you weren't right, and I knew it wasn't the time to ask. Somehow the time never did seem right. So if I was to tell you that I got used to having Shae around, even as she was, maybe you can understand that, and I hope forgive me for it.

It never seemed like all of her was gone.

The Woodwalker could've done much worse to her body, and I think it's held on to her soul. What I believe is that it didn't end her life for good, but took it to hold onto awhile.

Why else would the Woodwalker have bothered to bring her back to the house?

◄○►

My sister saw the Woodwalker once, so she'd claimed, looking at two dead deer, and the reason she'd known it was no hunter was because hunters don't help dead deer back to their feet and send them on their way.

There's give and there's take. There's balance in everything. It was the one law none of us could hide from. Even life for life sometimes, but if Shae really did see what she thought she had, I wondered what she *hadn't* seen—what life the Woodwalker had deemed forfeit for the deer's.

As I went about the ugliest business of my life, I thought of the moonshiners from the tale Mrs. Tepovich had told Ray as a boy—how they'd burned out a stretch of woodland and fields, and the grotesque fate they'd all met. But Grandma Evvie, as it turned out, had a different take on what had happened, and why the woods and crops rebounded so quickly after the fire.

"That story about Old Hickory Bones your Aunt Pol told you?" This was the last thing I said to Ray. "It's basically true, except she was wrong about one thing. Or maybe she wanted to give you the lesson but spare you the worst. But the part about replacing the bones with hickory sticks? That's not something the Woodwalker does... that's the gift it expects us to give it."

Whatever else was true and wasn't, I knew this much: Grandma Evvie would never have lied about my grandfather taking part in such a grim

judgment when he was a very young man, able to swing a cast-iron mallet with ease.

Just as he must've done, I cut and sliced, pounded and pushed, hurry-
ing to get it finished before the last of the golden autumn light left the
sky, until what I'd made looked something like a crucified scarecrow. It
glistened and dripped, and for as terrible a sight as it was, I'd still seen
worse in war. When I stood back to take it in, wrapped in the enormous
roar of woodland silence, I realized that my grandmother's faith in me
to do such a thing wasn't entirely a compliment.

Gina hadn't watched, hadn't even been able to listen, so she'd spent the
time singing to Shae, any song she could think of, as she prepared my
sister's body. She curled her among the roots of a great oak, resting on a
bed of leaves and draped with a blanket of creepers and vines. How much
was instruction and how much was instinct grew blurred, but it seemed
right. She shivered beneath Shae's real blanket after she was done, and
after I'd cleaned myself up inside the trailer, I held her awhile as she cried
for any of a hundred good reasons. Then I built a fire and we waited.

You let yourself hope but explain things away. No telling why that pile
of leaves rustled, why that vine seemed to twitch. Anything could've done
it. Flames flickered and shadows danced, while something watched us
in the night—something tall enough to tangle clouds in its hair, small
enough to hide in an acorn—and the forest ebbed and flowed with the
magnitude of its slow, contemplative breath.

A hand first, or maybe it was a foot… something moved, too deliberate, too human, to explain away as anything else. Eight years since I'd
heard her voice, but I recognized it instantly in the cough that came
from beneath the shadows and vines. Gina and I dug, and we pulled, and
scraped away leaves, and in the tangled heart of it all there was life, and
now only one reason to cry. Shae coughed a long time, scrambling in a
panic across the forest floor, her limbs too weak to stand, her voice too
weak to scream, and I wondered if she was back at that moment eight
years gone, reliving what it was like to die.

We held her until, I hoped, she thought it was just another dream.

I cupped her face, her cheeks still cold, but the fire gave them a flush
of life. "Do you know me?"

Her voice was a dry rasp. "You look like my brother… only older."

She had so painfully much to learn. I wondered if the kindest thing wouldn't be to keep her at the house until we'd taught each other everything about where we'd been the last eight years, and the one thing I hadn't considered until now was what if she wasn't right, in ways we could never fix, in ways beyond wrong, and it seemed like the best thing for everybody would be to send her back again.

For now, though, I had too much to learn myself.

"Take her back to the house," I told Gina. "I'll catch up when I can."

They both looked at me like I was sending them out among the wolves. But somebody, somewhere, was expecting what had just been cooked up in the trailer.

"And tell them not to put the place up for sale. I'll need it myself."

It was Shae, with the wisdom of the dead, who intuited it first, with a look on her face that asked *What did you do, Dylan, what did you do?*

I kissed them both on their cold cheeks, and turned toward the trailer before I could turn weak, and renege on the harshest terms of the trade.

Because there's give and there's take. There are balances to be kept. And there's a time in everyone's life when we realize we've become what we hate the most.

I was the bringer of plague now. There could be no other way.

And though I knew it would be a blessed endeavor, they still couldn't die fast enough.

⟜⟨o⟩⟞

FINAL GIRL THEORY

A.C. WISE

Everyone knows the opening sequence of *Kaleidoscope*. Even if they've never seen any other part of the movie (and they have, even if they won't admit it), they know the opening scene. No matter what anyone tells you, it is the most famous two and a half minutes ever put on film.

The camera is focused on a man's hand. He's holding a small shard of green glass, no bigger than his fingernail. He tilts it, catching the light, which darts like a crazed firefly. Then, so very carefully and with loving slowness, he presses the glass into something soft and white.

The camera is so tight the viewer can't see what he's pushing the glass into (but they suspect). Can you imagine that moment of realization for someone who *doesn't* know? Watch the opening sequence with a *Kaleidoscope* virgin sometime, you'll understand. The man pushes the glass into the soft white, and moves his hand away. A bead of bright red blood appears.

As the blood threads away from the glass, the sound kicks in. Only then do most people notice its absence before and discover how unsettling silence can be. The first sound is a breath. Or is it? Kaleidophiles (yes, they really call themselves that) have worn out old copies of the film playing that split-second transition from silence to sound over and over again. They've stripped their throats raw arguing. *Does* someone catch their breath, and if so, *who*?

There are varying theories, the two most popular being the man with the glass and the director. The third, of course, is that the man with the glass and the director are the same person.

Breath or no breath, the viewer slowly becomes aware they are listening to the sound of muffled sobs. At that moment of realization, as if prompted by it thus making the viewer complicit right from the start, the camera swings up wildly. We see a woman's wide, rolling eyes, circled with too much make-up. The camera jerk-pans down to her mouth; it's stuffed with a dirty rag.

The soundtrack comes up full force—blaring terrible horns and dissonant chords. The notes jangle one against the next. It isn't music, it's instruments screaming. It's sound felt in your back teeth and at the base of your spine.

The camera zooms out, showing the woman spread-eagle and naked, tied to a massive wheel. Her skin is filled with hundreds of pieces of colored glass—red, blue, yellow, green. Her tormentor steps back; the viewer never sees his face. He rips the gag out, and spins the wheel. Thousands of firefly glints dazzle the camera.

The woman screams. The screen dissolves in a mass of spinning color, and the opening credits roll.

You know what the worst part is? The opening sequence has nothing to do with the rest of the film. It is what it is; it exists purely for its own sake.

But let's go back to the scream. It's important. It starts out high-pitched, classic scream queen, and devolves into something ragged, wet, and bubbling. If there was any nagging doubt left about what kind of movie *Kaleidoscope* really is, it's gone. But it's too late. Remember, the viewer is complicit; they agreed to everything that follows in that split second between silence and sound, between sob and catch of breath. They can't turn back—not that anyone really tries.

Here's another thing about *Kaleidoscope*—no one ever watches it just once; don't let them tell you otherwise.

The opening is followed by eighty-five minutes of color-soaked, blood-drenched, action. (Except—if you're paying attention—you know that's a lie.)

The movie is a cult classic. It's shown on football fields, on giant, impromptu screens made of sheets strung between goalposts. It flickers in midnight double feature theaters, lurid colors washing over men and women hunched and sweating in the dark, feet stuck to crackling floors, breathing air reeking of stale popcorn. It plays in the background, miniaturized on ghostly television screens, while burn-outs fuck at 3 a.m., lit by candles meant to disguise the scent of beer and pot.

Here's the real secret: *Kaleidoscope* isn't a movie, it's an infection, whispered from mouth to mouth in the dark.

Hardcore fans have every line memorized (not that there are many). They know the plot back and forth (though there isn't one of those, either). You see, that's the beauty of *Kaleidoscope*, its terrible genius. It is the most famous eighty-seven and a half minutes ever committed to film (don't ever let anyone tell you otherwise), but it doesn't exist. If you were to creep through the film, frame by frame (and people have) you would know this is true.

Kaleidoscope exists in people's minds. It exists in the brief, flickering space between frames. The *real* movie screen is the inside of their eyelids, the back of their skulls when they close their eyes and try to sleep. When the film rolls, there is action and blood, sex and drugs, and not a little touch of madness, but there are shadows, too. There are things seen from the corner of the eye, and that's where the true movie lies. There, and in the rumors.

Jackson Mortar has heard them all. Crew members died or went missing during the shoot (or there was no crew); a movie house burned to the ground during the first screening (the doors were locked from the inside); fans have been arrested trying to recreate the movie's most famous scenes (the very best never get caught); and, of course, the most persistent rumor of all: everything in the movie—the sex, the drugs, the violence, and yes, even the flickering shadows—is one hundred percent real.

◂•▸

"You know that scene in the graveyard, with Carrie, when Lance is leading the voodoo ceremony to bring Lucy back from the dead?" Kevin leans across the table, half-eaten burger forgotten in his hand.

Jackson nods. He traces the maze on the kiddie menu, and refuses to look up. Kevin is a fresh convert. Like moths to flame, somehow they always know—when it comes to *Kaleidoscope*, Jackson Mortar is the man. Jackson supposes that makes him part of the mythology, in a way, and he should be proud. But his stomach flips, growling around a knot of cold fries. He pushes the remains of his meal away, rescuing his soda from Kevin's enthusiastic hand-talking.

"And you know how Carrie is writhing on the tomb, and the big snake is crawling all over her body, between her tits and between her legs, like it's *doing* her, and she's moaning and Lance is pouring blood all over her?" Kevin grins, painful-wide; Jackson can hear it, even without looking up.

"Yeah, what about it?"

"Do you think it's real?"

Jackson finally raises his head. Sweat beads Kevin's upper lip; his burger is disintegrating in his hand. A trace of fear ghosts behind the bravado in his eyes.

"Maybe." Jackson keeps his tone as neutral.

The glimpse of fear gives him hope for Kevin, but Kevin's smile does him in. Maybe the kid sees more than the sex and drugs and blood, but that's all he *wants* to see. Kevin has seen *Kaleidoscope*, and wishes the movie was otherwise. That, Jackson cannot abide.

"Listen, I gotta get going." Jackson stands. "I got work to do."

"Oh, okay. Sure." Kevin's expression falls. Another flicker of unease skitters across his face.

Guilt needles Jackson—he can't leave the kid alone like this—but Kevin pastes it over with another goofy, sloppy grin. "Maybe we can catch a midnight screening together sometime?"

Jackson's pity dissolves; he shrugs into his worn, black trench coat, "Yeah, sure. Sometime."

Jackson squeezes out of the booth. Kevin turns back to his cold hamburger. Jackson wonders how the kid stays so skinny. As he pushes through the restaurant door, out into the near-blinding sun, Jackson tries to remember to hate Kevin for the right reasons, not just because he's young and thin.

Jackson steps off the curb, and freezes. Across the street, on the other side of the world and close enough to touch, Carrie Linden walks through a slant of sunlight. She glances behind her, peering over the top of bug-large sunglasses, which almost swallow her face. She hunches into her collar, pulls open the pharmacy door, and darts inside.

A car horn blares. Jackson leaps back, the spell broken. His heart pounds. No one has seen any of the actors from *Kaleidoscope* since the movie was filmed. There are no interviews, no 'Where Are They Now?' specials on late night TV. It plays into the mystique, as though *Kaleidoscope* might truly be a mass hallucination thrown up on the silver screen. No one real has ever been associated with the film. The credits list the director as B. Z. Bubb and the writer as Lou Cypher.

It's been nearly forty years since *Kaleidoscope* was filmed, five years before Jackson was born (but long before he was *really* born). But Jackson knows it's her; he would know Carrie Linden anywhere.

Jackson has been in love with Carrie Linden his whole life. (Yes, he considers the first time he saw *Kaleidoscope* as the moment he was born.)

When Carrie Linden first appeared on the screen, Jackson forgot how to breathe. The scene is burned into his retinas; it, more than anything else, is his private, skull-thrown midnight show. He sees it on thin, blood-lined lids every time he closes his eyes.

Jackson refrains from telling anyone this unless he knows they'll really understand (and fellow Kaleidophiles always do). The problem—the reason he can't say anything to converts and virgins—is that the first part of Carrie Linden to appear on screen is her ass.

It's during the party scene. She walks across the camera from left to right. Long hair hangs down her back, dirty blonde, wavy, split ends brushing the curve of her buttocks. She wears ropes of glittering beads, but the viewer doesn't know that yet. They are the same beads used to whip Elizabeth in the very next scene, horribly disfiguring her face, but the viewer doesn't know that yet, either.

What the viewer knows is this: Carrie Linden walks across the screen from left to right. She climbs onto the lap of a man at least twice her age. She fucks him as he lifts tiny scoops of cocaine up to her nose, balancing them delicately on the end of an over-long fingernail.

The first time the viewer sees Carrie's face, she is sprawled naked on the couch. The camera pans up from her toes, pausing at her chest. Her breathing is erratic, shallow, then deep, then panicked—fast—a jackrabbit lives under her skin. Her head lolls to one side, her eyes are blissfully (or nightmare-chokedly) closed. A trickle of blood runs from her nose.

While Carrie sleeps, but hopefully doesn't dream, Elizabeth is whipped with Carrie's beads. Elizabeth screams. She's on her knees, and sometimes it looks as though she's stretching her hands out toward Carrie. Some viewers (Kaleidophiles, all) have made the comparison to various religious paintings. Elizabeth's face is a sheet of blood. When she collapses, her torturer steps over her, and drops the bloody beads around Carrie's neck. Almost as an afterthought he sticks his hand between Carrie's legs before wandering away. She doesn't react at all.

Jackson stares at the pharmacy door for so long that the woman he *knows* is Carrie Linden has time to conclude her business and slip out again, still darting glances over her shoulder as she hurries away. Once she's disappeared around the corner, Jackson dashes across the street, ignoring traffic. He yanks open the pharmacy door, and runs panting to the back counter. Luckily, Justin is working. Justin is a *Kaleidoscope* fan, too. (Aren't we all?)

"Hey, buddy. Here to get your prescription filled?" Justin winks.

Jackson ignores him, trying to catch his breath. "The woman who just left, did you see her?"

"Yeah. Dark hair and glasses? Not bad for an older broad." Justin's grin reminds Jackson of Kevin. He wants to reach across the counter and throttle Justin, who is skinny too, but old enough to know better. He's older than Jackson (not counting *Kaleidoscope* years, of course).

"Percocet," Justin says as an afterthought. He has no compunctions about confidentiality. If he didn't know the owner too well, he'd have been fired a long time ago.

"Can you get me her address?" Jackson asks. His mind whirls (like colors dissolving behind a credit roll while a woman screams).

"Sure." Justin shrugs. No questions asked—that's what Jackson likes about him. Justin consults his computer and chicken scrawls an address on the back of an old receipt.

"Thanks, man. I owe you!" Jackson snatches the paper, spins, and sprints for the door.

"Hey, who is she?" Justin calls after him.

"Carrie Linden!" Jackson slams through the door, answering only because he knows Justin won't believe him.

The name written over the address Justin gave him is Karen Finch. The address isn't five blocks from the pharmacy. Jackson runs the whole way, heaving his bulk, dripping sweat, legs burning, breath wheezing. It's worth a heart attack, worth the return of his childhood asthma, worth anything.

The street he arrives on is tree-lined and shadow-dappled. Cars border both sides of the road, dogs bark in backyards, and two houses over a group of children run in shrieking circles on an emerald lawn.

Jackson approaches number forty-seven. He's shaking. His mouth is dry in a way that has nothing to do with his mad, panting run. His heart pounds, louder than the dying echoes of his fist knocking against Carrie Linden's door. What is he doing? He should leave. But *Kaleidoscope* isn't that kind of movie. It isn't a movie at all. It's an infection, deep in Jackson's blood.

The door opens; Jackson stares.

Light frames the woman in a soft-focus glow, falling through a window at the far end of the hall. Her hair is dyed dark, but showing threads of gray (or maybe they're dirty blonde). The ends are split and frayed. She isn't wearing sunglasses, but shadows circle her eyes, seeming just as large. She is thin—not in a pretty way; her cheekbones knife against her skin. But she *is* Carrie Linden, and Jackson forgets how to breathe.

The second most famous scene in *Kaleidoscope* is the carnival scene. It's the one most viewers (not Kaleidophiles, mind you) rewind to watch over and over again. It's spawned numerous chat groups, websites, message boards, and one doctoral thesis, which languishes untouched in a drawer.

The scene goes like this: the characters go to a carnival—Carrie, Lance, Mary, and Josh, even Elizabeth, even though her face is horribly scarred (but not Lucy, because she's dead). The carnival is abandoned, but all the lights are on and all the rides are running. The night flickers with halogen-sick lights, illuminating painted rides and gaudy-bright games. The whole scene drifts, strange and unreal.

The gang rides the funhouse ride. But it's not just a funhouse, it's a haunted house, a hall of mirrors, and tunnel of love all rolled into one. The cars crank along the track, but jerk to a stop in the first room, as if the ride is broken. They wander through the ride on foot. And this is where the movie gets weird.

It fragments. Time stops. (Do any two viewers see the same scene?)

The camera follows scarred Elizabeth; it follows meathead Lance. It follows Carrie Linden. Voices whisper, words play backwards, things slide, half-glimpsed, across the corners of the film, at the very *edges*, spilling off the celluloid and into the dark. (Is it any wonder the movie house burned down?)

The funhouse is filled with painted flats and cheesy rubber monsters loaded on springs. But there are also angles that shouldn't exist, reflections where there should be none.

There are odd, jerky cuts in the film itself, loops, backward stutters, and doubled scenes, as if bits of films are being run through a projector at the same time. It's impossible.

Everyone is separated, utterly alone. The strange twists of the mirrored corridors keep them apart, even when they are only inches away. And here debates rage, because something happens, but no one is quite sure what.

Maybe Carrie Linden steps through a mirror into the room where Elizabeth is raking bloody nails against the glass, trying to escape. Some viewers claim that it isn't really Carrie, because she stepped through a mirror too. (Inside the funhouse, is anyone who they used to be?) What follows is brutal. With eerie, cold precision Carrie tortures Elizabeth. Accounts vary. Is blood actually drawn, or is the pain more subtle, more insidious than that? (What did *you* see? What do you *think* you saw?)

What makes the violence even more shocking is that up until this point in the film, Carrie has been utterly passive. (Is it possible to watch her push a sliver of mirrored glass through Elizabeth's cheek and not feel it in your own?) Elizabeth's face fills with terror, but oddly, she doesn't seem to notice Carrie at all. Her gaze darts to the mirrors. Her panicked glances skitter into the shadows.

She look straight at the camera, and tears roll silently from her eyes.

Four people leave the funhouse at the end of the scene—Carrie, Josh, Elizabeth and Lance. (Do they?) Mary is never seen again. Her absence is never explained. It's that kind of film.

The crux of the movie hangs here. Kaleidophiles know if they could just unravel this scene, they'd understand everything. (Do they really want to?) When she leaves the funhouse, what is Carrie holding in her hand? Was there really a reflection in the mirror behind Elizabeth's head? When Carrie leans down and puts her mouth against Elizabeth's ear, what does she whisper?

"Can I help you?" The woman's voice snaps Jackson back to himself. His skin flushes hot; panic constricts his throat.

The woman flickers and doubles. Carrie Linden (or Karen Finch) is here and now, but she is there and then too. Jackson shudders.

Something passes through the woman's eyes, a kind of recognition. It's as though all these years Jackson has been watching her, she's been looking right back at him.

"You're Carrie Linden," he says. His voice is thick and far away.

Her expression turns hard. Jackson sees the cold impulse to violence; for a moment, she wants to hurt him. Instead, she steps aside, her voice tight. "You'd better come inside."

Jackson squeezes past her, close enough to touch. He catches her scent—patchouli, stale cigarettes, and even staler coffee. Her posture radiates hatred; her bones are blades, aching towards his skin. When they are face to face, Jackson glimpses the truth in her eyes—she's been expecting this moment. Carrie Linden has been running her whole life, knowing sooner or later someone will catch her.

She shuts the door—a final sound. Jackson's heart skips, jitters erratically, worse than when he ran all the way here. Carrie gestures to a room opening up to the left.

"Sit. I'll make coffee."

She leaves him, disappearing down the narrow hall. Jackson lowers himself onto a futon covered with a tattered blanket. Upended apple crates flank it at either end. A coffee table sits between the futon and a nest-shaped chair. The walls are painted blood-rust red; they are utterly bare.

Carrie returns with mismatched mugs and hands him one. It's spider-webbed with near-invisible cracks, the white ceramic stained beige around the rim. The side of the mug bears an incongruous rainbow, arching away from a fluffy white cloud. Jackson sips, and almost chokes. The coffee is scalding black; she doesn't offer him milk or sugar.

Carrie Linden sits in the nest chair, tucking bare feet beneath her. She wears a chunky sweater coat. It looks hand-knit, and it nearly swallows her. She meets Jackson's gaze, so he can't possibly look away.

"Well, what do you want to know?" Her voice snaps, dry-stick brittle and hard.

Jackson can't speak for his heart lodged in his throat. There's a magic to watching *Kaleidoscope* (unless you watch it alone). The people on screen dying and fucking and screaming and weeping, they're just shadows. It's *okay* to watch; it's safe. None of it is real.

Motes of dust fall through the light around Carrie Linden—tiny, erratic fireflies. The curtains are mostly drawn, but the sun knifes through, leaving the room blood hot.

"All of it," Carries says, when Jackson can't find the words.

"What?" He gapes, mouth wide.

"That's what you're wondering, isn't it? That's what they all want to know. The answer is—all of it. All of it was real."

Jackson flinches as though he's been punched in the gut. (In a way, he has.) Should he feel guiltier about the cracked light in her eyes, or the fact that his stomach dropped when she said "that's what they all want to know"? He isn't her first.

Carrie Linden's hands wrap around her mug, showing blue veins and fragile bones. Steam rises, curling around her face. When she raises the mug to sip, her sleeve slides back defiantly and unapologetically revealing scars.

"Well?" Carrie's gaze follows the line of Jackson's sight. "Why *did* you come, then?"

She bores into him with piercing-bright eyes, and Jackson realizes—even sitting directly across from her—he can't tell what color they are. They are every color and no color at once, as if her body is just a shell housing the infinite possibilities living inside.

"I wanted to talk about the movie. I thought maybe…" Jackson glances desperately around the bare-walled room—nowhere to run. In his head, he's rehearsed this moment a thousand times. He's *always* known exactly what he'll say to Carrie Linden when he finally meets her, but now it's all gone wrong.

I'm sorry, he wants to say, I shouldn't have come, but the words stick in his throat. His eyes sting. He's failed. In the end, he's no better than Justin, or Kevin. He's not a Kaleidophile, he hasn't transcended the sex and gore—he's just another wanna-be.

Unable to look Carrie in the eye, Jackson fumbles a postcard out of his coat pocket. The edges are frayed and velvet-soft through years of wear. It's the original movie poster for *Kaleidoscope*, wrought in miniature. Jackson found it at a garage sale last year, and he's been carrying it around ever since. He passes it to Carrie with shaking hands.

As Carrie looks down to study the card, Jackson finally looks up. Like the movie, Jackson knows the card by heart, but now he sees it through Carrie's eyes; he's never loathed himself more. His eyes burn with the lurid color, the jumbled images piled together and bleeding into one.

The backdrop is a carnival, but it's also a graveyard, or maybe an empty field backed with distant trees. A woman studded with fragments of glass lies spread-eagle on a great wheel. Between her legs, Carrie lies on an altar, covered in writhing snakes. Behind Carrie, Elizabeth's blood-sheeted face hangs like a crimson moon. From the black of her wide open eyes, shadowy figures seep out and stain the other images. They hide behind and inside everything, doubling and ghosting and blurring. The card isn't one thing, it's everything.

"I'm sorry." Jackson finally manages the words aloud.

Slowly, Carrie reaches for a pen lying atop of a half-finished crossword puzzle. Her hand moves, more like a spasm than anything voluntary. The nib scratches across the card's back, slicing skin and bone and soul. She lets the card fall onto the table between them, infinitely kind and infinitely cruel. Jackson thinks the tears welling in his eyes are the only things that save him.

"It's okay," she says. Her voice is not quite forgiving. For a moment, Jackson has the mad notion she might fold him in her bony arms and soothe him like a child, as though he's the one that needs, or deserves, comforting.

Instead, Carrie leans forward and opens a drawer in the coffee table, fishing out a pack of cigarettes. Something rattles and slithers against the wood as the drawer slides closed. Jackson catches a glimpse, and catches his breath. Even after forty years he imagines the beads still sticky and warm, still slicked with Elizabeth's blood.

Carrie lights her cigarette, and watches the patterns the smoke makes in the air, in shadows on the wall. They don't quite match.

"I'm the final girl," she says. The softness of her voice makes Jackson jump. He doesn't think she's even speaking to him anymore. She might as well be alone. (She's always been alone.)

"What?" Jackson says, even though he knows exactly what she's talking about. His voice quavers.

"It's fucking bullshit, you know that?" Her voice is just as soft as before if the words are harsher. "I wasn't a helpless fantasy at the beginning; I wasn't an empowered hero at the end. I was just me the whole time. I was just human."

She stands, crushing her cigarette against the cupped palm of her hand without flinching. "You can stay if you want. Or you can go. I don't really care."

And just like that she's gone. Jackson is alone with Carrie Linden's blood-red walls and her battered couch, with her beads hidden in the coffee table drawer, and her autograph on a worn-soft postcard. When she walked onto the screen, Carrie Linden stopped Jackson's heart; walking out of the room, she stops it again.

He sees Carrie Linden doubled, trebled—bony-thin hips hidden beneath a bulky sweater; the curve of her naked ass, teased by long blonde hair as she saunters across the screen; a hunted, haunted woman, glancing behind her as she darts into the drug store.

Jackson has sunk so low, he can't go any lower. (At least that's what he tells himself as he leaves to make it okay.)

At home, Jackson hides the postcard and Carrie Linden's beads at the bottom of his drawer. He covers them with socks and underwear, wadded t-shirts smelling of his sweat and late night popcorn, ripe with fear and desire.

It doesn't matter how rare the postcard is, never mind that it's signed by Carrie Linden; he'll never show it to anyone, or even take it out of the drawer. The beads are another matter.

◂◦▸

Everyone knows the opening sequence of *Kaleidoscope*, but it's the closing sequence plays in most people's minds, projected against the ivory curve of their dreaming skulls, etched onto the thinness of their eyelids. It bathes the late-night stupors of lone losers curled on their couches with the blankets pulled up to their chins against the flickering dark. It haunts midnight movie screens in rooms smelling of sticky-sweet spills and stale salt. It looms large on sheets stretched between goal posts, while orgies wind down on the battered turf below.

It is the third most famous scene in cinema history. (Don't let anyone tell you otherwise.)

Carrie is running. Everybody else is dead—Lance and Lucy, Elizabeth and Josh and Mary, and all the other brief phantoms who never even had names. She is covered in blood. Some of it is hers. She is naked.

Ahead of her is a screen of trees. More than once, Carrie stumbles and falls. When she does, the camera shows the soles of her feet, slick and red. But she keeps getting back up, again and again. The camera judders as it follows her. It draws close, but never quite catches up.

Carrie glances back over her shoulder, eyes staring wide at something the camera never turns to let the viewer see. (Imagination isn't always the worst thing.) Carrie's expression (hunted and haunted) says it all.

There is no soundtrack, no psychedelic colors. The only sound is Carrie's feet slapping over sharp stones and broken bottles and her breath hitching in her throat. She's running for the grass and the impossibly distant trees.

The credits roll.

The screen goes dark.

But Carrie is still there, between the frames, bleeding off the edges, flickering in the shadows. She'll always be right there, forever, running.

—◦—

OMPHALOS

LIVIA LLEWELLYN

Vacation doesn't begin when Father pulls the Volkswagen camper out of the driveway, and speeds through the sleepy Tacoma streets toward Narrows Bridge. It doesn't begin on the long stretches of Route 16 through Gig Harbor, Port Orchard, and Bremerton, your twin brother Jaime fast asleep beside you on the warm back seat, his dark blond hair falling over his eyes. It doesn't begin with the hasty lunch at the small restaurant outside Poulsbo, where your father converses with the worn folds of the triple-A map as your mother slips the receipt into a carefully labeled, accordioned envelope. 16 whittles down to 3, blossoms into 104 as the camper crosses Hood Canal onto the Olympic Peninsula, and still your vacation does not begin. Discovery Bay, Sequim, Dungeness: all the feral playgrounds of vacations and summers past: no. It is in Port Angeles, under a storm-whipped sky, against the backdrop of Canada-bound ferries gorging their wide, toothless mouths on rivers of slow-moving cars, when Father turns away from your mother, thin-lipped and tearful from the forced confession that another envelope holding four passports sits on the quiet kitchen counter back in Tacoma. You roll your eyes. Why do they go to such trouble of pretense? Oh, yes: for the neighbors. For the pastor, for colleagues and relatives, for all the strangers and passers-by who wouldn't understand, who want to hear only the

189

normal. Father sees the look on your face, and takes you aside as his large flat thumb rubs against your cotton-clad arm in that old familiar way, that way you've known all of your fifteen long and lonely years, the way that always sends your mind into the flat black void. Old Spice tickles your nose, and you rub the itch away as Jaime scowls, the color fading from his perfect face like the sun.

"Don't worry, June-Bug. I know a place. Better than Victoria. No distractions, no tourists. Where there's nothing at all. You know the place. You've been there, before. It's where you always go." He places his calloused finger at the center of your forehead, and you almost piss yourself in fear: does he know?

"Where we can—you know."

Your mother takes Jamie aside, her fingers sliding around his slender waist as she spins her own version of the same tale. Father winks and parts his lips, coffee and cigarette breath drifting across your face as he whispers in your ear.

"Be alone."

Vacation has begun.

◂∘▸

Salt ocean air and the cries of gulls recede as Father guides the camper through Port Angeles. You wish you could stay, walk through the postcard-pretty gingerbread-housed streets with Jaime, shop for expensive knick-knacks you don't need, daydream of a life you'll never have. Father drives on. Office buildings and shopping districts give slow way to industrial parks and oversized construction sheds surrounded by rusting bulldozers and dump trucks. None of it looks permanent, not even the highway. 101 lengthens like overworked taffy into a worn, three-lane patchwork of blacktop and tar. Campers and flat-beds, station wagons and Airstreams all whoosh across its surface, with you and against you. Port into town, town into suburbs, suburbs into the beyond. The sun has returned in vengeance, and all the grey clouds have whipped away over the waters, following the ferry you were never meant to take.

"Once we're off the highway, we can follow the logging roads," Father shouts over the roaring wind as he steers the camper down the Olympic Highway. He sounds excited, almost giddy. "They'll take us deep into the Park, past the usual campgrounds and tourist spots, past the Ranger Stations, right into the heart of the forest. And then, once the logging roads have ended—well, look at the map. Just see how far we can go."

You stare at the silhouette of his head, dark against the dirty brilliance of the window shield. One calloused hand rests on the steering wheel, one hand on your mother's shoulder. His fingers play with the gold hoop at her ear, visible under the short pixie cut of grey-brown hair. She turns to him, her cheek rising as she smiles. They remind you of how you and Jamie must look together: siblings, alike and in love, always together. Father and you used to look like that. Now you and he look different. You clench your jaw, look away, look down.

"It's not even noon, we should be able to make it to Lake Mills by this afternoon—"

Your mother interrupts him. "That far? We'll never make it to Windy Arm by then, it's too far." So that's your destination. You've been there before, you know how much she loves the lake, the floating, abandoned logs, the placid humming of birds.

"Not this time, remember? We're taking Hot Springs Road over to the logging roads. Tomorrow we'll start out early, and we should be there by sundown."

"But there's nothing—wait, isn't Hot Springs closed? Or parts of it? I thought we going down Hurricane Ridge." Your mother looks confused. Evidently, they didn't make all the vacation plans together. Interesting.

"It's still drivable, and there won't be any traffic—that's the point. To get away from everyone. Don't worry."

"Aren't we going back home?" Jaime asks. "Where are we going?"

"We're not going all the way to the end of Hot Springs, anyway," Father continues over Jamie. "I told you we're taking the logging roads, they go deeper into the mountains. We already mapped this all out, last week."

"We didn't discuss this." Your mother has put on her "we need to speak in private" voice.

"Take a look at the map. June has it," Father says.

"I don't need to look at the map, I know where we planned on going. I mean, this is ridiculous—where in heaven's name do you think you're taking us to?"

"I said we're going all the way." His hand slides away from her shoulder, back to the wheel.

"All the way to where?"

"All the way to the end."

The map Father gave you to hold is an ordinary one, a rectangular sheaf of thick paper that unfolds into a table-sized version of your state. Jamie scoots closer to you as you struggle with the folds, his free hand resting light on your bare thigh, just below your shorts. His hands are large and gentle, like the paws of a young German Shepherd. You move your forehead close, until your bangs mingle with his, and together you stare down at the state you were born in, and all its familiar nooks and crevices. In the upper corner is your small city—you trace your route across the water and up the right hand side of the peninsula to Port Angeles, then down. The park and mountains are a blank green mass, and there are no roads to be seen.

You lift the edge of the map that rests on your legs, and dark markings well up from the other side. "Turn it over to the other side," you say.

"Just a minute." He holds his side tight, so you lift your edge up as you lower your head, peering. The other side of the paper is the enlarged, fang-shaped expanse of the Olympic Mountain Range. Small lines, yellow and pink and dotted and straight, fan around and around an ocean devoid of the symbols of cartography, where even the logging roads have not thrust themselves into. You can see where your father has circled small points throughout various squares, connecting each circle with steady blue dashes that form a line. Underneath his lines, you see the lavender ink of your mother's hand, a curving line that follows Whiskey Road to its end just before Windy Arm. Over all those lines, though, over all those imagined journeys, someone has drawn another road, another way to the interior of the park. It criss-crosses back and forth, overlapping the forests like a net until it ends at the edges of a perfect circle—several perfect circles, in fact, one inside another inside another, like a three-lane road. Like a cage. The circles encloses nothing—nothing you can see on the map, anyway, because nothing is in the center except mountains and snow, nothing the mapmakers thought worth drawing, nothing they could see. The circles enclose only a single word:

Χάος

Someone has printed it in the naked center of the brown-inked circles, across the mountains you've only ever seen as if in a dream, as smoky grey ridges floating far above the neat rooftops of your little neighborhood, hundreds of miles away. Letters of brown, dark brown like dried-up scratches of blood—not Father's handwriting, and not your mother's.

"Do you see that?" you ask Jamie. "Did you write that?"

"Write what?" He's still on the other side of the state. He doesn't see anything. He doesn't care.

You brush a fingertip onto the word. It feels warm, and a bit ridged. "Help me," you whisper to it, even though you're not sure to who or what you're speaking, or why. The words come out of your mouth without thought. They are the same words you whisper at night, when Father presses against you, whispering his own indecipherable litany into your ears. Your finger presses down harder against the paper, until it feels you'll punch a hole all the way through the mountains. "Save me. Take me away. Take it all away."

The word squirms.

Goosebumps cascade across your skin, a brushfire of premonition. As you lower your edge of the map, Jamie's fingers clench down onto your thigh. Perhaps he mistakes the prickling heat of your skin for something else. You don't dissuade him. Under the thick protection of the paper, hidden from your parents' eyes, your fingers weave through his, soaking up his heat and sweat; and your legs press together, sticking in the roaring heat of engine and sun-soaked wind. Your hand travels onto his thigh, resting at the edge of his shorts where the whorls of your fingertips glide across golden strands of hair, until you feel the start, the beginning of him, silky soft, and begin to rub back and forth, gently. His cock twitches, stiffens, and his breath warms your shoulder in deep bursts, quickening. You know what he loves.

"Do you see where we're headed to?" Father asks.

Hidden and unseen, Jamie's hand returns the favor, traveling up your leg. You feel the center of yourself unclench, just a little. Just enough. Raising the map again, you peek at the word. After all these years and so many silent pleas, has something finally heard? Face flush with shock, you bite your lower lip so as not to smile. You stare out the window, eyes hidden behind sticky sunglasses, watching the decayed ends of Port Townsend dribble away into the trees, watching the woods rise up to meet the road, the prickly skin of an ancient beast, slumbering and so very, very ready to awaken.

You want to believe, but you shouldn't. Belief is an empty promise. Belief just leads back to the void. You shouldn't want to believe, but you will. This time, just this once, you will.

"Yes," you say. "Yes, I do."

◄o►

The beginning of a journey is always deception. The beginning always appears beautiful, as a mirage. Once you fold the map away, there's laughter and music, jokes and gentle pinches, and the heady anticipation of traveling someplace new, all of you together, a family like any other family in the world. Sunlight drenches the windows and you laugh at the sight—so many prisms and prickles of color, glitter-balling the camper's dull brown interior into a jewelry box. After half an hour, your mother unbuckles her seat belt and makes her way across the porta-potty, wedged in between the small refrigerator and the tiny bench with its fake leather cushions that hide the bulk of the food.

"Something to eat—a snack? We had lunch so early." Your mother raises the folding table up, fixing the single leg to the camper's linoleum floor, then pulls sandwiches and small boxes of juice from the fridge, passing them up to Father. She's a good wife, attentive. Jamie drinks a Coke, wiping beads of sweat from its bright red sides onto his t-shirt. You pick at your bread, rolling it into hard balls before popping them into your mouth. The camper is traveling at a slight incline, and the right side of the highway peels away, revealing sloping hills that form the eastern edge of the Peninsula. You think of the ferry, of all that cool, wide ocean, waters without end, in which all things are hidden, in which all things can be contained.

"Can we stop?" You point to a small grocery stand and gas station coming up ahead to the right, overlooking a rest stop and lookout point.

Your mother points to the porta-potty. "You need to go?"

"No." You feel yourself recoil. "No, I just—I just thought we could stop for a while. I'm getting a little queasy." It's true, you get carsick, sometimes. You think of the curved slope beyond the rest stop, and how easy it'd be to slip over the rail guard as you pretend to be sick. You think of the water, so close you can almost see it. "While we can."

Your father doesn't slow the camper. "Sorry, June-Bug. We need to keep going."

You nod your head. "Sure. No problem." You think about what you've just said, and decide that it's not a lie. Running away would mean you didn't really believe that the word moved, that something out there in the mountains is weaving its way to you, some beautiful, dangerous god coming to save the queen. You want to stay. Just this once, you want to see your miracle.

Outside, 101 splits off, part of it flying off and up the coast to Neah Bay as the newly-formed 112. Now the landscape morphs, too, sloughing off yet more buildings and houses. A certain raw, ugly quality descends all around. The highway curves away, and with it, the store, the land. You're going in a different direction now. No use to think of ferries and guard rails anymore.

Jamie pulls out a deck of cards. They fan out and snap back into themselves as he shuffles them again and again. Your mother leans back against the small bench, watching him deal the cards. Go Fish—their favorite game. You've never liked games. You don't believe in luck or chance. You believe in fate.

Reaching to the floor, you pull a fat book out of your backpack, and turn the pages in an absentminded haze, staring at nothing as words and illustrations flow past. Ignore her, you say, ignore the two small feet, bare and crowned with nails painted a pretty coral, that appear between you and Jaime, and nestle in cozy repose at his thigh. You press yourself against the edge of the seat, forehead flat against the window, legs clamped tight, ignoring the low hum of their voices calling out the cards. It's not as if you hate your mother—you have long talks with her sometimes, she's a good listener. And she's never touched you, never like that. Sometimes, she even comes to your defense, when you can't—just can't do it anymore, when you're tired or sick or just need a break, just need an evening to yourself, to sit in your pink-ruffled bedroom and pretend you're a normal girl in a normal world. Still, though. She's your mother, not your friend, and Jamie is her favorite, just as you are Father's favorite. Sometimes you wonder if Jamie might love her more than you. That would kill you. It would be like, she's rejecting one half of you for the other, without any real reason why.

"Where did you get the map?" Why did you ask her that? You curse yourself silently. Always too curious, always wanting to know everything, and more. Like father, like daughter.

Your mother looks up from her cards, mouth pursed. Clearly she doesn't like being reminded of the map, and doesn't want to answer—or she's going to answer, but she's buying a bit of time. It's her little not-so-secret trick, her way of rebelling. Jamie does the same. Like mother, like son.

"It's just a regular map," she finally says, adjusting her hand as she speaks. "I don't know where your father got it. Maybe the car dealership? Or the 76 station on Bridgeport." She lays down a card, as you wait for the shoe to drop. Your mother is often more predictable than she'd care to admit.

"Why do you want to know?" she asks.

"Never mind."

Your mother sighs. "You know I hate it when you say that. Why did you ask?"

Jamie looks up from his cards. "She wants to know who drew the third map and the circle on it."

"The third *what*?"

"Jamie." Your voice is calm, but the biting pinch of your fingers at his thigh tells him what he needs to know. "Nothing, I meant nothing," Jamie says, but it's too late, he's said too much.

"Did you draw on the map?" Your mother's voice is hushed, conspiratorial. Together, your heads lean toward each other, voices dropping so that Father won't hear.

"No, I swear. I thought *someone* had drawn on it. That's all. That Father drew over it, where we were going to go, and someone else drew another map over those two."

"Juney, there's no third map—there's no second map. What are you talking about?"

"I—"

Now you're the one who's said too much. She places her cards on the table, and holds out one hand. The diamond on her wedding ring catches the light, hurling tiny rainbow dots across your face. "Let me see it." Her voice is low. You realize she's not just angry but afraid, and it unsettles you. Your mother is often cautious, but never afraid.

"I didn't write on it, I swear."

"I hope to God you didn't. He'll kill you—"

"What's going on back there?" Father, up in the driver's seat.

"Nothing, honey. We're playing Go Fish." She motions for the map. You pull it out from underneath your jacket, and hand it over. Your mother opens it up, spreading it across the table. Cards flutter to the floor. She stares down, hands aloft as if physically shaping her question with the uplift of her palms. From where you sit, you can see what she sees, upside down. You look up at the front of the camper. Father's sea green eyes stare back from the mirror, watching.

"Sonavu*bitch*," she whispers.

"What do you see?" I don't want to know, but I have to know. What map does she see?

"June." She throws up her hands, as if exasperated. "I have no idea what you're talking about. I see my map, which obviously your Father can't see because he obviously is ignoring everything we've been planning for the last two months, but there is no second or third set of drawings here."

"How can you not see that?" You know you see the lines, drawn over her directions and Father's. You know you see the word in the circular void. It's right there, on the paper, right in front of her. And, you know you don't want her to see, you want it to be *your* destination, the secret place only you can travel to. But you place a trembling finger onto the middle of the circle, just below the word. You have to confirm it, that your map is unseen, safe. "All these new roads, leading to this circle in the middle, leading to this word—"

Your mother raises her hand, and your voice trails away. She stares down, her brow furrowing as if studying for a test. You want to believe that the small ticks and movements of her lips, her eyelids, are the tiny cracks of the truth, seeping up from the paper and through her skin. Her fingers move just above the lines, and then away, as if deflected from the void in the middle. She moves her fingers again, her eyes following as she touches the paper. Again, deflection, and confusion drawing lazy strokes across her face, as her fingers slide somewhere north. Relief flares inside you, prickly cold, followed by hot triumph. She does not see your map.

She sees the route and destination only meant for her.

"June, honey." She leans back, thrusting the map toward as if anxious to be rid of it. "It's just coffee stains. It's a stain from the bottom of a coffee cup. See how it's shaped? Probably from your father's thermos."

"Yeah, you're right. I didn't see it until now."

"All that fuss for nothing. What were you talking about, anyway—what, did you think it was some mysterious, magical treasure map?" She laughs in that light, infectious tone you loathe so much—although, the way she rubs at the small blue vein in her right temple reveals a hidden side to her mood. "Come on, now. You're not five anymore, you're too old for this."

"Ah," you say, cheeks burning with sudden, slow anger. She's done this before, playing games with you. Long ago, like when she'd hide drawings you'd made and replace them with white paper, only to slide them out of nowhere at the last minute, when you'd worked yourself into an ecstatic frenzy of conspiracies about intervening angels or gods erasing what you'd drawn. You'd forgotten about that part of her. You'd forgotten about that part of yourself.

"It just looked like," you grasp for an explanation, "it just looked like you'd drawn your own map of our vacation, and Father drew another, and the circles looked—I mean, look…" The explanation fades.

"Sweetie, calm down." Your mother tousles your hair, cropped like hers. She appears bemused now, with only a touch of concern. She doesn't believe in miracles or the divine, and sometimes she thinks you're a bit slow. "Honestly. You read too much into everything, and you get so overexcited. That's your father's fault, not yours. All those damn books he gives you—"

"I'm sorry," you stutter. "It was stupid, I know—it's so bright in here. The sun."

"Are you feeling alright?" She places a cool palm against your forehead. She does love you, as best she can, in her own way. "Maybe we should have stopped. Do you want some water? Let me get you some water."

"Don't tell Father," you say, touching her arm with more than a little urgency. She pats your hand, then squeezes it.

"Of course." A flicker of fear crosses her face again. "Absolutely not."

As your mother busies herself in the fridge with the tiny ice cube tray, you fold the map back up, turning it around as you collapse it into itself.

Your hand brushes the surface, casually, and you close your eyes. The paper is smooth to your touch. It's just our secret, the circle, you tell yourself. It's between us, between me and the void. That's what you call it: the void, that black, all-enveloping place you go to whenever Father appears in your doorway, the place where you don't have to think or remember or be. After all these years of traveling to it, perhaps now it is coming to you.

"Are you ok?" Jamie touches your arm. You shrug.

"I'm fine. Help me pick up the cards. I want to play Old Maid."

◄○►

"June, it's getting dark. How can you read that—scoot your chair over here before you hurt your eyes."

"It's ok. I can read it just fine," you lie.

If there's a sun left in the sky, you can't see it from the makeshift camp-site, a small flat spot Father found just off the one of the dead-ended offshoots of Hot Springs Road. He says that according to the map—his version of it—there's a lake nearby, but it's hidden from view—wherever it is Father has parked the camper, you get no sense of water or sloping hills, of the space a lake carves for itself out of hilly land. The earth is hard and flat, and piles of stripped logs lie in jumbled heaps at the edges, as thought matchsticks tossed by a giant. The woods here seems weak and tired, as if it never quite recovered from whatever culling happened decades ago. You sit on a collapsible camp stool, watching Father set up a small table for the Coleman stove and lanterns. No fire tonight, this time. Father says there isn't time, they have to be to bed early and up early. "It's ready," he says to your mother, as he lights the small stove. "I'll be back in a bit." He turns and walks off with the lighter, disappearing between tree trunks and the sickly tangle of ferns. His job is finished, and he's off to smoke a cigarette or two, an ill-kept secret no one in the family is supposed to notice. There are so many other secrets to keep track of, he can afford to let slip one. Besides, it calms him down. You note that the map is in his back pocket, sticking out like a small paper flag.

Your mother has become thin-lipped and subdued over the past hour—you know what she's thinking, even if she doesn't. No matter where the family goes, a vacation for all of you is never a vacation for her, only the usual cooking and serving and cleaning without any of the comforts of home. Jamie knows how she feels, and as usual, he helps her. Beef stew and canned green beans tonight, and store-bought rolls with margarine. Chocolate pudding cups for dessert. If she was in the mood, she'd make drop biscuits from the box, or cornbread. She's not in the mood tonight. It's more than just cooking, this time. Father and your mother are divided over the vacation, over the destination. This is a first for them, and a first for you. Usually they are united in all things, as you and Jamie are, because so much is always at stake for all of you, because everything must be done in secret, away from the eyes of those who wouldn't understand, which is everyone in the world. But things are off-balance, tonight. You stare up at the trees, trying to see past them to the heart of the mountains. Your mother couldn't see the brown ink lines, the map within the map. Does he? You think you know the answer. Otherwise, why would he ignore his own vacation plans, his own map and dotted blue lines, why would he take you all here?

"June." Your mother, her voice clipped and tired. "Go get your father. Dinner's ready."

You stand up, looking around. Nothing but trees. It's peaceful here without him, brooding over everyone. You don't see the need to change that.

"I don't know where he went…"

"June, please. It's been a long day. Just go get him."

"I don't even know where he went to!"

"Just follow the smoke," Jamie says.

"Hush!" Your mother slaps at his arm, a playful smile on her face. For a moment, her dour mood has lifted. You use it, slipping into the woods unnoticed. You'll follow the smoke only as far as you need to, before going in the opposite direction. He can come back on his own.

Five feet in, and the darkness seals up the space behind you, as though the cozy camper and the soft lights never existed at all. Up above, the sky is still blue, but starless and without light. There are no paths or trails here, only ground thick with fallen pine needles and cones, and large ferns that brush at your face as you push through them. No trace of smoke is in the air, you smell only wet earth and pitch and leaves. You should have grabbed a flashlight, but you've never been afraid of the dark before, so you push forward. After several thick strands of webbing lash your face, you raise your arm, holding the book up high before you like a shield.

It's a crumbling cloth-bound volume Father gave you years ago, for your seventh birthday. *Mythology of Yore.* Mythology of your what?, you'd joked when you unwrapped the book. Father stopped smiling: later, when you started reading, you stopped smiling as well. The stories are old, very old, and deliciously cruel, and when you touch the illustrations, red and silver bleeds off onto your skin. "This will explain everything," Father had said when he gave it to you. "This will explain why we do what we do, and why it is not wrong. Why it is as old as mankind itself, beautiful, divine."

He must not have read all the stories in the book.

"You know where we're going, don't you?" Father appears from behind the trees, and you let out a small gasp as you lower the book. He's barely visible in the gloom, the red tip of the cigarette the only real part of him you can fix your sight on. Yet, you can tell, even in the dark, even from a distance, that some strange mood has seized him, morphing his face into a mask. He wants something, he's seeking something. You remember what he told you on the piers at Port Angeles. Now is not the time for a smart-ass reply.

"We're going to the mountains. Into the center of the Olympics, like you said."

"We're going into the center." Smoke billows from his mouth as he speaks, and he crushes the remains of the cigarette with his finger and thumb, carefully so as not to create stray sparks. You watch him slip the butt into his front pocket—Father never approved of littering—and his hand is upon your throat, lifting you up and back into the solid wall of a tree. The book tumbles from your grasp, away into the dense brush. It's gone, you'll never find it in the dark. Once again, he places a finger at the center of your forehead. Small coughs erupt from your lips, wet with spittle, as you struggle to breathe, as your feet slide up and down the rough bark, trying to find some place to come to rest.

"And where are you going, where do you go?" Father asks. His voice is a whispered snarl, hard and tight. What little air your lungs clutch at is tinged with warm smoke and rank sweat. "Where do you go when I'm with you? Where are you when the light leaves your eyes and all that darkness pools out of them as you beg me to take you away? What do you see?"

"I—don't—know." The words are little more than croaks.

"You don't know? You don't know? I treat you like goddess, like a queen, and you slip away like some backstabbing little whore?"

"No—never."

The finger at your forehead disappears, and you hear the rustle of paper. The map. "Is it here? Oh yes, I see it. I don't know how you did it, when you drew it, but there it is. I drew my road to where I wanted to go, and she drew hers, and then your little web appeared, shitting itself all over our destinations. Except, I couldn't figure out how to get my road to the center of your map, to that nice big space inside you, no matter how many roads there were, no matter how many times the lines crossed. I always lost the way to the center of your little Tootsie Pop. *And it's just a fucking piece of paper!*"

"Guess—it's not—you stupid—fuck."

The map slams against your face, and there's a *crunch*. Blood streams from your nose, and pain explodes like lightning through your skull. And then Father wrenches your shorts and panties down and off your legs in a single motion and his zipper is down and your legs up as he parts them wide and he's against you and inside you in a single painful thrust, his cock spearing you against the tree like a butterfly.

For a moment he doesn't move, only breathes hard against your face as the branches rustle overhead, catching the evening wind. It's true night now, and there is no moon and there are no stars. What is he waiting for? You realize the map is still stuck against your face, stuck in the sweat and tears and blood. You move, listening to the rustling of paper so close you're your open eyes, your open eyes that see only liquid primordial night, and he begins to thrust. Long, hard strokes slamming your back and head against the rough bark, in and out, again, again, and you can feel it but you can't help it but you can feel it the old familiar vortex of pleasure forming somewhere deep down inside your traitorous thrusting body and you would give anything to not go there to not feel that and the words form silent in your blood-filled mouth *take me away take it away take it all away*, and even though you can't see, you feel it, you feel the blood-brown word expanding, burning through the layers of map, burning through bone and skin. Somewhere, a chain is being pulled, a hole unplugged, and your muscles slacken as the dark of night whorls around, thickens and deepens, as the flat black void opens wide to take you back in, even as something begins to spill out—

The map disappears, and the hand comes down hard against your cheek. You're back.

"I go everywhere with you. *Everywhere!* Do you hear me?" Your father's grip tightens, and you spasm against the tree, struggling as he pins your arms back against the trunk with his hands. Tears and snot drip down your face, plop onto your breasts.

"I go *everywhere*," he says. "You don't get to leave me behind. And the next time, the next time?—I go with you. The next time, I see everything you see." He leans in, kissing you hard as he thrusts deeper, harder, his tongue pushing into your mouth, filling it up until all you taste is him, all you breath is the air from his lungs, all you feel is what he feels, what he wants.

He lets go.

You fall, choking on your spit and pain, into the roots of the tree, your shorts and panties bunched at your feet. Father walks away, thin branches snapping under his feet as he zips up his pants. Then the metal rasp of his lighter, followed by the solitary blue-orange flame singing the tobacco into red. "Tomorrow night, when we get there, I'll be with you. All the way to the end." A moment of silence as he takes a deep drag, and exhales. You stay huddled in the knotted arms of the tree, hand at your throat, afraid to breath.

"Dinner's waiting, June-Bug. Hurry up." He walks away, crashing and cursing as he tries to find his way. It would be funny, if—When you no longer hear the sound of his footsteps, you crawl to your feet, clinging to the bark of the tree for support, then pull your shorts back on with trembling hands. The map is stuck to the bottom of your right sandal. You wipe the blood and dirt off with great care, then fold it small enough to tuck into your panties, small enough to not be noticed by anyone. He's done for the night, and you're not touching Jamie again tonight, not with your mother's smell all over him.

Off to your left, that's where the campsite was supposed to be, except, you don't know what left is anymore, or where it used to be. You walk forward, toes curled and back hunched as if worried that a single noise will bring him flying out of the darkness at you again. Your sandals slide over blacktop, flat and smooth. Overhead, the stars, and a sudden feeling of space and distance: the road. It's the same road Father drove down two hours ago, before he turned off onto the dirt road into the woods. You turn, looking back into the woods. All of the trees look the same, you can't tell which one Father pressed you against. All you know is that when he first did, you and he were not at the side of the road, there was no road at all. You closed your eyes and you traveled. You escaped, but you took him with you, and only this far.

Is this what he was waiting for?

How much farther can you go?

-◦►-

Dinner is a dream. Your mother pinches your nose and wipes the blood away without a word, then gives you cold water with miniature ice cubes from the tiny freezer, saying nothing as she hands you the glass. She must know what father did. Maybe she made him do it. Father has two beers, and your mother doesn't hesitate in bringing them to him. He's mad at her, which is when he drinks. She's subservient when she's mad, which makes him angrier, because he knows she's just pretending. Jamie's eyes look a bit puffy, not enough for anyone except you to notice. Your mother did or said something to him, that he didn't like. He touches his bangs constantly, keeps his head down. You eat your beef stew in small bites, careful to grind it down to a paste your tender throat can swallow. It all tastes the same. And as you force down your meal, you realize that all the things you know about your world, the normal things, aren't the right things. They aren't the things that are going to save you. You think of the book, lonely and cold, heroes and gods already festering in the damp of the undergrowth.

But the map… The map is folded into a tiny square, shoved deep into your underwear. It's your map now, it's not his or hers, he threw it away, and besides, it was never his map anyway. It was never his journey, his destination. He had his own, and besides—isn't what he gets from you enough? Does he have to go everywhere, see everything? Is there no place left for you and you alone? You bite down on the lip of the plastic tumbler. There's nothing you can do, really. It's not your fight, what they fight about. You, like any good map, can only point any number of ways. But if he wants to see everything, he's going to be surprised. Everything is not where you're headed. Everything is never where you go.

After dinner, it's quick to washing up and then to bed. You and Jamie each get five minutes alone in the camper to change before clambering up into the camper's upper bed. Father and your mother argue quietly in the front of the camper, behind a small plaid curtain your mother sewed. I can't believe you lost the map, she says. We don't need a map, I know where we are, and I'll know when we get there, he says. That doesn't even make sense, she says. We agreed to go to Windy Arm, we agreed to go where I wanted to go for once, she says. Wherever we go, we go together, he says. We do it for the family. That's how Mom and Dad taught us, it's how we survive. We do it as one.

Jamie and you lay on your sides in a shallow imitation of spooning, his arm draped across your waist. At first you didn't want him touching you, afraid they'd stick their heads up into the pop-top for a last good-night—you've long suspected that they know what you and Jamie do, what you are to each other. Still. You don't need them to have it confirmed. Finally, the lights click out: the night is so dark in contrast, for a second it seems bright as noon. You slide your hand across Jamie's, bring it up to between your breasts, as if to shield your heart. Your breath is shallow. Father and your mother zip themselves into their sleeping bags, and the camper settles into the ground, little creaks and ticks sounding out like metal insects. You wait. And, after what seems like half the night, gentle snores and deep breathing fill the small space. They're asleep. Nothing more will be needed of you and your brother tonight.

Your lips part, and you close your eyes, letting anxiety sieve out through the netting into the cool night air. Still, though, you don't move a muscle, and neither does Jamie. Let them fall sleep peacefully below, undisturbed. Let them lay together, like they should. Sometimes, after the school day was over, Jamie would whisk you into one of the crumbling old portable classrooms, unused for years since the new additions were build. There in the soft of the chalky air, he'd press you against the plaster walls, his body fitting neatly against and into yours. It was so different than with Father, it felt so good, so right. There was no need for the void with Jamie, no need to escape, because you wanted to be there, you wanted to remember every sigh, every moan. It's like Jamie was made for you, made to fit you, made to taste and smell exactly how you like. He *was* made for you, though, he was a part of you once, inside your mother's womb. Making love to him was the only way you could love yourself.

Jamie's hand opens, slides down around your right breast, cupping it gently. You feel protected, safe. And yet. And yet.

Another hour passes, and another. Jamie drifts off, you can hear it in the rhythm of his breath, feel it in the dead weight of his limbs. Below, Father and your mother are lost in sleep. Do you dare? Even as your mind asks the question, your body is answering, your hands slipping up to zip, inch by careful inch, the hard mesh that surrounds the pop-top of the camper. Jamie stirs, turns over and away. You stop, listening. Somewhere in the woods, a branch cracks, sharp like a gunshot, and silky rustling follows. Here, in this part of the world, the moon is of little use to you, and the stars are nothing. Here nothing can penetrate the blanket of wood and branch and needles. You move forward, sticking your face outside. You see nothing. You are blind as a worm.

The zipper moves again, and now your entire upper body is exposed to the night. If you try to climb down the camper's slick sides, you'll only fall, and that will mean noise, unnatural human noise, the kind that wakens other humans. This is the most you can do, the most you can be free. Hidden at the bottom of your sleeping bag is the map. Your toes grasp the folds of paper, and you bend your knees up, reaching down at the same time. Slowly the map travels into your hands. You hold it out into the open air, outside in the world, your finger brushing across the bumpy ridges of the circles and into the center, where it once again rests on that strange, lone word. Is this truly the place you travel toward, when Father visits you in the night? Do you really hold the map to that invisible place, and if so, how and when did you draw it? Or was it you? Perhaps there is more in the flat black void than sublime nothingness. You move your finger back and forth, coaxing the letters to respond.

The brownish ink, invisible in the night, leaps against the whorls of your fingertip, as if tracing a route, an escape from the center and into the world. The paper crackles, and you stiffen, holding your breath in. Again, you listen. Silence. For a wild second, you imagine Father and your mother, awake and perched at the edge of the bunk, pupils wide and oily-black as owls as they stare down at you and your sleeping twin, younger versions of themselves, when they were brother and sister, before they were husband and wife. You ignoring the cold fear as you send your plea, your command, out into the mountains, wherever in the night they are. *Save me. Take me away.*

But nothing happens, and your arms become stiff and cold. Soft hooting punctuates the silence, followed by another passage of the wind through the ferns and trees. Resisting the temptation to sigh, you curl your arms back into the camper, and fumble for the zipper. As you close the mesh screen, the wind picks up, and small cracks sound throughout the clearing. It's a familiar sound, but you can't place it. Something flaps against the screen then whooshes away: startled, you shiver and slide back from the netting, images of insects and bats filling your mind. Jamie stirs, turns away. Another object hits the mesh and slides away—this time you recognize the sound for what it is. Stretching one hand out, you press against the mesh as hard as possible, fingers outstretched, wiggling as if coaxing. When the page hits the flat of your hand, you grab and reel it back in. The wind dies down, and the flapping of loose paper fades. What's left of the book is gone for good, scattered into the sky. You take the page and insert it into the folds of the map. You fall into restless sleep, paper clutched against your chest like a rag doll. In the early morning before everyone else awakens, when the sky is the color of ash, you'll wake up and study the pen and ink drawing of an ancient maelstrom, its nebulous center leading somewhere you cannot see.

◄◦►

The road Father drives down while you fall asleep is smooth as silk compared to the road you wake up to. It had been beautiful before—unbroken lanes of blacktop, with perfect rows of evergreens lining each side, wildflowers of crimson red and white crowding at their roots. The magazine slipping from your hands, you'd grabbed a pillow from the storage area behind the bench and snuggled against the window, bare feet resting flat against Jamie's legs. You slept hard, so hard you didn't feel the vibration in your bones as the road shifted to gravel and dirt, pitted with potholes and large rocks. You didn't see the forest fall away, dissolve into ragged sweeps of ravaged land, green only in the brush and grasses sprouting around stumps of long-felled trees. You didn't see the land itself fall away, until all that remained of the road was a miserly ledge, barely wide enough for any car, clinging to the steep sides of barren hills. You only woke up when you heard your mother screaming.

"Don't ask," Jamie says, before you can. He's sitting on the porta-potty, ashen-faced and shoulders hunched over, methodically placing one green grape after another in his mouth. You rub your eyes, trying to make sense of the ugly, unexpected landscape. To your right, the hill rises in a steep incline, tree stumps clinging for their lives to the dirt like severed hands. To your left: nothing. There is more desolation in the distance, but right beside the camper, there is nothing but jagged space.

The camper lurches down and shoots up, sending books and backpacks sliding across the floor. Your mother screams again. "Turn around, goddammit!" Tears stain her face in shining streaks.

"I can't turn around," Father shouts. "There's nowhere to turn!"

"Where are we?"

Jamie shrugs. "A logging road, somewhere. It's not on the map. Dad says it is, but—" he shrugs again, and shoves several more grapes in his mouth, barely chewing before they're gone. He always eats mindlessly when he's stressed out.

"When did we leave the real road?"

"I don't know—an hour ago? It didn't get really bad until about twenty minutes ago. I can't believe you slept through all that. I thought you were dead." The camper lurches again, swaying wildly. Jamie stares out the window, a grape at his lip. "Yeah, I don't want to talk anymore. I just want to be quiet for a while, ok? I need to not—I need to be quiet."

"Yeah. Sure." Reaching for the grapes, you start to rise, and Jamie shoots out his hand to block you. "Stop, ok? Just—don't. Fucking. Move. Sit down." The camper lurches again, and for a wild second, you get the impression that there is nothing under the wheels, that you're all about to topple over and fall. The shriek is out of your mouth before you can stop it.

"Goddammit." Father, at the wheel. "Sit down, June, both of you sit down and shut up!" Your mother covers her face with her hands. You've never seen her cry. You've never seen her lose control of her emotions, or of Father. They've always done things as one. Now she's sobbing like a child. Father turns back to you, motioning.

"Come up here."

"I—" You're paralyzed.

"Look at the road—" your mother shrieks. Father's hand lashes out like a snake. You can't hear the slap of his hand over the roar of gravel and rock under spinning wheels.

"June, get up here *now*. Jamie, get off the goddamn toilet and help your mother to the back. Everybody, now!"

Jamie stands up, legs shaking, and grabs your mother's hand as she sidles out of the passenger seat. Mascara coats her face in wet streaks, except for where Father slapped it away, and her lipstick has bled around the edges, making her mouth voracious and wide. Jamie helps her across the porta-potty, while you stand to the side, fingernails biting into your palms. There'll be raw red crescents in the skin when you finally unclench your hands.

"Come on," Father snaps, and you crawl across the toilet, hitting your head against the edge of the refrigerator as the camper slams over a log. Father curses under his breath, but doesn't slow down. Sweat the color of dust dribbles down his face, collects at the throat of his t-shirt and under his arms. If his jaw was clenched any tighter, his teeth would break. "Sit down. Open up the map."

Up here, in your mother's seat, you see now how bad it is. The road before you is barely there, crumbling on the right side back into the mountain, gouged with giant potholes—more like depressions where the road simply dropped away. No guard rails or tree line, just a straight drop hundreds of yards down, the kind of fall the camper would never survive. And the road curves, so steep and sharp that you can't see more than ten or twenty yards ahead, assuming there's even a road ten or twenty yards beyond that. No wonder your mother was hysterical. Father's going to kill you all.

"June, the map."

"You threw it away in the woods, I don't have it—"

"Never mind the fucking seatbelt. Take out the fucking map!"

Reaching into your blouse, you pull out the warm square of paper.

"Open it up."

You do as he says, refolding it so that only the folds showing the Olympic Peninsula show. It fits perfectly in your lap, the land and the void.

"Tell me where we are."

"Ok, I—" Your finger traces over the hand-drawn roads, so many of the brown-red roads that start and end with each other as abrupt as squares of netting. Below them, somewhere, is Father's dotted blue ink line, along with your mother's wishful scrawl of lavender road. Frantic, you move your fingernail along Father's road, following, following— You lost it. No: it's simply gone.

"Where are we, June-Bug?" Father manages a tight smile. "How much further do we have to go? I'm counting on you to help us."

"I'm looking—it's hard to see, it's like a furnace up here." Panic sharpens your voice. Again, you find the start of Father's road, and you follow, follow—it disappears. And it's not like it simply stops, and you can see the end. The road is there and then it's not, and your gaze is somewhere else on the map, on another map altogether, on the one that was meant for you.

"I'm sorry." The words barely leave your dry mouth. "I just can't find it. It's not on here. I'm looking and I see all these lines but there aren't any logging roads, and I can't find the road you drew—"

Father puts his foot on the brake, and the camper grinds to a hard halt. When he cuts the engine, the silence almost makes you groan with pleasure. Only the ticking of the engine now, and the whisper of wind and rolling gravel outside. Father places a hand on your shoulder. It sits there like some cancerous growth, hot and heavy, pressing down until the bones grind together. "You can do better than that," he says. "You know what map I'm talking about." He leans toward you, his eyes still on the ever-thinning road ahead. "Look at your map, June-Bug. I want you to tell me where we are on *your* map, not mine. Because, every very time I try to read it, I can't quite make out the roads. You know what I mean. Read your map, and tell me where we are. How far we are from the center."

You look back at your mother. She holds Jamie in her arms. His face rests at her throat, lips on her skin, pressing gently, whispering words you cannot hear because they aren't meant for you. Those beautiful large hands, around her waist and thighs. He didn't love you most, after all.

"June-Bug." Father stares at you, and you return his glance. There can't be any lying now. He already knows, and, you're so tired. You just want this all to be done.

"It's not my map. I didn't draw it, you know. I don't know how it got there."

"I know. We didn't draw those other maps, either, your mother and me."

"What?" You lean back in the seat, astonished and angry as you stare at the limp paper. You wanted divine intervention for yourself, not for him, because *you* were the one who needed it, not him. Did the void betray you? "Why didn't you tell me?"

"It doesn't matter."

"Do you know how it got there?"

"I don't know. I got it at a gas station, I didn't open it till I got home, and there it was." He stares at the dusty windshield, beads of sweat matting his brown-grey hair. "I think—I think they appeared because that's where we wanted to go more than anywhere else in the world; and I think something in the world heard us and showed us the way. To a place where we can be ourselves without anyone else's eyes on us, to where we can be free to do and act as we please."

As animals, you think. As monsters. But you remember Jamie in the same breath, curving over you in the quiet corners of the school. Like father, like daughter. Animal, monster, too.

"Why can you see my map? Why can't we both see yours?"

"Because your map, that's where we both most want to go now. Because I love you, and I want to be with you. We need to go there together."

"All of us, together?"

Father's hand moves from your shoulder, gliding over your breast as he lowers it onto your thigh, the fingers rubbing hard against your sore crotch. "Us, together. Just the two of us. That's how it's supposed to be."

The sun boils the fabric of the seat, searing your skin. You stare out your window at all the desolation, feeling his hand, working, working. You barely see a thing in the glare, but you don't need to. You don't need to see anything at all. The cool, black edges of the void nip at the edges of your conscious, small nudges that leave smears of black in your vision, as though ink is trickling into your tears.

"I know the way to the center," you say.

"Good girl." Father leans in, kissing you on the cheek, almost chaste in his touch. "Good girl."

The engines roar, and the wheels whine as Father shifts into first, sending the camper rattling back up the small ledge. It's not that much further, you tell him, just a few more corners to round, and we'll be at the top, and the road will even out. You stare at the map as you speak, fingers moving back and forth as they trace the roads to the nothingness in the middle. Another corner comes and goes, and another, and you can see the anger in his face start to rise again, anger and impatience because he thinks *no he knows* that you lie, and you move your hand to his shoulder and squeeze it, then place it on his thigh. He smiles, takes your wrist and moves it in and down, wrenching the small bones in his haste. Repulsion fills your throat as you slide your hand past the folds of fabric, but you grab tight, grab as you slide to the edge of your seat, place your other hand on the wheel and your foot on the gas, down hard. And the road becomes a blur, the cliff is a blur and the screams and Father's fist against your face are mere blurs, and only the momentary silence under the wheels before the sharp weightless flip of the entire world strikes you as having any substance or weight, just the right weight and terror to send you into the flat black void, into the nothingness of the center, as you whisper to Father and Jamie and your mother and to anything else that can hear:

◄◦►

Can you see everything now?

◄◦►

You open your eyes.

You stand in an open field on a hill. Beyond this hill, more hills—small mountains bristling with dark green trees. Beyond those, the Olympics rise up from one end of the horizon to the other—endless, imperious, cold and white, their jagged peaks tearing through passing clouds like tissue. Until now, you never thought they were quite real. You never knew anything so colossal, so beautiful, could actually exist. Behind them, the sun is lowering, and long shadows are creeping toward you and the hill. The light is wrong: thin and pale. The air is cool, almost cold. It doesn't feel like summer anymore. It doesn't feel like June.

Both your hands are covered in clotted scars and blood—your right hand clutches a long, pitted bone. Many of your nails are gone, the rest have grown out hideous and sharp. It takes a moment to recognize the filthy strips hanging from your body as the remains of your pajamas. Your skin is deep blue: hands, arms, torso, legs, feet. Dye from the small septic tank in the porta-potty. You smell like shit and death.

An animal-like grunt sounds out. Startled, you turn. To your right, a small herd of elk graze on the short grass. They are large and thick-furred, the males with antlers high as tree branches. They pay no attention to you. To your left sits the camper, monstrously dented and mangled, windows shattered, sliding side door long gone. Inside, it's dark. There's no movement in or around it, save for several birds perched on the pop-top. Scattered all around you are bits of clothes, empty cans and boxes, plastic bags, with a larger pile by the front tire of the camper, like a large nest. The hill. The road. The fall. The camper should not be here. You should not be here, alive. This is not the remains of the logging road. This is the interior. This is the center. But of what, you do not know.

Turning to the camper again, you wait.

You wait for Jamie. You wait for anyone. You wait until the sun begins to lower behind the range. Waves of nausea roll through you, sending drool and bile spilling out from between your lips, and your muscles spasm and twitch. But you are not ill, and you are not hungry, and you hold a long clean bone in your hand. You raise the bone to your face. It's been scratched and scoured clean.

You know they will not appear. You know where they've gone.

As you lower your hand, you notice how rounded your belly is, like a little pillow, and how your naval sticks out like a round fat tongue. You're thin but not starved. Bending over slightly, you study your inner thighs: they, of all places on you that should be caked with blood, are clean. "Oh." It's the only word you can form. You know what this means, and you now know you've been on this mountainside longer than just three months. The tight, blue skin of your stomach is dotted with a latticework of markings as intricate as lace. You touch the blood, a roadmap of brown ink—it's the map, you realize, it's your map made flesh. You run your finger in a spiral around to your naval, circled three times in dried blood. Press at the soft nub of flesh, the place that still connects you to your mother's womb, and to all the women before her, to the beginning of time, the first woman, the first womb. It was always going to be like this. It has to end like this. It cannot begin again.

Behind the mountains, the clouds and skies deepen into vivid pinks and purples, rich and wonderful. A wind barrels down, sharp and stiff:

the herd raise their heads from the grass in a single movement, then shoot off down the slope. You smell the change in the air, see the shimmering dark gather around the high peaks as the first thread of lightning splits down and away. Shivering, you sit down in the grass, balancing the bone at the crest of your mounded stomach, and carefully, firmly, run your wrists across the sharpened edges. And the sunset begins its slow dissolve, while lightning dances around the mountaintops, as all light fades from the world, and you start to cry. It's not a mirage, you see it: a separate, circular mass of black flowing up from the heart of the mountains, up and over the peaks like a tidal wave. Clouds and lighting curve toward the darkness, sliding into the mouth of the maelstrom and away. Near the edges of the whorl, uprooted trees begin to swarm into the air like locusts, disappearing with the earth itself. The ground beneath you shifts, and the entire hill jerks forward: the camper topples over and rolls out of sight. This is it. This is it. Raising your arms high, you inhale as much as your cracked ribs allow, and shout as hard as you can.

Take me. Save me.

It's not very loud, or hard, and your broken voice can barely be heard. But it doesn't matter. It's widening, consuming everything, and it doesn't even care or know that you exist because this is chaos, this is nothing and not nothing, and this is where you want to go more than anyplace else at all, because inside that, there is no sorrow, there is no pain. Only everything you ever were, waiting to be reborn.

And while you can still feel, you feel joy.

Within your belly, movement—a deep watery ping of a push, like someone beating down against a drum, over and over. You cover the mound of flesh with your weeping arms, and crouch before the rising winds. Everything's going, this time. Nothing will return. Cherry red ribbons cover the blue stains and black scars, erase the circles, the roads. No new map this time. Only a river rushing into itself, only a girl striking out on her own, with no directions left behind that anyone can follow.

Which is as it should be. Where a girl goes, the world is not meant to know.

◂•▸

DERMOT

SIMON BESTWICK

The bus turns left off Langworthy Road and onto the approach to the A6. Just before it goes under the overpass, past the old Jewish cemetery at the top of Brindleheath Road and on past Pendleton Church, it stops and Dermot gets on.

He gets a few funny looks, does Dermot, as he climbs aboard, but then he always does. It's hard for people to put their fingers on it. Maybe it's the way his bald head looks a bit too big. Or the fishy largeness of his eyes behind the jar-thick spectacles. The nervous quiver of his pale lips, perhaps.

Or perhaps it's just how pale he is. How smooth. His skin—his face, his hands—are baby smooth and baby soft. Like they've never known work, and hardly ever known light.

All that and he's in a suit, too. Quite an old suit, and it's not a perfect fit—maybe a size too large—but it's neat and clean and well maintained. Pressed. Smooth.

And of course, there's the briefcase.

It's old fashioned, like something out of the seventies, made out of plain brown leather. He doesn't carry it by the handle. He hugs it close against his chest. Like a child.

Dermot finds his way to a seat and parks himself there. His hands glide and slide smoothly over one another, as if perpetually washing themselves. His lips are slightly parted and behind the thick glasses his pale, almost colourless eyes are fixed on some far distant vanishing point beyond the bus' ceiling.

After a moment, the man next to him grunts and gets up. Dermot blinks, snapped rudely out of his reverie, then gets up to let the man past. He thinks the man's going to ding the bell to get off but he doesn't, just goes and finds another seat. Another, Dermot-less seat.

Dermot doesn't care.

He sidles up closer to the window and watches Salford glide past him in the thickening dusk, street lamps glinting dully in the gathering grey of impending night.

But he gazes beyond what is there to be seen.

And licks his lips as the bus rides on.

⭌◦⭌

"Special Needs..." slurs Shires, outside the door. "Special *Needs*..."

Abbie stops tapping her pencil on the desktop and looks up at Carnegie.

They're alone in the little office, the little dusty old office that never has a proper clean and has phones and a fax machine and a desktop computer that were last updated in 1991. Well, maybe a little more recently in the computer's case, but only that.

They're the dirty little secret. They're the office in the police station that nobody wants to admit is there, nobody wants to acknowledge exists.

That nobody wants to admit there is a need for.

"Special *Needs*... Special fucking *Needs*..."

Shires is pressing himself up against the door's big frosted glass pane with its reinforcing wire mesh. Seen through it, he's blurred but she can make out enough. His arms are up, bent at the elbows and bent sharply in at the wrists, fingers splayed, a parody of some kid with cerebral palsy. He's making that stupid, that *fucking annoying* voice, by sticking his tongue down between his bottom lip and his teeth and gums. It's supposed to make him sound like a spastic.

They have to call their little office something, have to give it some kind of a name, and so they call it Special Projects. Shires and the other lads and lasses in the station who know about it call it Special Needs.

It passes for humour around here.

But it's fear, nothing more. It's not the drab little out-of-date office, caught perpetually in its early nineties time warp, that they're scared of. It's what it represents.

It's what they have to fight.

And how they have to fight it.

That's the theory, anyway. Abbie knows all about the theory. She knows all about what goes on in here, in theory. She's read all the reports, the rule books, the case files. She knows the score. In theory.

But this is the first time she's done it for real.

Carnegie, though, he's different. He's a big guy, solid looking. In his forties, she thinks. Late thirties, maybe, and feeling the strain. Dirty blond hair, washed out watery looking blue eyes and features that all look too closely gathered together in the middle of his face. Black jacket, long black coat, black trousers and shoes. White shirt. No tie. The washed out watery looking blue eyes are rolled up towards the ceiling and each new breath is blown out through his lips. Hard. A little harder each time, it seems, Shires lets out his stupid call.

"Special fucking *Neeeeeeeeds…*"

Shires slaps and bats a splayed bent hand weakly against the frosted, wire-meshed glass, pressing his face up close against it.

Carnegie grabs the door handle, twists and slams his shoulder back into it. The door opens outwards and the impact knocks Shires flying back into the corridor, arms flailing. There's a heavy crash as he lands.

Carnegie pulls the door shut again. He turns to face Abbie and shrugs.

"Argh! Carnegie you fucking cunt!" Shires' voice is muffled.

Abbie is biting her lips hard so as not to laugh. She has to stop herself doing that because if she starts she doesn't know if she'll stop.

Moaning, groaning and mumbling indistinct threats of revenge, Shires stumbles away down the corridor and out of earshot.

Carnegie spreads his hands in a *what-can-you-do* gesture.

Abbie can't restrain herself anymore and bursts out laughing.

Carnegie starts laughing too.

On the frosted glass pane behind him, around head height, there's a splash of red on the outside of the door.

They're laughing.

And then the phone rings and they stop.

They just look at the phone, Abbie sitting at her desk, Carnegie stand-ing by the door, and they watch it and listen to it ring and ring and ring.

◄○►

Dermot stands patiently before the desk. The desk sergeant is trying to keep his eyes off him, but they keep straying back and every time they meet Dermot feels the thrill of contact, the hatred and the loathing and the contempt like the charge that jolts down a live wire when a connec-tion gets made.

The desk sergeant motions with his eyes to one of the seats in the recep-tion area. The subtext of which is *get the fuck away from me*.

Dermot doesn't care. He'd rather sit down anyway.

He goes to the chair and he sits and waits. His hands flow over and over one another in their endless washing motions. He hugs the briefcase tightly to his chest. Like a baby.

He licks his lips.

And he waits.

◄○►

The phone rings.

"Gonna answer it?" Carnegie asks.

"No," Abbie says.

"Answer it," says Carnegie.

She looks up at him. The phone rings. She wants to say *you answer it*. The phone rings. Or maybe *you answer it, sir*. The phone rings. Maybe, even, *you answer it sir. Please*. The phone rings. But she doesn't. The phone rings. Because he is her superior officer. The phone rings. And this is her first time. The phone rings. This is her test. The phone rings. This is her rite of passage. The phone rings. And if she fails it, she's out. The phone rings—

She picks it up and answers it. "Special—" she nearly says *Special Needs*, stops herself just in time; turning tragedy into farce would just add insult to injury. "Special Projects."

"He's here," the desk sergeant says.

Send him up, she almost tells him, but she stops herself again, once more just in time. They won't sully their hands with Dermot. They'll kid themselves they're not involved; leave it to the tainted bastards in Special Needs to do the job.

"I'll be right down," she says.

◄◊►

There's a loud, definite click as the desk sergeant puts down the phone. He feels Dermot's eyes on him and looks his way. "They're coming down for you," he says, managing, just about, not to grit his teeth. *Now stop fucking looking at me or I'll break your filthy fucking neck, no matter what you are to them.* That's what the subtext is.

Dermot just smiles, a mild, milky smile, and the desk sergeant looks away.

Dermot knows they hate him, but he doesn't care. In fact, he rather likes it.

Because they need him. He knows they need him and they know they need him too.

They have to give him what he wants.

No-one in the reception area is looking at him. The lift door chimes and opens. A woman approaches. Girl, really. Trouser suit. Blonde hair. Pretty, rather. If she was his type… but she isn't. Pity really.

But then, if she was his type, this wouldn't be all the sweeter. Because it's all the sweeter for the power, and what he can make them do.

She comes over to Dermot. She smiles and tries to look civil, but Dermot notices she doesn't offer to shake hands. There are limits even for the people in Special Projects.

"Sir?"

He nods. He bets it hurt her to call him that.

"Detective Constable Stone. If you'll just come with me?"

Without waiting for a reply, she turns and walks away. The desk sergeant steals a glance at her small, taut behind, rolling beneath the clinging fabric of her trousers, then recoils, blushing, as Dermot catches his eye and smirks.

The desk sergeant's face is red. His knuckles, of the fists clenched on the desktop, are white.

Dermot follows the girl into the lift. No-one else looks at him, her, at them. No-one else wants to admit they're linked or connected in any way, shape or form.

But they are.

⊷

"Have you read my file?" he asks her as the lift ascends.

Abbie starts, nearly jumping, gets it under control. She's stolen a couple of quick glances at him, but that's all. She was hoping he'd stay quiet, stay silent, till she'd got him to the office. Hoped Carnegie would do all the talking with him. She'd just have to make the tea. Not get involved. Not be complicit. Tell herself she wasn't responsible.

Don't talk to me, you bastard, she thinks.

But he does. He has.

And they have to co-operate with him. Have to go softly-softly. Have to give him what he wants.

Even my complicity? Even my soul?

You're kidding yourself if you think you haven't given that already, she tells herself. *You're already part of this. Carry on.*

He's looking at her, eyebrows raised, waiting politely for her answer. "Yes," she says.

He nods. "Then you know all about me," he says. It's a statement, not a question, this time. His voice is wavery and weak, with a faint Irish accent. It goes with his pale face and bland features and colourless eyes. With his soft, smooth, hairless hands that have never known honest work.

"Yes," she says. She doesn't want to reply but she has to. "Yes, I know all about you." She tries to keep her voice neutral but can't, not quite. She wishes she could, especially when she sees the look on his face.

He likes this. Making us dance to his tune. He likes this. Almost as much as the other part.

She isn't going to think about the other part. That will come later. She has to get through this one stage at a time, step by step. If she thought about the other part she'd never be able to get this done. And she has to.

The lift chimes, and she'd never have believed that simple sound could fill her with such relief.

"We're here," she says, and steps out of the lift.

⊷

Dermot follows her down the same plain, dusty corridor he's come down how many dozens, how many hundreds, of times before? He doesn't know how many. Even he's lost count. Neither she—the pretty little Detective Constable Stone—nor whichever senior officer awaits him in the room—will know.

Will it be Ryan, or McDonald? No—Carnegie, he thinks. It will be Carnegie's turn now. Carnegie won't know how many times Dermot's come down this corridor and into this room. To perform his thankless task. To receive his grudging reward. But he could find out if he wanted. It will be in a file somewhere. In this country, everything has to go on file.

DC Stone opens the door that Dermot knows so well, the one with the frosted glass pane reinforced with its wire mesh. Odd. There's a smear of blood on it, slowly drying.

Inside, at the desk, is Carnegie.

I was right, thinks Dermot. *I always am.*

◄◦►

Carnegie smokes.

He doesn't offer one to Dermot. Or to Abbie, for that matter. Not that she cares. She has her own packet of Silk Cut. Carnegie favours Sovereign, a much stronger brand. High tar. There's an ashtray on the tabletop. Fuck the smoking ban.

"We know there's at least one in the city," he says. "We need you to tell us where it is."

Dermot pointedly wafts a hand in front of his face. Carnegie glowers and bashes out his half-smoked cigarette.

"What about my fee?" Dermot asks.

"Fee?" Carnegie spits the word out with loathing.

"My reward, then. For doing my bit. For being such a good boy. For saving so many lives."

Carnegie's eyes are slits. His hands are clenched, the knuckles white. His mouth looks like a half-healed scar. Then he breathes out and his face goes slack.

"Your reward's waiting downstairs," he says. "When you deliver your side of the bargain. You know what we want. Where is it?"

Dermot smiles, nods, licks his lips. It's the last that Abbie finds the worst. The anticipation in it.

He closes his eyes. Prayers his hands together. Smiles. Parts his lips oh-so-slightly and spit-bubbles go pop-pop-pop.

He opens his eyes and his hands drop. His eyes are bright.

He speaks, rapidly. Abbie's already scribbling, transcribing it in shorthand. Then he's done and she's picking up the phone.

◄○►

Sirens wail in the night, and three police vans tear up Oldham Road into an area of bleak, functional looking sixties era council housing and old mills and factories either abandoned or converted to new purposes. Most of the district's one big industrial estate.

At one point along the roadside, a rank of three shops. The buildings are abandoned, boarded up and covered in geological layers of flyposters. The vans screech to a halt outside them. Armed police officers pile out. Some carry shotguns, other submachine guns.

Doors are kicked in and boots thunder up the stairs.

What they're looking for is on the topmost floor.

All the upstairs rooms of the three shops have been knocked together, creating a huge open space.

Things lie on the floor. Five of them. Still asleep. Waiting to wake up. They are vast. They have long talons. Longer jaws. And worse.

Guns are aimed.

Yellow eyes open. Something wakes, leaps up, howling, screeching, clawed hands aloft.

A dozen guns fire simultaneously. The flat, thundery blasts of shotguns, the staccato splitting cracks of submachine guns. The rearing thing is danced back across the room and collapses to the bare, rotted floorboards, writhing, spurting, and then is still.

Then the guns aim down, at the other things, and they fire again.

They don't stop until nothing is left alive on the floors or walls of that upstairs room.

◄○►

The phone rings.

Dermot watches Carnegie pick it up. The big man nods and grunts.

DC Stone is watching all of this, her eyes darting back and forth from one of them to the other.

Carnegie replaces the handset.

"They found them. There were five of them. Just like you said. They got them all." He doesn't want to say the next bit, but Dermot has his eyebrows raised and is demanding it, tacitly. Just like he always does. And so Carnegie says it. "Thank you."

"You're welcome," says Dermot. "Now—" he strives to keep his voice level; to show excitement would be unseemly "—there's the small matter of my reward."

"Yes," says Carnegie thickly, not looking up at him, looking down at the surface of his desk instead. "Detective Constable Stone?"

"Sir?" says Stone at last.

Carnegie still doesn't look up from the top of his desk. "Take him down to the cells. It's cell number thirteen."

"Ah," says Dermot. "How apt."

Carnegie doesn't look up or reply.

Stone's face is ashen. She's even shaking slightly. "If you'll just come with me," she says.

◄o►

All the way downstairs in the lift, Abbie's thinking *this can't be real,* thinking *this has to be a dream,* thinking *please let me wake up before—*

But it is, it isn't, she can't.

The lift doors open in the basement and she heads out, Dermot following in her wake. He's trotting after her, she realises with disgust. Trying to hide his excitement and failing. Miserably.

But who's more disgusting, him or her?

The custody sergeant doesn't look up from his paper at either of them as they pass. Determinedly. He knew they were coming. And he knew, just as well, that he wasn't going to, didn't want to see them.

Abbie leads Dermot down past the row of cells. They're all empty tonight. That's been arranged.

There's a slap of paper, the sound of boots on a tiled floor. She glances round to see the custody sergeant walking out fast. Getting out before the sounds start. Well, there'll be nothing else in here demanding his attention tonight.

She puts the key in the lock and opens the cell door. Light from the corridor spills into the darkness.

"Mummy?" The voice is tiny, thin and blurred. "Daddy?"

Dermot stands at the threshold, not going in yet.

"Go on then," she says. He doesn't move.

"Mummy?"

This time she prods his shoulder. "*Go on.*"

Dermot's head snaps round and for a second Abbie is afraid. But he's only smiling. Smiling and holding her with his eyes. Till she drops her gaze.

Then he's moving, tired of the game, and into the cell. Abbie pulls the door shut behind him, but not fast enough to evade a glimpse of the child's face, bewildered and afraid, or shut out the beginnings of her cry.

◂◦▸

Dermot hears Stone's footsteps recede down the corridor. He puts the briefcase down on the floor and loosens his tie.

The little girl has backed up against the far wall.

Dermot opens the briefcase and takes his tools out one by one. He puts them on the floor beside the case. And then he starts to undress.

◂◦▸

In the pub, afterward, Carnegie is on his third double Scotch and Abbie's forsaken her usual white wine spritzer for a vodka tonic. She's on her third. There's been less and less tonic in each one.

"You did good today," he says. Thick and slurred, but drunkenly sincere.

"Doesn't feel like it."

"It's got to be done," he says. "They need us. Otherwise…"

She knows. Knows what would happen without Dermot to tell them where the latest batch of creatures are incubating, ready to wake to murderous life. Knows you do your time in Special Projects—a year, two, maybe three—and then the world's your oyster, a fast track to any job you want, or if you don't want one anymore, early retirement on a fat pension. There's a reason for that. A price you pay.

She downs her vodka, digs out her mobile, rings for a cab. She feels bad, a little, about leaving Carnegie to drink alone, but sharing the bar with him just makes her remember what she's now part of.

"What time do you need me in tomorrow?"

"Don't bother. Come in in the afternoon." His watery blue eyes are bloodshot. "You passed the test, Abbie. You're in. I'll handle the cleanup."

Normally, she'd object to being treated like the little woman. But this time around, she doesn't mind.

She weaves out the door to the waiting cab.

Alone now, Carnegie downs the last of his whisky. Without being asked, the barman brings him another.

Carnegie bolts half of it in one, feels it burn its way down. Tomorrow, he'll go to cell thirteen, like so many times before. Dermot will be lying there, naked and pallid as a grub, clothes bagged up in a Tesco plastic carrier, tools already wiped spotless and back in the briefcase.

Carnegie will wake him up and take him to the showers. Get the blood off. When he's clean and dressed, he'll drive Dermot home. But first he'll have to go back into the thirteenth cell, and before they come to hose it down, he'll have to gather the bones.

◄◊►

BLACK FEATHERS

ALISON LITTLEWOOD

There was a raven at the edge of the woods. It was huge—even its beak looked as long as Mia's fingers. She stared at it and Little Davey laughed at her. Mia wrinkled her nose. Little Davey was younger than her by a year, but he wasn't that little anymore. He was as tall as she was and twice as loud, and he rode a bike much quicker than she could. He stood in front of her now, him and Sam Oakey and Jack Harris from down the road, and Sarah Farnham who was more like a boy than one of the boys. Mia stared at the raven. She didn't want to go into the woods, could smell its rank green warmth even from here. It was loaded with dark, with mystery, with her brother's mocking laughter as he turned his bike towards the trees.

"Come on," he said. "Last one in's a chicken." He started pedalling and the others followed him one by one, Sarah giving one ring of her bicycle bell, but none of them saying a word.

Mia stared after them. Davey knew she didn't like the woods; she didn't like the way the branches closed over her head, making it impossible to know which way was in and which was out. She knew he only went in there because of her fear; and because it was forbidden.

The thought of forbidden things reminded Mia of her fairy tales. Somewhere deep in the woods would be a castle circled by thorns that could put you to sleep with a single scratch. She reminded herself that a princess wouldn't be afraid. Princesses were never afraid, and she was much more a princess than Sarah Farnham.

With that, Mia turned her own bike towards the woods. The raven let out a dry, rasping burr, the sound a chain might make as it slipped from its sprockets. Then the bird took to wing, lifting its heavy bulk into the air. Its eyes were sharp bright points and Mia thought it eyed her as it flew, but couldn't work out what the look was meant to say. She paused, though, to pick up the thing it left for her—a single, gloss-dark feather—before following the others into the dark.

◄◦►

She heard them up ahead, shouting and laughing. Davey's laugh was loudest of all, and Mia's heart sank. For as long as she could remember, she had been wishing that Little Davey was different. Sometimes she had even tried to turn him into something else. One of her first memories was her mother pulling her off him, laughing because Mia loved her brother so very much she wouldn't stop showering him with kisses. If a frog could be turned into a prince for the simple kissing, Mia had thought, perhaps this mewling thing could be turned into a frog. It stood to reason. It was worth the sour milk smell that clung to her clothes. Worth the feel of his faintly damp, slightly peeling scalp on her lips.

After that, whenever Mia blew out her candles or wished upon a star, she always wished for Davey to change.

Now he stood in front of everybody, leaning out over the place where the banking fell away. They weren't supposed to come here. Mainly they didn't want to, because this was where the bigger kids played; sometimes they found cigarette butts or crushed beer cans, still with foul smells trapped inside. There were no big kids here today though; there was only the swing. The swing was a rope tied around a tree branch with three fat knots at different heights, to sit on. And there was Davey, right on the edge of the banking, the rope held in his hand.

"Don't," said Mia, and the others laughed. But Mia saw what they didn't. The rope was too high for him. He could touch it, but he wouldn't be able to sit; even the lowest knot was barely within his reach. He'd swing wild, holding on with only his hands, and he'd let go. Mia knew what lay beneath. The banking ended. After that it was a sheer drop, nothing but mud walls and broken branches waiting in the bottom. Old leaves and slimy things, long-legged things. She swallowed. It was up to her; she was supposed to look after him. She, after all, was the eldest.

Once, Mia had made a potion out of all the nasty things she could find, dust and dirt and a hair she had found next to the toilet. She mushed them all up with water and gave it to him in their father's sports bottle, so he couldn't see what was inside. Then she had wished Little Davey dead.

She hadn't really wanted him dead. She had knocked the bottle out of his hand before Davey could drink it. He had cried and run to Mum, and Mia got into trouble; or rather, Miranda had. Mia was always 'Miranda' when someone was angry with her.

Miranda was Mia's real name. It wasn't a name fit for a princess. She knew two other Mirandas, and neither of them looked like princesses. If anyone called Mia Miranda, she wouldn't answer. She wouldn't even look at them. Even Davey called her Mia. Miranda, if anything, sounded more like the name for a witch. Mia sometimes wondered what happened to the spell she wove that day, when it missed its target and fell to the ground with the bottle.

Little Davey let go of the rope and stepped back. Then, impossibly, he launched himself out over the space. His hands reached, grasping the rope high. It moved with him and his legs followed, trying to catch up. And then he *was* sitting on it, and not even at its lowest; he was sitting on the middle knot, cheeks burning, his face split by an enormous grin. Mia caught her breath. And she knew she had been right: the rope *was* too high for him, but Davey, with his courage, had made it fit. He had worked his own magic with his recklessness, taken a little of the world and made himself its king. She found herself grinning too, looked around at the others; but they weren't looking at Mia. Their eyes were fixed on her brother as he swung higher and higher, and they were all smiling.

Mia put her hands in her pocket and felt the smooth feather. If she stroked it one way it was like glass; if she rubbed it the other it was rough and caught in her fingers. She could feel it splitting, each thread parting from the next in a way she would never be able to put back together. She did it anyway, thinking of the raven and the way it had looked at her. Its beady black eyes.

Mia wanted Davey to be a girl. They would have been princesses together. Of course, all the stories favoured the younger sister, but Mia wouldn't be like the older girls in tales—proud, haughty, cast aside when the prince came along. Her little sister would have looked up to her, astonished by her beauty and cleverness. The prince wouldn't have had eyes for anyone but her.

After a while Davey got down from the swing and Sam Oakey had a go, and then Jack said he couldn't be bothered but Sarah tried it and so Jack did too. Each of them held onto the rope with both hands and pushed out over the drop; no one managed to get seated the way Little Davey had. None of them seemed to expect Mia to try, and she didn't care. Instead she spread herself on the grass, pretending she wore some great sparkling dress. What princess would go on a swing like that? She waited until it was time to go, and rode back with them through the woods, and the others said goodbye and headed away.

"What did you think of that?" Davey asked.

Mia scowled and turned to him. What she saw, though, wasn't Davey the pain; it almost wasn't like her little brother at all. He still had a glow that lit him up from the inside. She remembered the way he'd leapt out over nothing, the small spell he'd woven there in the woods. And she found herself smiling.

"It was pretty cool," she said. "Really cool." And Davey looked surprised, and then he smiled back.

"It was like you were flying," she said, and she fingered the feather in her pocket.

⟨o⟩

Mia went outside and headed towards the woods. She looked for the raven and he wasn't there but she saw that he had left more feathers for her. She picked them up and put them in her bag. Then she looked into the trees. She had thought she would be more afraid, but she was not. It was easy to hide when you were alone, and besides, she had the feathers. She scanned the ground for them, found one among the exposed roots of a tree. She went on, looking for the next; it led her into a bramble patch and she stepped carefully, picking the black thing out with care. She was following a trail, she realised, like Hansel and Gretel, but this time it was the birds which had left it instead of eating it up.

She found another feather beneath a curling fern, then a whole pile of them on a knoll of grass. It was as if they had been left for her to find, as though the birds knew what she needed. Mia looked up. There must be a lot of ravens living in these woods. She wondered if they were watching her now through their little black eyes. She swallowed, but forced herself to go on. It wasn't so bad. There wasn't much time to be afraid when there was something you really needed to do.

◄○►

Mia's favourite story was *The Six Swans*. A maiden's brothers were bewitched and cursed to live their lives as the white birds. So the maid wove them special shirts to turn them back again, and it worked, except she hadn't time enough to make the youngest brother's sleeve and he was left with a swan's wing for an arm. The sister loved them dearly, and was dutiful and kind all her days; she married the king and lived happily ever after.

There weren't any swans near Mia's house, but there were the ravens. And she knew that they were good, really, that they had looked after her and Davey on that day in the woods. She knew because she had dreamed of it. In her dream, her little brother Davey had leapt for the rope, and his fingers had brushed it, making it shiver. Then he had started to fall.

He fell until there came a loud rasp like a chain coming free, and the raven swept in and bore Davey up. It saved him from the sharp branches and the long fall and the slimy wriggling things that waited, and carried him up, over the treetops and far away.

Mia took the glue and spread it on the fabric. It had been a skirt, but she had taken her mother's scissors and cut it so that it looked like a cloak. She knew her mother would be angry, but Mia had never liked the skirt, and anyway, it was black; that was good, because it wouldn't show if she missed a bit.

She pressed a feather into the glue. It shone for a moment, blue and green and white before returning to black, and she felt a throb of excitement. Davey would love this. He would be king of the air. She had always wanted to turn him into something else, but she knew by the tingle in her fingers that this time it would be different.

This time, she would turn him into a bird.

—◦—

Mia led Davey along the path to the woods. He huffed and puffed, kicking at loose sticks. She turned and put a finger to her lips. "It'll be great, Davey. You'll see." She smiled at him, and it must have been a good smile because he tossed his head and half smiled back.

She picked her way down the path, following old footprints and bicycle tracks. There weren't any feathers, she noticed that as she went, and that was a sign; the ravens had gifted the feathers just for her, and for her alone. Now they were done, and it was up to her, Mia, to do the rest.

She carried a bundle under her arm. It was bulky and Davey had cast odd glances at it as they set off, almost as though he knew.

The others hadn't been near the woods and that had been another sign, a good one. This was a thing for her and her brother, the one she had been dutiful for, had thought of all the time she had been making the cloak. That was why it would work: because she'd put herself into it, and all the care for him she could muster. Davey would see that. He would appreciate the time she'd spent, her caring.

She led the way to the swing and Davey turned on her. He shrugged. "Well? What is it?"

Mia ignored his words. She took the bundle and unrolled the fabric. She straightened it. And the cloak shone, but it wasn't like she'd imagined, some soft, glowing, magical thing. There were spaces between the feathers and in the bright light of day you could see the gaps after all, dull and glue-spotted. Feathers were falling off, or had split when she'd rolled it. At the top, where she'd tried to make a collar, you could see it was only a waistband after all.

Little Davey wrinkled his nose. "What's that?"

"I made it for you, Davey. So you can fly. It's special."

"It's a skirt."

"No, Davey, it's not. I mean, it was a skirt. Now it's a cloak, and I made it for you, because—"

But Mia could no longer think why she had made it. She looked at the thing in her hands and saw it was a sorry thing, a poor thing. It wasn't something you would present to someone as a gift. Not something that could hold magic within it.

"It stinks."

"It doesn't." But Mia realised it did stink, a mixture of animal and glue that almost burned her nostrils. She wondered why she hadn't noticed it before. She turned the cloak, trying to make the feathers catch the light. Some of them did and she looked at Davey, hoping he had seen. She started when she saw his eyes. He was rolling them, as if looking at something ridiculous. He was rolling them at her and the start of something painful rose in her chest.

Davey started to laugh. He put his hands on his hips and leaned into it, and she heard how he was forcing the sound out, making it as loud as he could.

"You idiot," he said. "Oh, you idiot. Wait till I tell the others."

Mia's cheeks flooded with heat. "Davey, no." She looked down at her work. It was already ruined. Feathers fell from it to the ground. And then she heard something coming towards them through the woods: the ching, ching of a bicycle bell. She looked at Davey in alarm.

"Go on the swing," he said.

"What?" Mia glanced at the old rope hanging down over nothing.

"Go on the swing and I won't tell."

Davey smiled a slow smile. Mia wished, harder than she had ever wished before, that he would turn into something else: anything else.

The sound came closer. She looked down at the feathered mess at her feet. She couldn't bear the thought of the others laughing at the work of her hands, throwing it between them, scattering the birds' gift. She picked it up and ran towards the swing. She heard Davey calling her name but she didn't stop, just went faster and faster over the ground. Then, when she was almost at the rope, she skidded to a halt and threw the cloak of feathers into the drop below. She watched it fall, spreading itself as if it was trying to take off. And then it hit a fallen tree trunk before slipping down into a gap among the earth and the slime and the beer cans and the spiders and the cigarette butts, and she wanted to cry.

"Hey, Davey," a voice said. Mia didn't have to turn round to know it was Jack. There were grunts and greetings and the laying down of bikes, but she didn't turn around. Then she heard someone at her side. She twitched when he spoke.

"Come on, sis," Davey said in a low voice.

"Oh, are you going on the swing?" It was Sarah. "Look everybody, Mia's going on the swing."

"No," said Davey. "No, she's not." And Mia felt his hand on her shoulder.

Sarah laughed. "Chicken. Your sister's always a chicken, Davey. She doesn't do anything."

"No," echoed Sam Oakey. "*Anything.*"

"She's been on it already," said Davey. "It's my turn now."

Mia turned and stared at him. He winked.

"She went really high," he said. "Higher than me."

The others stared at Mia, but she wouldn't look at him. They didn't say anything, either. She knew they wouldn't question Davey. They never did question him, just followed him and tried to do what he did. She felt a stab of pride for her brother.

"Go on then," said Jack.

Mia realised he was talking to Davey. She looked around as her brother backed off, then started to run. She opened her mouth to call him back; closed it again. She smiled as he raced, all boy, all freedom, towards the rope. It already felt better. He was doing that thing again, weaving his magic in the air between them. It was all right. It was his spell, Davey's spell, not her own; but it was all right.

He ran towards the rope and he leapt. His fingers stretched out and the rope trembled.

Then Davey began to fall.

Mia screamed. He went so fast; how could he have gone so fast? There was only his hair, floating above his head, and the weight of him, and there must have been sound, but Mia hadn't heard any sound at all because she had screamed so loud.

The others ran past her to the drop. The rope was still there, hanging quite still. Jack edged up and down in front of it. Then he turned and ran past Mia, his face white, mouth open. He grabbed his bike. "I'll get someone," he panted, and was gone, off into the woods.

Sarah looked over her shoulder. "Where's he gone?" she asked. Her voice wasn't like her voice. "Where?"

All Mia could do was look at her.

"We have to go," Sarah said to Sam Oakey. "We can't get to him. We have to get help." She walked past Mia, slow but without pausing, and grabbed her bike. After a moment Sam followed. He didn't look at Mia at all.

Mia stepped towards the drop. When she reached it, she looked down.

There was the tree trunk she'd seen before. Other branches, scattered about. There was an old car tyre she'd never noticed before. And Davey. Little Davey lay in the cleft, and his body was broken. She could see it in the way his back fitted to the shape of the branch on which he lay, a giant, twisted thing. His arm was bent in an unnatural way too, and Mia thought she could see blood on it. It wasn't bleeding now though. She could tell from the look on her brother's face that little Davey was dead.

She let out a sound, something between a sob and a wail. She stared at the rope, the evil thing that Davey's spell hadn't worked upon, and wondered where the spells went when they missed the thing they had been meant for. Old potions made of dust and dirt and hair. She felt sick. Bent to the ground, leaned further over the edge. Tried to see into the gaps between the old wood in the hole in the ground.

Then she looked from side to side.

The ground was sheer where she was, but a little further around there were breaks in it she thought she might be able to hold onto. She remembered she wasn't supposed to—*never does anything*—as she hurried over there, threw herself onto her stomach and slithered backwards over the edge.

It was hard, but she held on tight, and kicked her shoes into the dirt face to make footholds as she eased herself down. She forced herself to think it through, deciding where to step next and how to hold on. It didn't seem to take very long before she stood at the bottom, mud clumped to her shoes and smeared down her dress.

She saw the white shapes of Davey's face and arms from the corner of her eye and looked away. Instead she headed for the tree trunk, her feet sinking into the ground. It was spongy, layers of old grass and rubbish. She looked down and saw something dark and long-legged skitter over her shoe. Shook it off with a little cry. She climbed over the branches and they didn't feel dry like tree bark but clammy and damp like cool skin.

When she took her hands away they were tinged with green.

She could see the gap where the cloak had fallen. It was dark. She would have to lie flat against the biggest branch and reach in with her hand. She shivered but didn't hesitate, just threw herself down and let the wood dig into her belly and her knees and her chest. She put her arm down into the space and groped. Somewhere above her came the cry of a bird. She ignored it. It made her think of outside, of playing with the others, of watching Davey fly. She couldn't think about that now. She had to think of this, the darkness under her, the sudden smoothness she felt under her fingertip. She stretched down, pressing her face into cold wood. Felt its clammy touch rub onto her cheek. She felt feathers; pinched the fabric between her fingers and pulled it towards her.

She slithered back off the branch, clutching the cloak, feeling its dry weight. She held it close, pressed tight against her body. Davey still lay where he had fallen. Everything was motionless; everything quiet.

Mia walked towards him, trying not to see how white his face had become. His jaw was sticking out; it looked as though it was unhinged. She wondered if he had shouted anything as he had fallen. If he had, Mia hadn't heard; had been too busy with her own scream.

She held out the cloak, turned it so that all the feathers hung downwards, like they do on birds' wings. She straightened it, tried not to see the black flakes falling to the ground. "You're my brother, Davey," she said. Her words seemed wrong in the empty air, too loud. It was for them, she thought. It was because her words were only for the two of them. She put the cloak over her brother's face. Then she turned and ran back towards the slope.

◄•►

When Mia got home and looked into her mother's face she knew that no one had told her. The others must have run to their own homes and she felt a stab of anger. Their mothers knew, and Davey's mother didn't. It was unfair. The whole world was like that, out of kilter.

Then her mother ran to Mia and knelt down and put her arms around her, and Mia wondered if she had been wrong, if her mother had known after all. Then she realised her mother was saying something, over and over: what is it Mia, what's wrong Mia, and she remembered the mud all down her front, and the wood-slime on her face, and knew her mother knew nothing, that she had only seen what she had read in Mia's eyes, and the next thing was, that Mia was going to have to tell her. And Mia started to cry.

For a moment, Mia wasn't sure what she'd been saying. Something about birds, and Davey, and the woods, and a rope. She knew her mother didn't understand. She just kept stroking Mia's hair and making shushing noises. Mia took a deep breath because she had to tell her, couldn't let her not know any longer, and she opened her mouth to say that Davey was dead and then the door opened and she saw the thing that stood there and Mia screamed.

It was Davey, but not Davey. His face was white and expressionless; only his eyes stared, dark and bright. His hair was plastered tight to his head. Mia saw that his jaw didn't stick out anymore and she looked at his arms and saw that they were wings after all; pitch black, inky black, and shining so brightly they looked wet. The wings hunched over his shoulders and hung long and powerful all around him.

Then Davy moved and she saw it was only a cloak, her cloak, the one she had made for him. He threw it to the floor and brushed himself down, his arms shaped as they should be, moving as they should move. And he looked at her. "I'm back," he said, and that was all she remembered before she fell.

◂◦▸

At first, when Mia tried to tell her mother how Davey had been hurt, she listened to her and stroked her head and soothed her. Later she began to tut and brush Mia's words away; later, she became angry. *He's fine,* she said. *Your brother's fine.*

Mia knew that Little Davey wasn't fine. He wasn't even the same. He was like Davey and yet not like him. He was too pale, his eyes too bright. He didn't smile.

The others didn't like to play with him anymore. Mia didn't really know why because they didn't tell her, and Mia knew that was because they had always been Davey's friends and not her own. They had liked his smiles and his bravado, and they were things she didn't have. Now they were things Davey didn't have either. He sat around the house, scowling at the television or staring into space. He stared at her, too, if she tried to talk to him, to ask him about the woods or the ravens. He stared at her as if he didn't really know what words meant.

One day her mother was trying to clean up around them, and she kept darting little looks towards her son. Sharp, hard little looks. At last she stopped and turned on him. "Why don't you go out?" she said.

Davey stopped staring into space and stared at her instead.

Their mother straightened. She licked her lips. When she spoke again her tone was different: sweeter. "Why don't you take your sister for a walk?" she asked.

Mia heard this, and thought: *I'm the eldest.* But she didn't say anything.

Her mother said, "Why don't you take her to the woods?" and Mia knew then how much their mother wanted them to go because she never told them to go to the woods, it was somewhere they weren't supposed to be.

Her brother turned his head and looked at her. "Do you want to come to the woods, Miranda?" he said.

She looked at him and saw that he hadn't said that to be funny or mean. He hadn't meant it in any way at all, he'd just said it, and they were only words, things that didn't seem to mean anything to him.

Mia, she mouthed. She was Mia. Even Little Davey had always called her Mia. But she didn't say it out loud.

He got up and put on his coat and so did she. When he went out of the front door she followed him. She didn't try to talk; knew it would be easier that way. Instead she walked at his heels until they reached the woods. The raven wasn't there but Davey stopped and stared for a moment, at something only he could see.

"What is it?" asked Mia, and he just started walking again and so did she.

They went into the woods and Mia wasn't afraid, not really. She had learned there were other things to be afraid of; things that came into your home and slept in the room next to yours; things you weren't really sure were the people you had known or the ones you had loved, in spite of yourself, all the time you were wishing they were something else.

She followed Davey until they reached the swing. He walked over to it, leaned out until he grasped the rope with his fingers. He didn't jump for it, though, or do anything else. He just stood there with it clasped in his hand, looking down into the drop.

"You died," said Mia.

When he turned, she wasn't sure that he had heard. She saw his eyes, though, and they were dark, and small, and bright. She couldn't look away from them. Then Davey smiled, and although it was something Mia had wished for, she suddenly knew it wasn't a thing she wanted to see. It wasn't Davey's smile. It wasn't a good smile.

Davey opened his mouth and he spoke to her in the voice she'd known was inside him. His voice was the sound a raven made and she knew then that the birds hadn't been good, after all; that they hadn't meant well. They had taken her brother just as she had dreamed, and it was the birds which brought him back: except, when they did, they left a part of him behind them, in whatever dark place they had been.

Mia shuddered. She felt stinging at her eyes. She closed them and felt the tears come, no use now. So many times she had wished, and she wished again now, but she knew it wasn't any use. The magic had gone. It had gone with Davey, and he had known that. He had looked at her and called her by her name.

So many times she had wanted her brother to be something else, some strange and magical thing. Now she clenched her fists, still feeling Davey's stare, and wished harder than anything to have her brother back. To have Little Davey come home, just the same as he had always been.

-◦-

THE FINAL VERSE

CHET WILLIAMSON

Okay, this on? Yep, red light, guess I'm good to go. I carry this thing around in case I get any song ideas, never used more than the first few minutes of a tape, so this'll be a first. What I'm gonna do now is tell how I came to get the last verse of "Mother Come Quickly," and also what really became of Pete Waitkus. Then I'm gonna tuck this away in my safe-deposit box, and maybe someday everybody'll know the *real* story. So here goes.

Now you oughta know this anyway, but "Mother Come Quickly" is one of the best-known songs in popular music, a sure-fire classic. It's traditional, and because of that everybody and his brother's recorded it. It was around as a folk song for a good many years before it was really a hit, which was when Peter, Paul, and Mary put it on their first album. It was that year's "Tom Dooley." Joan Baez did it on one of her first records, Bob Dylan used just the tune and put his own lyrics to it. There's even been rock versions of it. Kurt Cobain did it on that "Unplugged" show, lotsa others. And country and bluegrass, hell yes. Doesn't matter it's really a woman's song, a lot of guys sung it—Johnny Cash, George Jones, even ole Hank did it live, but he never recorded it. Became a bluegrass standard after Bill Monroe brought it out on Decca in the fifties. The Stanleys, Jim and Jesse, hell, even I did it back when I was doing straight country.

Course, I'm bluegrass now—then *and* now, since I started out as one of Bill Monroe's Bluegrass Boys, playing rhythm guitar and singing lead for two months way back in the early seventies till Bill realized that good as my singing was I wasn't never gonna get that Lester Flatt lick, that *bum-bumma-dooba-dooba-do* that had become such a part of his sound. I could play it medium tempo, but real fast I hit it maybe two times out of five, and the other three it sounded like chickens dancing on the frets. He let me go, but not before one of them Nashville smoothies seen me and thought I had the voice and looks to make the big time.

He was right. In a few years I was just *holding* the damn guitar, letting the backup pickers play the tricky licks. Yeah, I had a shitload of songs on the charts back then—and I did "Mother Come Quickly" on my album, *Billy Lincoln Sings Songs from the Home Place*. That was around 1983, when I was starting to slip. Record sales were down, they weren't asking me on the Grand Ole Opry anymore, concerts weren't selling, and Columbia dropped me.

So I went back to bluegrass. Any port in a storm, and things had gotten pretty damn stormy by then. I'd spent a lot more than I'd saved, and what I had saved I'd put into dumbass investments. I played guitar with Doyle Lawson for a time, doing the festival and church circuit, and finally started my own group, Billy Lincoln and the Blue Mountaineers. We did okay, got a contract with Rounder, where a lot of the best bluegrass acts were, and sold enough CDs to hang on.

We did "Mother Come Quickly," not like the ballad version the folkies did, but more up-tempo, driving bluegrass, the way Monroe did it. In fact, let me do it now, just so you can hear what the song was like for the first seventy or so years, before the last part... came along, so to speak. I'll do it like a ballad, because I want the words to stick out, and because that's how I'm gonna do it tomorrow night....

I come from a lovin' family
That lives where the two creeks meet.
One day from the east a young man came
Who wooed me with words so sweet.
He found me in my dark holler,
Brought sunshine to my night,

Wove daisies and violets through my hair,
He was my heart's delight.

Mother come quickly, Father come quickly,
Brother and Sister, see.
The only man I ever did love
Is hanging in front of me.

Now that's the first verse and the chorus, so right off the bat you know something bad's gonna happen. It goes on…

Oh, the days passed by and still he came
And he asked me to be his wife,
But my family told me I never must be
Wed any day of my life.
You are a lovin' daughter,
My father said to me,
But before you wed I'll see him dead
And hangin' in front of thee.

So now you got your paternal opposition, and right away you know the kids are gonna get into this, because whatever their parents want, hell, they want the opposite too. But now *weird* shit starts happening…

They found a girl beside the creek,
A knife had pierced her through.
And the blade stuck fast within her breast
Belonged to my love so true.
He was not guilty of the crime,
Nor would he run away,
For the threat of hanging scared him not
And with me he would stay.

Okay, now we got a dead girl in the picture, and she's stabbed by this gal's lover's knife. Only he didn't do it. She says *he was not guilty of the crime*. I always thought maybe he told her he didn't and she believed him, or maybe she knew some other way. Still, guilty or not, she wants him to get out of there, because she loves him, she doesn't want to see him hang…

I begged him to go and save his dear life,
But alas he would not flee.
With the moon in the sky they hung him on high,
And the guilt sat hard on me.

Mother, come quickly, Father, come quickly…

…and blah blah blah, final chorus. Up till now. She loved this fella, her dad didn't approve, so maybe Dad framed him with his knife and got him hung, and the girl feels guilty about it. But you notice something? The last verse only has four lines, not like the other ones that have eight.

That's where the rumor got started that there was more to the song than what everybody knew. When it got hot with the folkies in the early sixties was when the rumor really started growing. There was this story that A. P. Carter of the Carter Family had found the whole thing but wouldn't sing it, and some folks claimed they'd heard Mother Maybelle confirm it, but I think that's bullshit. But Roger Waitkus—that's the old guy who first collected it way long ago—he never said nothing. Never even said where he got it other than that it was Appalachian traditional or some such.

Waitkus was a queer duck. He was the biggest rival to John and Alan Lomax as far as collecting songs, but he didn't go out of the country or out west and down to the Delta like the Lomaxes did. He just did the mountains—the Appalachians and the Ozarks, that whole Scotch-Irish-English tradition, looking for every variant he could find, and of course anything new that hadn't popped up before.

He started way back in the twenties and thirties, and had his own little dynasty too—his son Carl was doing stuff around the same time as Alan Lomax, and then there's… his grandson Peter. I met Pete when he was a little kid, and I always got along good with him. He had a bad case of hero worship for me, because, hell, there I was, little older than a kid myself, playing on stage with the father of bluegrass. I kind of took to Pete, he knew so damn much for a kid. We lost track of each other when

I went country, though I got Christmas cards from him, and I'd always write him back.

It sort of meant something, getting cards from him, because to most folk he was real standoffish, like his old man and his grandpa had been. They did what they did, and published a book from some little college press every few years. I never knew a thing about Roger or Carl's wives, though they must've had them. But Pete thought of me as a friend because we'd been friendly when we both were much younger.

When I went back to bluegrass, it was like I'd been born again to Pete. He came to a lot of my gigs and was plumb tickled when I got my own band. He'd give me songs he'd come across and thought might work for me, and I used a few, gave him a nod on the CD credits, or when we performed I'd say, "That song was give to me by a good old friend, Pete Waitkus," and he'd like that. He was still digging in the mountains for songs the way his daddy and grandpa did—they were both dead now—and he spent a lot of time going over the old tapes and discs and wire recordings they made, seeing what might've been overlooked.

Anyway, he calls me last spring and says he wants to see me. He's all excited, and he says, "Billy, I think I found a key to the Holy Grail." Well, I've seen that Indiana Jones movie, and I don't know if he's joking or what, but I say okay, come on over. He lives in Nashville too, so he's there pretty quick.

It's quiet at my house since Linda's gone. She left right after Christmas, but we've been keeping it mum. Bluegrass fans don't like it if you got family troubles, and she's still singing in the act with her mom and brothers, so we figure we'll just play it cool before we get an actual separation or divorce.

Pete doesn't want a beer or coffee or anything, he's that excited. He can't even sit down, and he's up and walking around, and says he's got the best clue ever about the rest of the "Mother Come Quickly" song. Hell, I figure if anybody would he would, since it's his grandpa that found it, but I nod like this is great news. Then he starts rattling on.

"Do you know the story of how my grandpa got that song?" he asks, and I tell him I heard it was some old lady sang it for him. "That's right," he says, "it was Bertha Echols. She was old back then, and she told him there was more, but it wasn't hers to sing. That's all I knew, until…."

And he takes this big old pause like he's waiting for a drumbeat, and I say, "Until what?"

And then he says he found the original aluminum disc Roger Waitkus made back in nineteen-thirty-something. "I heard the tape transcriptions dozens of times," Pete says, "but there was *more* on the disc."

"More of the song?" I asked. I'm getting a little excited now myself.

"No," he says, "just talk. I put it on a DAT. You got a machine?"

Of course I got a DAT, so he sticks it in there and I hear his grandpa's voice, and it's saying, close as I can recall, "Now, Mrs. Echols, it's very important that you sing the entire song for me. This is an important historical document," and he's going on like that for a while, really pressing this woman, and then it gets to back and forth.

He says, "Well, why can't you sing it for me?"

And she says, "It ain't mine to sing."

And he says, "Well, whose is it?"

And she says, "The family. Ask them."

And he says, "What family?"

And she says, "You *know*."

And he says, "No I *don't*."

And she says, "Yes you *do*, and that's all I'm a-sayin'."

And she says nothing and he says nothing and then Pete stops the tape. And I say, "That's clear as mud."

"No, she was right," Pete says. "My grandpa knew it but he didn't realize it. She'd sung it for him. The answer was right there in the lyrics." And Pete tells me to listen, and he rewinds the tape and plays the beginning:

I come from a lovin' family
That lives where the two creeks meet.

At least that's what I hear. It's tough, because the old lady is singing kind of screechy, and the recording is crap, all full of hiss and other junk.

Pete turns it off and asks me what she sang. I tell him what I heard and he shakes his head no. "She didn't say 'a lovin'," he says. "You heard her dialect, she'd have pronounced it 'luhvin,' but instead she sings almost a long 'o' like 'loavin.' And listen to the word before too."

So he plays it again, and damned if it doesn't sound like "loavin," and in front of what I thought was "a" I can just barely hear, over all the noise, a t-h sound.

"What did you hear?" Pete asks.

"The loavin' family?" I say, feeling stupid. "What the hell's that, folks that make loaves of bread?"

"The L-O-V-I-N family," he spells out. "Spelled like lovin', but pronounced 'loavin.' It's a name. Not a common one in the Appalachians, but a real one. Louvin is another version of it, like the Louvin Brothers?"

I nod my head. I've met Charlie Louvin—mighty nice man, though I hear his brother Ira was mean as a gutshot snake.

Then Pete tells me he's gone online and checked the records for the county where Bertha Echols lived, and there was a Lovin family who lived there around 1935, when Roger Waitkus made that recording, but Pete couldn't find anything about them after that.

So I asked him, "What are you sayin'? That this family's got the last verse to the song?"

"Why not?" he says. "That stuff gets handed down, and after all, it's their song. If anybody'd have it, one of the Lovins would."

So I ask if he can't find any modern records about them, what makes him think there's still any Lovins left. And he says there's still places up in the mountains where the census takers don't even go, still folks who don't pay taxes or social security, still people the government don't even know exist, and if they do, they couldn't care less, since they don't have any money to pay taxes anyway.

Well, it all sounds kind of dubious to me, and he can see it in my face, but then he starts pitching me. "Think about it, Billy," he says. "Think about the singer who introduces that last verse to the public. Think about TV appearances, think about record sales. Boy, this is the closest anybody's ever come to finding this verse—and maybe the real story of the Lovins beside. I always liked you, always liked your singing, always liked your company... so why don't you come with me?"

I thought maybe there was more to it than that. Pete's sort of a pipsqueak, and I figured he didn't like the thought of going up into those mountains alone. Me, I'm a pretty big guy, and I got a nice collection of pistols, which is two good reasons for wanting me to come along. It was probably a wild-goose chase, but hell, I didn't have to start touring for another two weeks, and if we *did* find that verse, well, he was right about the publicity, and I could use it. If you ain't been in *O Brother, Where Art Thou?*, bluegrass is still the poor cousin in the music business.

So I say sure and Pete says great, but don't tell a soul. He doesn't want anybody else knowing about this, which is fine with me.

Next day, six o'clock in the morning, God help me, I drive my car over to his place, park it in his garage, and we go off in his RV. It's a nice one, with a toilet and big bunks, just in case we got to spend a night or two someplace where there are no motels. Pete lives alone too, so nobody knows what we're doing except us.

We drive east about four hours into North Carolina, just stopping once to take a leak and get some Krispy Kremes, then up into the Smokies, and we go to this town where Bertha Echols lived. I stay in the RV, behind the tinted windows, and let Pete talk to the people, because they might recognize me and we're keeping a low profile. He checks first at the post office, this little building not much bigger than an outhouse, but they tell him there's no such family living around there.

So he comes back and tells me this, and says he's gonna poke around town and I say fine, so I read some magazines while he's poking. Around one o'clock he comes back and says he's talked to dang near every old fart in the village, and nobody knows a thing. Never heard of no Lovins around here, they say. Closest Pete gets to anything is one old black man who says there used to be Lovins living years ago way up in the hills. The old place might be there, but nobody'd be alive now.

That's good enough for Pete. I tell him that if there's nobody alive up there then there's nobody to sing any damn songs, but he's like a kid in a candy store. He pulls out these, whaddyacallem, topographical maps with all the mountains and streams on them, and starts looking, and I ask what he's looking for, and he says, "Like in the song—'I come from the Lovin family that lives where the two creeks meet.'"

"Jesus," I say, "where the hell *don't* two creeks meet?" But he kept looking and narrowed it down to four places he thought there could be a cabin. I said, "Pete, look at all those streams and creeks up there, and all the places they meet! Must be a hundred. How can you say these four are the right ones?" Well, he mumbled something about "cultural geography" or some such B.S., and I thought, hell, it's his dime.

So we start up into the mountains and it isn't long before we're on dirt roads, and with the dirt roads come the ruts and the limbs fallen down over the road, and since I'm the big guy and Pete's driving, I'm the one got to get out and move them. Even with the crappy roads, it's pretty up there. Spring's come, and the trees are greening and there are wildflowers all over. We see a few deer now and again, some rabbits, birds taking dust baths in the dirt, and none of them seem very scared of us, almost like it's annoying that they got to get out of the road.

We get near this one place, so we park and walk through the woods—Pete's got himself a compass—and soon we find a place where two creeks meet. I see now what Pete meant. There's a little open area at the base of a bluff, a good place for a cabin, but there isn't one there, not even a foundation, so we go back and drive on.

Next place it's the same thing. Pretty site, but nothing there. It's getting kind of late now, and I tell Pete we oughta head back, but he says just one more. So we go another ten or so windy miles of rotten road. At least this site's closer to where we park, about a hundred yards through the trees. And son of a bitch if we don't see a cabin there, nestled right sweet in this little hollow, just like a cover painting on one of those *Songs of the Mountains* CDs. A few outbuildings are near fallen down, and next to one of them is a pole about eight foot long and six foot in the air, its ends stuck in the forks of two trees, and I think all it needs is a swing hanging from it.

Only thing is, nobody's been swinging there in years, far as I can see. The cabin's door is wide open, and most all the glass has fell out of the windows. The chinking between the logs is out in a lot of places too, so you can look right inside between the cracks.

Still, Pete's jumping around like he found King Tut's tomb or something. He goes to the door and actually says, "Hello?" like somebody's gonna answer him, like the whole Lovin clan is just gonna come out on the porch with banjos and guitars and mandolins and sing him their song.

"Nobody here, Pete," I say. "Nobody been here for a good number of years." I push on past him and go inside. It's a shit pile. Everything's dusty and smells old and moldy. There's still some furniture, awful worse for wear, a big old square table with five spindly wooden chairs, all of them homemade, but not *good* homemade, not like antiques. More like crap wood just thrown together with cheap nails. There are another couple chairs, just as ugly, by a fireplace. There's an old iron cookstove, there's a cupboard the shelves have all fell out of, and there's what's left of a rope bed at the back of the room, ropes all tore and hanging down. I see a torn cord and what's left of a cloth curtain on the floor that might've made the bedroom a little more private.

There's a ladder along the side wall that goes up into the attic, and I figure kids must've slept up there, but the wood's all dry and rotten, so I'm not gonna risk it. "So," I say to Pete, "you think this is the Lovin mansion?"

He nods, like it's the greatest place he's ever seen. "Sure of it," he says, and he heads for the ladder.

"Whoa, hoss," I tell him. "That don't look any too safe to me. Besides, it's gettin' dark. Let's wait till morning to look for the hidden gold, okay?"

"You mean it?" he says. "We can stay here tonight?"

"Not *here*," I say, "but in the RV, sure. You brought stuff to cook, right?" Because by now I'm getting real hungry.

He says he did, so we go back to the RV, and it *is* getting dark, and we trip over some roots but we make it okay. Pete's got some burgers in the fridge that we fry up, and we have a couple of beers. I try to calm him down a little, tell him that even if this is the old Lovin place, we ain't gonna find shit, but he doesn't seem to care.

After we eat, he asks me if I'd sing the song for him, what there is of it, and he's got a little Martin Backpacker guitar, so I do, and he sits there grinning like a kid. I sing a few more songs, but I'm feeling pretty tired after getting up so early, so we open the RV windows, since it's a little stuffy, and crawl into our bunks and turn off the lights. It's dark and quiet, just the sound of bugs chirping, and I fall asleep as quick as that.

When I wake up it's still dark, and at first I think what I hear is an animal yowling, like a cat in heat. But as I get more awake I realize it's a human voice, and it's singing, and it's just awful, God, like nails on a chalkboard. I sit up and listen, and damned if I can't make out "'who wooed me with words so sweet.'"

I get out of the bunk and call Pete's name, but there's no answer. I feel around his bunk, but he's not there. Well, I don't know what the hell is going on, so I grab a flashlight from where I saw Pete put one, and I turn it on and open the little case I brought along and I get out a .38 revolver I'd brought and I shove it down the front of my pants, reminding myself not to blow my balls off.

That might seem a little extreme, but we're out there in the middle of nowhere and Pete's gone, and I don't know who the hell else is up in these hills. So I go outside and I don't need the light, because the full moon's come up over the horizon and it's plenty bright to see where I'm walking, even with all the trees around.

I get closer to the cabin and see there's lights on inside. The voice is still singing—it's up to the part now where they find the dead girl by the creek, and that voice is so weird I gotta look down at the creek to make sure there *isn't* a body lying there. Funny thing—even though I got closer to the cabin, the voice didn't seem to get any louder. It was like I was hearing it inside myself, like distance didn't have anything to do with it.

When I got to the cabin I didn't go in the door, but went around to the window instead and just raised my head up over the bottom of the sill. I damn near pissed myself. Pete was in there sitting on that dirty floor, in all the dust and the mouse turds, and sitting right next to him was the ugliest old woman I've ever seen. I don't have much of a gift for words outside of songs, but believe you me, I wouldn't write any kind of song about that woman. She was like somebody dug her up and barely squirted some juice into her old dry skin. Her hair was dirty gray-yellow, like week-old snow in the gutter, and her eyes were these little black beads that honed into Pete like a hawk on a baby rabbit. There were more lines on her face than there were on Pete's maps. How ugly was she? Think of the worst thing you can and go a hundred more miles. Then keep driving.

After that first glimpse, I shot my head back down again. Christ knows I didn't want her looking at me the way she was at Pete. There were plenty of chinks in the wall, and I found one to look through. I felt safer then, though I really didn't know why that old woman scared me so much. I'd find out. I saw that the light in the cabin was from a few candles, but everything else was the same, and I wondered where the hell that old woman had been keeping herself—up in the attic maybe, or could be there was a cellar with a trapdoor we hadn't noticed.

By then she was singing the fourth verse, that short one about the gal feeling guilty, and then the chorus. When she stopped, Pete said, "My

God, that was beautiful. I've heard that song sung hundreds of times, but never like that."

I thought maybe he was putting her on, because I'd never heard it sung like that neither. But he sounded sincere as could be, and he told her that her voice sounded wonderful. I could see him looking at her like she was an angel, and I wondered what the hell was wrong with him. And then he answered my question for me, or at least I thought.

"Would you sing me the rest?" he says. Bingo, I think to myself—*that's* why he's being so sweet to her. He thinks she's a Lovin. He's after the goddam song, that's all, and if it means telling a crazy old lady she looks like an angel and sings like a bird, old Pete'll be taping feathers to her arms if he has to.

The old woman doesn't say a thing at first. She just touches his face with those fingers like old bent twigs, and I wonder how Pete keeps from shuddering. Then she leans in that wrinkled old road map of a face and whispers something in his ear. I can't hear the words, but it sounds like paper scraping on a two-day growth of beard.

Then Pete nods and be damn if he doesn't touch *her* face, lets his fingers trail down her cheek and move over to her lips and then, Jesus Harvey Christ, he kisses her. And I don't mean like you kiss your grandma. He lays it right on her, open mouthed, and I see something kind of fat and black that I think is maybe her tongue, and man, that's all I want to see. I look down and take a few deep breaths, thinking about the *lengths* that people will go to to get what they want, and hoping I never get that desperate.

After I don't know how long, I look back up, and now, good God, it's even worse. I mean, he's doin' her, right there on the floor. They got their clothes off and he's on top of her, and I never saw anything like that in my life, it looked like he was trying to screw that thing in the basement in those *Evil Dead* movies. I near to puked, and I looked away again but I still heard them, Pete panting like he was, I don't know, in the throes of ecstasy, and that old woman just grunting like a pig, louder and louder till it seemed like something busted inside her, and she let out this howl like some crazy monkey with its tail on fire.

It got quiet then, and I looked through the chink. They were both lying there, and it wasn't pretty, and I started thinking about what an absolute *whore* Pete Waitkus was, and I'da bet dollars to donuts that Alan Lomax never would've done nothing like that for a lousy song.

It was almost like Pete heard me thinking, bringing him back to square one, because he said, "Now… now will you sing for me?"

And she did. She started with that shortened fourth verse, and I'm not gonna try and sound like her because there's no way, but it was all high and airy, not as screechy as before, but just plain spooky…

I begged him to go and save his dear life,
But alas he would not flee.
With the moon in the sky they hung him on high,
And the guilt sat hard on me.

She paused for a second, and I thought, oh shit, that's all. She screwed Pete *twice* tonight. But then she went on, and it was the money shot…

For I had slain that maiden fair
With my love's knife cold and straight,
In hope he would run toward the rising sun
And escape the Lovin fate.

Damn me, yes. We were getting there, all right. Nobody'd ever heard *that* one before. She started on the chorus…

Mother come quickly, Father come quickly…

Then I heard a rustling, shuffling kind of sound that seemed to be outside with me, and when I turned my head I froze. Up toward the front of the cabin there were some people walking. I counted four shapes in the moonlight, one after another. They were moving slow, but like they knew where they were headed.…

Brother and Sister, see…

The two shorter ones had on long skirts, and the two tall ones were wearing pants, so I figured two men and two women, but when they went through the door and I saw them in the candlelight, they could've been anything. What was left of their hair was long and straggly, and if the old woman on the floor was a little long in the tooth, then these four had already had the worms at them. And that's not just a figure of speech.

The only man I ever did love
Is hanging in front of me.

Then the old woman says, "It's time for the last verse," and she puts on her dress, thank God, pulls it over her head as fast as a young woman might, and quick gets on her feet while the others surround Pete, who's still naked.

The two in pants reach down and grab him, one by his legs and the other by his arms, and pick him up like a baby. They go outside with him, moving fast now, toward that pole in the forks of two trees that I thought was the frame for a swing. The one man drops the top half of Pete's body and the other one hauls up on the legs so he's got Pete's feet up in the air, one on either side of the pole. Then one of the women sticks Pete through the back of both ankles—Jesus, did he squeal—with a long wooden stake sharpened on both ends, and before I can shut my jaw, they got him hanging head-down from the pole, and I realize that it ain't no swing. It's a pole for slaughtering hogs.

I fumbled for the gun in my pants and started to pull it out, but it got caught, and before I could free it, the old woman started to sing again. It was the last verse. Oh Jesus, was it ever, and now her voice sounded almost sweet. And this is what she sang...

We hanged him up by his pretty white feet
So his hair near touched the ground,
We bled him and skinned him and butchered the meat,
The sweetest to be found.
We ate of the flesh, we drank of the blood,
And the power came over us then,
As strong as the rush of a springtime flood,
And the Lovins became young again.

Then one of the men cut Pete's throat.

I knew it was too late, my hand on the gun slumped. The blood just poured out of him, and one of the women caught it in a wooden bowl. He kept moving for a while, but he was dead. I couldn't have saved him. I keep telling myself that, and I hope it's the truth.

Then they did what she said they'd do in the song. And I could only crouch there in the shadows and watch, afraid to move, praying the moon wouldn't light me up. Hell, I didn't know what they were, I didn't know if I even *could* shoot them, if it'd do any good. It wouldn't do Pete any good, that was for sure.

After they got done with Pete—taking what they wanted from him— they went into the cabin, and they ate and drank like the song said, and I was still too scared to move, to make a sound. But after a while the sounds inside the cabin, like pigs eating from a trough, they stopped, and it got quiet, and it was darker too. I'd just started to move when I heard the old woman's voice—at least I think it was hers. It sounded different, soft but... *stronger*. It was singing.

It was singing a final chorus, a chorus that maybe nobody outside this hollow had ever heard.

When it was finished, I looked into the cabin through the chinks. All the candles but one had burned out. The Lovins, all five of them, were lying on the floor, like hogs that had eaten their fill and fallen asleep.

I stood up and took a step away from the cabin, and my foot lit right on a dry branch that snapped loud as a breaking bone. I held still. I could feel sweat just oozing out of me. I waited for footsteps crossing the cabin floor to the door, but they didn't come.

So I got a little braver and looked in through the window. None of them were moving at all. It was like they were dead drunk. And then I knew what I had to do.

I thought about it as I picked my way through the trees toward the RV. Whatever these things were, they were evil. I didn't know if they'd magicked Pete or what, but my folks are from the hills, and my grandpas and grandmas and aunts and uncles told me things that people would say were crazy, but which they really believed in. They saw things happen with their own eyes that we'd say were impossible. And I saw something tonight that made no sense at all in the real world. At the very best, these... *people* were murderers. Pete was dead, and they'd killed him. And worse.

I'd seen the two-gallon can of gas in the back of the RV, so I took it and a pack of matches and went back to the cabin. It was still dark but for the moon, and I finally looked at my watch. Two thirty-five. There was plenty night left—too much of it.

It took me some nerve to go inside, but I did. The Lovins weren't moving. Hell, they didn't even seem to be breathing now. The last candle was burnt out, but the moon gave me just enough light to work. I slopped the gas all up the dry wood walls and over the floor. I didn't splash any on the Lovins, though, just in case they might wake up, but they didn't. The tallest man, who I took to be the father, was lying in a patch of moonlight, and he wasn't what he'd been before. His hair was full and long and dark, except for gray at the temples, and his skin was whole again.

That was enough. I didn't want to look at the others.

I poured a trail of gas out through the front door and then touched a match to it. It ran inside quick as a snake and the whole shebang went up at once. That dry wood took to fire like kindling, and in less than a minute the cabin was blazing. Nothing moved inside. I don't think even the burning woke them up.

The hollow was pretty well hid, so I doubted anybody'd see the flames, and there was enough of a clearing around the cabin that I didn't think it'd set the woods on fire, though I didn't give a damn if it did or not. I wasn't thinking real clear.

But clear enough to haul down what was left of Pete. I found an old shovel in an outbuilding and buried him away from the cabin, back in the woods. It would've been quicker to toss him in the fire, but I didn't want him with them. Not any more than he was.

I said some words over him, climbed in the RV, and drove through the dark back toward Nashville. I got lost a couple times on those dirt roads, but finally hit a blacktop and got my bearings. Back at Pete's I put the RV in his driveway and pulled my car out of his garage without anybody seeing me, and drove home.

I had the song with me. I had it in my head. And by God, I was gonna do something with it. I couldn't tell the truth about how I got it, so I figured I pull that journalistic thing and say I couldn't reveal my sources. If people don't believe me, the hell with them. One thing in my favor is that it makes something terrible out of a song everybody loves, and if I'd made it up on my own, I sure wouldn't have done that.

I kept Pete's DAT copy of Bertha Echols and played it again and heard something else different. That line about "You are a lovin' daughter/My father said to me/But before you wed I'll see him dead…" That wasn't transcribed right either. Bertha Echols sings it "You are *the Lovin* daughter" and not "but"— "*So* before you wed I'll see him dead," like one thing follows the other, and for the Lovins it did.

Once I had *all* the lyrics in my head, I told my manager about it and he got to work. Boy, did he ever. I'm recording it next week, and Sony's already offered to buy out my Rounder contract. I'm getting a full hour with Terry Gross on National Public Radio, twenty minutes with Larry King, I'm booked on *Prairie Home Companion*, but we're actually gonna spring the song on *60 Minutes*. I get the final segment, and they're flying to Nashville and broadcasting me *live* singing it for the first time. A straight ahead ballad with guitar, no banjos or bluegrass from now on. Oh no, I'm looking to get back into country, where the money is.

Hell, I can wear a cowboy hat as well as the next guy, and lose a few pounds around my middle, too. Besides, the country crowd aren't as tough on you as those tightass bluegrass folks if you wanta split from your wife and remarry—or hell, maybe just be a swinger again.

Since Linda left, my love life's been drier than a west Texas August, but it looks like my luck might be changing. Met a real honey in the Station Inn a few nights ago. Incredible. A ten. Eyes to drown in, sweetest voice you ever did hear, and we been goin' out every night since. Kinda surprised me she'd be rubbin' up on a guy my age, but maybe she's got one of those daddy complexes you hear about. I know she's got her sights set on this old songbird, because she says she wants to take me home tonight to meet her kin. What the hell, maybe her mama can cook.

A certain chubby mandolin player made a crack about the "old hag" I was with—I knew that boy's eyesight was bad from the diabetes and the booze, but not *that* much. He must be near blind as a bat. Or just jealous. Can't blame him, I guess. It's pretty damn amazing that a girl like her is sweet on a guy like me. Yep, my luck's just runnin' good for a change.

That's about it, I guess. Tomorrow's *60 Minutes*, and I get famous again. I have to confess, though, I guess my conscience is bothering me a little—not over what I did up there in the mountains, but about whether

I should do it or not, you know, take a song that people have loved their whole lives and turn it into something else, something… ugly. But hey, you can't buy this kind of publicity. If I hadn't have gotten it, maybe somebody else might've. And the money'll be nice—I got the copyright, and whoever covers it—and there'll be plenty in years to come—will have to pay old Billy Lincoln.

Yeah, like I say, the luck's runnin' good as a spring stream.

But I never did play that last chorus, did I? The last one I heard the old lady sing. Well, okay then, here we go, just in case I get hit by a meteor or struck by lightning before tomorrow night…

Mother come quickly, Father come quickly,
Brother and Sister see.
Every man I ever did love
Has given more years to thee.

Sweet.

◄○►

IN THE ABSENCE OF MURDOCK

TERRY LAMSLEY

"Oh, it's you Franz, come on in."

"I've come to see Jerry. Is he at home?"

"Of course he is. Where else would he be? He's always at home nowadays, remember. He's upstairs, waiting for you, I expect."

Franz gave his sister a curious look. "How do you know that?"

"I suggested that he call you or another of his old friends."

"Is something wrong?"

"Possibly. Probably," Barbara said, pulling the front door shut behind him.

Franz said, "I can hear it in your voice and Jerry sounded very strange when he phoned."

"Yes, I expect he did."

"Are you going to tell me what it is?"

"The—problem? Well, I'm not sure about that. I'd better let Jerry explain. It would sound better coming from him."

"Really? Why's that?"

Barbara gave Franz a wild, slightly irritated look. "Please," she said, "go on up. He'll be pleased to see you."

"You seem almost embarrassed about something, Barbara."

"Not really, no—it's not that, exactly—but we've both been under a bit of a strain recently, for the past few days, in fact."

"It shows."

"Well, you're here now. Perhaps you can sort things out."

Franz started to climb the stairs. "At least I'll try," he said.

Barbara waited until he was passing the chair lift waiting at the top of the stairs before she called out, "Thanks for coming, Franz. Jerry will be so pleased to see you."

Franz said, "So you said, just now."

He walked along the landing, stopped outside his brother-in-law's room, and waited a few moments before lifting his fist and rapping rather loudly on the door.

"Is that you, Franz? Come on in."

Franz walked in to the room Jerry called his office. It resembled an office in as much as it contained a large desk covered with a certain amount of paper and a typewriter. Jerry called himself an 'old-fashioned' writer. He claimed to despise computers and people who used them and was proud of his antiquated method of producing his and Murdock's scripts. As far as Franz could remember, Murdock transferred the finished script to respectable Word form, but Jerry was not supposed to be aware of that. Murdock was not present but Franz thought he could detect the faint smell of the man's horrible cigars hanging in the air.

Jerry was sitting in a wheelchair near the window. The heavy curtains were drawn and the only light in the room came from a big lamp hanging over the desk.

Franz said, "What have you been up to Jerry?"

"Not a lot. We've just about put the new series to bed, I'm pleased to say."

"You didn't invite—summon—me here to tell me that."

"True enough. I'd forgotten what an extremely no-nonsense sort of person you were Franz. Forgive my attempted polite small talk."

"Barbara thinks you've got a problem."

"Hum. Well, it's not exactly a problem. One that you might be able to solve, that is."

"What is it then?"

"Something inexplicable, Franz."

"Go on then, astonish me."

"Okay. Murdock has gone missing."

"He's walked out on you? Doesn't surprise me at all, you can be a pain in the neck at times, as I'm sure you're aware. I'm surprised that the working relationship has lasted so long. He's probably had enough or too much of you. Needs a break. I expect he'll turn up in his own good time."

"I fear not."

"Why?"

"The circumstances of his disappearance were… peculiar."

For some reason Franz found this funny. He laughed then said, "Just what exactly is on your mind, Jerry. Do you want me to go and look for him?"

"No, that may not be necessary, but I'd like your opinion. Just let me explain."

"Do, by all means."

Jerry put his hands together in a prayerful attitude, tapped his fingers together one by one, than hauled his wheelchair round so it was exactly facing Franz. Franz supposed he was attempting to appear relaxed, but he had the same mildly embarrassed expression on his face that Franz had seen on his sister's face a few minutes earlier.

He said, "I assume you know how we work together, Murdock and I?"

Franz had watched an episode of the comedy Murdock and Jerry were responsible for, *Dead Funny Ted,* set in a funeral parlor run by a doddering old fool called Edward and set in a picturesque seaside town populated almost entirely by elderly people. He had found it gormless and not the least bit funny, but he didn't think it necessary to tell Jerry that. Besides, the public were supposed to love it. Instead he said, "I read something somewhere, in one of the TV Sunday supplements I guess, how you work as a team. About how you read the papers together in the morning in search of ideas then get down to work in the afternoon."

Jerry nodded, "Murdock enjoys what he calls 'our daily disaster sessions'. Always seems to be something terrible happening somewhere. You have to laugh."

"I believe it mentioned something about that too."

Jerry permitted himself an uneasy smile of satisfaction on hearing this. "That's right. That gets us going. Anyway, we both have our different roles. I provide the plots and situations and Murdock handles the characterization and dialogue. Believe it or not, he's good at jokes. Or, rather, a humorous turn of phrase. Myself, I'm less so."

Jerry paused as though he expected Franz to make some comment. Franz didn't so Jerry continued, "It always worked well enough for both of us. We were just about finishing up on our fifth series, you know."

"I didn't."

"Yes, it's been what you might call a runaway success."

"That's very good."

"We were working on putting the finishing touches to the last episode a few days ago. Murdock was going through his paces, speaking every character's part aloud, as he has always insisted on doing, searching about for the humor in the situation we've reached in the script. I had turned my chair away from him and wheeled it up to the window for some fresh air. My lungs and heart, as you know, are not good, especially in the presence of Murdock's cigar smoke."

"I don't know how or why you stand it."

"As I said, we have to work as a team, all for one and one for all. Murdock says he can't think without a smoke and we each need the support of the other. It's the way we get things done."

"Humm. It once occurred to me that he uses those particularly pungent cigars to hide another more personal smell."

"Barbara told me she sometimes has the same suspicions. She keeps her distance."

Franz, resisting the temptation to yawn, said, "Anyway, carry on."

"It's going to be a bit tricky explaining the next bit. Barbara, usually so sympathetic, can't follow me at all after this point. Anyway, see what you think."

"You had your back to Murdock and you were looking out of the window."

"I was doing a bit of free thinking, I call it, searching for inspiration, letting my mind wander, and was not really aware of my surroundings. While I was daydreaming I realised that Murdock's voice had stopped and the room had fallen very silent. Even when he's not mumbling away to himself Murdock fidgets about and makes noises. He giggles to himself and coughs and sighs a lot. I couldn't hear a thing from him so I looked round to see if he was alright."

"And he wasn't."

"No, he really wasn't. He wasn't there at all."

"He'd left the room."

"He certainly wasn't in it. It took me just a few seconds to establish that fact. Then I smelt burning and that worried me, as you can imagine. I thought the house might be on fire but then I saw smoke rising from over there," he pointed, "just where Murdock had been sitting and I found a cigar end smoldering on the carpet."

Franz leaned forward and rested his hand on his forehead in hope of concealing the smile that he couldn't avoid. Jerry said, "What's the matter?"

"Nothing, please continue."

"Yes, well, I had to call Barbara then, because if I reached down for it I risked falling out of my wheelchair. I mean, I could have killed myself, it was that risky. My condition is very delicate. Luckily she heard me and ran up at once." He pulled a peculiar face, like a cautious rat sniffing the air, then said, "There's what's left of the cigar. I thought I'd better keep it." He stretched out and slid a large glass ashtray towards Franz.

After giving the tray and its contents a brief inspection Franz said, "Why?"

"Did I keep it? I suppose as some sort of evidence."

"Evidence of what? Surely, at that time it didn't occur to you that something had gone wrong."

"Oh yes it did. No doubt about it. There was a *feeling* in this room. Barbara noticed it I think, but she didn't say anything, so as not to upset me even more, bless her."

"She could see that you were upset, then?"

"I couldn't hide it. And she was furious about the burnt carpet. I tried to explain but she didn't, couldn't, understand what had happened and I was too confused to make much sense. I mean, I wasn't sure myself. She got the message that Murdock had gone after dropping his cigar but she wasn't much surprised because she's said many a time that the man was a clumsy lout."

"Well, let's face it, she's not far wrong."

Jerry looked mildly disapproving of that. "Murdock has his faults, no doubt about it, but together we bring in the money. I may not be around much longer, and there's seven years left before the mortgage on this house is paid. I frequently have to remind Barbara of that when she criticizes Murdock."

"Anyway, you say he's gone missing for the moment," Franz said.

"I said he's vanished."

"And you saw and heard nothing when he went?"

"Umm, well, there was a slight sound, just before I looked round and found he had gone. At least, I think so."

Franz was tired. It had been a long, hard day in the library where he had been doing some research since it had opened at nine in the morning. He took a discrete look at his watch and found it was now almost eleven in the evening. He got out of his chair and yawned. Jerry got the message and said, "You are leaving. I'm sorry to have kept you. It was good of you to come."

"What was it though, this sound you heard?"

Jerry sought the precise expression to describe the noise he thought he had perceived, then said, "It was like a sharp inhalation and exhalation of air."

"Of breath?"

"Almost certainly."

"Like a sigh, then. Perhaps Murdock's last sigh? Or gasp?"

"It's no joke. I'm deadly serious about this."

"I'll go away and think about what you've told me but perhaps, if Murdock really has disappeared or had some sort of accident, wouldn't it be better to call the police?"

"No, no way am I having anything to do with them. They'll question me and I will have to tell the truth and they'll think I'm mad. Do you think I've gone insane?"

"It crossed my mind," Franz confessed, "but I think it more likely you just got it all wrong. Maybe you fell asleep for a short while that day and Murdock left without waking you."

"He couldn't do that. He makes too much noise, I told you. He bellows about and blunders into everything. Knocks things over."

"He's a big man. Anyway, I'm off now. I'll have a fish about and I'll be in touch."

"What do you mean 'fish about'?"

"I'm not sure. I'll see if I can dig into things a bit, if you know what I mean?"

"I don't. But that's fine. Thank you Franz. I'm sorry to have off-loaded all this on you. But I felt I had to tell someone who was not too… judgmental."

Franz slipped out of the room and almost ran downstairs. At the bottom he found his sister waiting for him.

"What do you think?" she said. "Has he told you the whole story?"

"He told me too much. More than I can believe."

"When he called me up on Wednesday, to extinguish a cigar Murdock had dropped, I had no idea that he was up there alone. Usually I hear Murdock leaving the house. He can only manage three stairs then he has to have a rest. Like a bloody elephant coming down. And he usually calls out goodbye to me before he leaves. I didn't hear a thing that day."

"Perhaps he was in a hurry for some reason. Late for an appointment. Wanted to get away without causing a fuss."

"I expect you're right but people do disappear under odd circumstances. Strange things do happen, Franz."

"Not to me they don't. I've lived for almost fifty years and nothing remotely strange has ever happened to me."

"That's why I suggested Jerry get in touch with you to hear his story. You're so down to earth. Jerry believes what he says though. I can't get him away from that."

"He's delusional in my opinion. Not that I know anything about unusual psychological states. But you said yourself you've both been under a lot of strain recently. Perhaps he's been working too hard."

"We were doing okay before Murdock went missing, Franz."

◄◦►

Next morning, Sunday, Franz lay in bed until just before noon, thinking about the work he was planning to do on his new project and trying not to think about Jerry or Murdock. It was a perfect day for working indoors, with a constant drizzle falling outside. But, after he had dressed and eaten a late breakfast, he phoned Barbara and asked for Murdock's address. As it happened it turned out to be quite near where he lived. After establishing that Murdock was not answering his phone he told Barbara that he was going to call round to see what, if anything, was going on.

"Murdock probably isn't aware that he's caused this upset Barbara," he told her. "I'll see if I can get him to explain himself."

"That's really good of you Franz, but be careful."

"What?"

"You heard what I said."

"Are you suggesting Murdock might pose some sort of threat?"

"Not really, no. But we don't know what might happen next, do we? I mean the man's disappeared, hasn't he?"

Franz put the phone down, grimaced at his reflection in a mirror, and went out to his car.

⊷◇⊶

Franz recognised the spot as soon as he saw it. He'd passed it many times going in and out of town. A thirty yard square of grass, still covered by an inch of grimy snow from weeks before. It was surrounded by a mixture of bungalows and cheaply built houses of various vintages and with little or no individual parking space so their occupants had to squat their vehicles in front or on a makeshift and crumbling area of cement set in the among the unkempt grass. The higher walls of a larger and grander estate recently built behind loomed above them, giving the impression that the older group of houses had clung on where they were not wanted.

After finding space for his car on the cracked cement Franz looked about for number 15 which proved to be the largest of the bungalows. Obviously the script writing didn't bring in as much money as he had supposed or, for some reason, Murdock chose to live in one of the less salubrious parts of town.

Franz walked in the continuously drizzling rain through a creaky gate and up to Murdock's front door. As soon as he rapped his knuckles on the glass something, probably a small animal, went berserk in the hall beyond. He could hear it leaping and scratching frantically. He tried to get sight of it through the letter box but could not do so because a flap of canvas hung behind the door. He whispered what he hoped were words of comfort to the creature, whatever it was, which only made it wilder in its desperation. Franz withdrew and took stock of the rest of the building, which was much bigger than he had supposed, by circumnavigating it. When he got round to the front door again he was pretty sure that Murdock was not at home. He tried peering into the gloom beyond the front windows when a voice said, "Would you be looking for Mr. McFee, by any chance?"

It took Franz a few seconds to recognise Murdock's surname, it was so long since he'd used it.

He turned and saw a bald man in a boiler suit carrying aloft an open umbrella. He said, "Yes, have you any idea where he is?"

"No," the man said. He seemed to be measuring Franz up carefully.

Franz said, "There is some kind of animal in there that obviously wants to be let out."

"That will be Mr. McFee's dog, Rasputin."

"Is it hungry?"

"If Mr. McFee is not at home and it's not been fed, then it will be, yes."

"Is he in the habit of going away and leaving it?"

"No. He gives my lad charge of it."

"Your lad?"

"I'll fetch him. He's got a key." The man went swiftly off towards the house next door and returned at once with a boy of about fourteen huddled up next to him under the umbrella. "This is the feller, Clive," he said. "Says he's a friend of Mr. McFee."

Franz saw at once that Clive, unfortunately, was not all there. His father's words seemed to mean nothing to him and he stared steadily at the ground in front of him.

"Clive is a bit slow, but he loves that dog. Mr. McFee isn't here to let him in but if you say so he'll open the door and let it out."

"Well, certainly, yes, let's do that."

The man said, "Go on Clive," and the boy sauntered away holding the key out in front of him. A moment later the dog burst out of the open door like a flood of bathwater, and squirmed round and round Clive's legs. The boy knelt down and Rasputin licked his face voluptuously.

"It doesn't bark," Franz observed. "Why's that?"

"Mr. McFee had it operated on, I believe."

That seemed an odd remark to Franz. "I'd better take a look round in the house, to make sure nothing unfortunate has happened," he said and, when the man made no objection, he made his way into the bungalow.

The stale smell of Murdock's cigars hung about the place, particularly the kitchen, which was obviously the room most used. A few small piles of dog shit were scattered about on the floor, which Franz grubbed up with some paper towels. Not as many turds as might be expected but then the dog hadn't eaten for possibly three or four days. Franz opened the fridge. Not much there either—some wilting salad, a pint of milk beginning to turn blue and a few cheese rinds. Relics of meals. Obviously, Murdock was not a fancy eater. On a shelf next to the refrigerator he spotted some tins of dog food. He eased the lid off one and turned its contents out into a saucer and set it down on the linoleum.

The large table obviously served Murdock for many purposes as its entire area was covered with books, magazine, DVDs, some dirty mugs and dishes, a computer and various other, to Franz, unrecognisable electrical gadgets. Two large scrapbooks of newspaper cuttings contained reviews of *Dead Funny Ted,* some of them surprisingly ancient, and reports of various disasters, both at home and in distant parts of the world.

Having seen enough of the kitchen Franz set about inspecting the rest of the house for signs of a possibly sick or even dead Murdock, perhaps in the bedroom.

The bungalow was surprisingly spacious, and contained more rooms than Franz had expected. Some of them were completely empty. Murdock hadn't even bothered to put bulbs in the light sockets, others contained oddments of furniture stacked without thought any which way. Murdock lived a far more desolate life than Franz had imagined. And this from a man who laughed a lot. But not, Franz reminded himself, at particular jokes and incidents. He seemed to find amusement in life itself.

At the rear of the bungalow Franz became confused because someone, Murdock presumably, though he didn't seem a likely candidate to be a master of DIY, had fitted neat partitions into two rooms to divide them up into a number of smaller spaces. Finding his way round them in the semi-darkness kept Franz fully occupied for some time and he was relieved when he came upon a wooden door which he took to be at the back of the house. He tried the handle, found it wasn't locked, and hurried through it, only to find himself in a large, windowless room lit only by some slight luminescence originating in what at first he took to be some indoor plants. He stopped to get a better look at them and saw that in fact they were what appeared to be the upper—in fact the topmost—branches of a large tree and, looking down, he realised that they continued down into a space below the bungalow.

Bemused, he ventured forward a couple of steps and peered into what he thought might be a cellar and saw that the space below was too wide and deep to be anything of the kind. He could see a very long way down—so much so that he felt himself reeling. His fear of heights made him almost topple forward and it was with some effort that he managed to scramble back some distance towards the door. He held his right hand up to his brow as his head had for some reason begun to ache and glared again at the branches that protruded through the floor.

He noticed that some of them were beginning to move and sway a little where they were closest together, at the back, and thought he could see a clump of something in amongst them, like a platform, or maybe it was—could it be—a nest? It appeared to be a good four feet across and three or more feet deep.

Yes, he knew then that that was what it had to be, some kind of nest made of branches and the tattered remains of what appeared to be curtains, bed sheets and various scraps of clothing. And the reason that the branches were swaying and bending was because something, some creature, had been aroused by his presence, and was coming out of its nest to investigate the cause of its disturbance.

After a couple of quite violent shudders the nest tipped forwards at the side nearest Franz, far enough for him to get a glimpse of what could have been the top of a large hairless head and perhaps the tips of the fingers of a chubby, grasping hand.

Franz must have fled then, though he had no memory later of going through the wooden door and closing it behind him. He found himself in the partitioned rooms trying frantically to find his way out.

He fumbled and tumbled about in the near darkness for some time then, before he managed to relocate Murdock's kitchen where he stopped for a moment to listen for any sounds of anything following him. There were no indications of that at all. All around him was perfect silence.

He sat at Murdock's table just long enough to recover his breath and steady his head, then left the bungalow, slamming the door behind him.

He found the father of the boy who had gone off with Murdock's dog waiting for him near the front step. The man, still holding his umbrella, looked at him and said. "You've cut your hand. It's bleeding all down your jacket."

Franz couldn't think of anything to say to this but he realised it was true. He held the key out to the man who took it and said, "I'll give it to the boy."

Franz nodded.

"He's not in there dead or anything then, Mr. McFee?"

Franz shook his head this time.

"Don't worry about the dog. My boy will look after him in the meantime."

This time Franz forced himself to speak.

"Does he go into the house to collect it?"

"My boy? No, *never*. Mr. McFee wouldn't want him to."

"Hum. Does he often go away, Murdock? I mean Mr. McFee."

"Oh, from time to time, yes. That's when he tells my boy to look after the dog. Usually he gives him something to buy food for it. We don't have much money."

Franz reached into his pocket for his wallet. He had no intention of going back into the kitchen where the tins of dog food were stashed. He held out a note and said, "Is that enough?"

"I should think it will be, yes. Have you no idea when your friend is coming back then?"

Franz shook his head again and went off to his car.

⤙◇⤚

He drove home slowly, cautiously, not really concentrating on what he was doing. His mind was on other things. At one point he drove off the road down a side street and stopped while he sorted through his thoughts. What had he seen back in the bungalow? A hallucination or some kind of tableau devised by Murdock to scare away burglars? It would certainly have that effect but surely it would be better placed in the front of the building instead of hiding away behind a maze of wooden partitions where he, Franz, had only come across it as an afterthought, after searching the whole bungalow.

It then seemed to him that perhaps it had been that his brain had simply misinterpreted the information it was receiving and things were not as they seemed. He had never experienced any kind of hallucination before but that seemed a more reasonable solution to what he now began to think of as his "vision". He thought that might be the explanation for all such visions, religious and otherwise. If he, a determinedly unbelieving person, could think he saw such sights, then surely it could happen to anyone?

He drew comfort from that thought. He even began to wish he had stayed a little longer in Murdock's back room and even considered returning to take another look, but decided not to.

And he wouldn't mention anything about his visit to Barbara, apart from telling her that he had not been able to contact Murdock at all. No point in upsetting her even more.

He went back to the main road and drove home.

⫍⊙⫎

The phone rang twice that evening but Franz did not answer it. He felt guilty and slightly irritated about not doing so but his mind was not sufficiently calm to deal with his sister and her worries. He was certain it was her who was calling as hardly anyone else ever did.

Next day, Monday, he worked on his computer at home then, in the afternoon, returned to the library to continue his research on his project. When the library closed he went to a supermarket to buy supplies. He was loaded down with bags of food as he approached his front door behind which he could clearly hear his phone ringing. Flustered by the urgent sound he tried his best to get to it in time but fumbled with his key and almost dropped some of his bags. Meanwhile the phone stopped ringing.

He knew he ought to call his sister but was still unready to do so. No doubt she would call back.

She did, almost an hour later. This time he picked up the receiver.

"Hello, you're there at last then," Barbara said, then seemed to whisper something that he didn't catch.

"Sorry, could you repeat that?"

"No Franz, it doesn't matter."

"I went round to Murdock's place yesterday. He wasn't there. No sign of him. Did you know he has a dog though? That was a surprise. He's never seemed to me to be a pet loving sort of person."

"No, he's never mentioned a dog to me. What kind of dog?"

Franz realised he had no idea. The boy had run away with the creature so quickly he'd not been able to get a look at it. He explained as much to his sister who did not sound particularly interested.

"Anyway," she said, "I'll be able to ask him about it. He's back now."

"What!"

"Yes, it was all a misunderstanding. He's been ill and he didn't want to tell us for some reason, so he slipped away."

"Slipped away?"

"And he's done it again now. He's coming to see you. He should be there in ten minutes."

"Ten minutes."

"That's correct. Stop repeating what I say please."

"But why would he want to come here. Did you give him my address? He's never been here before."

"No, I didn't need to. He must know it. Anyway, he's heading in your direction now. He left as soon as you answered the phone and I told him you were in."

"But Barbara, you shouldn't have done that."

"Why on earth not?"

"I don't want to see him. I *particularly* don't. The bastard. What does he want with me?"

"Franz, it's not like you to talk of anybody like that. He said he just wants to thank you."

"For what?"

"Oh, I don't know. For caring enough to take the trouble to call on him?"

"Did you tell him I'd done that?"

"Not that I can remember, no. I didn't know you had."

"He was supposed to be ill wasn't he?"

"Perhaps he was too ill to answer the door."

"No he bloody wasn't."

"Franz, what's got into you? You're not normally like this."

Realising he had to end the conversation to prepare for Murdock's visit, Franz gruffly apologised, said he'd probably call her back later, and put down the phone. He went round his house checking all the doors and windows were shut and pulled all the curtains on the ground floor. Then he went up to his bedroom to watch and wait.

◄○►

He waited in the darkest part of his bedroom and kept watch on the street in front of his house. After about ten minutes a small unmarked white van drew up against the opposite pavement. The driver turned off the engine but didn't get out immediately, confirming, somehow, Franz's guess that Murdock was the occupant of the vehicle. This proved correct when the door suddenly swung open some time later and Murdock's huge bulk clambered into view. He was dressed in some kind of duffle coat with a hood concealing his face but Franz recognized the shuffling glide of his feet as he went round to the back of the van and opened the rear door. The dog ran out.

It doesn't look too happy, Franz thought. It had its tail between its legs and slunk along with its belly almost touching the ground. Murdock closed the back of the van and crossed the street towards Franz's house with the dog following close behind.

Franz moved backward a couple of steps, fearing he might be visible from the street. Murdock moved up to his front door and Franz expected him to knock or ring the bell but it didn't happen.

Guessing that Murdock was reconnoitering his house Franz waited to see what move his visitor would make next. After a long silence he heard his letter box squeak. Then Murdock appeared in his little front garden again, pursued by the dog. As he got to the point where the garden ended and the street began he stopped, turned, looked up to where Franz had concealed himself, and raised an arm in some sort of salute. At the same time the hood fell back and Franz saw that he was smiling broadly, almost laughing. He turned, crossed the street, let the dog in the back of the van, got in himself and drove away.

After waiting a few minutes in the dark Franz ventured out of his bedroom and went downstairs without turning on any lights. He saw that a folded piece of paper had been posted through his letterbox. There was enough light from the street lamp outside his house for him to see, when he unfolded the paper, that there was nothing written on it at all. But he got the message.

He spent the next half hour going round his house with a little torch and filling his rucksack with essentials for travel. He made sure he had his passport, credit cards in his wallet, and some folding money.

Then, after checking to make sure there was no sign of the white van anywhere nearby, he ran out to his car and drove swiftly away. After parking in the airport lot he checked the departures board then walked up to the Scandinavian Airlines stand and bought a one way ticket. He wasn't sure how long he was going to be away but it was definitely time he took a break. He'd decided he had a lot to get away from.

◄○►

Next morning, at about eleven o'clock as usual, Murdock lumbered into Jerry's room without knocking, with a selection of daily newspapers under his arm. He lit a cigar, sat down close to Jerry's wheelchair, and spread the papers on the table in front of him.

"Anything especially grim today?" Jerry asked, genuinely expectant of some entertaining bad news.

Murdock made a play of searching through the sheets of paper as he said, "Well, not much actually, it's been a good day for the world, all things considered, but I did spot one small item of interest. Now let me see… ah, here we have it." He held up a page of newspaper and said, "It seems a 747 came off the runway in Oslo last night and hit a luggage vehicle."

"Much harm done?"

"A few people hurt in the ensuing fire but only one fatality."

"Oh. Hardly worth mentioning, then."

"It says here that the dead man was believed to carry an English passport but the body was too badly burned to be identified. Next of kin have yet to be informed."

"They'll soon sort that out," Jerry said, without much interest.

Murdock, who seemed to be very pleased about something, perhaps just himself, said, "I expect they already have done."

Downstairs, sounding faintly mournful and further away than it actually was, a phone began to ring.

◄○►

YOU BECOME THE NEIGHBORHOOD

GLEN HIRSHBERG

"How'd it *start*?" Mom asks, taking a step back toward the curb. Her long-fingered hands have curled up at her sides like smacked daddy longlegs, and her braid has come loose and swings back and forth, gray and heavy, across her back. "How'd it start? How do I know?"

She tears her eyes away from the little triplex, just for a moment, and looks at me. I flinch, start to take her hand, but I'm afraid to. For so many years, after we left here, I'd see that expression bubble up, triggered by nothing: a bus sighing on a nearby streetcorner, or the sight of a tent-*sukka* billowing off the side of someone's porch, or a flying beetle landing on her hand, or a summer wind. Then she'd start screaming at me, or whoever was near. Even then, I knew it wasn't really me, and that did help, some.

Behind her, the sunset has ignited the smog, and the evening redness rises on the horizon behind the hazy towers of Century City, barely visible less than a mile from here. The traffic on Olympic is Sunday-evening sparse, the noise and the heat of it lapping around us rather than crashing down, the way it mostly did when we lived here. Low tide.

"I'm sorry," I murmur, starting back around the corner toward the side-street where we parked. "I didn't mean to bring you here. I actually forgot this place was so near. I just thought you'd want to see the building where Danny and I are going to be liv—"

"Do you remember the turtle?" my mother asks. And then she just folds her legs under her and sits down in the square of grass in front of the triplex. The angry expression has vanished. But there are tears. "Ry? Do you remember?"

She pats the grass. My legs are bare under my skirt, and if I sit there, they're going to itch. I do it anyway. For a moment, I wonder what who-ever currently lives in the front apartment will think, two women camped on their lawn with their backs to the traffic and their eyes riveted to those bay windows like *paparazzi*. But if the existing tenants are anything like we were, they'll never open those curtains—too many cars passing, too stark a reminder of the carbon monoxide seeping through every little gap in the walls and window frames—so they'll never see us.

All at once, I *do* remember. And I find myself glancing toward the hedge, then the back alley where the dumpster is, half-expecting to see that little, darker-green hump in the grass. That tiny, wrinkled head turned slightly sideways. "*So it can see the sky.*" That's what Evie used to tell me.

"A hundred years after we die," I say.

"What?" snaps my mother.

"Sorry. It's what she used to say. Evie. She said that turtle of hers could live 250 years. She'd already had it for like twenty. She said we could come back here a hundred years after we die and there it would be. Just being."

"Evie," my mother says, and for the first time all night—in a long while, really, at least around me—she offers up her gentle, close-lipped smile. Her softest one, that I loved so much when I was little, and lost when we left here. "Oh, God, Ry, you should have seen her."

"Mom, you used to make me call her Adopted Grandma. Didn't she walk me home from nursery school when you were at work? I saw her all the time."

"Not this time, you didn't. Oh, wow." To my amazement, my mother starts to laugh. Right on cue, from all the way down Olympic, comes a whiff of ocean breeze, just strong enough to blow out the laughter like a candle. Her shoulders tremble, though she can't possibly be cold. My shins have begun to itch.

I put my palms in the grass and make to stand, saying, "Well, I guess we should go."

But my mother is still smiling. At least, I think she is. "You asked how it started."

"Yeah. I did."

"Maybe this is it. I mean, obviously, it's not the beginning, it had to have been in full swing by then, but this is the first one I really remember. This is as close to the beginning as I can get."

Her shoulders tremble again. "Leyton," she says. "Mr. Busby, I mean…"

"I know who you meant, Mom."

"I actually don't know why he didn't blame me. Because it was kind of my fault."

I sigh, roll my head back on my neck to watch the ribbons of orange run the rim of the sky like a brush fire along a ridge. My mother follows my eyes up, and she goes rigid. She says something, too, but I can't make it out. I sigh again. "I'm not sure this qualifies as starting at the beginning."

"Mr. Busby'd moved in… I don't know… six months before? Fall of '95. I think."

"Did Evie always hate him?"

"I don't think she ever hated him, Ry."

"What are you talking about? Why else would—"

"She hated his being here. Totally different, in this case."

"Okay. Why did she hate him being here?"

My mom looks at me, and I want to weep. I've never actually seen the expression I unleash on her every fifteen minutes or so during our Sunday-night outings. But I suspect it looks like that. If that's true, at least my mother can't be as fragile as she generally appears.

"Why do you think?" she asks.

"Yeah. Okay. I just meant that that always surprised me about Evie. She seemed so open about everything, and everyone. Always talking about the Clintons, and propositions, and Greenpeace. I'm pretty sure she taught me all those words."

My mother nods. I'm still surprised she's let us sit here this long. "I think the riots really spooked her. Remember, she was eighty-four years old. She'd lived here a long, long time. For most of that, this neighborhood was one hundred percent Jews."

"A lulav in every window," I say, and my mother laughs.

"An etrog on every plate. Where'd she even get that? I've never seen an etrog on anyone's plate. Have you?"

I laugh, too. And my surprise tilts toward amazement. I am sitting with my mother in front of our childhood home—the one we left for the last time in an ambulance, with my mother in restraints and screaming—and we're laughing.

"So anyway," my mother says. "Here's our coal-skinned new retiree neighbor Mr. Busby, walking around the yard all the time in his half-buttoned, purple satin shirts—"

"That's right, those shirts!"

"—with his barrel chest stuck out. And there's little Evie, trapped upstairs tending to Stan—that was her husband—who was pretty much just a pool to pour morphine in by then. So mostly, she just stared out the window."

"'You become the neighborhood,'" I say, gliding my hands across the tops of the blades of grass, feeling their chemically treated ends prickle like gelled hair. "Do you remember her saying that?"

My mother pauses a moment, then shakes her head. "No, actually."

I do. More than once. Though I can't remember when. And even now, I don't know what it means.

My mother shakes her head again, but harder, like a dog shedding water. "You know, I really do have no idea how the pranks started. I think he might have brought her up a cold shrimp platter the first weekend he lived here. As a new-neighbor gesture, you know, not realizing. I don't think he'd ever met a Jew before, either, let alone known anything about keeping Kosher. But not long after that, she got him the gift subscription to *Hustler*, with the note that said '*To go with your shirts.*' Then he hid a bunch of those black, rubber June bugs all over that *sukka* she put up every year around back, on strings so he could make them scuttle across her little folding picnic table. Do you remember any of that?"

I shake my head. "Just the picnic table. And ears of corn? Did she hang ears of corn in there?"

"He put rubber bugs in those, too. After that, it was *on*. Seemed like one of them came up with a new torture for the other every single week."

Instead of smiling some more, my mother starts muttering again. At least now I can hear her. "She was so lonely," she says. "They both were." Then some things that I don't catch. The sky purples over our heads, and the breeze brushes past.

"So, this one time…" I finally prod.

She looks surprised, as though she thought she'd still been talking to me. Her braid swings like the tongue of a bell, and her body vibrates. "Sorry. Yes. This one time. I assume she got the clothes from Madolyn, Tell me you remember Madolyn."

"Good God, how could I forget them," I say, and my mother says *them* right with me, holding her hands a good two feet in front of her breasts, and there we are smiling again. Mother and daughter. We glance together across the street toward Madolyn's duplex. "You don't think she still lives there?" I ask.

My mother doesn't respond.

"Whose ex was she again? The *Family Affair* guy?"

"Not him. The one from the knock-off. With the beard."

"Oh my God, Mom, do you remember what she told me? When I was just sitting out here with the turtle, minding my seven year-old business? She came across the street in this tiny black dress, and she had to have been as old as Mr. Busby, right? Sixty, at least."

"Older," says my mother.

"So it's just me and the turtle, looking at the sky. And here comes Madolyn and her shadows. And she stands over us. And she puts her hands right on her boobs. And then she says…" I try for a smoker's rasp, though it doesn't quite come off. "*Just remember, Girlie. I got these for the husband. But I kept 'em for me.*" And then she turned around and went right back home."

My mother just nods, and takes a long time doing it. Her voice comes out sad. "That would be Madolyn. She was always so nice."

Nice?

More silence. Another sudden, nervous glance up in the air from my mother, and I know this can't last long. "Sorry I interrupted. You said Evic got something from her?"

"Oh. Right. Very possibly the same little black dress you just mentioned."

"What are you talking about?"

"And some fishnets. And some red lipstick. And some stilettos. Jesus, Ry, they had to have been seven inches high."

"Wait… she borrowed that stuff *for herself*? To *wear*?"

"For Mr. Busby."

At the gurgle in my throat, my mom actually grins. "It was horrible, really. And ingenious. You wouldn't think that sweet old woman… Mr. Busby's daughter was worried about him skulking around here by himself. She got him to take out a Personals ad in the *L.A. Weekly.* I helped him write it. And then I guess, maybe when I was trying to convince Evie to let me watch her husband sleep for a couple hours so she could go out and see a movie or something some evening, I must have let it slip. And that's what gave her the idea, which is why it was kind of my fault."

"You're telling me she answered his ad?"

"Made a date, told him she'd be by to pick him up. She didn't tell him who she was, of course."

"She actually went through with it? Went to his door dressed like that? What did he do?"

"I don't know, exactly. That is, I couldn't quite see. She made Madolyn and me hide in the hedge. All I could hear over our laughter was his screaming."

"That's…" I start, and don't know how to continue. I want to keep her talking about this forever, or at least long enough for me to get the picture straight in my head. Not of Evie, but of my mother crouched in a hedge with a friend, laughing. "I can't believe you haven't told me this before."

I know it's the wrong comment even before I finish. My mom's mouth twists, and her shoulders clench inward. She folds her arms across her chest.

"What happened after that?" I keep my voice light.

"Stan died," says my mother.

The sun goes, dragging all that color behind it, and around us, the apartment buildings lose their depth like false fronts on a set. Across the street is Beverly Hills. A whole other world. You can tell by the curlicues on the street signs.

Without warning, my mother starts to swell. Her arms come loose and drop to her sides, and her spine arches and her head tilts all the way back as her mouth falls open. The moan seems to surge out of the grass and up her throat, rattling her teeth as it bursts out of her.

"*Mom*," I gasp, grabbing for her hand, scrambling up on my knees to try getting an arm around her.

The moan stops. My mother holds her position, completely frozen, like a sculpture of my mother moaning. Then her eyes pop open.

"Do you remember that sound, Ry?"

"Remember it? What the hell are you—"

"You don't," she says. "I'm glad." Then she folds her arms back across her chest and lowers her chin and sits there, holding herself. "I'm so glad."

Usually, by this point on our Sunday evenings, I've dutifully offered up the most innocuous details of my work life and my grad-school plans and my relationship with Danny (since I have no intention of actually *bringing* Danny), for which my mother trades seemingly grateful nods and sometimes an anecdote about women's feet from the shoe store where she works. Most weeks, she doesn't break down, especially if I have her back in her apartment and ensconced in front of her Tivo'd *American Idol* episodes—all of which she also watched when they were first broadcast—by eight. This is the first night in years where I've lost track of the time, even for a little while. And yet, I'm all too aware we're on dangerous ground.

"Do you want to go home?" I ask gently. I even touch her shoulder, and she doesn't pull away, though she also doesn't unclench.

"It usually started around 2 a.m.," she says. "Sometimes earlier than that. Mostly not, though. You really don't remember?" There are no tears, now, just a gauntness that seems to have surfaced in her chin and cheeks.

This is what she'll look like, old, I think, for no good reason.

"The most amazing thing is that I really think she had no idea she was doing it. I think she did it in her sleep. By the third or fourth night after Stan died, *I* couldn't sleep at all for knowing it was coming. Somehow, being woken up by that, *to* that... it was just too much world, too fast.

"There wasn't any lead up. It came like an earthquake. That sound I just made, only a lot louder. And a thousand times as heartbroken. It went on and on and on, like she didn't even need to breathe. Then it would stop for maybe an hour, and then there'd be aftershocks, these quicker, more jagged moans. Those were so loud that that suspended light in my bedroom started swinging back and forth. You couldn't drown them out. I tried the fan. I tried headphones. *Nothing* worked. It was like they'd crawled inside my head.

"Which reminds me. This was also when the spiders came."

That, at least, triggers a memory. Up until now, it's been like watching my mother recount a completely separate life. Part of which she's made up, or at least exaggerated, because I may have only been seven, and I've always slept heavy, but surely I would have heard what she's describing. And retained it.

But those webs. Everywhere, on everything. "I remember them," I say.

Mostly, I remember the wolf spider outside our front door. We had bougainvillea climbing the iron grating on either side of our little stoop. And for months that spring and early summer—the last months we lived here—this one bulbous, pregnant wolf spider would weave a new web between them every single night. We discovered the web the first time when I raced out the door one morning, headed for the park, and wrapped most of the strands around my face. I don't think I started screaming until my mom did, and she didn't start, she later said, until she saw the spider itself dangling just under my earlobe like some outsized, nightmare earring, clawing with its hairy legs as it tried to scuttle up the air into my hair to hide. My mom whacked it into the bushes with her hand, then spent half an hour calming us both down and picking the insect carcasses and threading out of my curls.

We weren't laughing, then. Or ever, really, about the spiders. There were too many of them, attracted, the tv said, by the freakishly humid spring, the eruption of greenery and insects that draped the hillsides and gardens of midtown L.A. and made it look, for just that short while, like somewhere living things actually belonged.

But we developed a sort of affection for our lone wolf. Or fascination, at least. The way one might for a house ghost. Some nights, before sending me to bed, my mother would bring me to the front couch, draw back those bay-window curtains, flick on the porch light. And there she'd be, gray and translucent and hairy, scuttling back and forth seemingly in mid-air between the columns of bougainvillea, floating on her milky white egg-sac as though it were a balloon. Every morning, we took a broom, said we were sorry, and brought the web down so we could get out of the apartment. But we left the spider herself alone.

"Ry?" says my mother, startling me by brushing a fallen curl out of my eyes. She's never touched me, much. Not since I was very young. "What are you thinking about?"

I catch myself leaning away and feel bad, but too late. My mother has already withdrawn her hand. I try to smile, get some nostalgia into my voice. I'm surprisingly close to feeling some. I gesture toward the front stoop. "Our furry-legged friend."

She looks at my hands. Then the front of the apartment. Then she bursts into tears.

"Sorry," she says fast. "Sorry, sorry, sorry."

I reach to comfort her. But it never did any good when I was a kid, and it doesn't now. The sobs grab her by the shoulders and shake her.

They stop sooner than usual, though. And when my mother lowers her hands from her face, there's a steeliness in her jaw I don't remember seeing. "I'm just being stupid, as usual," she says. "It wasn't really that. It wasn't real. Obviously. It was just that time, those moans. I hadn't slept in so long, and those things were crawling over the place, and I missed your fucking asshole father, and…" her voice drops into its murmur. But lo and behold, it climbs back out. She looks at me. "It wasn't real," she says. "I want you to know I know."

I have no idea what to say to that. "We should get you home," I say eventually.

"Evie came down a few times that week after Stan died. Mostly in the evening, just to sit. You and I used to steal lemons off the trees by that condo complex around the corner, and I made lemonade, and the three of us would come right out here. Right about this time. We'd watch the spiders dancing up the walls and the sun going down and that turtle nosing around in the grass. Mr. Busby was away, I think his daughter'd taken him to Bermuda or something, and it was so quiet around here.

"I kept trying to ask Evie how she was doing, but she wouldn't talk about it. She talked about maybe going to see her sister in Maine, but not like she was really planning to do it. You showed her our wolf spider. She said there were lots more up under the eaves. She claimed she could hear them on the roof at night, and that she had a resident, too, who hung out by her bedroom window. An even bigger one. She didn't like its eyes.

"One night, later than usual—I was in a robe, and I'm sure you'd already gone to bed—she knocked on the door in tears and asked me to come out. She was in a robe, too. This horrible cream thing with blue lilies all over it. She was grabbing her arms to her chest.

"'They're biting him,' she kept saying. 'They're biting him. My poor Stan.' Then she showed me her hand. It was all purple on the back, she had this *huge* spider bite. Really nasty.

"'Evie, my God, you've got to treat that. Come in,' I told her. But she wouldn't. She said she had to get back. That they kept climbing on Stan and running around on him. She wasn't making much sense. Mostly, she was sobbing.

"I do remember one thing. At some point, she just started saying the word 'Gone.' And when I'd gotten her some lemonade and held her for a while—and I swear, Ry, she was thinner than you, it was like holding a garden rake except that she was so *soft*—she stuck her fingers under her glasses and wiped her eyes and said it again. 'Gone. What do people even mean when they say that? How can someone *go*? Go where? To me, he's as here as he ever was. He's right in the next room.'

"Know the worst part, Ry? What I remember thinking was that that was true. The guy'd been gone for ages. Months and months before he died. In a way, she was right.

"And somehow, between comforting her while she cried and getting her lemonade and wrapping her poor, old, squishy hand, I missed that part about the spiders biting him. I didn't think a single thing about what that meant until later that night, when Mr. Busby came home from his trip."

The silence seems almost peaceful at first, an organic lull in the conversation. But it lasts too long. My mother's staring up toward the windows of the upstairs apartment, and her mouth has formed an O. Her shadow stretches out long beside her on the grass, like a web she's spun, or gotten stuck in.

"Mom. Seriously. I don't need another moan-demonstration."

She blinks as though I've dumped water over her head. As though she has no idea what I'm talking about. Yet again, I feel horrible. But this has gone on for so many years.

"I didn't know he was back," she says. "I mean, we were friendly, he even had me bring in his mail sometimes. But it wasn't like with Evie. He kind of kept to himself.

"If I'd known he was back, I would have warned him. But I didn't, and

right on time at about 2:40 a.m., Evie went off. It was particularly horrible that night. God, Ry. Lying there in the dark, I think I started doing
it along with her, under my breath, just to keep from going crazy. Only
then—remember, I hadn't slept through the night since Stan died, so for
maybe eight days running—I started thinking maybe it *was* me making
the sounds, and that really freaked me out. And then the music exploded."

And there it is again. A surprising wisp of smile floating over her
face. "His choice was *inspired*, in a way. I mean, he must have put some
thought into it, after the moans woke him up. All of a sudden, these fat,
thudding drums boom out his windows. And this bass. *Buum, buum,
buum-bumm, dugga-dugga.* Rattled that picture of you on the Griffith
Park merry-go-round right off my wall.

"I could hear him yelling, too. Mr. Busby. 'Hear that?' he was shouting.
'Cause I'm sure hearing you, Old Bat.

"You know, you slept through that, too? I swear, Ry, sleeping through
the Northridge quake must have trained you, because you never even
moved. I jumped up, threw on my robe, and ran around to Mr. Busby's.
He was holding one of his stereo speakers out his living room window,
aimed straight up at Evie's. Every time the bass hit, his whole body quivered like the windshield of a car.

"Well he saw me. I'll never forget it, he was wearing these flashy green
pajamas, I'm pretty sure they were the most reflective article of clothing
I've ever seen on anyone. And he was having the time of his life. Grinning
ear to ear. He was kind of irresistible that way, like a big overgrown lab.
In reflective green pajamas. And he shouts to me, 'Evening, Girl. Think
the old woman knows I'm home?'

"'Stan died,' I told him.

"'Sorry,' he yelled. 'Lot of moaning going on. Can't hear ya.'

"I told him again. That time, he understood. 'Ah, shit,' he said, and
quivered when the bass hit him. He ducked inside and shut off the music.
There were lights on halfway down the block, and Madolyn was out on
her lanai, yelling.

"Mr. Busby stuck his head back out, shouting, 'Yeah, yeah, go back to
bed' to the whole world. Then he threw his hands up to his hair, and he
started rooting around and saying 'Goddamn. Is it on me? Can you see it?'

"I helped him get rid of the rest of the web he'd stuck his face through.

Then I got lemonade, and he got a box of Wheat Thins. And we just stood together at his window, all night. Him and me. He kept looking up at Evie's windows. Sometimes he'd say, 'So she's been doing that a lot? That sound? Every night?' And sometimes he'd say, 'Poor old bat.' Finally, sometime around dawn, right when I told him I had work and got up to go in, he said, 'Hey. Want to see my wheels?' And he took me around to the driveway to show me the car his daughter had bought him."

"I'll bet it was shiny," I say, though I'm entranced yet again. How is it possible that I know so little about the life my mother led here, before she became the way she is?

"You bet right. And not just shiny. *Pink* and shiny. And a Jag."

My jaw drops. "I didn't know they made pink Jags. Or that anyone on this side of Olympic had that kind of money."

"His daughter bought it for him. And this is the thing about Leyton Busby, Ry. This is what I think Evie never understood. That was all he wanted to talk about. It was all he cared about. I don't think he cared about the car itself one little bit. 'She paid half down,' he told me. He never even walked around it, he just stood there in his shiny pajamas, which his daughter also bought him, beaming away. '*Half.* To cheer me up, she says. Like I need so much cheering.'"

"But he *was* cheerier that morning. Just not about the car. I always hoped..." The sudden turn of my mother's head catches me off-guard. Headlights from a passing car sweep her face, and her eyes flare like fireflies in the gloom. Guilt blows through and past me, faint and salty.

"Well," says my mother. "I just hope his daughter knew that. Somehow, I got the impression maybe she didn't." Shadows have settled back over her face, but I can still feel her eyes on me. Another one of those near-smiles flutters across her lips without landing there. "For a long time, Mr. Busby and I just looked at his car. Once, he said, 'Watch this,' and then he jumped from one side of the bumper to the other, then pointed into the paint job. 'You see that?' he said. 'There's a pink me in there.' I was about to go inside when he asked, 'You figure she's awake? The old bat?'

"I told him I didn't even know what time it was.

"'Sun's up,' he said. 'She's super-old. And I don't hear moaning, do you?' When I shook my head, he said, 'Right. Let's go see what we can do.'

"I was too surprised to do anything but follow. And... I remember the air, right then. It was so clean. Like it never is here. There were hum-mingbirds beating around the bougainvillea. And bees buzzing. You could actually see the outlines of all the trees and cars and people, without that haze around them, you know? Everything just seemed so *substantial*, or something. Like we were really here, for once. If that makes any sense."

"I actually know exactly what you mean," I say quietly.

This time, for one moment, that smile actually lands. Beats its wings on her lips. Lifts away again. I want to reach out, snatch it back. But it's too late already. Again.

"We got upstairs, and Mr. Busby banged on Evie's door, and he was right, she was up, dressed, had her hair out of her curlers. I think she maybe forgot herself, because she just threw the door open, then shut it halfway real fast, but not fast enough. That's when I realized Stan was still in there."

Now it's my turn to stare. My mother's staring, too. But at the building, not me.

"Mom. What?"

"It'd been eight days. Maybe longer, I don't know. I just caught a glimpse. The hospital bed, the i.v. stand with the tubing wrapped around it for disposal. And Stan. He was half-curled up in the sheets. This little cocoon husk she'd been married to for sixty-three years."

"Wait. You mean his body? She *kept* it?"

"'Oh my God,' I remember saying. I tried to elbow Mr. Busby out of the way, but he wasn't going.

"'Is that Stan?' he kept saying. 'Mary Mother of God, woman, is that Stan?'

"She tried to slam the door on us. But Mr. Busby wedged himself in the frame and wouldn't let her. I think she hit him. He didn't budge. She looked terrible. Bloated and pale and patchy. Maybe it was the light, but even her skin had gone gray. She was practically transparent. Like a column of dust motes you could scatter with one hand.

"'Oh, Evie,' I told her. 'Come downstairs. Let me take care of this for you.'

"She didn't put up much fight. She hit Mr. Busby a few more times. Then she said she'd appreciate that. But that she'd wait up here with Stan.

"So I went down and woke you and showered and looked in the Yellow Pages and found an undertaker who said he'd come. And then I went to work. When I got home, I knocked on Evie's door, just to check on her, but no one answered.

"And then you got the mumps. And my work went crazy, and I almost lost my job because I kept having to take off to care for you. And your dad got himself thrown in jail again. And the spiders got into everything. And somehow, weeks passed…"

This time, instead of muttering, she goes completely still. Sits there in the grass. Until, with a shriek, she scuttles backwards on her hands, smacking at her legs and jabbing her hands up the sleeves of her summer blouse and raking downward with clawed fingers. Welts well up in her skin and boil over. I try to grab her wrists, but she claws me, too, then scrambles all the way to the sidewalk and stands up.

All this time, she's kept her eyes glued to the upstairs windows. My tears surprise me. I'm not even sure what they're for. It's not like this is atypical behavior.

"Mom," I whisper. "I'm sorry I brought you here. I didn't mean to."

"It wasn't real," she says again, spitting the words. "You need to know I know."

"Okay. I know you know."

"No you don't."

I close my eyes. "Okay, I don't."

"Maybe you want to know what I saw. Maybe you should. Maybe then you'd stop looking at me like that."

"I'm not looking at you like anything," I sigh, standing to start negotiating her back toward my car.

"That's what I mean," she says, starting to cry. "So I'm going to tell you."

We've attracted attention, finally. A curtain has stirred in the apartment next to our old one. Mr. Busby's old place. And across the side-street, a stoop-backed old woman with a basket on her wrist and a long, white cane has emerged onto the sidewalk. Her hair is some crazy L.A. old-lady color, practically fuchsia in the twilight. She has a hand shading her eyes, as though even the echoes of orange in the west are too bright for her.

"Hey, Mom? We should probably go. I think it's time to get you home. Simon Cowell and the gang are waiting."

"I don't know what made me call them," she says. "The undertakers." The sky has gone royal blue, and even the blue is draining away as though it's being siphoned. The breeze has developed a bite, too, and the old woman across the street has made her way to the crosswalk, and now she's inching in our direction. She's thin, all in white, her stoop so pronounced that she almost looks likes a cane herself, for the shadows to lean on.

"Mom?" I say, with even more force than I intend. "I want to go, even if you don't."

"I hadn't seen Evie in a while. I went up and knocked a few times. Mostly, there was no answer. I thought she'd finally gone away to see her sister or something. But then sometimes I'd hear her through the door. She sounded so small. I could hardly understand her.

"Mr. Busby tried a few pranks. 'Going to lure her out,' he'd say. 'Get her blood going. Leyton knows what the ladies need.' He'd stop every Jehovah's Witness and Mormon missionary he saw and direct them to Evie's door. One night around midnight, he came out on the grass with a ukulele and sang 'Tiny Bubbles' at the top of his lungs, except he kept saying 'Tiny Evie' instead. But she never appeared at the window. We had this possum family that took up residence by the dumpster, and he made a trail with orange peels and lettuce right to her door and got the whole family to camp outside it. But as far as I know, she never saw them.

"And then one day… you were still so sick. I was so worried about you. I'd spent all my summer pay to bail out your dad, and my reward was having him call in a drunken stupor every night to tell me either that he was going to make it up to me, somehow, or that he was going to kill me. Depended what he'd been drinking. I think it must have been the possums that made me even think of it, because to be honest, I didn't have time or energy to worry about Evie. She'd stopped moaning. But instead, she kept prowling around up there, every single night, at any hour. I think she was barefoot, at least. I could barely hear her. Just these little scratches. Little slides. Back and forth, in little lurches. All blessed night. Just enough to keep me awake. It also made me even more sad. And tired. I'd never been so tired in my whole life. This went on and on.

"Until that one day. The last day." She takes a huge breath and holds it, as though trying to cure hiccoughs. She does that for so long that her knees start to wobble.

"Mom, come on," I say.

"I came home." Her voice shakes. "And I saw the possum family at the top of her steps. And the spider webs all up and down the stairwell, as though no one had used it for years, which was ridiculous. The mailman went up there every day, for one.

"But something about it gave me this weird feeling. And it set me thinking. I hadn't been invited to Stan's funeral. Evie hadn't said anything about it whatsoever. I was sure she would have invited me, or talked to me. I went inside and found the number of the undertakers, and I called them.

"And that's when I found out. They'd come, alright, on the day I'd summoned them, and knocked at the door. Evie had answered them through it. She said everything was taken care of. And the undertakers said okay and left.

"I hung up. I had no idea what to think. Then you started crying. And your father called. Then he called again. And you cried some more. And I started crying. I think I just switched on the tv and left you in the living room with a popsicle and a blanket and ignored you when you yelled for me. I locked myself in the bedroom to try to get some sleep before Evie started pacing again. I think somehow I must have got some, too. Because this time it was the screaming that woke me up."

"Jesus," rasps the old woman in white, right next to us, and I jump forward and whirl around. How is it possible for something that slow to sneak up?

She's got a crooked, stumpy hand in my mother's hair. Holding on to her braid, like a child grabbing a cat's tail.

"It really is you," she rasps, her voice so honeycombed that it might be the wind talking.

Even then, several stunned seconds pass before I recognize her. And my mother ignores her completely. She just rambles on, as though the woman isn't even there.

"I hurtled out bed and came racing out the door. I thought it was you, even though it sounded nothing like you. I just felt so bad. So guilty. About so many things." Tears stream down her face. To my astonishment, she lays her head on the old woman's shoulder. The woman strokes her braid.

"*Madolyn?*" I gasp. While thinking, *where's the rest of you?* The shapeless dress drops without interruption past her waist. The sight is horrifying to me. Incomprehensible. Sad. Wrong. New York without the Trade Centers.

"It took me a minute to realize the screams were coming from out-side. From the driveway." My mother burrows deeper into Madolyn's collarbone, which looks bony, now, and can't be comfortable. "I raced around the building. And there was Mr. Busby, standing by what was left of his Jag."

Madolyn still holds onto my mother's braid. I have to stifle an urge to grab her wrist, shake her loose. It's like my mother is a child's pull-toy, and as long as Madolyn keeps yanking her hair, she's got no choice but to keep talking.

"I never thought you'd come back here," the old woman rasps. "Either one of you. You look good, Ry. Like you made it. I thought you might."

"They'd broken every single window," says my mother. "Bashed the windshield to pieces. Stolen all the tires. Knifed the seats." She speaks faster and faster. One of her hands has snared itself in Madolyn's dress. "On both sides, into that beautiful pink paint, they'd keyed the words *Black Fag*."

I blink. "What? Who?"

"Leyton was just shaking, when he wasn't shouting. I felt awful. I tried to say something comforting, but he wasn't having it. I didn't even hear what he was saying at first. That he was actually accusing Evie of this. And even if I had, it was so crazy. But how could he not be crazy, after that? 'Oh, Leyton,' I told him.

"'Too far,' he was shouting. 'Too far, Old Bat. Not funny. Way too far.' And then…" my mother twitches in place, and Madolyn gives a gentle tug on her braid. "Then…" Again, the twitch and tug. Like she's stuck.

"Mom," I say. "Let's get out of here."

"He started for the stairs. He was still screaming 'Old Bat' at the top of his lungs, and—"

"Come *on*," I snarl, yanking her away from Madolyn. A shudder ripples from her neck all the way down into her feet, and she stumbles against me and then straightens up.

She's holding my hand. Standing tall. Somehow, I've forgotten that my mother is taller than me. She's blinking furiously. She reaches up and at least smears the wetness flooding her face. Only then does she seem to see Madolyn.

"Oh," she says. "Hello."

Madolyn eyes her up and down. Her skin is tanning-bed orange, her brow surgically lifted so high that it seems pinned to the crest of her head. She looks like a doll, a Madolyn action-figure, denuded of its most characteristic elements. Sanitized.

"*You*, on the other hand, don't look so different from the night you left. I'm sorry to say."

My mother tries a laugh. As if Madolyn were kidding. "I was just telling Ry the story. It seems so silly, now."

"Silly," says Madolyn.

The urge to get my mother away from here, and from this woman, has become overwhelming. I'm way past questioning it. I start to pull her toward the curb. But she digs in her feet and won't budge.

"I just thought she should know." She's practically chirping, trying so hard to sound like an ordinary, comfortable person that it breaks my heart.

"I agree," says Madolyn. "She should."

"You know," my mother says, forces a laugh, waves an airy hand. "What caused me to… it seems so ridiculous, in retrospect. What I thought I saw."

"Thought?" says Madolyn, very quietly.

"It was just such a hard year for me, you know? Such a terrible time. Watching that poor old woman go completely to pieces. And Leyton stomping around his place and the yard, not knowing what to do with himself or how to go on, and you across the street—" she's talking to Madolyn, almost accusing her— "in your little mausoleum to yourself, with all those pictures of you and a guy you don't love on the cover of *People* or whatever, blown up to cover every inch of wallspace. And that moaning and pacing upstairs every single goddamn night." She turns to me. "And you. My sweet, sweet daughter. Sitting out here by yourself day after day, with no one to look after you properly. With a turtle for a playmate. We were all so lonely. So, so lonely. I guess I got lonely, too."

"You become the neighborhood," I blurt, and tear up again.

"I guess it all just boiled over. Messed up my head. And when Leyton got up the stairs and started banging on that door, screaming for Evie to come out… When he kept banging and banging and banging, while I was screaming for him to stop…

"That's right, you were there, too, Madolyn. You saw it all happen.

My big breakdown." She laughs that laugh again; it's horrible, like a CD skipping. "You were there when the door opened."

Madolyn has straightened over her cane. The botox injections have made actual facial expressions impossible. But her eyes are ice-cold. "Yep," she says.

"She was there," my mother tells me, patting my hand. "She helped me when I broke down. When I started screaming. When the paramedics came. You probably called the paramedics, didn't you, Madolyn? She helped them get me in the ambulance. Made sure they knew about you. I never thanked you for that. How'd I even get that picture in my head, Madolyn? I still don't know."

"The one you saw, you mean."

"The one I thought I saw. When Evie's door opened."

"So you think you didn't see it? Is that what you're telling me?"

"Mom, please." My own voice starts to crack. *I'm too late*, I think. *One more time.*

"You mean, giant spiderlegs scuttling out onto the landing?" The skipping laugh crescendos. "Grabbing Leyton and yanking him inside?"

"That," says Madolyn. "And those sounds. Like a cat being ripped inside out while it was still alive." She nods her fuchsia-haired, copper-skinned head. "Sounds about right to me. Pretty much what I saw and heard."

My mother stops laughing. Stops breathing again. Sways on her feet. "Stop it," she says.

With a shrug, Madolyn steps toward her. "I'm just saying your memory matches pretty perfectly with mine."

"Oh, you bitch." My mother's voice is a pig-squeal, now. She's shaking all over. "Stop right now."

"You better bring her inside," Madolyn says to me. "She's going to collapse."

"You cunt whore, stop," squeals my mother, throws her head back, and screams.

"*Mom!*" I try to grab her, but she jabs her elbows into my ribs, staggers away, and drops to her knees in the grass.

"Say you're joking," she hisses. "Say it right now."

If Madolyn gets any closer to my mother, I'm thinking I will bowl her over. Drive her into the ground, cane, basket and all.

"Get away," I tell her.

Instead, she plants the cane and sits. My mother folds into a little hump, then tilts sideways against the old woman, and lays her head in her lap.

"There, now," Madolyn says, and strokes my mother's braid. And there they sit.

It's insane, the stupidest sensation of this stupid evening yet. But most of what I feel right then is jealousy. And guilt, for the last fifteen years. Especially the last few. I've been old enough to treat my mother differently for a long time, now.

Abruptly, Madolyn lifts the lid of her basket, reaches inside, and pulls out the turtle. I gasp, folding down beside them. My mother lies in Madolyn's lap and shakes and coos like a baby. Madolyn lays the turtle in the grass, where it begins to nose about. Head sideways. Eying the sky.

"That's him? Evie's?" I stammer.

Madolyn nods.

"You saved him?"

"Afterward. Yeah. When the police were done."

"Police…" I reach my finger in front of the turtle's nose, the way one does with a kitten. The turtle pulls its head into its shell. Noses out again. Sidles sideways to get at more grass.

Madolyn watches him, too, shaking her head. "I found him under the couch. Under all the webbing."

In her lap, my mother twitches.

"What the hell are you talking about?" I snap.

"What there was. A lot of ugly smears of God knows what, all over the walls and the floor and even the ceiling. A lot of web. A lot of mess. All the windows smashed out, and wind just whipping everything around. No bodies. Not Stan's. Not Leyton Busby's. Not Evie's. No one's."

"Are you…" I don't want to say it, or think it. Most of all, I don't want my mother to hear it. It comes out anyway. "Are you seriously saying she was…?"

Madolyn strokes a curved, clawed hand down my mother's cheek. Her face is so blank, you could project anything there. At the moment, insanely, I'm projecting grandmotherly kindness. The moon has just started to rise behind her, and there's this white nimbus floating around her fuchsia head.

"Well, that's one of the possibilities, I suppose," she says. "I've thought of a few others, down the years. Mostly, I try not to think about it, to be honest. All I know for sure is that Evie wasn't in there when the cops came. No one was. And no one saw or heard from her, or from Leyton Busby, ever again. And that ever since, I've been keeping a good watch. I don't know what for, exactly. But I watch that building real close. The whole neighborhood, really. Just… seems like what I'm here for, maybe. And I keep my own house *clean*."

It's the way my mother's lying there, I think, that makes me break down and weep. The way her knees have drawn up. The shudders wracking her. "You become the neighborhood," I whisper.

"Second time you've said that," said Madolyn. "What's it mean?"

"Hell if I know. Evie used to say it."

Leaning back on her hands with my mother in her lap and Evie's turtle nosing around near her hip, Madolyn glances down at what's left of herself, or maybe my mother, both of them suspended in pale moonlight. Then she looks across the street toward her own home, where she's lived alone, I'm all but certain, for going on thirty years. Then she looks up at Evie's windows.

"You know what I think?" Her voice is like a rainstick, a rattlesnake's warning, a fire going out. Like she's praying and fighting and giving up all at the same time. "I think maybe if you live long enough, and you see enough…" Again, she glances down. "And you lose enough, and life gets at you enough, and does what it's going to do…"

Then she looks at me. Actually reaches out and wipes some of my tears away, while the shakes seem to sizzle out of my mother, through the grass like lightning, and up into me.

"Sooner or later, Hon. For better or worse. You become you."

◄○►

IN PARIS,
IN THE MOUTH OF KRONOS

JOHN LANGAN

I

"**Y**ou know how much they want for a Coke?"

"How much?" Vasquez said.

"Five euros. Can you believe that?"

Vasquez shrugged. She knew the gesture would irritate Buchanan, who took an almost pathological delight in complaining about everything in Paris, from the lack of air conditioning on the train ride in from De Gaulle to their narrow hotel rooms, but they had an expense account, after all, and however modest it was, she was sure a five-euro Coke would not deplete it. She didn't imagine the professionals sat around fretting over the cost of their sodas.

To her left, the broad Avenue de la Bourdonnais was surprisingly quiet; to her right, the interior of the restaurant was a din of languages: English, mainly, with German, Spanish, Italian, and even a little French mixed in. In front of and behind her, the rest of the sidewalk tables were occupied by an almost even balance of old men reading newspapers and young-ish couples wearing sunglasses. Late afternoon sunlight washed over her surroundings like a spill of white paint, lightening everything several shades, reducing the low buildings across the Avenue to hazy rectangles. When their snack was done, she would have to return to one of the souvenir shops they had passed on the walk here and buy a pair of sunglasses. Another expense for Buchanan to complain about.

"*M'sieu? Madame?*" Their waiter, surprisingly middle-aged, had returned. "*Vous êtes—*"

"You speak English," Buchanan said.

"But of course," the waiter said. "You are ready with your order?"

"I'll have a cheeseburger," Buchanan said. "Medium-rare. And a Coke," he added with a grimace.

"Very good," the waiter said. "And for Madame?"

"*Je voudrais un crêpe de chocolat,*" Vasquez said, "*et un café au lait.*"

The waiter's expression did not change. "*Très bien, Madame. Merçi,*" he said as Vasquez passed him their menus.

"A cheeseburger?" she said once he had returned inside the restaurant.

"What?" Buchanan said.

"Never mind."

"I like cheeseburgers. What's wrong with that?"

"Nothing. It's fine."

"Just because I don't want to eat some kind of French food—ooh, *un crêpe, s'il vous-plait.*"

"All this," Vasquez nodded at their surroundings, "it's lost on you, isn't it?"

"We aren't here for 'all this,'" Buchanan said. "We're here for Mr. White."

Despite herself, Vasquez flinched. "Why don't you speak a little louder? I'm not sure everyone inside the café heard."

"You think they know what we're talking about?"

"That's not the point."

"Oh? What is?"

"Operational integrity."

"Wow. You pick that up from the *Bourne* movies?"

"One person overhears something they don't like, opens their cellphone and calls the cops—"

"And it's all a big misunderstanding officers, we were talking about movies, ha ha."

"—and the time we lose smoothing things over with them completely fucks up Plowman's schedule."

"Stop worrying," Buchanan said, but Vasquez was pleased to see his face blanch at the prospect of Plowman's displeasure.

For a few moments, Vasquez leaned back in her chair and closed her eyes, the sun lighting the inside of her lids crimson. *I'm here*, she thought, the city's presence a pressure at the base of her skull, not unlike what she'd felt patrolling the streets of Bagram, but less unpleasant. Buchanan said, "So you've been here before."

"What?" Brightness overwhelmed her vision, simplified Buchanan to a dark silhouette in a baseball cap.

"You parlez the français pretty well. I figure you must've spent some time—what? In college? Some kind of study abroad deal?"

"Nope," Vasquez said.

"'Nope,' what?"

"I've never been to Paris. Hell, before I enlisted, the farthest I'd ever been from home was the class trip to Washington senior year."

"You're shittin me."

"Uh-uh. Don't get me wrong: I wanted to see Paris, London—everything. But the money—the money wasn't there. The closest I came to all this were the movies in Madame Antosca's French 4 class. It was one of the reasons I joined up: I figured I'd see the world and let the Army pay for it."

"How'd that work out for you?"

"We're here, aren't we?"

"Not because of the Army."

"No, precisely because of the Army. Well," she said, "them and the spooks."

"You still think Mr.—oh, sorry—*You-Know-Who* was CIA?"

Frowning, Vasquez lowered her voice. "Who knows? I'm not even sure he was one of ours. That accent... he could've been working for the Brits, or the Aussies. He could've been Russian, back in town to settle a few scores. Wherever he picked up his pronunciation, dude was not regular military."

"Be funny if *he* was on Stillwater's payroll."

"Hysterical," Vasquez said. "What about you?"

"What about me?"

"I assume this is your first trip to Paris."

"And there's where you would be wrong."

"Now you're shittin me."

"Why, because I ordered a cheeseburger and a Coke?"

"Among other things, yeah."

"My senior class trip was a week in Paris and Amsterdam. In college, the end of my sophomore year, my parents took me to France for a month." At what she knew must be the look on her face, Buchanan added, "It was an attempt at breaking up the relationship I was in at the time."

"It's not that. I'm trying to process the thought of you in college."

"Wow, anyone ever tell you what a laugh riot you are?"

"Did it work—your parents' plan?"

Buchanan shook his head. "The second I was back in the US, I knocked her up. We were married by the end of the summer."

"How romantic."

"Hey." Buchanan shrugged.

"That why you enlisted, support your new family?"

"More or less. Heidi's dad owned a bunch of McDonald's; for the first six months of our marriage, I tried to assistant manage one of them."

"With your people skills, that must have been a match made in Heaven."

The retort forming on Buchanan's lips was cut short by the reappearance of their waiter, encumbered with their drinks and their food. He set their plates before them with a, "*Madame,*" and, "*M'sieu,*" then, as he was distributing their drinks, said, "Everything is okay? *Ça va?*"

"*Oui,*" Vasquez said. "*C'est bon. Merçi.*"

With the slightest of bows, the waiter left them to their food.

While Buchanan worked his hands around his cheeseburger, Vasquez said, "I don't think I realized you were married."

"*Were,*" Buchanan said. "She wasn't happy about my deploying in the first place, and when the shit hit the fan…" He bit into the burger. Through a mouthful of bun and meat, he said, "The court martial was the excuse she needed. Couldn't handle the shame, she said. The humiliation of being married to one of the guards who'd tortured an innocent man to death. What kind of role model would I be for our son?

"I tried—I tried to tell her it wasn't like that. It wasn't that—you know what I'm talking about."

Vasquez studied her neatly-folded crêpe. "Yeah." Mr. White had favored a flint knife for what he called *the delicate work*.

"If that's what she wants, fine, fuck her. But she made it so I can't see my son. The second she decided we were splitting up, there was her dad with money for a lawyer. I get a call from this asshole—this is right in the middle of the court martial—and he tells me Heidi's filing for divorce—no surprise—and they're going to make it easy for me: no alimony, no child support, nothing. The only catch is, I have to sign away all my rights to Sam. If I don't, they're fully prepared to go to court, and how do I like my chances in front of a judge? What choice did I have?"

Vasquez tasted her coffee. She saw her mother, holding open the front door for her, unable to meet her eyes.

"Bad enough about that poor bastard who died—what was his name? If there's one thing you'd think I'd know…"

"Mahbub Ali," Vasquez said. *What kind of a person are you?* her father had shouted. *What kind of person is part of such things?*

"Mahbub Ali," Buchanan said. "Bad enough what happened to him; I just wish I'd know what was happening to the rest of us, as well."

They ate the rest of their meal in silence. When the waiter returned to ask if they wanted dessert, they declined.

II

Vasquez had compiled a list of reasons for crossing the Avenue and walking to the Eiffel Tower, from, *It's an open, crowded space: it's a better place to review the plan's details*, to, *I want to see the fucking Eiffel Tower once before I die, okay?* But Buchanan agreed to her proposal without argument; nor did he complain about the fifteen euros she spent on a pair of sunglasses on the walk there. Did she need to ask to know he was back in the concrete room they'd called the Closet, its air full of the stink of fear and piss?

Herself, she was doing her best not to think about the chamber under the prison's sub-basement Just-Call-Me-Bill had taken her to. This was maybe a week after the tall, portly man she knew for a fact was CIA had started spending every waking moment with Mr. White. Vasquez had followed Bill down poured concrete stairs that led from the labyrinth of the basement and its handful of high-value captives in their scattered cells (not to mention the Closet, whose precise location she'd been unable to fix), to the sub-basement, where he had clicked on the large yellow flashlight he was carrying. Its beam had ranged over brick walls, an assortment of junk (some of it Soviet-era aircraft parts, some of it tools to repair those parts, some of it more recent: stacks of toilet paper, boxes of plastic cutlery, a pair of hospital gurneys). They had made their way through that place to a low doorway that opened on carved stone steps whose curved surfaces testified to the passage of generations of feet. All the time, Just-Call-Me-Bill had been talking, lecturing, detailing the history of the prison, from its time as a repair center for the aircraft the Soviets flew in and out of here, until some KGB officer decided the building was perfect for housing prisoners, a change everyone who subsequently held possession of it had maintained. Vasquez had struggled to pay attention, especially as they had descended the last set of stairs and the air grew warm, moist, the rock to either side of her damp. *Before*, the CIA operative was saying, *oh, before. Did you know a detachment of Alexander the Great's army stopped here? One man returned.*

The stairs had ended in a wide, circular area. The roof was flat, low, the walls no more than shadowy suggestions. Just-Call-Me-Bill's flashlight had roamed the floor, picked out a symbol incised in the rock at their feet: a rough circle, the diameter of a manhole cover, broken at about eight o'clock. Its circumference was stained black, its interior a map of dark brown splotches. *Hold this*, he had said, passing her the flashlight, which had occupied her for the two or three seconds it took him to remove a plastic baggie from one of the pockets of his safari vest. When Vasquez had directed the light at him, he was dumping the bag's contents in his right hand, tugging at the plastic with his left to pull it away from the dull red wad. The stink of blood and meat on the turn had made her step back. *Steady, specialist.* The bag's contents had landed inside the broken circle with a heavy, wet smack. Vasquez had done her best not to study it too closely.

A sound, the scrape of bare flesh dragging over stone, from behind and to her left, had spun Vasquez around, the flashlight held out to blind, her sidearm freed and following the light's path. This section of the curving wall opened in a black arch like the top of an enormous throat. For a moment, that space had been full of a great, pale figure. Vasquez had had a confused impression of hands large as tires grasping either side of the arch, a boulder of a head, its mouth gaping amidst a frenzy of beard, its eyes vast, idiot. It was scrambling towards her; she didn't know where to aim—

And then Mr. White had been standing in the archway, dressed in the white linen suit that somehow always seemed stained, even though no discoloration was visible on any of it. He had not blinked at the flashlight beam stabbing his face; nor had he appeared to judge Vasquez's gun pointing at him of much concern. Muttering an apology, Vasquez had lowered gun and light immediately. Mr. White had ignored her, strolling across the round chamber to the foot of the stairs, which he had climbed quickly. Just-Call-Me-Bill had hurried after, a look on his bland face that Vasquez took for amusement. She had brought up the rear, sweeping the flashlight over the floor as she reached the lowest step. The broken circle had been empty, except for a red smear that shone in the light.

That she had momentarily hallucinated, Vasquez had not once doubted. Things with Mr. White already had raced past what even Just-Call-Me-Bill had shown them, and however effective his methods, Vasquez was afraid that she—that all of them had finally gone too far, crossed over into truly bad territory. Combined with a mild claustrophobia, that had caused her to fill the dark space with a nightmare. However reasonable that explanation, the shape with which her mind had replaced Mr. White had plagued her. Had she seen the Devil stepping forward on his goat's feet, one red hand using his pitchfork to balance himself, it would have made more sense than that giant form. It was as if her subconscious was telling her more about Mr. White than she understood. Prior to that trip, Vasquez had not been at ease around the man who never seemed to speak so much as to have spoken, so that you knew what he'd said even though you couldn't remember hearing him saying it. After, she gave him still-wider berth.

Ahead, the Eiffel Tower swept up into the sky. Vasquez had seen it from a distance, at different points along hers and Buchanan's journey from their hotel towards the Seine, but the closer she drew to it, the less real it seemed. It was as if the very solidity of the beams and girders weaving together were evidence of their falseness. *I am seeing the Eiffel Tower*, she told herself. *I am actually looking at the goddamn Eiffel Tower.*

"Here you are," Buchanan said. "Happy?"

"Something like that."

The great square under the Tower was full of tourists, from the sound of it, the majority of them groups of Americans and Italians. Nervous men wearing untucked shirts over their jeans flitted from group to group—street vendors, Vasquez realized, each one carrying an oversized ring strung with metal replicas of the Tower. A pair of gendarmes, their hands draped over the machine guns slung high on their chests, let their eyes roam the crowd while they carried on a conversation. In front of each of the Tower's legs, lines of people waiting for the chance to ascend it doubled and redoubled back on themselves, enormous fans misting water over them. Taking Buchanan's arm, Vasquez steered them towards the nearest fan. Eyebrows raised, he tilted his head towards her.

"Ambient noise," she said.

"Whatever."

Once they were close enough to the fan's propeller drone, Vasquez leaned into Buchanan. "Go with this," she said.

"You're the boss." Buchanan gazed up, a man debating whether he wanted to climb *that* high.

"I've been thinking," Vasquez said. "Plowman's plan's shit."

"Oh?" He pointed at the Tower's first level, three hundred feet above.

Nodding, Vasquez said, "We approach Mr. White, and he's just going to agree to come with us to the elevator."

Buchanan dropped his hand. "Well, we do have our… persuaders. How do you like that? Was it cryptic enough? Or should I have said, 'Guns'?"

Vasquez smiled as if Buchanan had uttered an endearing remark. "You really think Mr. White is going to be impressed by a pair of .22s?"

"A bullet's a bullet. Besides," Buchanan returned her smile, "isn't the plan for us not to have to use the guns? Aren't we relying on him remembering us?"

"It's not like we were BFFs. If it were me, and I wanted the guy, and I had access to Stillwater's resources, I wouldn't be wasting my time on a couple of convicted criminals. I'd put together a team and go get him. Besides, twenty grand a piece for catching up to someone outside his hotel room, passing a couple of words with him, then escorting him to an elevator: tell me that doesn't sound too good to be true."

"You know the way these big companies work: they're all about throwing money around. Your problem is, you're still thinking like a soldier."

"Even so, why spend it on us?"

"Maybe Plowman feels bad about everything. Maybe this is his way of making it up to us."

"Plowman? Seriously?"

Buchanan shook his head. "This isn't that complicated."

Vasquez closed her eyes. "Humor me." She leaned her head against Buchanan's chest.

"What have I been doing?"

"We're a feint. While we're distracting Mr. White, Plowman's up to something else."

"Like?"

"Maybe Mr. White has something in his room; maybe we're occupying him while Plowman's retrieving it."

"You know there are easier ways for Plowman to steal something."

"Maybe we're keeping Mr. White in place so Plowman can pull a hit on him."

"Again, there are simpler ways to do that that would have nothing to do with us. You knock on the guy's door, he opens it, pow."

"What if we're supposed to get caught in the crossfire?"

"You bring us all the way here just to kill us?"

"Didn't you say big companies like to spend money?"

"But why take us out in the first place?"

Vasquez raised her head and opened her eyes. "How many of the people who knew Mr. White are still in circulation?"

"There's Just-Call-Me-Bill—"

"You think. He's CIA. We don't know what happened to him."

"Okay. There's you, me, Plowman—"

"Go on."

Buchanan paused, reviewing, Vasquez knew, the fates of the three other guards who'd assisted Mr. White with his work in the Closet. Long before news had broken about Mahbub Ali's death, Lavalle had sat on the edge of his bunk, placed his gun in his mouth, and squeezed the trigger. Then, when the shitstorm had started, Maxwell, on patrol, had been stabbed in the neck by an insurgent who'd targeted only him. Finally, in the holding cell awaiting his court martial, Ruiz had taken advantage of a lapse in his jailers' attention to strip off his pants, twist them into a rope, and hang himself from the top bunk of his cell's bunkbed. His guards had cut him down in time to save his life, but Ruiz had deprived his brain of oxygen for sufficient time to leave him a vegetable. When Buchanan spoke, he said, "Coincidence."

"Or conspiracy."

"Goddammit." Buchanan pulled free of Vasquez, and headed for the long, rectangular park that stretched behind the Tower, speedwalking. His legs were sufficiently long that she had to jog to catch up to him. Buchanan did not slacken his pace, continuing his straight line up the middle of the park, through the midst of bemused picnickers. "Jesus Christ," Vasquez called, "will you slow down?"

He would not. Heedless of oncoming traffic, Buchanan led her across a pair of roads that traversed the park. Horns blaring, tires screaming, cars swerved around them. *At this rate*, Vasquez thought, *Plowman's motives won't matter.* Once they were safely on the grass again, she sped up until she was beside him, then reached high on the underside of Buchanan's right arm, not far from the armpit, and pinched as hard as she could.

"Ow! Shit!" Yanking his arm up and away, Buchanan stopped. Rubbing his skin, he said, "What the hell, Vasquez?"

"What the hell are you doing?"

"Walking. What did it look like?"

"Running away."

"Fuck you."

"Fuck you, you candy-ass pussy."

Buchanan's eyes flared.

"I'm trying to work this shit out so we can stay alive. You're so concerned about seeing your son, maybe you'd want to help me."

"Why are you doing this?" Buchanan said. "Why are you fucking with my head? Why are you trying to fuck this up?"

"I'm—"

"There's nothing to work out. We've got a job to do; we do it; we get the rest of our money. We do the job well, there's a chance Stillwater'll add us to their payroll. That happens—I'm making that kind of money—I hire myself a pit bull of a lawyer and sic him on fucking Heidi. You want to live in goddamn Paris, you can eat a croissant for breakfast every morning."

"You honestly believe that."

"Yes I do."

Vasquez held his gaze, but who was she kidding? She could count on one finger the number of stare-downs she'd won. Her arms, legs, everything felt suddenly, incredibly heavy. She looked at her watch. "Come on," she said, starting in the direction of the Avenue de la Bourdonnais. "We can catch a cab."

III

Plowman had insisted they meet him at an airport café before they set foot outside De Gaulle. At the end of those ten minutes, which had consisted of Plowman asking details of their flight and instructing them how to take the RUR to the Metro to the stop nearest their hotel, he had passed Vasquez a card for a restaurant, where, he had said, the three of them would reconvene at 3:00 pm local time to review the evening's plans. Vasquez had been relieved to see Plowman seated at a table outside the café. Despite the ten thousand dollars gathering interest in her checking account, the plane ticket that had been Fed-Ex'd to her apartment, followed by the receipt for four nights' stay at the Hôtel Resnais, she had been unable to shake the sense that none of this was as it appeared, that it was the set up to an elaborate joke whose punchline would come at her expense. Plowman's solid form, dressed in a black suit whose tailored lines announced the upward shift in his pay grade, had confirmed that everything he had told her the afternoon he had sought her out at Andersen's farm had been true.

Or true enough to quiet momentarily the misgivings that had whispered ever-louder in her ears the last two weeks, to the point that she had held her cell open in her left hand, the piece of paper with Plowman's number on it in her right, ready to call him and say she was out, he could have his money back, she hadn't spent any of it. During the long, hot train ride from the airport to the Metro station, when Buchanan had complained about Plowman not letting them out of his sight, treating them like goddamn kids, Vasquez had found an explanation on her lips.

It's probably the first time he's run an operation like this, she had said. *He wants to be sure he dots all his i's and crosses all his t's.* Buchanan had harrumphed, but it was true: Plowman obsessed over the minutiae; it was one of the reasons he'd been in charge of their detail at the prison. Until the shit had buried the fan, that attentiveness had seemed to forecast his steady climb up the chain of command. At his court martial, however, his enthusiasm for exact strikes on prisoner nerve clusters, his precision in placing arm restraints so that a prisoner's shoulders would not dislocate when he was hoisted off the floor by his bonds, his speed in obtaining the various surgical and dental instruments Just-Call-Me-Bill requested, had been counted liabilities rather than assets, and he had been the only one of their group to serve substantial time at Leavenworth, ten months.

Still, the Walther Vasquez had requested had been waiting where Plowman had promised it would be, wrapped with an extra clip in a waterproof bag secured inside the tank of her hotel room's toilet. A thorough inspection had reassured her that all was in order with the gun, its ammunition. If he were setting her up, would Plowman have wanted to arm her? Her proficiency at the target range had been well-known, and while she hadn't touched a gun since her discharge, she had no doubts of her ability. Tucked within the back of her jeans, draped by her blouse, the pistol was easily accessible.

That's assuming, of course, that Plowman's even there tonight. But the caution was a formality. Plowman being Plowman, there was no way he was not going to be at Mr. White's hotel. Was there any need for him to have made the trip to West Virginia, to have tracked her to Andersen's farm, to have sought her out in the far barns, where she'd been using a high-pressure hose to sluice pig shit into gutters? An e-mail, a phone call would have sufficed. Such methods, however, would have left too much outside Plowman's immediate control, and since he appeared able to dunk his bucket into a well of cash deeper than any she'd known, he had decided to find Vasquez and speak to her directly. (He'd done the same with Buchanan, she'd learned on the flight over, tracking him to the suburb of Chicago where he'd been shift manager at Hardee's.) If the man had gone to such lengths to persuade them to take the job, if he had been there to meet them at the Charles de Gaulle and was waiting for them even now, as their taxi crossed the Seine and headed towards the

Champs-Élysées, was there any chance he wouldn't be present later on?

Of course, he wouldn't be alone. Plowman would have the reassurance of God-only-knew-how-many Stillwater employees, which was to say, mercenaries (no doubt, heavily-armed and armored) backing him up. Vasquez hadn't had much to do with the company's personnel; they tended to roost closer to the center of Kabul, where the high-value targets they guarded huddled. Iraq: that was where Stillwater's bootprint was the deepest; from what Vasquez had heard, the former soldiers riding the re-inforced Lincoln Navigators through Baghdad not only made about five times what they had in the military, they followed rules of engagement that were, to put it mildly, less robust. While Paris was as far east as she was willing to travel, she had to admit, the prospect of that kind of money made Baghdad, if not appealing, at least less unappealing.

And what would Dad have to say to that? No matter that his eyes were failing, the center of his vision consumed by Macular Degeneration, her father had lost none of his passion for the news, employing a standing magnifier to aid him as he pored over the day's *New York Times* and *Washington Post*, sitting in his favorite chair listening to *All Things Considered* on WVPN, even venturing online to the BBC using the computer whose monitor settings she had adjusted for him before she'd deployed. Her father would not have missed the reports of Stillwater's involvement in several incidents in Iraq that were less shoot-outs than turkey-shoots, not to mention the ongoing Congressional inquiry into their policing of certain districts of post-Katrina and Rita New Orleans, as well as an event in Upstate New York last summer, when one of their employees had taken a camping trip that had left two of his three companions dead under what could best be described as suspicious circumstances. She could hear his words, heavy with the accent that had accreted as he'd aged: *Was this why I suffered in the Villa Grimaldi? So my daughter could join the* Caravana de la Muerte? The same question he'd asked her the first night she'd returned home.

All the same, it wasn't as if his opinion of her was going to drop any further. *If I'm damned,* she thought, *I might as well get paid for it.*

That said, she was in no hurry to certify her ultimate destination, which returned her to the problem of Plowman and his plan. You would have expected the press of the .22 against the small of her back to have been reassuring, but instead, it only emphasized her sense of powerlessness, as if Plowman were so confident, so secure, he could allow her whatever firearm she wanted.

The cab turned onto the Champs-Élysées. Ahead, the Arc de Triomphe squatted in the distance. Another monument to cross off the list.

IV

The restaurant whose card Plowman had handed her was located on one of the sidestreets about halfway to the Arc; Vasquez and Buchanan departed their cab at the street's corner and walked the hundred yards to a door flanked by man-sized plaster Chinese dragons. Buchanan brushed past the black-suited host and his welcome; smiling and murmuring, "*Padonnez, nous avons un rendez-vous içi,*" Vasquez pursued him into the dim interior. Up a short flight of stairs, Buchanan strode across a floor that glowed with pale light—glass, Vasquez saw, thick squares suspended over shimmering aquamarine. A carp the size of her forearm darted underneath her, and she realized that she was standing on top of an enormous, shallow fishtank, brown and white and orange carp racing one another across its bottom, jostling the occasional slower turtle. With one exception, the tables supported by the glass were empty. Too late, Vasquez supposed, for lunch, and too early for dinner. Or maybe the food here wasn't that good.

His back to the far wall, Plowman was seated at a table directly in front of her. Already, Buchanan was lowering himself into a chair opposite him. *Stupid*, Vasquez thought at the expanse of his unguarded back. Her boots clacked on the glass. She moved around the table to sit beside Plowman, who had exchanged the dark suit in which he'd greeted them at De Gaulle for a tan jacket over a cream shirt and slacks. His outfit caught the light filtering from below them and held it in as a dull sheen. A metal bowl filled with dumplings was centered on the tablemat before him; to its right, a slice of lemon floated at the top of a glass of clear liquid. Plowman's eyebrow raised as she settled beside him, but he did not comment on her choice; instead, he said, "You're here."

Vasquez's, "Yes," was overridden by Buchanan's, "We are, and there are some things we need cleared up."

Vasquez stared at him. Plowman said, "Oh?"

"That's right," Buchanan said. "We've been thinking, and this plan of yours doesn't add up."

"Really." The tone of Plowman's voice did not change.

"Really," Buchanan nodded.

"Would you care to explain to me exactly how it doesn't add up?"

"You expect Vasquez and me to believe you spent all this money so the two of us can have a five-minute conversation with Mr. White?"

Vasquez flinched.

"There's a little bit more to it than that."

"We're supposed to persuade him to walk twenty feet with us to an elevator."

"Actually, it's seventy-four feet three inches."

"Whatever." Buchanan glanced at Vasquez. She looked away. To the wall to her right, water chuckled down a series of small rock terraces through an opening in the floor into the fishtank.

"No, not 'whatever,' Buchanan. Seventy-four feet, three inches," Plowman said. "This is why the biggest responsibility you confront each day is lifting the fry basket out of the hot oil when the buzzer tells you to. You don't pay attention to the little things."

The host was standing at Buchanan's elbow, his hands clasped over a pair of long menus. Plowman nodded at him and he passed the menus to Vasquez and Buchanan. Inclining towards them, the host said, "May I bring you drinks while you decide your order?"

His eyes on the menu, Buchanan said, "Water."

"*Moi aussi*," Vasquez said. "*Merçi*."

"Nice accent," Plowman said when the host had left.

"Thanks."

"I don't think I realized you speak French."

Vasquez shrugged. "Wasn't any call for it, was there?"

"Anything else?" Plowman said. "Spanish?"

"I understand more than I can speak."

"You folks were from—where, again?"

"Chile," Vasquez said. "My Dad. My Mom's American, but her parents were from Argentina."

"That's useful to know."

"For when Stillwater hires her," Buchanan said.

"Yes," Plowman answered. "The company has projects underway in a number of places where fluency in French and Spanish would be an asset."

"Such as?"

"One thing at a time," Plowman said. "Let's get through tonight, first, and then you can worry about your next assignment."

"And what's that going to be," Buchanan said, "another twenty K to walk someone to an elevator?"

"I doubt it'll be anything so mundane," Plowman said. "I also doubt it'll pay as little as twenty thousand."

"Look," Vasquez started to say, but the host had returned with their water. Once he deposited their glasses on the table, he withdrew a pad and pen from his jacket pocket and took Buchanan's order of crispy duck and Vasquez's of steamed dumplings. After he had retrieved the menus and gone, Plowman turned to Vasquez and said, "You were saying?"

"It's just—what Buchanan's trying to say is, it's a lot, you know? If you'd offered us, I don't know, say five hundred bucks apiece to come here and play escort, that still would've been a lot, but it wouldn't—I mean, *twenty thousand dollars*, plus the air fare, the hotel, the expense account. It seems too much for what you're asking us to do. Can you understand that?"

Plowman shook his head yes. "I can. I can understand how strange it might appear to offer this kind of money for this length of service, but..." He raised his drink to his lips. When he lowered his arm, the glass was half-drained. "Mr. White is... to say he's high-value doesn't begin to cover it. The guy's been around—he's been around. Talk about a font of information: the stuff this guy's forgotten would be enough for a dozen careers. What he remembers will give whoever can get him to share it with them permanent tactical advantage."

"No such thing," Buchanan said. "No matter how much the guy says he knows—"

"Yes, yes," Plowman held up his hand like a traffic cop. "Trust me. He's high value."

"But won't the spooks—what's Just-Call-Me-Bill have to say about this?" Vasquez said.

"Bill's dead."

Simultaneously, Buchanan said, "Huh," and Vasquez, "What? How?"

"I don't know. When my bosses greenlighted me for this, Bill was the first person I thought of. I wasn't sure if he was still with the Agency, so I did some checking around. I couldn't find out much—goddamn spooks keep their mouths shut—but I was able to determine that Bill was dead. It sounded like it might've been that chopper crash in Helmand, but that's a guess. To answer your question, Vasquez, Bill didn't have a whole lot to say."

"Shit," Buchanan said.

"Okay," Vasquez exhaled. "Okay. Was he the only one who knew about Mr. White?"

"I find it hard to believe he was," Plowman said, "but thus far, no one's nibbled at any of the bait I've left out. I'm surprised: I'll admit it. But it makes our job that much simpler, so I'm not complaining."

"All right," Vasquez said, "but the money—"

His eyes alight, Plowman leaned forward. "To get my hands on Mr. White, I would have paid each of you ten times as much. That's how important this operation is. Whatever we have to shell out now is nothing compared to what we're going to gain from this guy."

"Now you tell us," Buchanan said.

Plowman smiled and relaxed back. "Well, the bean counters do appreciate it when you can control costs." He turned to Vasquez. "Well? Have your concerns been addressed?"

"Hey," Buchanan said, "I was the one asking the questions."

"Please," Plowman said. "I was in charge of you, remember? Whatever your virtues, Buchanan, original thought is not among them."

"What about Mr. White?" Vasquez said. "Suppose he doesn't want to come with you?"

"I don't imagine he will," Plowman said. "Nor do I expect him to be terribly interested in assisting us once he is in our custody. That's okay." Plowman picked up one of the chopsticks alongside his plate, turned it in his hand, and jabbed it into a dumpling. He lifted the dumpling to his mouth; momentarily, Vasquez pictured a giant bringing its teeth together on a human head. While he chewed, Plowman said, "To be honest, I hope the son of a bitch is feeling especially stubborn. Because of him, I lost everything that was good in my life. Because of that fucker, I did time in prison—fucking *prison*." Plowman swallowed, speared another dumpling. "Believe me when I say, Mr. White and I have a lot of quality time coming."

Beneath them, a half-dozen carp that had been floating lazily, scattered.

V

Buchanan was all for finding Mr. White's hotel and parking themselves in its lobby. "What?" Vasquez said. "Behind a couple of newspapers?" Stuck in traffic on what should have been the short way to the Concorde Opera, where Mr. White had the Junior Suite, their cab was full of the reek of exhaust, the low rumble of the cars surrounding them.

"Sure, yeah, that'd work."

"Jesus—and I'm the one who's seen too many movies?"

"What?" Buchanan said.

"Number one, at this rate, it'll be at least six before we get there. How many people sit around reading the day's paper at night? The whole point of the news is, it's new."

"Maybe we're on vacation."

"Doesn't matter. We'll still stick out. And number two, even if the lobby's full of tourists holding newspapers up in front of their faces, Plowman's plan doesn't kick in until eleven. You telling me no one's going to notice the same two people sitting there, doing the same thing, for five hours? For all we know, Mr. White'll see us on his way out and coming back."

"Once again, Vasquez, you're overthinking this. People don't see what they don't expect to see. Mr. White isn't expecting us in the lobby of his plush hotel, ergo, he won't notice us there."

"Are you kidding? This isn't 'people.' This is Mr. White."

"Get a grip. He eats, shits, and sleeps same as you and me."

For the briefest of instants, the window over Buchanan's shoulder was full of the enormous face Vasquez had glimpsed (hallucinated) in the caves under the prison. Not for the first time, she was struck by the crudeness of the features, as if a sculptor had hurriedly struck out the approximation of a human visage on a piece of rock already formed to suggest it.

Taking her silence as further disagreement, Buchanan sighed and said, "All right. Tell you what: a big, tony hotel, there's gotta be all kinds of stores around it, right? Long as we don't go too far, we'll do some shopping."

"Fine," Vasquez said. When Buchanan had settled back in his seat, she said, "So. You satisfied with Plowman's answers?"

"Aw, no, not this again…"

"I'm just asking a question."

"No, what you're asking is called a leading question, as in, leading me to think that Plowman didn't really say anything to us, and we don't know anything more now than we did before our meeting."

"You learned something from that?"

Buchanan nodded. "You bet I did. I learned that Plowman has a hard-on for Mr. White the size of your fucking Eiffel Tower, from which, I deduce that anyone who helps him satisfy himself stands to benefit enormously." As the cab lurched forward, Buchanan said, "Am I wrong?"

"No," Vasquez said. "It's—"

"What? What is it, now?"

"I don't know." She looked out her window at the cars creeping along beside them.

"Well that's helpful."

"Forget it."

For once, Buchanan chose not to pursue the argument. Beyond the car to their right, Vasquez watched men and women walking past the windows of ground-level businesses, tech stores and clothing stores and a bookstore and an office whose purpose she could not identify. Over their wrought-iron balconies, the windows of the apartments above showed the late-afternoon sky, its blue deeper, as if hardened by a day of the sun's baking. *Because of him, I lost everything that was good in my life. Because of that fucker, I did time in prison—fucking prison.* Plowman's declaration sounded in her ears. Insofar as the passion on his face authenticated his words, and so the purpose of their mission, his brief monologue should have been reassuring. And yet, and yet…

In the moment before he drove his fist into a prisoner's solar plexus, Plowman's features, distorted and red from the last hour's interrogation, would relax. The effect was startling, as if a layer of heavy makeup had melted off his skin. In the subsequent stillness of his face, Vasquez initially had read Plowman's actual emotion, a clinical detachment from the pain he was preparing to inflict that was based in his utter contempt for the man standing in front of him. While his mouth would stretch with his screams to the prisoner to *Get up! Get the fuck up!* in the second after his blow had dropped the man to the concrete floor, and while his mouth and eyes would continue to express the violence his fists and boots were concentrating on the prisoner's back, his balls, his throat, there would be other moments, impossible to predict, when, as he was shuffle-stepping away from a kick to the prisoner's kidney, Plowman's face would slip into that non-expression and Vasquez would think that she had seen through to the real man.

Then, the week after Plowman had brought Vasquez on board what he had named the White Detail, she'd found herself sitting through a Steven Seagal double-feature—not her first or even tenth choice for a way to pass three hours, but it beat lying on her bunk thinking, *Why are you so shocked? You knew what Plowman was up to—everyone knows.* An hour into *The Patriot*, the vague sensation that had been nagging at her from Seagal's first scene crystallized into recognition: that the blank look with which the actor met every ebb and flow in the drama was the same as the one that Vasquez had caught on Plowman's face, was, she understood, its original. For the remainder of that film and the duration of the next (*Belly of the Beast*), Vasquez had stared at the undersized screen in a kind of horrified fascination, unable to decide which was worse: to be serving under a man whose affect suggested a sociopath, or to be serving under a man who was playing the lead role in a private movie.

How many days after that had Just-Call-Me-Bill arrived? No more than two, she was reasonably sure. He had come, he told the White Detail, because their efforts with particularly *recalcitrant* prisoners had not gone unnoticed, and his superiors judged it would be beneficial for him to share his knowledge of enhanced interrogation techniques with them—and no doubt, they had some things to teach him. His back ramrod straight, his face alight, Plowman had barked his enthusiasm for their collaboration.

After that, it had been learning the restraints that would cause the prisoner maximum discomfort, expose him (or occasionally, her) to optimum harm. It was hoisting the prisoner off the ground first without dislocating his shoulders, then with. Waterboarding, yes, together with the repurposing of all manner of daily objects, from nail files to pliers to dental floss. Each case was different. Of course you couldn't believe any of the things the prisoners said when they were turned over to you, their protestations of innocence. But even after it appeared you'd broken them, you couldn't be sure they weren't engaged in a more subtle deception, acting as if you'd succeeded in order to preserve the truly valuable information. For this reason, it was necessary to keep the interrogation open, to continue to revisit those prisoners who swore they'd told you everything they knew. *These people are not like you and me*, Just-Call-Me-Bill had said, confirming the impression that had dogged Vasquez when she'd walked patrol, past women draped in white or slate *burqas*, men whose *pokool* proclaimed their loyalty to the *mujahideen*. *These are not a reasonable people. You cannot sit down and talk to them*, Bill went on, *come to an understanding with them. They would rather fly an airplane into a building full of innocent women and men. They would rather strap a bomb to their daughter and send her to give you a hug. They get their hands on a nuke, and there'll be a mushroom cloud where Manhattan used to be. What they understand is pain. Enough suffering, and their tongues will loosen.*

Vasquez could not pin down the exact moment Mr. White had joined their group. When he had shouldered his way past Lavalle and Maxwell, his left hand up to stop Plowman from tilting the prisoner backwards, Just-Call-Me-Bill from pouring the water onto the man's hooded face, she had thought, *Who the hell?* And, as quickly, *Oh—Mr. White.* He must have been with them for some time for Plowman to upright the prisoner, Bill to lower the bucket and step back. The flint knife in his right hand, its edge so fine you could feel it pressing against your bare skin, had not been unexpected. Nor had what had followed.

It was Mr. White who had suggested they transfer their operations to the Closet, a recommendation Just-Call-Me-Bill had been happy to embrace. Plowman, at first, had been noncommittal. Mr. White's... call it his taking a more active hand in their interrogations, had led to him and Bill spending increased time together. Ruiz had asked the CIA man what he was doing with the man whose suit, while seemingly filthy, was never touched by any of the blood that slicked his knife, his hands. *Education*, Just-Call-Me-Bill had answered. *Our friend is teaching me all manner of things.*

As he was instructing the rest of them, albeit in more indirect fashion. Vasquez had learned that her father's stories of the Villa Grimaldi, which he had withheld from her until she was fifteen, when over the course of the evening after her birthday she had been first incredulous, then horrified, then filled with righteous fury on his behalf, had little bearing on her duties in the Closet. Her father had been an innocent man, a poet, for God's sake, picked up by Pinochet's *Caravana de la Muerte* because they were engaged in a program of terrorizing their own populace. The men (and occasional women) at whose interrogations she assisted were terrorists themselves, spiritual kin to the officers who had scarred her father's arms, his chest, his back, his thighs, who had scored his mind with nightmares from which he still fled screaming, decades later. They were not like you and me, and that difference authorized and legitimized whatever was required to start them talking.

By the time Mahbub Ali was hauled into the Closet, Vasquez had learned other things, too. She had learned that it was possible to concentrate pain on a single part of the body, to the point that the prisoner grew to hate that part of himself for the agony focused there. She had learned that it was preferable to work slowly, methodically— religiously, was how she thought of it, though this was no religion to which she'd ever been exposed. This was a faith rooted in the most fundamental truth Mr. White taught her, taught all of them, namely, that the flesh yearns for the knife, aches for the cut that will open it, relieve it of its quivering anticipation of harm. As junior member of the Detail, she had not yet progressed to being allowed to work on the prisoners directly, but it didn't matter. While she and Buchanan sliced away a prisoner's clothes, exposed bare skin, what she saw there, a fragility, a vulnerability whose thick, salty taste filled her mouth, confirmed all of Mr. White's lessons, every last one.

Nor was she his best student. That had been Plowman, the only one of them to whom Mr. White had entrusted his flint knife. With Just-Call-Me-Bill, Mr. White had maintained the air of a senior colleague; with the rest of them, he acted as if they were mannequins, placeholders. With Plowman, though, Mr. White was the mentor, the last practitioner of an otherwise-dead art passing his knowledge on to his chosen successor. It might have been the plot of a Steven Seagal film. And no Hollywood star could have played the eager apprentice with more enthusiasm than Plowman. While the official cause of Mahbub Ali's death was sepsis resulting from improperly tended wounds, those missing pieces of the man had been parted from him on the edge of Mr. White's stone blade, gripped in Plowman's steady hand.

VI

Even with the clotted traffic, the cab drew up in front of the Concorde Opera's three sets of polished wooden doors with close to five hours to spare. While Vasquez settled with the driver, Buchanan stepped out of the cab, crossed the sidewalk, strode up three stairs, and passed through the center doors. The act distracted her enough that she forgot to ask for a receipt; by the time she remembered, the cab had accepted a trio of middle-aged women, their arms crowded with shopping bags, and pulled away. She considered chasing after it, before deciding that she could absorb the ten euros. She turned to the hotel to see the center doors open again, Buchanan standing in them next to a young man with a shaved head who was wearing navy pants and a cream tunic on whose upper left side a name tag flashed. The young man pointed across the street in front of the hotel and waved his hand back and forth, all the while talking to Buchanan, who nodded attentively. When the young man lowered his arm, Buchanan clapped him on the back, thanked him, and descended to Vasquez.

She said, "What was that about?"

"Shopping," Buchanan said. "Come on."

The next fifteen minutes consisted of them walking a route Vasquez wasn't sure she could retrace, through clouds of slow-moving tourists stopping to admire some building or piece of public statuary; alongside briskly-moving men and women whose ignoring those same sights marked them as locals as much as their *chic* haircuts, the rapid-fire French they delivered to their cellphones; past upscale boutiques and the gated entrances to equally upscale apartments. Buchanan's route brought the two of them to a large, corner building whose long windows displayed teddy bears, model planes, dollhouses. Vasquez said, "A toy store?"

"Not just 'a' toy store," Buchanan said. "This is *the* toy store. Supposed to have all kinds of stuff in it."

"For your son."

"Duh."

Inside, a crowd of weary adults and overexcited children moved up and down the store's aisles, past a mix of toys Vasquez recognized—Playmobil, groups of army vehicles, a typical assortment of stuffed animals—and others she'd never seen before—animal-headed figures she realized were Egyptian gods, replicas of round-faced cartoon characters she didn't know, a box of a dozen figurines arranged around a cardboard mountain. Buchanan wandered up to her as she was considering this set, the box propped on her hip. "Cool," he said, leaning forward. "What is it, like, the Greek gods?"

Vasquez resisted a sarcastic remark about the breadth of his knowledge; instead, she said, "Yeah. That's Zeus and his crew at the top of the mountain. I'm not sure who those guys are climbing it…"

"Titans," Buchanan said. "They were monsters who came before the gods, these kind of primal forces. Zeus defeated them, imprisoned them in the underworld. I used to know all their names: when I was a kid, I was really into myths and legends, heroes, all that shit." He studied the toys positioned up the mountain's sides. They were larger than the figures at its crown, overmuscled, one with an extra pair of arms, another with a snake's head, a third with a single, glaring eye. Buchanan shook his head. "I can't remember any of their names, now. Except for this guy," he pointed at a figurine near the summit, "I'm pretty sure he's Kronos."

"Kronos?" The figure was approximately that of a man, although its arms, its legs, were slightly too long, its hands and feet oversized. Its head was surrounded by a corona of gray hair that descended into a jagged beard. The toy's mouth had been sculpted with its mouth gaping, its eyes round, idiot. Vasquez smelled spoiled meat, felt the cardboard slipping from her grasp.

"Whoa." Buchanan caught the box, replaced it on the shelf.

"Sorry," Vasquez said. *Mr. White had ignored her, strolling across the round chamber to the foot of the stairs, which he had climbed quickly.*

"I don't think that's really Sam's speed, anyway. Come on," Buchanan said, moving down the aisle.

When they had stopped in front of a stack of remote-controlled cars, Vasquez said, "So who was Kronos?" Her voice was steady.

"What?" Buchanan said. "Oh—Kronos? He was Zeus's father. Ate all his kids because he'd heard that one of them was going to replace him."

"Jesus."

"Yeah. Somehow, Zeus avoided becoming dinner and overthrew the old man."

"Did he—did Zeus kill him?"

"I don't think so. I'm pretty sure Kronos wound up with the rest of the Titans, underground."

"Underground? I thought you said they were in the underworld."

"Same diff," Buchanan said. "That's where those guys thought the underworld was, someplace deep underground. You got to it through caves."

"Oh."

In the end, Buchanan decided on a large wooden castle that came with a host of knights, some on horseback, some on foot, a trio of princesses, a unicorn, and a dragon. The entire set cost two hundred and sixty euros, which struck Vasquez as wildly overpriced but which Buchanan paid without a murmur of protest—the extravagance of the present, she understood, being the point. Buchanan refused the cashier's offer to gift-wrap the box, and they left the store with him carrying it under his arm.

Once on the sidewalk, Vasquez said, "Not to be a bitch, but what are you planning to do with that?"

Buchanan shrugged. "I'll think of something. Maybe the front desk'll hold it."

Vasquez said nothing. Although the sky still glowed blue, the light had begun to drain out of the spaces among the buildings, replaced by a darkness that was almost granular. The air was warm, soupy. As they stopped at the corner, Vasquez said, "You know, we never asked Plowman about Lavalle or Maxwell."

"Yeah, so?"

"Just—I wish we had. He had an answer for everything else, I wouldn't have minded hearing him explain that."

"There's nothing to explain," Buchanan said.

"We're the last ones alive—"

"Plowman's living. So's Mr. White."

"Whatever—you know what I mean. Christ, even Just-Call-Me-Bill is dead. What the fuck's up with that?"

In front of them, traffic stopped. The walk signal lighted its green man.

They joined the surge across the street. "It's a war, Vasquez," Buchanan said. "People die in them."

"Is that what you really believe?"

"It is."

"What about your freakout before, at the Tower?"

"That's exactly what it was, me freaking out."

"Okay," Vasquez said after a moment, "okay. Maybe Bill's death was an accident; maybe Maxwell, too. What about Lavalle? What about Ruiz? You telling me it's normal two guys from the same detail try to off themselves?"

"I don't know." Buchanan shook his head. "You know the Army isn't big on mental health care. And let's face it, that was some pretty fucked-up shit went on in the Closet. Not much of a surprise if Lavalle and Ruiz couldn't handle it, is it?"

Vasquez waited another block before asking, "How do you deal with it, the Closet?" Buchanan took one more block after that to answer: "I don't think about it."

"You don't?"

"I'm not saying the thought of what we did over there never crosses my mind, but as a rule, I focus on the here and now."

"What about the times the thought does cross your mind?"

"I tell myself it was a different place with different rules. You know what I'm talking about. You had to be there; if you weren't, then shut the fuck up. Maybe what we did went over the line, but that's for us to say, not some panel of officers don't know their ass from a hole in the ground, and damn sure not some reporter never been closer to war than a goddamn showing of *Platoon*." Buchanan glared. "You hear me?"

"Yeah." How many times had she used the same arguments, or close enough, with her father? He had remained unconvinced. *So only the criminals are fit to judge the crime?* he had said. *What a novel approach to justice.* She said, "You know what I hate, though? It isn't that people look at me funny—*Oh, it's her*—it isn't even the few who run up to me in the supermarket and tell me what a disgrace I am. It's like you said, they weren't there, so fuck 'em. What gets me are the ones who come up to you and tell you, 'Good job, you fixed them Ay-rabs right,' the crackers who wouldn't have anything to do with someone like me, otherwise."

"Even crackers can be right, sometimes," Buchanan said.

VII

Mr. White's room was on the sixth floor, at the end of a short corridor that lay around a sharp left turn. The door to the Junior Suite appeared unremarkable, but it was difficult to be sure, since both the bulbs in the wall-sconces on either side of the corridor were out. Vasquez searched for a light switch and, when, she could not find one, said, "Either they're blown, or the switch is inside his room."

Buchanan, who had been unsuccessful convincing the woman at the front desk to watch his son's present, was busy fitting it beneath one of the chairs to the right of the elevator door.

"Did you hear me?" Vasquez asked.

"Yeah."

"Well?"

"Well what?"

"I don't like it. Our visibility's fucked. He opens the door, the light's behind him, in our faces. He turns on the hall lights, and we're blind."

"For like, a second."

"That's more than enough time for Mr. White to do something."

"Will you listen to yourself?"

"You saw what he could do with that knife."

"All right," Buchanan said, "how do you propose we deal with this?"

Vasquez paused. "You knock on the door. I'll stand a couple of feet back with my gun in my pocket. If things go pear-shaped, I'll be in a position to take him out."

"How come I have to knock on the door?"

"Because he liked you better."

"Bullshit."

"He did. He treated me like I wasn't there."

"That was the way Mr. White was with everyone."

"Not you."

Holding his hands up, Buchanan said, "Fine. Dude creeps you out so much, it's probably better I'm the one talking to him." He checked his watch. "Five minutes till showtime. Or should I say, 'T-minus five and counting,' something like that?"

"Of all the things I'm going to miss about working with you, your sense of humor's going to be at the top of the list."

"No sign of Plowman, yet." Buchanan checked the panel next to the elevator, which showed it on the third floor.

"He'll be here at precisely eleven ten."

"No doubt."

"Well…" Vasquez turned away from Buchanan.

"Wait—where are you going? There's still four minutes on the clock."

"Good: it'll give our eyes time to adjust."

"I am so glad this is almost over," Buchanan said, but he accompanied Vasquez to the near end of the corridor to Mr. White's room. She could feel him vibrating with a surplus of smart-ass remarks, but he had enough sense to keep his mouth shut. The air was cool, floral-scented with whatever they'd used to clean the carpet. Vasquez expected the minutes to drag by, for there to be ample opportunity for her to fit the various fragments of information in her possession into something like a coherent picture; however, it seemed practically the next second after her eyes had adapted to the shadows leading up to Mr. White's door, Buchanan was moving past her. There was time for her to slide the pistol out from under her blouse and slip in into the right front pocket of her slacks, and then Buchanan's knuckles were rapping the door.

It opened so quickly, Vasquez almost believed Mr. White had been positioned there, waiting for them. The glow that framed him was soft, orange, an adjustable light dialed down to its lowest setting, or a candle. From what she could see of him, Mr. White was the same as ever, from his unruly hair, more gray than white, to his dirty white suit. Vasquez could not tell whether his hands were empty. In her pocket, her palm was slick on the pistol's grip.

At the sight of Buchanan, Mr. White's expression did not change. He stood in the doorway regarding the man, and Vasquez three feet behind him, until Buchanan cleared his throat and said, "Evening, Mr. White. Maybe you remember me from Bagram. I'm Buchanan; my associate is Vasquez. We were part of Sergeant Plowman's crew; we assisted you with your work interrogating prisoners."

Mr. White continued to stare at Buchanan. Vasquez felt panic gathering in the pit of her stomach. Buchanan went on, "We were hoping you would accompany us on a short walk. There are matters we'd like to discuss with you, and we've come a long way."

Without speaking, Mr. White stepped into the corridor. The fear, the urge to sprint away from here as fast as her legs would take her, that had been churning in Vasquez's gut, leapt up like a geyser. Buchanan said, "Thank you. This won't take five minutes—ten, tops."

Behind her, the floor creaked. She looked back, saw Plowman standing there, and in her confusion, did not register what he was holding in his hand. Someone coughed, and Buchanan collapsed. They coughed again, and it was as if a snowball packed with ice struck Vasquez's back low and to the left.

All the strength left her legs. She sat down where she was, listing to her right until the wall stopped her. Plowman stepped over her. The gun in his right hand was lowered; in his left, he held a small box. He raised the box, pressed it, and the wall sconces erupted in deep purple—black light, by whose illumination Vasquez saw the walls, the ceiling, the carpet of the short corridor covered in symbols drawn in a medium that shone pale white. She couldn't identify most of them: she thought she saw a scattering of Greek characters, but the rest were unfamiliar, circles bisected by straight lines traversed by short, wavy lines, a long, gradual curve like a smile, more intersecting lines. The only figure she knew for sure was a circle whose thick circumference was broken at about the eight o'clock point, inside which Mr. White was standing and Buchanan lying. Whatever Plowman had used to draw them made the symbols appear to float in front of the surfaces on which he'd marked them, strange constellations crammed into an undersized sky.

Plowman was speaking, the words he was uttering unlike any Vasquez had heard, thick ropes of sound that started deep in his throat and spilled into the air squirming, writhing over her eardrums. Now Mr. White's face showed emotion: surprise, mixed with what might have been dismay, even anger. Plowman halted next to the broken circle and used his right foot to roll Buchanan onto his back. Buchanan's eyes were open, unblinking, his lips parted. The exit wound in his throat shone darkly. His voice rising, Plowman completed what he was saying, gestured with both hands at the body, and retreated to Vasquez.

For an interval of time that lasted much too long, the space where Mr. White and Buchanan were was full of something too big, that had to double over to cram itself into the corridor. Eyes the size of dinner plates stared at Plowman, at Vasquez, with a lunacy that pressed on her like an animal scenting her with its sharp snout. Amidst a beard caked and clotted with offal, a mouth full of teeth cracked and stained black formed sounds Vasquez could not distinguish. Great pale hands large as tires roamed the floor beneath the figure—Vasquez was reminded of a blind man investigating an unfamiliar surface. When the hands found Buchanan, they scooped him up like a doll and raised him to that enormous mouth.

Groaning, Vasquez tried to roll away from the sight of Buchanan's head surrounded by teeth like broken flagstones. It wasn't easy. For one thing, her right hand was still in her pants pocket, its fingers tight around the Walther, her wrist and arm bent in at awkward angles. (She supposed she should be grateful she hadn't shot herself.) For another thing, the cold that had struck her back was gone, replaced by heat, by a sharp pain that grew sharper still as she twisted away from the snap and crunch of those teeth biting through Buchanan's skull. *God.* She managed to move onto her back, exhaling sharply. To her right, the sounds of Buchanan's consumption continued, bones snapping, flesh tearing, cloth ripping. Mr. White—what had been Mr. White—or what he truly was—that vast figure was grunting with pleasure, smacking its lips together like someone starved for food given a gourmet meal.

"For what it's worth," Plowman said, "I wasn't completely dishonest with you." One leg to either side of hers, he squatted over her, resting his elbows on his knees. "I do intend to bring Mr. White into my service; it's just the methods necessary for me to do so are a little extreme."

Vasquez tried to speak. "What… is he?"

"It doesn't matter," Plowman said. "He's old—I mean, if I told you how old he is, you'd think…." He looked to his left, to the giant sucking the gore from its fingers. "Well, maybe not. He's been around for a long time, and he knows a lot of things. We—what we were doing at Bagram, the interrogations, they woke him. I guess that's the best way to put it; although you could say they called him forth. It took me a while to figure out everything, even after he revealed himself to me. But there's nothing like prison to give you time for reflection. And research.

"That research says the best way to bind someone like Mr. White is—

actually, it's pretty complicated." Plowman waved his pistol at the symbols shining around them. "The part that will be of most immediate interest to you is the sacrifice of a man and woman who are in my command. I apologize. I intended to put the two of you down before you knew what was happening; I mean, there's no need to be cruel about this. With you, however, I'm afraid my aim was off. Don't worry. I'll finish what I started before I turn you over to Mr. White."

Vasquez tilted her right hand up and squeezed the trigger of her gun. Four pops rushed one after the other, blowing open her pocket. Plowman leapt back, stumbled against the opposite wall. Blood bloomed across the inner thigh of his trousers, the belly of his shirt. Wiped clean by surprise, his face was blank. He swung his gun towards Vazquez, who angled her right hand down and squeezed the trigger again. The top of Plowman's shirt puffed out; his right eye burst. His arm relaxed, his pistol thumped on the floor, and, a second later, he joined it.

The burn of suddenly hot metal through her pocket sent Vasquez scrambling up the wall behind her before the pain lodged in her back could catch her. In the process, she yanked out the Walther and pointed it at the door to the Junior Suite—

—in front of which, Mr. White was standing, hands in his jacket pockets. A dark smear in front of him was all that was left of Buchanan. *Jesus God...* The air reeked of black powder and copper. Across from her, Plowman stared at nothing through his remaining eye. Mr. White regarded her with something like interest. *If he moves, I'll shoot,* Vasquez thought, but Mr. White did not move, not the length of time it took her to back out of the corridor and retreat to the elevator, the muzzle of the pistol centered on Mr. White, then on where Mr. White would be if he rounded the corner. Her back was a knot of fire. When she reached the elevator, she slapped the call button with her left hand while maintaining her aim with her right. Out of the corner of her eye, she saw Buchanan's gift for his son, all two hundred and sixty euros worth, wedged under its chair. She left it where it was. A faint glow shone from the near end of the corridor: Plowman's black-lighted symbols. Was the glow changing, obscured by an enormous form crawling towards her? When the elevator dinged behind her, she stepped into it, the gun up in front of her until the doors had closed and the elevator had commenced its descent.

The back of her blouse was stuck to her skin; a trickle of blood tickled the small of her back. The interior of the elevator dimmed to the point of disappearing entirely. The Walther weighed a thousand pounds. Her legs wobbled madly. Vasquez lowered the gun, reached her left hand out to steady herself. When it touched, not metal, but cool stone, she was not as surprised as she should have been. As her vision returned, she saw that she was in a wide, circular area, the roof flat, low, the walls no more than shadowy suggestions. The space was lit by a symbol incised on the rock at her feet: a rough circle, the diameter of a manhole cover, broken at about eight o'clock, whose perimeter was shining with cold light. Behind and to her left, the scrape of bare flesh dragging over stone turned her around. This section of the curving wall opened in a black arch like the top of an enormous throat. Deep in the darkness, she could detect movement, but was not yet able to distinguish it.

As she raised the pistol one more time, Vasquez was not amazed to find herself here, under the ground with things whose idiot hunger eclipsed the span of the oldest human civilizations, things she had helped summon. She was astounded to have thought she'd ever left.

For Fiona.

—o—

LITTLE PIG

ANNA TABORSKA

iotr waited nervously in the International Arrivals hall of Heathrow Airport's Terminal 1. Born and bred in London, Piotr had never thought of himself as the type of guy who would import a wife from Poland. His parents had made sure that he'd learnt Polish from an early age; while his English friends had played football or watched *Swap Shop* on Saturday mornings, Piotr had been dragged kicking and screaming to Polish classes in Ealing. But it had all paid off in the end when he went to Poland one summer and met Krystyna. Since that time, Krystyna had moved to London and moved in with Piotr. They were engaged to be married, and it seemed to Piotr that all the members of Krystyna's family had already visited London and stayed with them—all, that is, except Krystyna's grandmother, and that was who Piotr was now waiting for. Krystyna had not been able to get the day off work, and Piotr was now anxiously eyeing every elderly woman who came through the arrival gate, in the hope that one of them would match the tattered photograph that Krystyna had given him.

Eventually a little old lady came out alone. Piotr recognised her immediately and started to walk towards her, stopping abruptly as he saw the woman slip, drop her glasses and, in a desperate effort to right herself, step on them, crushing them completely. Upset for the woman, Piotr began to rush forward, only to halt as she started to laugh hysterically. She muttered something under her breath and, had he not known any better, Piotr could have sworn that what she said was "little pig!"

-◦-

The sleigh sped through the dark forest, the scant moonlight reflected by the snow lighting up the whites of the horse's eyes as it galloped along the narrow path, nostrils flaring and velvet mouth spitting foam and blood into the night. The woman cried out as the reins cut into her hands, and screamed to her children to hang on.

The three little girls clung to each other and to the sides of the sleigh, their tears freezing onto their faces as soon as they formed. The corner of the large blanket in which their mother had wrapped them for the perilous journey to their grandparents' house had come loose and was flapping violently in the icy air.

"Hold on to Vitek!" the woman screamed over her shoulder at her eldest child, her voice barely audible over the howling wind. But the girl did not need to be told; only two days away from her seventh birthday, she clung onto her baby brother, fear for her tiny sibling stronger than her own terror. The other two girls, aged two and four, huddled together, lost in an incomprehensible world of snow and fear and darkness.

The woman whipped the reins against the horse's heaving flanks, but the animal was already running on a primal fear stronger than pain. The excited yelps audible over the snowstorm left little doubt in the woman's mind: the pack was gaining on the sleigh—the hungry wolves were getting closer.

That winter had been particularly hard on the wolf pack. The invading Russian army had taken the peasants' livestock and, with no farm animals to snatch, the wolves had been limited to seeking out those rabbits and wild fowl that the desperate peasants and fleeing refugees had not killed and eaten. Driven half-mad with starvation, the wolves had already invested an irrevocable amount of energy in chasing the horse, and instinct informed them that it was too late to give up now—they had to feed or had to die.

The horse was wheezing, the blood freezing in its nostrils as it strained through the snow. Its chestnut coat was matted with sweat whipped up into a dirty foam. Steam rose off its back like smoke, giving the bizarre impression that the animal was on fire.

The woman shouted at the horse, willing it on, and brought the reins down against its flanks. She had only been fending for herself for three days—since the soldiers had tied her husband to a tree, cut off his genitals and sawn him in half with a blunt saw—but she knew instinctively that without the horse she and her children would die. If the starving wolves did not kill them, the cold would. They still had many miles to travel—and they would never make it on foot. The time had come to resort to the last hope her children had left.

The woman pulled on the reins, slowing the horse to a more controlled pace. She tied the reins to the sleigh, the horse running steadily along the forest path. She tried not to look at her shaking, crying children, clinging onto each other as they were thrown around the sleigh—the pitiful sight would break her, and she must not break. She must not lose the battle to keep her children alive.

"Good girls," she muttered, without looking back, "hold on to your brother." She stood up carefully in the speeding sleigh and reached over the side, unfastening the buckles on the wicker basket attached there. She opened the lid as slowly and as carefully as the shaking sleigh would allow. The sight that greeted her made her stomach turn, as fear for her children gave way to shock and panic. She howled in despair. A sudden jerky movement sent her sprawling back into the sleigh. She pulled herself up and clawed at the basket again, tearing the whole thing off in an effort to change the unchangeable.

"Little pig!" screamed the woman, her eyes wild and unseeing. The children screamed too, the madness in their mother's voice destroying the last remnant of safety and order in their world. "Little pig!" she screamed. "They took the little pig!"

The woman fell back onto her seat. The horse was slowing. An expectant howl pierced the darkness behind the sleigh. The woman grabbed the reins and struck at the horse's flanks again. The animal snorted and strained onwards, but even in her panic the woman knew that if she tried to force any more speed out of it, she would kill it, and all her children with it.

The howling and snarling grew closer, forcing the horse's fear onto a new level. It reared and tried to bolt, almost overturning the sleigh, but its exhaustion and the snow prevented its escape from the hungry pack.

The wolves were beginning to fan out on either side of the sleigh, still behind it, but not far off. One of the beasts—a battle-scarred individual with protruding ribs and cold yellow eyes—broke away from the others and made a dash for the horse, nipping at its heels. The horse screamed and kicked out, catching the wolf across the snout and sending it tumbling into the trees. It pulled itself up in seconds and started back after its companions.

The reins almost slipped from the woman's bleeding, freezing hands. She tightened her grip, wrapping the reins around her wrists. If only they were closer to her parents' village, she could let the wolves have the horse—it was the horse that they were after. But without the horse they would all freeze in the snow long before they reached safety.

The pack was catching up with the sleigh now; the wolves spilled forward, biting at the horse. The woman shouted at the wolves, whipped at them and at the horse with the reins, but there was nothing she could do. She cast a glance at her daughters: the two little ones pale as sheets, Irena holding onto Vitek as if he were life itself. And Vitek—her perfect little boy. The woman remembered her husband's face when she first told him he had a son. His face had lit up; he had taken the little boy from her and held him in his big, strong arms... her husband... then an image of the last time she had seen him—seen his mutilated corpse tied to the old walnut tree in the orchard...

She was back in the present, fighting to save her children—losing the fight to save her children. The little pig was gone—she had put it in the wicker basket at the side of the sleigh and fastened the straps when the soldiers were getting drunk inside her house. She had gone back to the barn to get the children, to flee with them under cover of darkness to what she hoped would be the relative safety of her parents' village. Someone must have seen her put the piglet in the basket, someone cruel enough to take the time to do up the straps after sentencing her children to death in the wolf-infested forest.

The little pig was gone and another sacrifice was needed in its place to protect the horse. The woman prepared to jump out of the sleigh. She turned to Irena and shouted, "Give Vitek to Kasia!" Irena stared at her mother blankly. "Give your brother to Kasia!" The woman's voice rose to a hysterical pitch. Four-year-old Kasia clung onto her two-year-old sister, and Irena began to cry, clutching her brother even tighter. "Give him to her!" screamed the woman, "I need you to hold the reins!" But even as she said it, she knew that the six-year-old would never be able to control the terrified horse. Her own hands were a bloody ruin and she wondered how she was able to hang on as the frantic animal fought its way forward.

"Irena! Give Vitek to Kasia—now!" But Irena saw something in her mother's eyes that scared her more than the dark and the shaking sleigh and even the wolves. She clutched her brother to her chest and shook her head, fresh tears rolling down her face and freezing to her cheeks.

A large silver wolf clamped its jaws onto the horse's left hind leg. The horse stumbled, but managed to right itself and the wolf let go, unable to keep up with the horse in the deep snow—but not for long. As the chestnut reeled, the sleigh lurched and the woman panicked. She had to act now or lose all her children. She could not give her life for them because they would never make it to safety without her. But a sacrifice had to be made. If she could not die to save her children, then one of them would have to die to save the others. She would not lose them all. One of them would have to die and she would have to choose. The delicate fabric of the woman's sanity was finally stretched to its limits and gave way. She threw back her head and howled her anguish into the night. All around her the night howled back.

The woman turned and looked into the faces of her children. A sharp intake of breath—like that taken by one about to drown. She took the reins in one hand, and with the other she reached out for her beloved son—her husband's greatest joy; the frailest of her children, half-frozen despite his sister's efforts to keep him warm, too exhausted even to cry, and the least likely to survive the journey.

"Give him to me!" she screamed at Irena. The girl struggled with her mother. The woman wrenched her baby out of her daughter's grasp and held him to her, gazing for a moment into his eyes. The woman smiled through her tears at her son. Snow was falling on the baby's upturned face, the frost had tinged his lips a pale blue, but in the woman's fevered mind, her baby smiled back at her.

Two of the wolves had closed in on the horse and were trying to bring it down. The woman screamed and threw Vitek as far from the sleigh as she could. There was a moment's silence, then a triumphant yelping as the wolves turned their attention away from the horse, and rushed away into the night. Irena cried out, and her little sisters stared uncomprehendingly at their mother, who screamed and screamed as she grabbed the reins in both hands and whipped the horse on into the dark.

As the first light of dawn broke across the horizon, an eerie sight greeted the sleepy village. The sleigh rolled in slowly, as the exhausted horse made it within sight of the first farmhouse. It stood for a moment, head drooping, blood seeping from its nostrils, its mouth, from open wounds along its flanks. Then it dropped silently to the ground and lay still. In the sleigh sat a wild-eyed woman, staring but unseeing, her black hair streaked with white, reins clenched tightly in her bloody hands. Behind her were three little girls. Two were slumped together, asleep. The third girl, the eldest of the three, was awake—she sat very still, eyes wide, silent as her mother.

—⟨⟩—

"Irena?" Piotr reached the old lady and touched her arm. "I'm Piotr." He bent down and picked up what was left of Irena's glasses. "I'm sorry about your glasses," he told her, handing the crushed frames back to her.

"No need to be sorry," said Irena. "It's just a little pig."

Piotr was taken aback. It was bad enough taking care of Krystyna's relatives, but she had never said that her grandmother was senile.

Irena read Piotr like an open book.

"A little pig," she explained, "a small sacrifice to make sure nothing really terrible happens… during my visit."

"I understand," said Piotr. He did not understand, but at least there was some method in the old lady's madness, and that was good enough for him. He paid the parking fee at the ticket machine, and they left the building: a tall young man pushing a trolley and a little old lady clutching a pair of broken glasses.

—⟨⟩—

THE BALLAD OF BALLARD AND SANDRINE

PETER STRAUB

1997

"**S**o, do we get lunch again today?" Ballard asked. They had reached the steaming, humid end of November.

"We got fucking lunch yesterday," replied the naked woman splayed on the long table: knees bent, one hip elevated, one boneless-looking arm draped along the curves of her body, which despite its hidden scars appeared to be at least a decade younger than her face. "Why should today be different?"

After an outwardly privileged childhood polluted by parental miscon-duct, a superior education, and two failed marriages, Sandrine Loy had evolved into a rebellious, still-exploratory woman of forty. At present, her voice had a well-honed edge, as if she were explaining something to a person of questionable intelligence.

Two days before joining Sandrine on this river journey, Ballard had celebrated his sixty-fifth birthday at a dinner in Hong Kong, one of the cities where he conducted his odd business. Sandrine had not been in-vited to the dinner and would not have attended if she had. The formal, ceremonious side of Ballard's life, which he found so satisfying, interested her not at all.

Without in any way adjusting the facts of the extraordinary body she had put on display, Sandrine lowered her eyes from the ceiling and examined him with a glance brimming with false curiosity and false innocence. The glance also contained a flicker of genuine irritation.

Abruptly and with vivid recall, Ballard found himself remembering the late afternoon in 1969 when, nine floors above Park Avenue, upon a carpet of almost unutterable richness in a room hung with paintings by Winslow Homer and Albert Pinkham Ryder, he had stood with a rich scapegrace and client named Lauritzen Loy, his host, to greet Loy's daughter on her return from another grueling day at Dalton School, then observed the sidelong, graceful, slightly miffed entrance of a fifteen-year-old girl in pigtails and a Jackson Brown sweatshirt two sizes too large, met her gray-green eyes, and felt the very shape of his universe alter in some drastic way, either expanding a thousand times or contracting to a pinpoint, he could not tell. The second their eyes met, the girl blushed, violently.

She hadn't liked that, not at all.

"I didn't say it was going to be different, and I don't think it will." He turned to look at her, making sure to meet her gaze before letting his eye travel down her neck, over her breasts, the bowl of her belly, the slope of her pubis, the length of her legs. "Are you in a more than ordinarily bad mood?"

"You're snapping at me."

Ballard sighed. "You gave me that *look*. You said, 'Why should today be different?'"

"Have it your way, old man. But as a victory, it's fucking pathetic. It's hollow."

She rolled onto her back and gave her body a firm little shake that settled it more securely onto the steel surface of the table. The metal, only slightly cooler than her skin, felt good against it. In this climate, nothing not on ice or in a freezer, not even a corpse, could ever truly get cold.

"Most victories are hollow, believe me."

Ballard wandered over to the brass-bound porthole on the deck side of their elaborate, many-roomed suite. Whatever he saw caused him momentarily to stiffen and take an involuntary step backwards.

"What's the view like?"

"The so-called view consists of the filthy Amazon and a boring, muddy bank. Sometimes the bank is so far away it's out of sight."

He did not add that a Ballard approximately twenty years younger, the Ballard of, say, 1976, dressed in a handsome dark suit and brilliantly white shirt, was leaning against the deck rail, unaware of being under the eye of his twenty-years-older self. Young Ballard, older Ballard observed, did an excellent job of concealing his dire internal condition beneath a mask of deep, already well-weathered urbanity: the same performance, enacted day after day before an audience unaware of being an audience and never permitted backstage.

Unlike Sandrine, Ballard had never married.

"Poor Ballard, stuck on the *Endless Night* with a horrible view and only his aging, moody girlfriend for company."

Smiling, he returned to the long steel table, ran his mutilated right hand over the curve of her belly, and cupped her navel. "This is exactly what I asked for. You're wonderful."

"But isn't it funny to think—everything could have been completely different."

Ballard slid the remaining fingers of his hand down to palpate, lightly, the springy black shrub-like curls of her pubic bush.

"Everything is completely different right now."

"So take off your clothes and fuck me," Sandrine said. "I can get you hard again in a minute. In thirty seconds."

"I'm sure you could. But maybe you should put some clothes *on*, so we could go into lunch."

"You prefer to have sex in our bed."

"I do, yes. I don't understand why you wanted to get naked and lie down on this thing, anyhow. Now, I mean."

"It isn't cold, if that's what you're afraid of." She wriggled her torso and did a snow angel movement with her legs.

"Maybe this time we could catch the waiters."

"Because we'd be early?"

Ballard nodded. "Indulge me. Put on that sleeveless white French thing."

"Aye, aye, *mon capitaine*." She sat up and scooted down the length of the table, pushing herself along on the raised vertical edges. These were of dark green marble, about an inch thick and four inches high. On both sides, round metal drains abutted the inner side of the marble. At the end of the table, Sandrine swung her legs down and straightened her arms, like a girl sitting on the end of a diving board. "I know why, too."

"Why I want you to wear that white thing? I love the way it looks on you."

"Why you don't want to have sex on this table."

"It's too narrow."

"You're thinking about what this table is for. Right? And you don't want to combine sex with *that*. Only I think that's exactly why we *should* have sex here."

"Everything we do, remember, is done by mutual consent. Our Golden Rule."

"Golden Spoilsport," she said. "Golden Shower of Shit."

"See? Everything's different already."

Sandrine levered herself off the edge of the table and faced him like a strict schoolmistress who happened momentarily to be naked. "I'm all you've got, and sometimes even I don't understand you."

"That makes two of us."

She wheeled around and padded into the bedroom, displaying her plush little bottom and sacral dimples with an absolute confidence Ballard could not but admire.

Although Sandrine and Ballard burst, in utter defiance of a direct order, into the dining room a full nine minutes ahead of schedule, the unseen minions had already done their work and disappeared. On the gleaming rosewood table two formal place settings had been laid, the plates topped with elaborately chased silver covers. Fresh irises brushed blue and yellow filled a tall, sparkling crystal vase.

"I swear, they must have a greenhouse on this yacht," Ballard said.

"Naked men with muddy hair row the flowers out in the middle of the night."

"I don't even think irises grow in the Amazon basin."

"Little guys who speak bird-language can probably grow anything they like."

"That's only one tribe, the Piraha. And all those bird-sounds are actual words. It's a human language." Ballard walked around the table and took the seat he had claimed as his. He lifted the intricate silver cover. "Now what is that?" He looked across at Sandrine, who was prodding at the contents of her bowl with a fork.

"Looks like a cut-up sausage. At least I hope it's a sausage. And something like broccoli. And a lot of orangey-yellowy goo." She raised her fork and licked the tines. "Um. Tastes pretty good, actually. But...."

For a moment, she appeared to be lost in time's great forest.

"I know this doesn't make sense, but if we ever did this before, *exactly* this, with you sitting over there and me here, in this same room, well, wasn't the food even better, I mean a *lot* better?"

"I can't say anything about that," Ballard said. "I really can't. There's just this vague...." The vagueness disturbed him far more than seemed quite rational. "Let's drop that subject and talk about bird language. Yes, let's. And the wine." He picked up the bottle. "Yet again a very nice Bordeaux," Ballard said, and poured for both of them. "However. What you've been hearing are real birds, not the Piraha."

"But they're talking, not just chirping. There's a difference. These guys are saying things to each other."

"Birds talk to one another. I mean, they sing."

She was right about one thing, though: in a funky, down-home way, the stew-like dish was delicious. He thrust away the feeling that it should have been a hundred, a thousand times more delicious: that once it, or something rather like it, had been paradisal.

"Birds don't sing in sentences. Or in paragraphs, like these guys do."

"They still can't be the Piraha. The Piraha live about five hundred miles away, on the Peruvian border."

"Your ears aren't as good as mine. You don't really hear them."

"Oh, I hear plenty of birds. They're all over the place."

"Only we're not talking about *birds*," Sandrine said.

1982

On the last day of November, Sandrine Loy, who was twenty-five, constitutionally ill-tempered, and startlingly good-looking (wide eyes, long mouth, black widow's peak, columnar legs), formerly of Princeton and Clare College, Cambridge, glanced over her shoulder and said, "Please tell me you're kidding. I just showered. I put on this nice white frock you bought me in Paris. And I'm *hungry*." Relenting a bit, she let a playful smile warm her face for nearly a second. "Besides that, I want to catch sight of our invisible servants."

"I'm hungry, too."

"Not for food, unfortunately." She spun from the porthole and its ugly view—a mile of brown, rolling river and low, muddy banks where squat, sullen natives tended to melt back into the bushes when the *Sweet Delight* went by—to indicate the evidence of Ballard's arousal, which stood up, darker than the rest of him, as straight as a flagpole.

"Let's have sex on this table. It's a lot more comfortable than it looks."

"Kind of defeats the fucking purpose, wouldn't you say? Comfort's hardly the point."

"Might as well be as comfy as we can, I say." He raised his arms to let his hands drape from the four-inch marble edging on the long steel table. "There's plenty of space on this thing, you know. More than in your bed at Clare."

"Maybe you're not as porky as I thought you were."

"Careful, careful. If you insult me, I'll make you pay for it."

At fifty Ballard had put on some extra weight, but it suited him. His shoulders were still wider far than his hips, and his belly more nascent than actual. His hair, longer than that of most men his age and just beginning to show threads of gray within the luxuriant brown, framed his wide brow and executive face. He looked like an actor who had made a career of playing senators, doctors, and bankers. Ballard's real profession was that of fixer to an oversized law firm in New York with a satellite office in Hong Kong, where he had grown up. The weight of muscle in his arms, shoulders, and legs reinforced the hint of stubborn determination, even perhaps brutality in his face: the suggestion that if necessary he would go a great distance and perform any number of grim deeds to do what was needed. Scars both long and short, scars like snakes, zippers, and tattoos bloomed here and there on his body.

"Promises, promises," she said. "But just for now, get up and get dressed, please. The sight of you admiring your own dick doesn't do anything for me."

"Oh, really?"

"Well, I do like the way you can still stick straight up into the air like a happy little soldier—at your age! But men are so soppy about their penises. You're all queer for yourselves. You more so than most, Ballard."

"Ouch," he said, and sat up. "I believe I'll put my clothes on now, Sandrine."

"Don't take forever, all right? I know it's only the second day, but I'd like to get a look at them while they're setting the table. Because someone, maybe even two someones, does set that table."

Ballard was already in the bedroom, pulling from their hangers a pair of white linen slacks and a thick, long-sleeved white cotton T-shirt. In seconds, he had slipped into these garments and was sliding his sun-tanned feet into rope-soled clogs.

"So let's move," he said, coming out of the bedroom with a long stride, his elbows bent, his forearms raised.

From the dining room came the sharp, distinctive chirping of a bird. Two notes, the second one higher, both clear and as insistent as the call of a bell. Ballard glanced at Sandrine, who seemed momentarily shaken.

"I'm not going in there if one of those awful jungle birds got in. They have to get rid of it. We're paying them, aren't we?"

"You have no idea," Ballard said. He grabbed her arm and pulled her along with him. "But that's no bird, it's *them*. The waiters. The staff."

Sandrine's elegant face shone with both disbelief and disgust.

"Those chirps and whistles are how they talk. Didn't you hear them last night and this morning?"

When he pulled again at her arm, she followed along, reluctance visible in her stance, her gait, the tilt of her head.

"I'm talking about birds, and they weren't even on the yacht. They were on shore. They were up in the air."

"Let's see what's in here." Six or seven minutes remained until the official start of dinner time, and they had been requested never to enter the dining room until the exact time of the meal.

Ballard threw the door open and pulled her into the room with him. Silver covers rested on the Royal Doulton china, and an uncorked bottle of a distinguished Bordeaux stood precisely at the mid-point between the two place settings. Three inches to its right, a navy-blue-and-royal-purple orchid thick enough to eat leaned, as if languishing, against the side of a small square crystal vase. The air seemed absolutely unmoving. Through the thumb holes at the tops of the plate covers rose a dense, oddly meaty odor of some unidentifiable food.

"Missed 'em again, damn it." Sandrine pulled her arm from Ballard's grasp and moved a few steps away.

"But you have noticed that there's no bird in here. Not so much as a feather."

"So it got out—I know it was here, Ballard."

She spun on her four-inch heels, giving the room a fast 360-degree inspection. Their dining room, roughly oval in shape, was lined with glassed-in bookshelves of dark-stained oak containing perhaps five hundred books, most of them mid-to-late nineteenth and early twentieth century novels ranked alphabetically by author, regardless of genre. The jackets had been removed, which Ballard minded, a bit. Three feet in front of the bookshelves on the deck side, which yielded space to two portholes and a door, stood a long wooden table with a delicately inlaid top—a real table, unlike the one in the room they had just left, which was more like a work station in a laboratory. The real one was presumably for setting out buffets.

The first door opened out onto the deck; another at the top of the oval led to their large and handsomely-furnished sitting room, with reading chairs and lamps, two sofas paired with low tables, a bar with a great many bottles of liquor, two red lacquered cabinets they had as yet not explored, and an air of many small precious things set out to gleam under the parlor's low lighting. The two remaining doors in the dining room were on the interior side. One opened into the spacious corridor that ran the entire length of their suite and gave access to the deck on both ends; the other revealed a gray passageway and a metal staircase that led up to the Captain's deck and cabin and down into the engine room, galley, and quarters for the yacht's small, unseen crew.

"So it kept all its feathers," said Sandrine. "If you don't think that's possible, you don't know doodly-squat about birds."

"What isn't possible," said Ballard, "is that some giant parrot got out of here without opening a door or a porthole."

"One of the waiters let it out, dummy. One of those handsome *Spanish-speaking* waiters."

They sat on opposite sides of the stately table. Ballard smiled at Sandrine, and she smiled back in rage and distrust. Suddenly and without warning, he remembered the girl she had been on Park Avenue at the end of the sixties, gawky-graceful, brilliantly surly, her hair and wardrobe goofy, claiming him as he had claimed her, with a glance. He had rescued her father from ruinous shame and a long jail term, but as soon as he had seen her he understood that his work had just begun, and that it would demand restraint, sacrifice, patience, and adamantine caution.

"A three-count?" he asked.

She nodded.

"One," he said. "Two." They put their thumbs into the round holes at the tops of the covers. "Three." They raised their covers, releasing steam and smoke and a more concentrated, powerful form of the meaty odor.

"Wow. What is that?"

Yellow-brown sauce or gravy covered a long, curved strip of foreign matter. Exhausted vegetables that looked a little like okra and string beans but were other things altogether lay strewn in limp surrender beneath the gravy.

"All of a sudden I'm really hungry," said Sandrine. "You can't tell what it is, either?"

Ballard moved the strip of unknown meat back and forth with his knife. Then he jabbed his fork into it. A watery yellow fluid oozed from the punctures.

"God knows what this is."

He pictured some big reptilian creature sliding down the riverbank into the meshes of a native net, then being hauled back up to be pierced with poison-tipped wooden spears. Chirping like birds, the diminutive men rioted in celebration around the corpse, which was now that of a hideous insect the size of a pony, its shell a poisonous green.

"I'm not even sure it's a mammal," he said. "Might even be some organ. Anaconda liver. Crocodile lung. Tarantula heart."

"You first."

Ballard sliced a tiny section from the curved meat before him. He half-expected to see valves and tubes, but the slice was a dense light brown all the way through. Ballard inserted the morsel into his mouth, and his taste buds began to sing.

"My god. Amazing."

"It's good?"

"Oh, this is way beyond 'good.'"

Ballard cut a larger piece off the whole and quickly bit into it. Yes, there it was again, but more sumptuous, almost floral in its delicacy and grounded in some profoundly satisfactory flavor, like that of a great single-barrel bourbon laced with a dark, subversive French chocolate. Subtlety, strength, sweetness. He watched Sandrine lift a section of the substance on her fork and slip it into her mouth. Her face went utterly still, and her eyes narrowed. With luxuriant slowness, she began to chew. After perhaps a second, Sandrine closed her eyes. Eventually, she swallowed.

"Oh, yes," she said. "My, my. Yes. Why can't we eat like this at home?"

"Whatever kind of animal this is, it's probably unknown everywhere but here. People like J. Paul Getty might get to eat it once a year, at some secret location."

"I don't care what it is, I'm just extraordinarily happy that we get to have it today. It's even a little bit sweet, isn't it?"

A short time later, Sandrine said, "Amazing. Even these horrible-looking vegetables spill out amazing flavors. If I could eat like this every day, I'd be perfectly happy to live in a hut, walk around barefoot, bathe in the Amazon, and wash my rags on the rocks."

"I know exactly what you mean," said Ballard. "It's like a drug. Maybe it is a drug."

"Do the natives really eat this way? Whatever this animal was, before they serve it to us, they have to hunt it down and kill it. Wouldn't they keep half of it for themselves?"

"Be a temptation," Ballard said. "Maybe they lick our plates, too."

"Tell me the truth now, Ballard. If you know it. Okay?"

Chewing, he looked up into her eyes. Some of the bliss faded from his face. "Sure. Ask away."

"Did we ever eat this stuff before?"

Ballard did not answer. He sliced a quarter sized piece off the meat and began to chew, his eyes on his plate.

"I know I'm not supposed to ask."

He kept chewing and chewing until he swallowed. He sipped his wine. "No. Isn't that strange? How we know we're not supposed to do certain things?"

"Like see the waiters. Or the maids, or the Captain."

"Especially the Captain, I think."

"Let's not talk anymore, let's just eat for a little while."

Sandrine and Ballard returned to their plates and glasses, and for a time made no noise other than soft moans of satisfaction.

When they had nearly finished, Sandrine said, "There are so many books on this boat! It's like a big library. Do you think you've ever read one?"

"Do you?"

"I have the feeling… well, of course that's the reason I'm asking. In a way, I mean in a *real* way, we've never been here before. On the Amazon? Absolutely not. My husband, besides being continuously unfaithful, is a total asshole who never pays me any attention at all unless he's angry with me, but he's also tremendously jealous and possessive. For me to get here to be with you required an amazing amount of secret organization. D-Day didn't take any more planning than this trip. On the other hand, I have the feeling I once read at least one of these books."

"I have the same feeling."

"Tell me about it. I want to read it again and see if I remember anything."

"I can't. But… well, I think I might have once seen you holding a copy of *Little Dorrit*. The Dickens novel."

"I went to Princeton and Cambridge, I know who wrote *Little Dorrit*," she said, irritated. "Wait. Did I ever throw a copy of that book overboard?"

"Might've."

"Why would I do that?"

Ballard shrugged. "To see what would happen?"

"Do you remember that?"

"It's tough to say what I remember. Everything's always different, but it's different *now*. I sort of remember a book, though—a book from this library. *Tono-Bungay*. H. G. Wells. Didn't like it much."

"Did you throw it overboard?"

"I might've. Yes, I actually might have." He laughed. "I think I did. I mean, I think I'm throwing it overboard right now, if that makes sense."

"Because you didn't—don't—like it?"

Ballard laughed and put down his knife and fork. Only a few bits of the vegetables and a piece of meat the size of a knuckle sliced in half remained on his plate. "Stop eating and give me your plate." It was almost exactly as empty as his, though Sandrine's plate still had two swirls of the yellow sauce.

"Really?"

"I want to show you something."

Reluctantly, she lowered her utensils and handed him her plate. Ballard scraped the contents of his plate onto hers. He got to his feet and picked up a knife and the plate that had been Sandrine's. "Come out on deck with me."

When she stood up, Sandrine glanced at what she had only briefly and partially perceived as a hint of motion at the top of the room, where for the first time she took in a dun-colored curtain hung two or three feet before the end of the oval. What looked to be a brown or suntanned foot, smaller than a normal adult's and perhaps a bit grubby, was just now vanishing behind the curtain. Before Sandrine had deciphered what she thought she had seen, it was gone.

"Just see a rat?" asked Ballard.

Without intending to assent, Sandrine nodded.

"One was out on deck this morning. Disappeared as soon as I spotted it. Don't worry about it, though. The crew, whoever they are, will get rid of them. At the start of the cruise, I think there are always a few rats around. By the time we really get in gear, they're gone."

"Good," she said, wondering: *If the waiters are these really, really short Indian guys, would they hate us enough to make us eat rats?*

She followed him through the door between the two portholes into pitiless sunlight and crushing heat made even less comfortable by the dense, invasive humidity. The invisible water saturating the air pressed against her face like a steaming washcloth, and moisture instantly coated her entire body. Leaning against the rail, Ballard looked cool and completely at ease.

"I forgot we had air conditioning," she said.

"We don't. Vents move the air around somehow. Works like magic, even when there's no breeze at all. Come over here."

She joined him at the rail. Fifty yards away, what might have been human faces peered at them through a dense screen of jungle—weeds with thick, vegetal leaves of a green so dark it was nearly black. The half-seen faces resembled masks, empty of feeling.

"Remember saying something about being happy to bathe in the Amazon? About washing your clothes in the river?"

She nodded.

"You never want to go into this river. You don't even want to stick the tip of your finger in that water. Watch what happens, now. Our native friends came out to see this, you should, too."

"The Indians knew you were going to put on this demonstration? How could they?"

"Don't ask me, ask them. *I* don't know how they do it."

Ballard leaned over the railing and used his knife to scrape the few things on the plate into the river. Even before the little knuckles of meat and gristle, the shreds of vegetables, and liquid strings of gravy landed in the water, a six-inch circle of turbulence boiled up on the slow-moving surface. When the bits of food hit the water, the boiling circle widened out into a three-foot, thrashing chaos of violent little fish tails and violent little green shiny fish backs with violent tiny green fins, all in furious motion. The fury lasted about thirty seconds, then disappeared back under the river's sluggish brown face.

"Like Christmas dinner with my husband's family," Sandrine said.

"When we were talking about throwing *Tono-Bungay* and *Little Dorrit* into the river to see what would happen—"

"The fish ate the books?"

"They'll eat anything that isn't metal."

"So our little friends don't go swimming all that often, do they?"

"They never learn how. Swimming is death, it's for people like us. Let's go back in, okay?"

She whirled around and struck his chest, hard, with a pointed fist. "I want to go back to the room with the table in it. *Our* table. And this time, you can get as hard as you like."

"Don't I always?" he asked.

"Oh," Sandrine said, "I like that 'always.'"

"And yet, it's always different."

"I bet *I'm* always different," said Sandrine. "You, you'd stay pretty much the same."

"I'm not as boring as all that, you know, " Ballard said, and went on, over the course of the long afternoon and sultry evening, to prove it.

After breakfast the next morning, Sandrine, hissing with pain, her skin clouded with bruises, turned on him with such fury that he gasped in joy and anticipation.

1976

End of November, hot sticky muggy, a vegetal stink in the air. Motionless tribesmen four feet tall stared out from the overgrown bank over twenty yards of torpid river. They held, seemed to hold, bows without arrows, though the details swam backward into the layers of folded green.

"Look at those little savages," said Sandrine Loy, nineteen years old and already contemplating marriage to handsome, absurdly wealthy Antonio Barban, who had proposed to her after a chaotic Christmas dinner at his family's vulgar pile in Greenwich, Connecticut. That she knew marriage to Antonio would prove to be an error of sublime proportions gave the idea most of its appeal. "We're putting on a traveling circus for their benefit. Doesn't that sort of make you detest them?"

"I don't detest them at all," Ballard said. "Actually, I have a lot of respect for those people. I think they're mysterious. So much gravity. So much *silence*. They understand a million things we don't, and what we do manage to get they know about in another way, a more profound way."

"You're wrong. They're too stupid to understand anything. They have mud for dinner. They have mud for brains."

"And yet...." Ballard said, smiling at her.

As if they knew they had been insulted and seemingly without moving out of position, the river people had begun to fade back into the network of dark, rubbery leaves in which they had for a long moment been framed.

"And yet what?"

"They knew what we were going to do. They wanted to see us throwing those books into the river. So out of the bushes they popped, right at the time we walked out on deck."

Her conspicuous black eyebrows slid nearer each other, creating a furrow. She shook her beautiful head and opened her mouth to disagree.

"Anyway, Sandrine, what did you think of what happened just now? Any responses, reflections?"

"What do I think of what happened to the books? What do I think of the fish?"

"Of course," Ballard said. "It's not *all* about us."

He leaned back against the rail, communicating utter ease and confidence. He was forty-four, attired daily in dark tailored suits and white shirts that gleamed like a movie star's smile, the repository of a thousand feral secrets, at home everywhere in the world, the possessor of an understanding it would take him a lifetime to absorb. Sandrine often seemed to him the center of his life. He knew exactly what she was going to say.

"I think the fish are astonishing," she said. "I mean it. Astonishing. Such concentration, such power, such complete *hunger*. It was breathtaking. Those books didn't last more than five or six seconds. All that thrashing! My book lasted longer than yours, but not by much."

"*Little Dorrit* is a lot longer than *Tono-Bungay*. More paper, more thread, more glue. I think they're especially hot for glue."

"Maybe they're just hot for Dickens."

"Maybe they're speed readers," said Sandrine. "What do we do now?"

"What we came here to do," Ballard said, and moved back to swing open the dining room door, then froze in mid-step.

"Forget something?"

"I was having the oddest feeling, and I just now realized what it was. You read about it all the time, so you think it must be pretty common, but until a second ago I don't think I'd ever before had the feeling that I was being watched. Not really."

"But now you did."

"Yes." He strode up to the door and swung it open. The table was bare, and the room was empty.

Sandrine approached and peeked over his shoulder. He had both amused and dismayed her. "The great Ballard exhibits a moment of paranoia. I think I've been wrong about you all this time. You're just another boring old creep who wants to fuck me."

"I'd admit to being a lot of things, but paranoid isn't one of them." He gestured her back through the door. That Sandrine obeyed him seemed to take both of them by surprise.

"How about being a boring old creep? I'm not really so sure I want to stay here with you. For one thing, and I know this is not related, the birds keep waking me up. If they are birds."

He cocked his head, interested. "What else could they be? Please tell me. Indulge a boring old creep."

"The maids and the waiters and the sailor guys. The cook. The woman who arranges the flowers."

"You think they belong to that tribe that speaks in bird calls? Actually, how did *you* ever hear about them?"

"My anthropology professor was one of the people who first discovered that tribe. The Piranhas. Know what they call themselves? The tall people. Not very observant, are they? According to the professor, they worshipped a much older tribe that had disappeared many generations back—miracle people, healers, shamans, warriors. The Old Ones, they called them, but the Old Ones called themselves **We**, you always have to put it in boldface. My professor couldn't stop talking about these tribes—he was so full of himself. *Sooo* vain. Kept staring at me. Vain, ugly, and lecherous, my favorite trifecta!"

The memory of her anthropology professor, with whom she had clearly gone through the customary adoration-boredom-disgust cycle of student-teacher love affairs, had put Sandrine in a sulky, dissatisfied mood.

"You made a lovely little error about thirty seconds ago. The tribe is called the Piraha, not the Piranhas. Piranhas are the fish you fell in love with."

"Ooh," she said, brightening up. "So the Piraha eat piranhas?"

"Other way around, more likely. But the other people on the *Blinding Light* can't be Piraha, we're hundreds of miles from their territory."

"You *are* tedious. Why did I ever let myself get talked into coming here, anyhow?"

"You fell in love with me the first time you saw me—in your father's living room, remember? And although it was tremendously naughty of me, in fact completely wrong and immoral, I took one look at your stupid sweatshirt and your stupid pigtails and fell in love with you on the spot. You were perfect—you took my breath away. It was like being struck by lightning."

He inhaled, hugely.

"And here I am, thirty-eight years of age, height of my powers, capable of performing miracles on behalf of our clients, exactly as I pulled off, not to say any more about this, a considerable miracle for your father, plus I am a fabulously eligible man, a tremendous catch, but what do you know, still unmarried. Instead of a wife or even a steady girlfriend, there's this succession of inane young women from twenty-five to thirty, these Heathers and Ashleys, these Morgans and Emilys, who much to their dismay grow less and less infatuated with me the more time we spend together. 'You're always so distant,' one of them said, 'you're never really *with* me.' And she was right, I couldn't really be with her. Because I wanted to be with you. I wanted us to be *here*."

Deeply pleased, Sandrine said, "You're such a pervert."

Yet something in what Ballard had evoked was making the handsome dining room awkward and dark. She wished he wouldn't stand still; there was no reason why he couldn't go into the living room, or the other way, into the room where terror and fascination beckoned. She wondered why she was waiting for Ballard to decide where to go, and as he spoke of seeing her for the first time, was assailed by an uncomfortably precise echo from the day in question.

Then, as now, she had been rooted to the floor: in her family's living room, beyond the windows familiar Park Avenue humming with the traffic she only in that moment became aware she heard, Sandrine had been paralyzed. Every inch of her face had turned hot and red. She felt intimate with Ballard before she had even begun to learn what intimacy meant. Before she had left the room, she waited for him to move between herself and her father, then pushed up the sleeves of the baggy sweatshirt and revealed the inscriptions of self-loathing, self-love, desire and despair upon her pale forearms.

"You're pretty weird, too. You'd just had your fifteenth birthday, and here you were, gobsmacked by this old guy in a suit. You even showed me your arms!"

"I could tell what made *you* salivate." She gave him a small, lop-sided smile. "So why were you there, anyhow?"

"Your father and I were having a private celebration."

"Of what?"

Every time she asked this question, he gave her a different answer. "I made the fearsome problem of his old library fines disappear. *Poof!*, no more late-night sweats." Previously, Ballard had told her that he'd got her father off jury duty, had cancelled his parking tickets, retroactively upgraded his B- in Introductory Chemistry to an A.

"Yeah, what a relief. My father never walked into a library, his whole life."

"You can see why the fine was so great." He blinked. "I just had an idea." Ballard wished her to cease wondering, to the extent this was possible, about the service he had rendered for her father. "How would you like to take a peek at the galley? Forbidden fruit, all that kind of thing. Aren't you curious?"

"You're suggesting we go down those stairs? Wasn't *not* doing that one of our most sacred rules?"

"I believe we were given those rules in order to make sure we broke them."

Sandrine considered this proposition for a moment, then nodded her head.

That's my girl, he thought.

"You may be completely perverted, Ballard, but you're pretty smart." A discordant possibility occurred to her. "What if we catch sight of our extremely discreet servants?"

"Then we know for good and all if they're little tribesmen who chirp like bobolinks or handsome South American yacht bums. But that won't happen. They may, in fact they undoubtedly do, see us, but we'll never catch sight of them. No matter how brilliantly we try to outwit them."

"You think they watch us?"

"I'm sure that's one of their main jobs."

"Even when we're in bed? Even when we... you know."

"Especially then," Ballard said.

"What do we think about that, Ballard? Do we love the whole idea, or does it make us sick? You first."

"Neither one. We can't do anything about it, so we might as well forget it. I think being able to watch us is one of the ways they're paid—these tribes don't have much use for money. And because they're always there, they can step in and help us when we need it, at the end."

"So it's like love," said Sandrine.

"Tough love, there at the finish. Let's go over and try the staircase."

"Hold on. When we were out on deck, you told me that you felt you were being watched, and that it was the first time you'd ever had that feeling."

"Yes, that was different—I don't *feel* the natives watching me, I just assume they're doing it. It's the only way to explain how they can stay out of sight all the time."

As they moved across the dining room to the inner door, for the first time Sandrine noticed a curtain the color of a dark camel hair coat hanging up at the top of the room's oval. Until that moment, she had taken it for a wall too small and oddly shaped to be covered with bookshelves. The curtain shifted a bit, she thought: a tiny ripple occurred in the fabric, as if it had been breathed upon.

There's one of them now, she thought. *I bet they have their own doors and their own staircases.*

For a moment, she was disturbed by a vision of the yacht honeycombed with narrow passages and runways down which beetled small red-brown figures with matted black hair and faces like dull, heavy masks. Now and then the little figures paused to peer through chinks in the walls. It made her feel violated, a little, but at the same time immensely proud of the body that the unseen and silent attendants were privileged to gaze at. The thought of these mysterious little people watching what Ballard did to that body, and she to his, caused a thrill of deep feeling to course upward through her body.

"Stop daydreaming, Sandrine, and get over here." Ballard held the door that led to the gray landing and the metal staircase.

"You go first," she said, and Ballard moved through the frame while still holding the door. As soon as she was through, he stepped around her to grasp the gray metal rail and begin moving down the stairs.

"What makes you so sure the galley's downstairs?"

"Galleys are always downstairs."

"And why do you want to go there, again?"

"One: because they ordered us not to. Two: because I'm curious about what goes on in that kitchen. And three: I also want to get a look at the wine cellar. How can they keep giving us these amazing wines? Remember what we drank with lunch?"

"Some stupid red. It tasted good, though."

"That stupid red was a '55 Chateau Petrus. Two years older than you."

Ballard led her down perhaps another dozen steps, arrived at a landing, and saw one more long staircase leading down to yet another landing.

"How far down can this galley be?" she asked.

"Good question."

"This boat has a bottom, after all."

"It has a hull, yes."

"Shouldn't we actually have gone past it by now? The bottom of the boat?"

"You'd think so. Okay, maybe this is it."

The final stair ended at a gray landing that opened out into a narrow gray corridor leading to what appeared to be a large, empty room. Ballard looked down into the big space, and experienced a violent reluctance, a mental and physical refusal, to go down there and look further into the room: it was prohibited by an actual taboo. That room was not for him, it was none of his business, period. Chilled, he turned from the corridor and at last saw what was directly before him. What had appeared to be a high gray wall was divided in the middle and bore two brass panels at roughly chest height. The wall was a doorway.

"What do you want to do?" Sandrine asked.

Ballard placed a hand on one of the panels and pushed. The door swung open, revealing a white tile floor, metal racks filled with cast-iron pans, steel bowls, and other cooking implements. The light was a low, diffused dimness. Against the side wall, three sinks of varying sizes bulged downward beneath their faucets. He could see the inner edge of a long, shiny metal counter. Far back, a yellow propane tank clung to a range with six burners, two ovens, and a big griddle. A faint mewing, a tiny *skritch skritch skritch* came to him from the depths of the kitchen.

"Look, is there any chance…?" Sandrine whispered.

In a normal voice, Ballard said "No. They're not in here right now, whoever they are. I don't think they are, anyhow."

"So does that mean we're supposed to go inside?"

"How would I know?" He looked over his shoulder at her. "Maybe we're not *supposed* to do anything, and we just decide one way or the other. But here we are, anyhow. I say we go in, right? If it feels wrong, smells wrong, whatever, we boogie on out."

"You first," she said.

Without opening the door any wider, Ballard slipped into the kitchen. Before he was all the way in, he reached back and grasped Sandrine's wrist.

"Come along now."

"You don't have to drag me, I was right behind you. You bully."

"I'm not a bully, I just don't want to be in here by myself."

"All bullies are cowards, too."

She edged in behind him and glanced quickly from side to side. "I didn't think you could have a kitchen like this on a yacht."

"You can't," he said. "Look at that gas range. It must weigh a thousand pounds."

She yanked her wrist out of his hand. "It's hard to see in here, though. Why is the light so fucking weird?"

They were edging away from the door, Sandrine so close behind that Ballard could feel her breath on his neck.

"There aren't any light fixtures, see? No overhead lights, either."

He looked up and saw, far above, only a dim white-gray ceiling that stretched away a great distance on either side. Impossibly, the "galley" seemed much wider than the *Blinding Light* itself.

"I don't like this," he said.

"Me, neither."

"We're really not supposed to be here," he said, thinking of that other vast room down at the end of the corridor, and said to himself, *That's what they call the "engine room", we absolutely can't even glance that way again, can't can't can't, the "engines" would be way too much for us.*

The mewing and skritching, which had momentarily fallen silent, started up again, and in the midst of what felt and tasted to him like panic, Ballard had a vision of a kitten trapped behind a piece of kitchen equipment. He stepped forward and leaned over to peer into the region beyond the long counter and beside the enormous range. Two funny striped cabinets about five feet tall stood there side by side.

"Do you hear a cat?" he asked.

"If you think that's a cat..." Sandrine said, a bit farther behind him than she had been at first.

The cabinets were cages, and what he had seen as stripes were their bars. "Oh," Ballard said, and sounded as though he had been punched in the stomach.

"Damn you, you started to bleed through your suit jacket," Sandrine whispered. "We have to get out of here, fast."

Ballard scarcely heard her. In any case, if he were bleeding, it was of no consequence. They knew what to do about bleeding. Here on the other hand, perhaps sixty feet away in this preposterous "galley," was a phenomenon he had never before witnessed. The first cage contained a thrashing beetle-like insect nearly too large for it. This gigantic insect was the source of the mewing and scratching. One of its mandibles rasped at a bar as the creature struggled to roll forward or back, producing noises of insect-distress. Long smeary wounds in the wide middle area between its scrabbling legs oozed a yellow ichor.

Horrified, Ballard looked hastily into the second cage, which he had thought empty but for a roll of blankets, or towels, or the like, and discovered that the blankets or towels were occupied by a small boy from one of the river tribes who was gazing at him through the bars. The boy's eyes looked hopeless and dead. Half of his shoulder seemed to have been sliced away, and a long, thin strip of bone gleamed white against a great scoop of red. The arm half-extended through the bars concluded in a dark, messy stump.

The boy opened his mouth and released, almost too softly to be heard, a single high-pitched musical note. Pure, accurate, well defined, clearly a word charged with some deep emotion, the note hung in the air for a brief moment, underwent a briefer half-life, and was gone.

"What's that?" Sandrine said.

"Let's get out of here."

He pushed her through the door, raced around her, and began charging up the stairs. When they reached the top of the steps and threw themselves into the dining room, Ballard collapsed onto the floor, then rolled onto his back, heaving in great quantities of air. His chest rose and fell, and with every exhalation he moaned. A portion of his left side pulsing with pain felt warm and wet. Sandrine leaned against the wall, breathing heavily in a less convulsive way. After perhaps thirty seconds, she managed to say, "I trust that was a bird down there."

"Um. Yes." He placed his hand on his chest, then held it up like a stop sign, indicating that he would soon have more to say. After a few more great heaving lungfuls of air, he said, "Toucan. In a big cage."

"You were that frightened by a kind of parrot?"

He shook his head slowly from side to side on the polished floor. "I didn't want them to catch us down there. It seemed dangerous, all of a sudden. Sorry."

"You're bleeding all over the floor."

"Can you get me a new bandage pad?"

Sandrine pushed herself off the wall and stepped toward him. From his perspective, she was as tall as a statue. Her eyes glittered. "Screw you, Ballard. I'm not your servant. You can come with me. It's where we're going, anyhow."

He pushed himself upright and peeled off his suit jacket before standing up. The jacket fell to the floor with a squishy thump. With blood-dappled fingers, he unbuttoned his shirt and let that, too, fall to the floor.

"Just leave those things there," Sandrine said. "The invisible crew will take care of them."

"I imagine you're right." Ballard managed to get to his feet without staggering. Slow-moving blood continued to ooze down his left side.

"We have to get you on the table," Sandrine said. "Hold this over the wound for right now, okay?"

She handed him a folded white napkin, and he clamped it over his side. "Sorry. I'm not as good at stitches as you are."

"I'll be fine," Ballard said, and began moving, a bit haltingly, toward the next room.

"Oh, sure. You always are. But you know what I like about what we just did?"

For once he had no idea what she might say. He waited for it.

"That amazing food we loved so much was Toucan! Who would've guessed? You'd think Toucan would taste sort of like chicken, only a lot worse."

"Life is full of surprises."

In the bedroom, Ballard kicked off his shoes, pulled his trousers down over his hips, and stepped out of them.

"You can leave your socks on," said Sandrine, "but let's get your undies off, all right?"

"I need your help."

Sandrine grasped the waistband of his boxers and pulled them down, but they snagged on his penis. "Ballard is aroused, surprise number two." She unhooked his shorts, let them drop to the floor, batted his erection down, and watched it bounce back up. "Barkis is willin', all right."

"Let's get into the workroom," he said.

"Aye aye, *mon capitaine*." Sandrine closed her hand on his erection and said, "Want to go there on-deck, give the natives a look at your magnificent manliness? Shall we increase the index of penis envy among the river tribes by a really big factor?"

"Let's just get in there, okay?"

She pulled him into the workroom and only then released his erection.

A wheeled aluminum tray had been rolled up beside the worktable. Sometimes it was not given to them, and they were forced to do their work with their hands and whatever implements they had brought with them. Today, next to the array of knives of many kinds and sizes, cleavers, wrenches, and hammers lay a pack of surgical thread and a stainless steel needle still warm from the autoclave.

Ballard sat down on the worktable, pushed himself along until his heels had cleared the edge, and lay back. Sandrine threaded the needle and, bending over to get close to the wound, began to do her patient stitching.

1982

"Oh, here you are," said Sandrine, walking into the sitting room of their suite to find Ballard lying on one of the sofas, reading a book whose title she could not quite make out. Because both of his hands were heavily bandaged, he was having some difficulty turning the pages. "I've been looking all over for you."

He glanced up, frowning. "All over? Does that mean you went down the stairs?"

"No, of course not. I wouldn't do anything like that alone, anyhow."

"And just to make sure…. You didn't go up the stairs, either, did you?"

Sandrine came toward him, shaking her head. "No, I'd never do that, either. But I want to tell you something. I thought *you* might have decided to take a look upstairs. By yourself, to sort of protect me in a way I never want to be protected."

"Of course," Ballard said, closing his book on an index finger that protruded from the bulky white swath of bandage. "You'd hate me if I ever tried to protect you, especially by doing something sneaky. I knew that about you when you were fifteen years old."

"When I was fifteen, you did protect me."

He smiled at her. "I exercised an atypical amount of restraint."

His troublesome client, Sandrine's father, had told him one summer day that a business venture required him to spend a week in Mexico City. Could he think of anything acceptable that might occupy his daughter during that time, she being a teenager a bit too prone to independence and exploration? Let her stay with me, Ballard had said. The guest room has its own bathroom and a TV. I'll take her out to theaters at night, and to the Met and Moma during the day when I'm not doing my job. When I *am* doing my job, she can bat around the city by herself the way she does now. Extraordinary man you are, the client had said, and allow me to reinforce that by letting you know that about a month ago my daughter just amazed me one morning by telling me that she liked you. You have no idea how god-damned fucking unusual that is. That she talked to me at all is staggering, and that she actually announced that she liked one of my friends is stupefying. So yes, please, thank you, take Sandrine home with you, please do, escort her hither and yon.

When the time came, he drove a compliant Sandrine to his house in Harrison, where he explained that although he would not have sex with her until she was at least eighteen, there were many other ways they could express themselves. And although it would be years before they could be naked together, for the present they would each be able to be naked before the other. Fifteen-year-old Sandrine, who had been expecting to use all her arts of bad temper, insult, duplicity, and evasiveness to escape ravishment by this actually pretty interesting old guy, responded to these conditions with avid interest. Ballard announced another prohibition no less serious, but even more personal.

"I can't cut myself any more?" she asked. "Fuck you, Ballard, you loved it when I showed you my arm. Did my father put you up to this?" She began looking frantically for her bag, which Ballard's valet had already removed to the guest rooms.

"Not at all. Your father would try to kill me if he knew what I was going to do to you. And you to me, when it's your turn."

"So if I can't cut myself, what exactly happens instead?"

"*I* cut you," Ballard said. "And I do it a thousand times better than you ever did. I'll cut you so well no one ever be able to tell it happened, unless they're right on top of you."

"You think I'll be satisfied with some wimpy little cuts no one can even see? Fuck you all over again."

"Those cuts no one can see will be incredibly painful. And then I'll take the pain away, so you can experience it all over again."

Sandrine found herself abruptly caught up by a rush of feelings that seemed to originate in a deep region located just below her ribcage. At least for the moment, this flood of unnamable emotions blotted out her endless grudges and frustrations, also the chronic bad temper they engendered.

"And during this process, Sandrine, I will become deeply familiar, profoundly familiar with your body, so that when at last we are able to enjoy sex with each other, I will know how to give you the most amazing pleasure. I'll know every inch of you, I'll have your whole gorgeous map in my head. And you will do the same with me."

Sandrine had astonished herself by agreeing to this program on the spot, even to abstain from sex until she turned eighteen. Denial, too, was a pain she could learn to savor. At that point Ballard had taken her upstairs to her the guest suite, and soon after down the hallway to what he called his "workroom."

"Oh my God," she said, taking it in, "I can't believe it. This is real. And you, you're real, too."

"During the next three years, whenever you start hating everything around you and feel as though you'd like to cut yourself again, remember that I'm here. Remember that this room exists. There'll be many days and nights when we can be here together."

In this fashion had Sandrine endured the purgatorial remainder of her days at Dalton. And when she and Ballard at last made love, pleasure and pain had become presences nearly visible in the room at the moment she screamed in the ecstasy of release.

"You dirty, dirty, dirty old man," she said, laughing.

Four years after that, Ballard overheard some Chinese bankers, clients of his firm for whom he had several times rendered his services, speaking in soft Mandarin about a yacht anchored in the Amazon Basin; he needed no more.

"I want to go off the boat for a couple of hours when we get to Manaus,"

Sandrine said. "I feel like getting back in the world again, at least for a little while. This little private bubble of ours is completely cut off from everything else."

"Which is why—"

"Which is why it works, and why we like it, I understand, but half the time I can't stand it, either. I don't live the way you do, always flying off to interesting places to perform miracles…"

"Try spending a rainy afternoon in Zurich holding some terminally anxious banker's hand."

"Not that it matters, especially, but you don't mind, do you?"

"Of course not. I need some recuperation time, anyhow. This was a little severe." He held up one thickly bandaged hand. "Not that I'm complaining."

"You'd better not!"

"I'll only complain if you stay out too late—or spend too much of your father's money!"

"What could I buy in Manaus? And I'll make sure to be back before dinner. Have you noticed? The food on this weird boat is getting better and better every day?"

"I know, yes, but for now I seem to have lost my appetite," Ballard said. He had a quick mental vision of a metal cage from which something hideous was struggling to escape. It struck an oddly familiar note, as of something half-remembered, but Ballard was made so uncomfortable by the image in his head that he refused to look at it any longer.

"Will they just know that I want to dock at Manaus?"

"Probably, but you could write them a note. Leave it on the bed. Or on the dining room table."

"I have a pen in my bag, but where can I find some paper?"

"I'd say, look in any drawer. You'll probably find all the paper you might need."

Sandrine went to the little table beside him, pulled open its one drawer and found a single sheet of thick, cream-colored stationery headed *Sweet Delight*. An Omas roller-ball pen, much nicer than the Pilot she had liberated from their hotel in Rio, lay angled atop the sheet of stationery. In her formal, almost italic handwriting, Sandrine wrote *Please dock at Manaus. I would like to spend two or three hours ashore.*

"Should I sign it?"

Ballard shrugged. "There's just the two of us. Initial it."

She drew a graceful, looping S under her note and went into the din-ing room, where she squared it off in the middle of the table. When she returned to the sitting room, she asked, "And now I just wait? Is that how it works? Just because I found a piece of paper and a pen, I'm supposed to trust this crazy system?"

"You know as much as I do, Sandrine. But I'd say, yes, just wait a little while, yes, that's how it works, and yes, you might as well trust it. There's no reason to be bitchy."

"I have to stay in practice," she said, and lurched sideways as the yacht bumped against something hard and came to an abrupt halt.

"See what I mean?"

When he put the book down in his lap, Sandrine saw that it was *Tono-Bungay.* She felt a hot, rapid flare of irritation that the book was not something like *The Women's Room*, which could teach him things he needed to know: and hadn't he already read *Tono-Bungay*?

"Look outside, try to catch them tying us up and getting out that walkway thing."

"You think we're in Manaus already?"

"I'm sure we are."

"That's ridiculous. We scraped against a barge or something."

"Nonetheless, we have come to a complete halt."

Sandrine strode briskly to the on-deck door, threw it open, gasped, then stepped outside. The yacht had already been tied up at a long yel-low dock at which two yachts smaller than theirs rocked in a desultory brown tide. No crewmen were in sight. The dock led to a wide concrete apron across which men of European descent and a few natives pushed wheelbarrows and consulted clipboards and pulled on cigars while pointing out distant things to other men. It looked false and stagy, like the first scene in a bad musical about New Orleans. An avenue began in front of a row of warehouses, the first of which was painted with the slogan MANAUS AMAZONA. The board walkway with rope handrails had been set in place.

"Yeah, okay," she said. "We really do seem to be docked at Manaus."

"Don't stay away too long."

"I'll stay as long as I like," she said.

The avenue leading past the facades of the warehouses seemed to run directly into the center of the city, visible now to Sandrine as a gathering of tall office buildings and apartment blocks that thrust upwards from the jumble of their surroundings like an outcropping of mountains. The skyscrapers were blue-gray in color, the lower surrounding buildings a scumble of brown, red, and yellow that made Sandrine think of Cezanne, even of Seurat: dots of color that suggested walls and roofs. She thought she could walk to the center of the city in no more than forty-five minutes, which left her about two hours to do some exploring and have lunch.

Nearly an hour later, Sandrine trudged past the crumbling buildings and broken windows on crazed, tilting sidewalks under a domineering sun. Sweat ran down her forehead and cheeks and plastered her dress to her body. The air seemed half water, and her lungs strained to draw in oxygen. The office buildings did not seem any nearer than at the start of her walk. If she had seen a taxi, she would have taken it back to the port, but only a few cars and pickups rolled along the broad avenue. The dark, half-visible men driving these vehicles generally leaned over their steering wheels and stared at her, as if women were rare in Manaus. She wished she had thought to cover her hair, and was sorry she had left her sunglasses behind.

Then she became aware that a number of men were following her, how many she could not tell, but more than two. They spoke to each other in low, hoarse voices, now and then laughing at some remark sure to be at Sandrine's expense. Although her feet had begun to hurt, she began moving more quickly. Behind her, the men kept pace with her, neither gaining nor falling back. After another two blocks, Sandrine gave in to her sense of alarm and glanced over her shoulder. Four men in dark hats and shapeless, slept-in suits had ranged themselves across the width of the sidewalk. One of them called out to her in a language she did not understand; another emitted a wet, mushy laugh. The man at the curb jumped down into the street, trotted across the empty avenue, and picked up his pace on the sidewalk opposite until he had drawn a little ahead of Sandrine.

She felt utterly alone and endangered. And because she felt in danger, a scorching anger blazed up within her: at herself for so stupidly putting herself at risk, at the men behind her for making her feel frightened, for ganging up on her. She did not know what she was going to have to do, but she was not going to let those creeps get any closer to her than they were now. Twisting to her right, then to her left, Sandrine removed her shoes and rammed them into her bag. They were watching her, the river scum; even the man on the other side of the avenue had stopped moving and was staring at her from beneath the brim of his hat.

Literally testing the literal ground, Sandrine walked a few paces over the paving stones, discovered that they were at any rate not likely to cut her feet, gathered herself within, and, like a race horse bursting from the gate, instantly began running as fast as she could. After a moment in which her pursuers were paralyzed with surprise, they too began to run. The man on the other side of the street jumped down from the curb and began sprinting toward her. His shoes made a sharp *tick-tick* sound when they met the stony asphalt. As the ticks grew louder, Sandrine heard him inhaling great quantities of air. Before he could reach her, she came to a cross street and wheeled in, her bag bouncing at her hip, her legs stretching out to devour yard after yard of stony ground.

Unknowingly, she had entered a slum. The structures on both sides of the street were half-collapsed huts and shanties made of mismatched wooden planks, of metal sheeting, and tarpaper. She glimpsed faces peering out of greasy windows and sagging, cracked-open doors. Some of the shanties before her were shops with soft drink cans and bottles of beer arrayed on the window sills. People were spilling from little tarpaper and sheet-metal structures out into the street, already congested with abandoned cars, empty pushcarts, and cartons of fruit for sale. Garbage lay everywhere. The women who watched Sandrine streak by displayed no interest in her plight.

Yet the slum's chaos was a blessing, Sandrine thought: the deeper she went, the greater the number of tiny narrow streets sprouting off the one she had taken from the avenue. It was a feverish, crowded warren, a *favela*, the kind of place you would never escape had you the bad luck to have been born there. And while outside this rat's nest the lead man chasing her had been getting dangerously near, within its boundaries the knots of people and the obstacles of cars and carts and mounds of garbage had slowed him down. Sandrine found that she could dodge all of these obstacles with relative ease. The next time she spun around a corner, feet skidding on a slick pad of rotting vegetables, she saw what looked to her like a miracle: an open door revealing a hunched old woman draped in black rags, beckoning her in.

Sandrine bent her legs, called on her youth and strength, jumped off the ground, and sailed through the open door. The old woman only just got out of the way in time to avoid being knocked down. She was giggling, either at Sandrine's athleticism or because she had rescued her from the pursuing thugs. When Sandrine had cleared her doorway and was scrambling to avoid ramming into the wall, the old woman darted forward and slammed her door shut. Sandrine fell to her knees in a small room suddenly gone very dark. A slanting shaft of light split the murk and illuminated a rectangular space on the floor covered by a threadbare rug no longer of any identifiable color. Under the light, the rug seemed at once utterly worthless and extraordinarily beautiful.

The old woman shuffled into the shaft of light and uttered an incomprehensible word that sounded neither Spanish nor Portuguese. A thousand wayward wrinkles like knife cuts, scars, and stitches had been etched into her white, elongated face. Her nose had a prominent hook, and her eyes shone like dark stones at the bottom of a fast, clear stream. Then she laid an upright index finger against her sunken lips and with her other hand gestured toward the door. Sandrine listened. In seconds, multiple footsteps pounded past the old woman's little house. Leading the pack was *tick tick tick.* The footsteps clattered up the narrow street and disappeared into the ordinary clamor.

Hunched over almost parallel to the ground, the old woman mimed hysterical laughter. Sandrine mouthed *Thank you, thank you,* thinking that her intention would be clear if the words were not. Still mock-laughing, her unknown savior shuffled closer, knitting and folding her long, spotted hands. She had the ugliest hands Sandrine had ever seen, knobbly arthritic fingers with filthy, ragged nails. She hoped the woman was not going stroke her hair or pat her face: she would have to let her do it, however nauseated she might feel. Instead, the old woman moved right past her, muttering what sounded like *Munna, munna, num.*

Outside on the street, the ticking footsteps once again became audible. Someone began knocking, hard, on an adjacent door.

Only half-visible at the rear of the room, the old woman turned toward Sandrine and beckoned her forward with an urgent gesture of her bony hand. Sandrine moved toward her, uncertain of what was going on.

In an urgent, raspy whisper: *Munna! Num!*

The old woman appeared to be bowing to the baffled Sandrine, whose sense of peril had begun again to boil up within her. A pane of greater darkness slid open behind the old woman, and Sandrine finally understood that her savior had merely bent herself more deeply to turn a doorknob.

Num! Num!

Sandrine obeyed orders and *nummed* past her beckoning hostess. Almost instantly, instead of solid ground, her foot met a vacancy, and she nearly tumbled down what she finally understood to be a staircase. Only her sense of balance kept her upright: she was grateful she still had all of her crucial toes. Behind her, the door slammed shut. A moment later, she heard the clicking of a lock.

◦

Back on the yacht, Ballard slipped a bookmark into *Tono-Bungay* and for the first time, at least for what he thought was the first time, regarded the pair of red lacquered cabinets against the wall beside him. Previously, he had taken them in, but never really examined them. About four feet high and three feet wide, they appeared to be Chinese and were perhaps moderately valuable. Brass fittings with latch pins held them closed in front, so they were easily opened.

The thought of lifting the pins and opening the cabinets aroused both curiosity and an odd dread in Ballard. For a moment, he had a vision of a great and forbidden room deep in the bowels of the yacht where enormous spiders ranged across rotting, heaped-up corpses. (With wildly variant details, visions of exactly this sort had visited Ballard ever since his adolescence.) He shook his head to clear it of this vision, and when that failed, struck his bandaged left hand against the padded arm of the sofa. Bright, rolling waves of pain forced a gasp from him, and the forbidden room with its spiders and corpses zipped right back to wherever had given it birth.

Was this the sort of dread he was supposed to obey, or the sort he was supposed to ignore? Or if not ignore, because that was always unwise and in some sense dishonorable, acknowledge but persist in the face of anyway? Cradling his throbbing hand against his chest, Ballard let the book slip off his lap and got to his feet, eyeing the pair of shiny cabinets. If asked to inventory the contents of the sitting room, he would have forgotten to list them. Presumably that meant he was supposed to overlook his foreboding and investigate the contents of these vertical little Chinese chests. *They* wanted him to open the cabinets, if *he* wanted to.

Still holding his electrocuted left hand to his chest, Ballard leaned over and brought his exposed right index finger in contact with the box on the left. No heat came from it, and no motion. It did not hum, it did not quiver, however delicately. At least six or seven coats of lacquer had been applied to the thing—he felt as though he were looking into a deep river of red lacquer.

Ballard hunkered and used his index finger to push the brass latch pin up and out of the ornate little lock. It swung down on an intricate little cord he had not previously noticed. The door did not open by itself, as he had hoped. Once again, he had to make a choice, for it was not too late to drop the brass pin back into its latch. He could choose not to look; he could let the *Sweet Delight* keep its secrets. But as before, Ballard acknowledged the dread he was feeling, then dropped his hip to the floor, reached out, and flicked the door open with his fingernail. Arrayed on the cabinet's three shelves were what appeared to be photographs in neat stacks. Polaroids, he thought. He took the first stack of photos from the cabinet and looked down at the topmost one. What Ballard saw there had two contradictory effects on him. He became so light-headed he feared he might faint; and he almost ejaculated into his trousers.

◄○►

Taking care not to tumble, Sandrine moved in the darkness back to the top of the staircase, found the door with her fingertips, and pounded. The door rattled in its frame but did not give. "Open up, lady!" she shouted. "Are you *kidding*? Open this door!" She banged her fists against the unmoving wood, thinking that although the old woman undoubtedly did not speak English, she could hardly misunderstand what Sandrine was saying. When her fists began to hurt and her throat felt ragged, the strangeness of what had just happened opened before her: it was like…

like a fairy tale! She had been duped, tricked, flummoxed; she had been trapped. The world had closed on her, as a steel trap snaps shut on the leg of a bear.

"Please!" she yelled, knowing it was useless. She would not be able to beg her way out of this confinement. Here, the Golden Shower of Shit did not apply. "Please let me out!" A few more bangs of her fist, a few more shouted pleas to be set free, to be *let go*, *released*. She thought she heard her ancient captor chuckling to herself.

Two possibilities occurred to her: that her pursuers had driven her to this place and the old woman was in league with them; and that they had not and she was not. The worse by far of these options was the second, that to escape her rapists she had fled into a psychopath's dungeon. Maybe the old woman wanted to starve her to death. Maybe she wanted to soften her up so she'd be easy to kill. Or maybe she was just keeping her as a snack for some monstrous get of hers, some overgrown looney-tunes son with pinwheel eyes and horrible teeth and a vast appetite for stray women.

More to exhaust all of her possibilities than because she imagined they possessed any actual substance, Sandrine turned carefully around, planted a hand on the earthen wall beside her, and began making her way down the stairs in the dark. It would lead to some spider-infested cellar, she knew, a foul-smelling hole where ugly, discarded things waited thug-like in the seamless dark to inflict injury upon anyone who entered their realm. She would grope her way from wall to wall, feeling for another door, for a high window, for any means to escape, knowing all the while that earthen cellars in shabby slum dwellings never had separate exits.

Five steps down, it occurred to Sandrine that she might not have been the first woman to be locked into this awful basement, and that instead of broken chairs and worn-out tools she might find herself knocking against a ribcage or two, a couple of femurs, that her foot might land on a jawbone, that she might step on somebody's forehead! Her body of a sudden shook, and her mind went white, and for a few moments Sandrine was on the verge of coming unglued: she pictured herself drawn up into a fetal ball, shuddering, weeping, whimpering. For a moment this dreadful image seemed unbearably tempting.

Then she thought, *Why the FUCK isn't Ballard here?*

Ballard was one hell of a tricky dude, he was full of little surprises, you could never really predict what he'd feel like doing, and he was a brilliant problem-solver. That's what Ballard did for a living, he flew around the world mopping up other people's messes. The only reason Sandrine knew him at all was that Ballard had materialized in a New Jersey motel room where good old Dad, Lauritzen Loy had been dithering over the corpse of a strangled whore, then caused the whore to vanish, the bloody sheets to vanish, and for all she knew the motel to vanish also. Two hours later a shaken but sober Lauritzen Loy reported to work in an immaculate and spotless Armani suit and Brioni tie. (Sandrine had known the details of her father's vile little peccadillo for years.) Also, and this quality meant that his presence would have been particularly valuable down in the witch-hag's cellar, although Ballard might have looked as though he had never picked up anything heavier than a briefcase, he was in fact astonishingly strong, fast, and smart. If you were experiencing a little difficulty with a dragon, Ballard was the man for you.

While meditating upon the all-round excellence of her longtime lover and wishing for him more with every fresh development of her thought, Sandrine had been continuing steadily on her way down the stairs. When she reached the part about the dragon, it came to her that she had been on these earthen stairs far longer than she had expected. Sandrine thought she was now actually beneath the level of the cellar she had expected to enter. The fairy tale feeling came over her again, of being held captive in a world without rational rules and orders, subject to deep patterns unknown to or rejected by the daylit world. In a flash of insight, it came to her that this fairytale world had much in common with her childhood.

To regain control of herself, perhaps most of all to shake off the sense of gloom-laden helplessness evoked by thoughts of childhood, Sandrine began to count the steps as she descended. Down into the earth they went, the dry firm steps that met her feet, twenty more, then forty, then fifty. At a hundred and one, she felt light-headed and weary, and sat down in the darkness. She felt like weeping. The long stairs were a grave, leading nowhere but to itself. Hope, joy, and desire had fled, even boredom and petulance had fled, hunger, lust, and anger were no more. She felt tired and empty. Sandrine leaned a shoulder against the earthen wall, shuddered once, and realized she was crying only a moment before she fled into unconsciousness.

In that same instant she passed into an ongoing dream, as if she had wandered into the middle of a story, more accurately a point far closer to its ending. Much, maybe nearly everything of interest, had already happened. Sandrine lay on a mess of filthy blankets at the bottom of a cage. The Golden Shower of Shit had sufficiently relaxed, it seemed, as to permit the butchering of entire slabs of flesh from her body, for much of the meat from her right shoulder had been sliced away. The wound reported a dull, wavering ache that spoke of those wonderful objects, Ballard's narcotic painkillers. So close together were the narrow bars, she could extend only a hand, a wrist, an arm. In her case, an arm, a wrist, and a stump. The hand was absent from the arm Sandrine had slipped through the bars, and someone had cauterized the wounded wrist.

The Mystery of the Missing Hand led directly to Cage Number One, where a giant bug-creature sat crammed in at an angle, filling nearly the whole of the cage, mewing softly, and trying to saw through the bars with its remaining mandible. It had broken the left one on the bars, but it was not giving up, it was a bug, and bugs don't quit. Sandrine was all but certain that when in possession of both mandibles, that is to say before capture, this huge *thing* had used them to saw off her hand, which it had then promptly devoured. The giant bugs were the scourge of the river tribes. However, the Old Ones, the Real People, the Cloud Huggers, the Tree Spirits, the archaic Sacred Ones who spoke in birdsong and called themselves **We** had so shaped the River and the Forest, which had given them birth, that the meat of the giant bugs tasted exceptionally good, and a giant bug guilty of eating a person or parts of a person became by that act overwhelmingly delicious, like manna, like the food of paradise for human beings. **We** were feeding bits of Sandrine to the captured bug that it might yield stupendous meals for the Sandrine and Ballard upstairs.

Sandrine awakened crying out in fear and horror, scattering tears she could not see.

Enough of that. Yes, quite enough of quivering; it was time to decide what to do next. Go back and try to break down the door, or keep going down and see what happens? Sandrine hated the idea of giving up and going backwards. She levered herself upright and resumed her descent with stair number one hundred and two.

At stair three hundred she passed through another spasm of weepy trembling, but soon conquered it and moved on. By the four hundredth stair she was hearing faint carnival music and seeing sparkly light-figments flit through the darkness like illuminated moths. Somewhere around stair five hundred she realized that the numbers had become mixed up in her head, and stopped counting. She saw a grave that wasn't a grave, merely darkness, and she saw her old tutor at Clare, a cool, detached Don named Quentin Jester who said things like, "If I had a lifetime with you, Miss Loy, we'd both know a deal more than we do at present," but she closed her eyes and shook her head and sent him packing.

Many stairs later, Sandrine's thigh muscles reported serious aches, and her arms felt extraordinarily heavy. So did her head, which kept lolling forward to rest on her chest. Her stomach complained, and she said to herself, *Wish I had a nice big slice of sautéed giant bug right about now*, and chuckled at how crazy she had become in so short a time. Giant bug! Even good old Dad, old LL, who often respected sanity in others but wished for none of it himself, drew the line at dining on giant insects. And here came yet another proof of her deteriorating mental condition, that despite her steady progress deeper and deeper underground, Sandrine could almost sort of half-persuade herself that the darkness before her seemed weirdly less dark than only a moment ago. This lunatic delusion clung to her step after step, worsening as she went. She said to herself, I'll hold up my hand, and if I think I see it, I'll know it's good-by, real world, pack Old Tillie off to Bedlam. She stopped moving, closed her eyes, and raised her hand before her face. Slowly, she opened her eyes, and beheld... her hand!

The problem with the insanity defense lay in the irrevocable truth that it was really her hand before her, not a mad vision from Gothic literature but her actual, entirely earthly hand, at present grimy and crusted with dirt from its long contact with the wall. Sandrine turned her head and discovered that she could make out the wall, too, with its hard-packed earth showing here and there the pale string of a severed root, at times sending in her direction a little spray or shower of dusty particulate. Sandrine held her breath and looked down to what appeared to be the source of the illumination. Then she inhaled sharply, for it seemed to her that she could see, dimly and a long way down, the bottom of the stairs. A little rectangle of light burned away down there, and from it floated the luminous translucency that made it possible for her to see.

Too shocked to cry, too relieved to insist on its impossibility, Sandrine moved slowly down the remaining steps to the rectangle of light. Its warmth heated the air, the steps, the walls, and Sandrine herself, who only now registered that for most of her journey she had been half-paralyzed by the chill leaking from the earth. As she drew nearer to the light, she could finally make out details of what lay beneath her. She thought she saw a strip of concrete, part of a wooden barrel, the bottom of a ladder lying on the ground: the intensity of the light surrounding these enigmatic objects shrank and dwindled them, hollowed them out even as it drilled painfully into her eyes. Beneath her world existed another, its light a blinding dazzle.

When Sandrine had come within thirty feet of the blazing underworld, her physical relationship to it mysteriously altered. It seemed she no longer stepped downward, but moved across a slanting plane that leveled almost imperceptibly off. The dirt walls on either side fell back and melted to ghostly gray air, to nothing solid, until all that remained was the residue of dust and grime plastered over Sandrine's white dress, her hands and face, her hair. Heat reached her, the real heat of an incendiary sun, and human voices, and the clang and bang and underlying susurrus of machinery. She walked toward all of it, shading her eyes as she went.

Through the simple opening before her Sandrine moved, and the sun blazed down upon her, and her own moisture instantly soaked her filthy dress, and sweat turned the dirt in her hair to muddy trickles. She knew this place; the dazzling underworld was the world she had left. From beneath her shading hand Sandrine took in the wide concrete apron, the equipment she had noticed all that harrowing time ago and the equipment she had not, the men posturing for the benefit of other men, the sense of falsity and stagecraft and the incipient swelling of a banal unheard melody. The long yellow dock where on a sluggish umber tide three yachts slowly rocked, one of them the *Sweet Delight*.

In a warm breeze that was not a breeze, a soiled-looking scrap of paper flipped toward Sandrine over the concrete, at the last lifting off the ground to adhere to her leg. She bent down to peel it off and release it, and caught a strong, bitter whiff, unmistakably excremental, of the Amazon. The piece of paper wished to cling to her leg, and there it hung until the second tug of Sandrine's dirty fingers, when she observed that she was gripping not a scrap of paper but a Polaroid, now a little besmudged by contact with her leg. When she raised it to her face, runnels of dirt obscured portions of the image. She brushed away much of the dirt, but could still make no sense of the photograph, which appeared to depict some pig-like animal.

In consternation, she glanced to one side and found there, lounging against bollards and aping the idleness of degenerates and river louts, two of the men in shabby suits and worn-out hats who had pursued her into the slum. She straightened up in rage and terror, and to confirm what she already knew to be the case, looked to her other side and saw their companions. One of them waved to her. Sandrine's terror cooled before her perception that these guys had changed in some basic way. Maybe they weren't idle, exactly, but these men were more relaxed, less predatory than they had been on the avenue into Manaus.

They had their eyes on her, though, they were interested in what she was going to do. Then she finally got it: they were different because now she was where they had wanted her to be all along. They didn't think she would try to escape again, but they wanted to make sure. Sandrine's whole long adventure, from the moment she noticed she was being followed to the present, had been designed to funnel her back to the dock and the yacht. The four men, who were now smiling at her and nodding their behatted heads, had pushed her toward the witch-hag, for they were all in it together! Sandrine dropped her arms, took a step backward, and in amazement looked from side to side, taking in all of them. It had all been a trick; herded like a cow, she had been played. Falsity again; more stagecraft.

One of the nodding, smiling men held his palm up before his face, and the man beside him leaned forward and laughed into his fist, as if shielding a sneeze. Grinning at her, the first man went through his meaningless mime act once again, lifting his left hand and staring into its palm. Grinning even more widely, he pointed at Sandrine and shouted, "*Munna!*"

The man beside him cracked up, *Munna!*, what a wit, then whistled an odd little four note melody that might have been a birdcall.

Experimentally, Sandrine raised her left hand, regarded it, and realized that she was still gripping the dirty little Polaroid photograph of a pig. Those two idiots off to her left waved their hands in ecstasy. She was doing the right thing, so *Munna!* right back atcha, buddy. She looked more closely at the Polaroid and saw that what it pictured was not actually a pig. The creature in the photo had a head and a torso, but little else. The eyes, nose, and ears were gone. A congeries of scars like punctuation marks, like snakes, like words in an unknown language, decorated the torso.

I know what Munna *means, and* Num, thought Sandrine, and for a moment experienced a spasm of stunning, utterly sexual warmth before she fully understood what had been given her: that she recognized the man in the photo. The roar of oceans, of storm-battered leaves, filled her ears and caused her head to spin and wobble. Her fingers parted, and the Polaroid floated off in an artificial, wind-machine breeze that spun it around a couple of times before lifting it high above the port and winking it out of sight, lost in the bright hard blue above the *Sweet Delight.*

Sandrine found herself moving down the yellow length of the long dock.

Tough love, Ballard had said. To be given and received, at the end perfectly repaid by that which she had perhaps glimpsed but never witnessed, the brutal, exalted, slow-moving force that had sometimes rustled a curtain, sometimes moved through this woman her hair and body now dark with mud, had touched her between her legs, Sandrine, poor profane lost deluded most marvelously fated Sandrine.

1997

From the galley they come, from behind the little dun-colored curtain in the dining room, from behind the bookcases in the handsome sitting room, from beneath the bed and the bloodstained metal table, through wood and fabric and the weight of years, **We** come, the Old Ones and Real People, the Cloud Huggers, **We** process slowly toward the center of the mystery **We** understand only by giving it unquestioning service. What remains of the clients and patrons lies, still breathing though without depth or force, upon the metal work-table. It was always going to end this way, it always does, it can no other. Speaking in the high-pitched, musical language of birds that **We** taught the Piraha at the beginning of time, **We** gather at the site of these ruined bodies, **We** worship their devotion to each other and the Great Task that grew and will grow on them, **We** treat them with grave tenderness as we separate what can and must be separated. Notes of the utmost liquid purity float upward from the mouths of **We** and print themselves upon the air. **We** know what they mean, though they have long since passed through the realm of words and gained again the transparency of music. **We** love and accept the weight and the weightlessness of music. When the process of separation is complete, through the old sacred inner channels **We** transport what the dear, still-living man and woman have each taken from the other's body down down down to the galley and the ravening hunger that burns ever within it.

Then. Then. With the utmost tenderness, singing the deep tuneless music at the heart of the ancient world, **We** gather up what remains of Ballard and Sandrine, armless and legless trunks, faces without features, their breath clinging to their mouths like wisps, carry them (in our arms, in baskets, in once-pristine sheets) across the deck and permit them to roll from our care, as they had always longed to do, and into that of the flashing furious little river-monarchs. **We** watch the water boil in a magnificence of ecstasy, and **We** sing for as long as it lasts.

◄◦►

HONORABLE MENTIONS

Atkins, Peter "Dancing Like We're Dumb," *Rumours of the Marvellous*.

Ballingrud, Nathan "Sunbleached," *Teeth*.

Barron, Laird "The Carrion Gods in Their Heaven," *Supernatural Noir*.

Barron, Laird "The Men From Porlock," (novella) *The Book of Cthulhu*.

Barron, Laird "The Siphon," *Blood and Other Cravings*.

Baxter, Alan "Punishment of the Sun," *Dead Red Heart*.

Bear, Elizabeth "Needles," *Blood and Other Cravings*.

Bowes, Richard "Blood Yesterday, Blood Tomorrow," *Blood and Other Cravings*.

Braunbeck, Gary A. "And Still you Wonder Why Our First Impulse is to Kill You," *The Monster's Corner*.

Carroll, Jonathan "East of Furious," Conjunctions: 56, Terra Incognita.

Colangelo, Michael R. "Blacklight," *Chilling Tales*.

Cowdrey, Albert E. "The Bogle," *F&SF* January/February.

Davidson, Craig "The Burn," *The Cincinnati Review*, April.

Dowling, Terry "The Shaddowesbox," *Ghosts by Gaslight*.

Fowler, Christopher "An Injustice," *House of Fear*.

Frost, Gregory "The Dingus," *Supernatural Noir*.

Gresh, Lois "Wee Sweet Girlies," *Eldritch Evolutions*.

Hand, Elizabeth "Near Zennor," (novella) *A Book of Horrors*.

Hand, Elizabeth "Uncle Lou," *Conjunctions 57: Kin*.

Harwood, John "Face to Face," *Ghosts by Gaslight*.

Hirshberg, Glen "After-Words," *The Janus Tree and Other Stories*.

Hodge, Brian "Hate the Sinner, Love the Sin," *Picking the Bones*.

Hodge, Brian "Scars in Progress," *Demons*.

Johnstone, Carole "Electric Dreams," *Black Static 23*, July/August.

Jones, Stephen Graham "Little Monsters," *Creatures: Thirty Years of Monsters*.

Kiernan, Caitlín R. "The Maltese Unicorn," *Supernatural Noir*.

King, Stephen "Under the Weather," *Full Dark, No Stars*.

Langan, John "The Third Always Beside You," *Blood and Other Cravings*.

Langan, John "The Unbearable Proximity of Mr. Dunn's Balloons," *Ghosts by Gaslight*.

Lees, Tim "Durgen's Party," *Black Static 22*, April/May.

McMahon, Gary "What They Hear in the Dark," chapbook.

Miéville, China "Covehithe," *Guardian*, May.

Nate Southard "The Blisters on My Heart," *Supernatural Noir*.

Oliver, Reggie "A Child's Problem," (novella) *A Book of Horrors*.

Oliver, Reggie "Dancer in the Dark," *Mrs Midnight and Other Stories*.

Oliver, Reggie "Hand to Mouth," *Haunts: Reliquaries of the Dead*.

Partridge, Norman "Vampire Lake," *Subterranean Tales of Dark Fantasy 2*.

Piccirilli, Tom "But For Scars," *Supernatural Noir*.

Pinborough, Sarah "The Screaming Room," *The Monster's Corner*.

Shearman, Robert "Alice Through the Plastic Sheet," *A Book of Horrors*.

Shepard, Lucius "Ditch Witch," *Supernatural Noir*.

Smith, Michael Marshall "Sad, Dark Thing," *A Book of Horrors*.

Stalter, K. Harding "A Summer's Day," *Black Static 24*.

Tem, Melanie "Afraid of Snakes," *Portents*.

Thomas, Lee "Comfortable in Her Skin," *Supernatural Noir*.

Travis, Tia V. "Still," *Portents*.

Tremblay, Paul G. "The Getaway," *Supernatural Noir*.

Valentine, Genevieve "Bufonidae," *Phantasmagorium #1*.

Wall, Alan "The Salt of Eliza," *Black Static 22*, April/May.

Warren, Kaaron "All You Can Do is Breathe," *Blood and Other Cravings*.

ABOUT THE AUTHORS

LAIRD BARRON is the author of two collections: *The Imago Sequence*, and *Occultation*. His work has appeared in many magazines and anthologies. His novella, "The Light is the Darkness," was recently published in a limited edition by Infernal House. His first novel, *The Croning* is being published June 2012. An expatriate Alaskan, Barron currently resides in Upstate New York.

"Blackwood's Baby" was originally published in *Ghosts by Gaslight*, edited by Jack Dann and Nick Gevers.

Born in Wolverhampton, **SIMON BESTWICK** escaped at the age of two and now lives in the wilds of Lancashire. So far he's published two short story collections, *A Hazy Shade of Winter* and *Pictures of The Dark*, a chapbook, *Angels of The Silences* and two novels, *Tide of Souls* and *The Faceless*. Forthcoming are a chapbook, *Cold Havens*, from Spectral Press and a collection, *The Condemned*, from Gray Friar Press. In between working on his next novel and reams of new stories, novelettes and novellas, he tries in vain to have a life and catch up on his sleep.

"The Moraine," the first of Bestwick's two stories reprinted herein, was originally published in *Terror Tales of the Lake District*, edited by Paul Finch.

Simon Bestwick's second story reprinted in this volume, "Dermot," was originally published in *Black Static #24*.

LEAH BOBET drinks tea, wears feathers in her hair, and plants gardens in alleyways. Her short fiction has appeared in numerous venues including *Strange Horizons*, *Realms of Fantasy*, and several year's best anthologies, and her first novel, *Above*, will be published by Arthur A. Levine Books in April 2012. For more, visit http://www.leahbobet.com.

"Stay," was originally published in *Chilling Tales*, edited by Michael Kelly.

GLEN HIRSHBERG's 2011 collection, *The Janus Tree and Other Stories*, includes both "You Become the Neighborhood" and the Shirley Jackson Award-Winning title novelette. Each of his previous collections, *American Morons*, and *The Two Sams*, won the International Horror Guild Award. He is also the author of two novels, *The Snowman's Children* and *The Book of Bunk*. A new novel, *Motherless Child*, will be published in 2012. With Dennis Etchison and Peter Atkins, he co-founded the Rolling Darkness Revue, a traveling ghost story performance troupe that tours the west coast of the United States and elsewhere each October. His fiction has appeared frequently in *The Year's Best Fantasy and Horror*, *The Mammoth Book of Best New Horror*, and *The Best Horror of the Year*.

BRIAN HODGE is the award-winning author of ten novels of horror and crime/noir, over 100 short stories, novelettes, and novellas, and four full-length collections. His most recent collection, *Picking the Bones*, became the first of his books to be honored with a *Publishers Weekly* starred review. His first collection, *The Convulsion Factory*, was listed by critic Stanley Wiater as one of the 113 best books of modern horror.

Works slated for 2012 include a collection of crime fiction, *No Law Left Unbroken*; a novella, *Without Purpose, Without Pity*; and hardcover editions of a couple of early novels.

He lives with his soulmate, Doli, in Boulder, Colorado, where he's currently engaged in a locked-cage death match with his next novel. He also dabbles in music, sound design, and photography; loves everything about organic gardening except the thieving squirrels; and trains in Krav Maga and Brazilian Jiu Jitsu, which are of no use at all against the squirrels.

Connect through his web site (www.brianhodge.net) or on Facebook (www.facebook.com/brianhodgewriter), and follow his blog, Warrior Poet (www.warriorpoetblog.com).

"Roots and All" was originally published in *A Book of Horror*.

STEPHEN KING needs little introduction. Since the publication of his first novel, *Carrie*, in 1974, King has been entertaining readers with novels such as *Salem's Lot*, *The Dead Zone*, *The Stand*, *Cujo*, *The Dark Half*, *The Green Mile*, *Duma Key*, *Under the Dome*, and most recently *11/22/63*. The author's short fiction and novellas have been collected in *Night Shift*, *Different Seasons*, *Skeleton Crew*, *Four Past Midnight*, *Nightmares and Dreamscapes*, *Hearts in Atlantis*, *Everything's Eventual*, *The Secretary of Dreams* (two volumes), *Just After Sunset* and *Full Dark, No Stars*. He has won numerous awards, including the O'Henry Award, the Horror Writers' Association and World Fantasy Lifetime Achievement Awards, and a Medal for Distinguished Contribution to American Letters from the National Book Foundation.

"The Little Green God of Agony" was originally published in *A Book of Horrors*, edited by Stephen Jones.

TERRY LAMSLEY's first collection, set in his then home-town, Buxton in Derbyshire, was nominated for three World Fantasy Awards and the title story "Under the Crust" won in the Best Novella category, 1994. Since then he has had numerous stories published in a wide range of collections, magazines and anthologies, most recently in *The Very Best of Best New Horror* and *House of Fear*. He no longer writes about Buxton and lives in Amsterdam in The Netherlands.

"In the Absence of Murdock" was originally published in *House of Fear*, edited by Jonathan Oliver.

MARGO LANAGAN has written four collections of short stories: *White Time*, *Black Juice*, *Red Spikes* and *Yellowcake*, and two dark fantasy novels, *Tender Morsels* and *The Brides of Rollrock Island*, which will be published in late 2012. She is a four-time World Fantasy Award winner, for Short Story, Collection, Novel and Novella. Lanagan lives in Sydney, and day-jobs as a contract technical writer. She was an instructor at Clarion South in 2005, 2007 and 2009, and taught at Clarion West in 2011.

"Mulberry Boys" was originally published in *Blood and Other Cravings* edited by Ellen Datlow.

JOHN LANGAN is author of the collections *Mr. Gaunt and Other Uneasy Encounters, Technicolor and Other Revelations,* and of the novel *House of Windows.* His stories have been published in *The Magazine of Fantasy & Science Fiction* and in numerous anthologies, including *Supernatural Noir, Blood and Other Cravings,* and *Ghosts by Gaslight.* He lives in upstate New York with his wife, son, dog, cats, and several tanks full of fish.

"In Paris, In the Mouth of Kronos" was originally published in *Supernatural Noir,* edited by Ellen Datlow

ALISON LITTLEWOOD is a writer of dark fantasy and horror fiction. Her first novel, *A Cold Season,* is published by Jo Fletcher Books, a new imprint of Quercus. It was selected as a Richard and Judy Book Club read for spring 2012. Alison's short stories have appeared in magazines including *Black Static, Crimewave* and *Not One Of Us,* as well as the British Fantasy Society's Dark Horizons. She also contributed to the charity anthology *Never Again* as well as *Read by Dawn Vol 3, Midnight Lullabies,* and *Festive Fear 2.* Her nonfiction has appeared in *The Guardian.*

"Black Feathers" was originally published in *Black Static #22.*

Visit her at www.alisonlittlewood.co.uk.

LIVIA LLEWELLYN is the author of the short story collection *Engines of Desire: Tales of Love & Other Horrors,* published by Lethe Press. Her fiction has appeared in numerous magazines and anthologies, including *Subterranean, ChiZine,* and *Postscripts.* She's currently working on her first novel.

"Omphalos" was originally published in *Engines of Desire: Tales of Love & Other Horrors.*

DAVID NICKLE has been writing and publishing fiction for the past twenty years, with stories appearing in places like the *Northern Frights* anthology series, the *Tesseracts* and *Queer Fear* anthologies, *The Year's Best Fantasy and Horror,* and magazines like *Cemetery Dance* and *On Spec.* He's a past winner of the Bram Stoker Award and Canada's Aurora Award for short fiction. Lately, he's been publishing books with Toronto's ChiZine Publications. His story collection *Monstrous Affections* received a Black Quill Readers' Choice award in 2010. His historical horror novel *Eutopia: A Novel of Terrible Optimism* was released from CZP in 2011. In late spring of 2012, his novel of psychic spies, giant squid and outdoor sporting equipment, *Rasputin's Bastards*, is set for release.

He lives and works as a journalist in Toronto, where he presides over the city hall press gallery, covering local politics for a chain of community newspapers.

"Looker" was originally published in *Chilling Tales*, edited by Michael Kelly.

PRIYA SHARMA is a medical doctor in the UK, where she spends as much free time as she can devouring books and writing speculative fiction. She has a computer but prefers a fountain pen and a notebook. Her short stories have appeared in publications such as *Albedo One, On Spec, Alt Hist* and *Fantasy Magazine*. More will appear in 2012 in *Dark Tales, On Spec*, and *Bourbon Penn*. She is currently working on a historical fantasy novel set in North Wales, not far from where she lives. More information can be found at www.priyasharmafiction.co.uk

"The Show" was originally published in *Box of Delights*, edited by John Kenny.

PETER STRAUB is the author of eighteen novels, including *Ghost Story, Koko, Mr. X*, two collaborations with Stephen King, *The Talisman* and *Black House*, and his most recent *A Dark Matter*. He has also written two volumes of poetry and two collections of short fiction. He edited *Conjunctions 39: The New Wave Fabulists*, Library of America's *H. P. Lovecraft: Tales*, the LoA's *American Fantastic Tales* and *Poe's Children*. He has won the British Fantasy Award, nine Bram Stoker Awards, two International Horror Guild Awards, and three World Fantasy Awards. In 1998, he was named Grand Master at the World Horror Convention. He has also won WFC's Lifetime Achievement Award and the Barnes & Noble Writers For Writers Award. The University of Wisconsin and Columbia University gave him Distinguished Alumnus Awards.

"The Ballad of Ballard and Sandrine" was originally published in *Conjunctions 56*.

ANNA TABORSKA was born in London, England. She studied Experimental Psychology at Oxford University and went on to gainful employment in public relations, journalism and advertising, before throwing everything over to become a filmmaker and horror writer.

Taborska has directed two short films (Ela and The Sin), two documentaries (*My Uprising* and *A Fragment of Being*) and a one-hour television drama (*The Rain Has Stopped*), which won two awards at the British Film Festival Los Angeles in 2009. She has also worked on seventeen other films, including *Simon Magus* and *Number One Longing. Number Two Regret.*

Taborska's feature length screenplays include *Chainsaw, The Camp,* and *Pizzaman.* Her short stories have been published in *52 Stitches, Daily Flash, The Horror Zine,* and in several volumes of *The Black Book of Horror.* "Little Pig" was originally published in *The Eighth Black Book of Horror.*

You can watch clips from Taborska's films and view her full resume here: http://www.imdb.com/name/nm1245940/

CHET WILLIAMSON is the author of over twenty books, the latest of which are *Defenders of the Faith* and *Hunters.* Among his other published novels are *Second Chance, The Story of Noichi the Blind, Ash Wednesday, Soulstorm, Lowland Rider, Reign,* and *McKain's Dilemma.* Most of his early work remains in print as e-books from Crossroad Press and Amazon's Kindle store. Over a hundred of his short stories have appeared in such magazines as *The New Yorker, Playboy, Esquire,* and *The Magazine of Fantasy & Science Fiction,* and many other magazines and anthologies. *Figures in Rain,* a collection of his short stories, was given the International Horror Guild Award for Outstanding Collection.

His work has also been adapted for television, radio, and recorded books. His *New Yorker* short story, "Gandhi at the Bat," was made into a short film and has been shown in festivals worldwide.

"The Last Verse" was originally published in *The Magazine of Fantasy & Science Fiction,* May/June issue.

A.C. WISE was born in Montreal and currently lives in the Philadelphia area with a spouse, two cats, and one very short dog. Her fiction has appeared in publications such as *Clarkesworld, Strange Horizons,* and *Fantasy Magazine,* among others. In addition to her writing, she co-edits the online 'zine of bug-related fiction, *The Journal of Unlikely Entomology.* You can find her online at www.acwise.net.

"Final Girl Theory" was originally published in *Chizine #48.*

COPYRIGHT ACKNOWLEDGMENTS

Night Shade Books is an Independent Publisher of Quality Science-Fiction, Fantasy and Horror

ISBN: 978-1-59780-230-7 ❅ $24.99 ❅ Look for it in e-Book!

Strange things exist on the periphery of our existence, haunting us from the darkness looming beyond our firelight. Black magic, weird cults and worse things loom in the shadows. The Children of Old Leech have been with us from time immemorial. And they love us...

Donald Miller, geologist and academic, has walked along the edge of a chasm for most of his nearly eighty years, leading a charmed life between endearing absent-mindedness and sanity-shattering realization. Now, all things must converge. Donald will discover the dark secrets along the edges, unearthing savage truths about his wife Michelle, their adult twins, and all he knows and trusts. For Donald is about to stumble on the secret...

...of The Croning.

From Laird Barron, Shirley Jackson Award-winning author of *The Imago Sequence* and *Occultation*, comes *The Croning*, a debut novel of cosmic horror.

Night Shade Books is an Independent Publisher of Quality Science-Fiction, Fantasy and Horror

ISBN: 978-1-59780-219-2 ❧ $15.99 ❧ Look for it in e-Book!

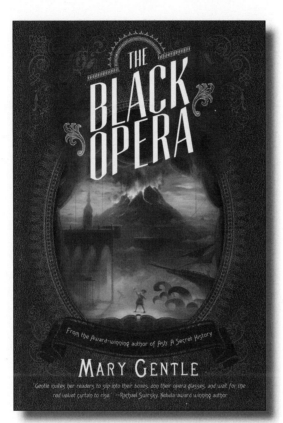

NAPLES, THE 19TH CENTURY.

In the Kingdom of the Two Sicilies, holy music has power. Under the auspices of the Church, the Sung Mass can bring about actual miracles like healing the sick or raising the dead. But some believe that the musicodramma of grand opera can also work magic by channeling powerful emotions into something sublime. Now the Prince's Men, a secret society, hope to stage their own black opera to the empower the Devil himself—and change Creation for the better.

Conrad Scalese is a struggling librettist whose latest opera has landed him in trouble with the Holy Office of the Inquisition. Rescued by King Ferdinand II, Conrad finds himself recruited to write and stage a counteropera that will, hopefully, cancel out the apocalyptic threat of the black opera, provided the Prince's Men, and their spies and saboteurs, don't get to him first.

And he only has six weeks to do it. . .

Night Shade Books is an Independent Publisher of Quality Science-Fiction, Fantasy and Horror

ISBN: 978-1-59780-398-4 ❦ $14.99 ❦ Look for it in e-Book!

The World Snake is coming, devourer of Thrace and Atlantis... and the only one standing in its way is Amber, a sixteen-year-old runaway, recently arrived in Los Angeles.

Amber is more than just a girl with a stolen ID and an attitude; she is a daughter of the wolf-kind, a shapeshifter able to change forms at will. One night, as Amber prowls the Hollywood Hills in wolf form, she stumbles onto an occult ceremony, interrupting the ritual. As a result, Amber finds herself the unwilling mistress of a handsome demonic servant, Richard.

Appearing as a fair youth of eighteen years, Richard is a demon accidentally summoned, then captured, by Dr. John Dee, court magician to Queen Elizabeth I. Richard has been trying for four centuries to free himself from a succession of masters and mistresses, but finds himself bound to Amber, the only one who can protect him from his greatest fear, the herald of the World Snake, the Eater of Souls.

The last thing a girl of the wolf-kind needs is a boy following her around like a lap-dog, but Amber agrees to help Richard reclaim his soul from two of his old foes, hoping to grant Richard his freedom. But all hell is about to break loose, and Amber and Richard are going to need some allies to stop the Eater of Souls and avert the World Snake, and the battle has only begun.

From Carol Wolf comes the urban fantasy debut *Summoning*, a novel of a wolf girl, a demon boy, and a city on the edge of disaster.

Night Shade Books is an Independent Publisher of Quality Science-Fiction, Fantasy and Horror

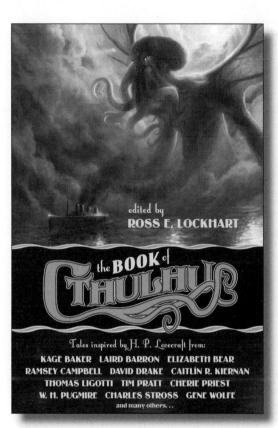

Ia! Ia! Cthulhu Fhtagn!

First described by visionary author H. P. Lovecraft, the Cthulhu mythos encompass a pantheon of truly existential cosmic horror: Eldritch, uncaring, alien god-things, beyond mankind's deepest imaginings, drawing ever nearer, insatiably hungry, until one day, when the stars are right....

As that dread day, hinted at within the moldering pages of the fabled *Necronomicon*, draws nigh, tales of the Great Old Ones: Cthulhu, Yog-Sothoth, Hastur, Azathoth, Nyarlathotep, and the weird cults that worship them have cross-pollinated, drawing authors and other dreamers to imagine the strange dark aeons ahead, when the dead-but-dreaming gods return.

Now, intrepid anthologist Ross E. Lockhart has delved deep into the Cthulhu canon, selecting from myriad mind-wracking tomes the best sanity-shattering stories of cosmic terror. Featuring fiction by many of today's masters of the menacing, macabre, and monstrous, *The Book of Cthulhu* goes where no collection of Cthulhu mythos tales has before: to the very edge of madness... and beyond!

Do you dare open *The Book of Cthulhu*? Do you dare heed the call?

Night Shade Books is an Independent Publisher of Quality Science-Fiction, Fantasy and Horror

ISBN: 978-1-59780-285-7 ❦ $14.99 ❦ Look for it in e-Book!

Recent World War II veteran Bull Ingram is working as muscle when a Memphis DJ hires him to find Ramblin' John Hastur. The mysterious blues man's dark, driving music—broadcast at ever-shifting frequencies by a phantom radio station—is said to make living men insane and dead men rise.

Disturbed and enraged by the bootleg recording the DJ plays for him, Ingram follows Hastur's trail into the strange, uncivilized backwoods of Arkansas, where he hears rumors the musician has sold his soul to the Devil.

But as Ingram closes in on Hastur and those who have crossed his path, he'll learn there are forces much more malevolent than the Devil and reckonings more painful than Hell . . .

In a masterful debut of Lovecraftian horror and Southern gothic menace, John Hornor Jacobs reveals the fragility of free will, the dangerous power of sacrifice, and the insidious strength of blood.

Night Shade Books is an Independent Publisher of Quality Science-Fiction, Fantasy and Horror

ISBN: 978-1-59780-290-1 ❦ $14.99 ❦ Look for it in e-Book!

"Terrifying, darkly hilarious, tougher and meaner and faster than a .45 hole-in-the-head—Roche delivers a fast-paced, gripping thriller where the showdowns make other zombie novelists look like they're playing with dollies."

—Violet Blue, author of *The Smart Girl's Guide to Porn* and many others

THE PANAMA LAUGH
THOMAS S. ROCHE

Ex-mercenary, pirate, and gun-runner Dante Bogart knows he's screwed the pooch after he hands one of his shady employers a biological weapon that made the dead rise from their graves, laugh like hyenas, and feast upon the living. Dante tried to blow the whistle via a tell-all video that went viral—but that was before the black ops boys deep-sixed him at a secret interrogation site on the Panama-Colombia border.

When Dante wakes up in the jungle with the five intervening years missing from his memory, he knows he's got to do something about the laughing sickness that has caused a world-wide slaughter. The resulting journey leads him across the nightmare that was the Panama Canal, around Cape Horn in a hijacked nuclear warship, to San Francisco's Mission District, where a crew of survivalist hackers have holed up in the pseudo-Moorish-castle turned porn-studio known as The Armory.

This mixed band of anti-social rejects has taken Dante's whistle blowing video as an underground gospel, leading the fight against the laughing corpses and the corporate stooges who've tried to profit from the slaughter. Can Dante find redemption and save civilization?

Night Shade Books is an Independent Publisher of Quality Science-Fiction, Fantasy and Horror

NECROPOLIS
MICHAEL DEMPSEY

Michael Dempsey's *Necropolis* reads the way stepping over a wasted body in the rain feels. It's a noir science fiction gut punch from a strong new voice.
— Richard Kadrey, author of *Sandman Slim*

In a future where death is a thing of the past...
...how far would you go to solve your own murder?

Paul Donner is a NYPD detective struggling with a drinking problem and a marriage on the rocks. Then he and his wife get dead—shot to death in a "random" crime. Fifty years later, Donner is back—revived courtesy of the Shift, a process whereby inanimate DNA is re-activated.

This new "reborn" underclass is not only alive again, they're growing younger, destined for a second childhood. The freakish side-effect of a retroviral attack on New York, the Shift has turned the world upside down. Beneath the protective geodesic Blister, clocks run backwards, technology is hidden behind a noir facade, and you can see Bogart and DiCaprio in *The Maltese Falcon III*. In this unfamiliar retro-futurist world of flying Studebakers and plasma tommy guns, Donner must search for those responsible for the destruction of his life. His quest for retribution, aided by Maggie, his holographic Girl Friday, leads him to the heart of the mystery surrounding the Shift's origin and up against those who would use it to control a terrified nation.

Night Shade Books is an Independent Publisher of Quality Science-Fiction, Fantasy and Horror

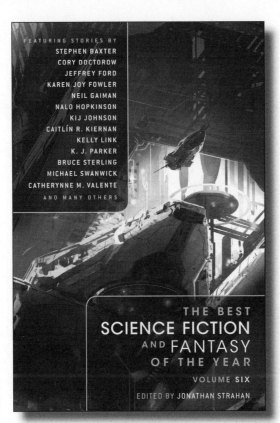

FEATURING STORIES BY
STEPHEN BAXTER
CORY DOCTOROW
JEFFREY FORD
KAREN JOY FOWLER
NEIL GAIMAN
NALO HOPKINSON
KIJ JOHNSON
CAITLÍN R. KIERNAN
KELLY LINK
K. J. PARKER
BRUCE STERLING
MICHAEL SWANWICK
CATHERYNNE M. VALENTE
AND MANY OTHERS

THE BEST
SCIENCE FICTION
AND FANTASY
OF THE YEAR
VOLUME SIX
EDITED BY JONATHAN STRAHAN

AN ANCIENT SOCIETY OF CARTOGRAPHER WASPS create delicately inscribed maps; a bodyjacking parasite is faced with imminent extinction; an AI makes a desperate gambit to protect its child from a ravenous dragon; a professor of music struggles with the knowledge that murder is not too high a price for fame; living origami carries a mother's last words to her child; a steam girl conquers the realm of imagination; aliens attack Venus, ignoring an incredulous earth; a child is born on Mars...

The science fiction and fantasy fiction fields continue to evolve, setting new marks with each passing year. For the sixth year in a row, master anthologist Jonathan Strahan has collected stories that captivate, entertain, and showcase the very best the genre has to offer. Critically acclaimed, and with a reputation for including award-winning speculative fiction, *The Best Science Fiction and Fantasy of the Year* is the only major "best of" anthology to collect both fantasy and science fiction under one cover.

Jonathan Strahan has edited more than twenty anthologies and collections, including *The Locus Awards* (with Charles N. Brown), *The New Space Opera* (with Gardner Dozois), and *The Starry Rift*. He has won the Ditmar, William J. Atheling Jr., and Peter McNamara awards for his work as an anthologist and reviewer, and was nominated for a Hugo Award for his editorial work. Strahan is currently the reviews editor for *Locus*.

ABOUT THE EDITOR

Ellen Datlow has been editing science fiction, fantasy, and horror short fiction for over twenty-five years. She was fiction editor of *OMNI* Magazine and *SCIFIC-TION* and has edited more than fifty anthologies, including *The Best Horror of the Year, Inferno, Poe: 19 New Tales Inspired by Edgar Allan Poe, Darkness: Two Decades of Modern Horror, Lovecraft Unbound, Supernatural Noir, Naked City: Tales of Urban Fantasy, Blood and Other Cravings, The Beastly Bride* and *Teeth: Vampire Tales* (the latter two young adult anthologies with Terri Windling), and *Haunted Legends* (with Nick Mamatas).

Forthcoming is the young adult dystopian anthology *After* and the adult fantasy anthology *Queen Victoria's Book of Spells* (both with Windling).

She's has tied for the most World Fantasy Awards (nine), and has also won multiple Locus Awards, Hugo Awards, Stoker Awards, International Horror Guild Awards, and The Shirley Jackson Award for her editing. She was named recipient of the 2007 Karl Edward Wagner Award, given at the British Fantasy Convention for "outstanding contribution to the genre." She has also been honored with the Life Achievement Award given by the Horror Writers Association, in acknowledgment of superior achievement over an entire career.

She co-curates the long-running Fantastic Fiction at KGB reading series in New York City's east village.

More information can be found at www.datlow.com or at her blog: http://ellen-datlow.livejournal.com/. She tweets as https://twitter.com/#!/ellendatlow